CW00507486

ARTIFICIAL WISDOM

ARTIFICIAL WISDOM

THOMAS R. WEAVER

CHAINMAKER
PRESS

First published in the United Kingdom in 2023 by Chainmaker Press

ISBN: 978-1-7394343-0-4

Typeset using Atomik ePublisher from Easypress Technologies

Printed and bound by CPI Group (UK) Ltd, Croydon, CR0 4YY

Cover design by Mecob

http://chainmaker.press
@chainmakerpress

To all those stricken by nature's fury,
And to the young souls inheriting our storm-tossed world:
May hope always light your path.

KUWAIT CITY

❧

She held her swollen belly and rolled over, the hot tarmac sticking to her face. "Oh, my child." She looked up, and the sun blinded her last moments. "Oh, my love."

1

LONDON, JULY 1st 2050

⤳

Marcus Tully pitched the tumbler as hard as he could at the screen. It slipped through the floating image and shattered against his study wall in a burst of golden rum. He glowered at the undamaged display, still hovering in his vision six feet away. Afternoon sun from the dusty floor-to-ceiling windows glinted from the crystal shards now scattered across the carpet tiles.

"Well," a pundit sneered at the newscast host, "I just don't accept the premise of your question. Ten years since this so-called *tabkhir* hit the Persian Gulf, and I see no credible evidence the heatwave really killed anyone. It was a coup, nothing more."

Damn all tabkhir-deniers to a humid hell. Ten years since the threads of a hundred million lives were cut from those left behind. Ten years since Zainab, his wife, had died. Ten years of holding tight onto every memory in case they slipped away when his back was turned.

Shit, he was drunk.

The faint whirr of cleaning bots sounded across the room. He staggered over to the window, placing his palms against the cool glass, then his forehead. Far below, the poor and desperate of London scurried around in the baking summer heat.

Ten years. Ten years today, but it still felt so fresh. Move on, they said. Get over her. But what if he didn't want to? What if the day he forgot her voice was when she was truly gone?

3

Play call recording, he told his neuro-assistant. *Marcus Tully and Zainab Tully, July the first, 2040.*

There was a beep—the sound of the old phone systems.

"*My love?*" Zainab said.

He squeezed his eyes shut at the sound of her voice, so alive, so real, as if he could reach out and touch her.

"*Hey, I'm here, Zee,*" he said, a man with no idea his world was about to change. "*You okay?*"

"*I've been better. Didn't sleep well. None of us did. It's too hot, and we're having brownouts.*"

"*Pretty warm here too, today, though it's early. Must be 8 a.m. in Kuwait?*"

There was a pause. "*Marcus, it's really, really humid here this morning, and the heat ... I can barely move.*" Another pause. "*It can't be good for the baby.*"

He could still remember the feeling of that first flickering moment of worry, that sudden sharpening of his attention. He opened his eyes again and stared at the skyline.

"*But your father has good aircon, right?*" Tully said.

"*The brownouts, Marcus.*" There was a crackle and she cut out for a moment. "*—Aircon isn't working. Nothing's working apart from the phones.*"

"*Maybe you should come home early? I know your mother wanted to spend time with you, before the birth, but—*"

"*I'll come,*" she said, too fast. "*Let me know when you've booked the ticket, I can't do it from here. The connection is as bad as the air—*"

There was another crackle, then nothing more.

"*Zee?*" he said. "*Zainab? Can you hear me?*"

But she was gone. It burned him up, not to know what really happened to her in the hours after that call, like a fathomless acid in his belly.

He lurched over to the desk and grabbed the rum bottle. Where the hell was the glass?

He sensed a *pang*—warning a notification was impending, like an artificial tingle deep within his forehead. A second later he could see the message teasing at the upper right periphery of his vision. Red-edged, for unknown contact. He ignored it and pulled the cork stopper, then took a gulp of the rum.

There was another pang, also red. He shook his head now and took another sip. A third pang made him groan, but he looked up.

Tully, read the first message. *Got a story you need to hear. Can we meet? Has to be right now.*

The second message read, *Government secrets, okay? Not safe.*

A third followed. *You got two mins, big shot, or I'm going to your competitors. Bradley maybe. Oh, this also concerns your wife.*

The bottle slipped from his hands and smashed on the edge of the desk, releasing a sickly stench. The cleaning bots bleeped disapprovingly. Tully blinked at the last message, reread the first two, then stared again at the third.

She'd been dead for ten years. What the hell would a whistleblower know about it?

2

Adrenalin began to clear the boozy fog from Tully's head, but nowhere near fast enough. *One moment,* he managed to reply.

He jerked open a desk drawer and rifled through the mess inside before slamming it shut again and yanking open a second one. He grabbed a pack of disposable jet injectors and pulled one free. He hesitated only a moment. He'd rather have faced the hangover, but he jammed it to his forearm and pressed the release, grunting at the jolt of chems blasting through his skin, spreading a cold sensation up his arm. He sucked in air as pain hit his chest, his lungs, his liver, wracking his muscles in a spasm, but within seconds it'd decelerated his drunkenness with a kick like a parachute ripping out a backpack at five thousand feet.

He steadied himself, blood alcohol level painfully back to normal, and looked again at the messages. He subspoke the follow up, lips barely moving. *Neuro-reality?*

Yeah NR. What the fuck else? came the reply.

He took a deep breath and pulled up his chair, sniffing and surveying the study, hoping his team hadn't heard the noise. There was a price to pay for having them live and work on site—a complete and utter abdication of privacy.

The cleaning bots were working their magic on the wall and carpet stains, and one was heading for the bottle. He left them to it, took off his earset, and grabbed the bigger, heavier neuro-reality headset. He pulled it on and powered it up, pulled a pill dispenser out of his pocket and pressed a button. It spat a tiny bubble of gelatinous liquid into his hand which he let dissolve beneath his tongue. Billions of neurograins would swarm his brain in seconds. The idea of the nanobots crawling around his skull like microscopic spiders made him shiver, but it was better than getting a permanent chip surgically implanted. The sights, sounds and smells of his study faded to a black void for the briefest moment as the headset jacked straight into his consciousness. A Mindscape logo appeared in white and vanished again.

His personal neural 'home'—or egospace, to use the jargon—faded in. The sweet and sharp tang of rum in the air mellowed into a light musk of orange blossom. The sensation of soft carpet beneath his bare feet hardened to a mosaic stone under leather shoes. The hum and chill of aircon had gone, too, and now there was a warm peacefulness, a comfortable absence of other life around him. He didn't take a moment to appreciate the beautiful space, however, and certainly didn't look around—there were some things he didn't want to see, not today—but just loaded the meeting app.

His egospace melted into a marble-floored hotel lobby, columned and triple-height. The nostalgic scent of a log fire—now illegal outside of NR—filled the air. He sat in a comfortable cuboid sofa chair with high arms, facing a second, empty sofa over a low marble table. Three tall aquarium tanks acted as dividers from other meeting spaces—not that they were actually there—making it into a snug.

A lean, wiry, androgynous individual flickered into existence in the second chair. Head shaved, face hairless, no sign of stubble. Casually dressed in an army-green hoodie and black baggy trousers. Amused eyes, mouth working at some chewing gum.

This one would have an attitude, Tully was sure of it. "I'm Tully." He held out his hand; it was ignored.

"No shit. Not gonna tell you my real name, though you can call me Whistle. Not gonna tell you where I'm from, who I work for, my sexual preferences or how I identify, the name of my first pet or any other pigeon shit that'd help you figure out who I am. And you're not gonna try find out, right?" The genderless accent was like a cheap cocktail that had lost all hint of its individual flavours.

Tully shook his head. "Whistle, huh? Well, no, I don't work like that. I need to know who my sources are, so my readers can trust I've done my due diligence."

"Maybe you gonna wanna make an exception this time," Whistle said.

Maybe this was going to be a complete waste of time. He sat back in his chair and steepled his fingers. "So you're whistle-blowing? May I ask, on who?"

Whistle grinned. "On every shithead in power doing things they shouldn't be."

"You're after justice, then? Or perhaps you just want to see the world burn."

"The world is already burning. Seems you're one of the only journos actually trying to expose the bastards holding the flamethrowers."

A compliment? Not generously delivered, but he'd take it. He wouldn't let it soften him up, though. Tully leaned forward and put on the hardest, iciest stare he could summon, the kind of stare that says, the chit-chat is over. The kind of stare that says, it's time for business. The kind of stare that says, get to the fucking point, or I'll get back to getting drunk. "What's this got to do with my wife?"

Whistle pulled a white data cube from a hoodie pocket and placed it carefully in the centre of the table, then gestured at it with one hand and sat back. "Go for it."

Tully picked up the cube and his neuro-assistant automatically initiated a scan. *No virus, contents include one neuro-reality video file, file size of two hundred zettabytes, file creation date of July the second, 2040.*

He froze.

Whistle winked. "Got your attention, right? Go on, take a look. I'll wait."

"What…" Tully's voice was gruff, and he cleared his throat. "What is it?"

"You know what it is—what it has to be, with a date like that."

"How did you get it?"

"You don't wanna know. Get on with it, or I'm taking it back."

Tully grimaced and ran his fingers over the smooth cube. Just an imaginary object in an imaginary reality that someone had decided should feel like porcelain. Would it break if he threw it in neuro-reality? Did he really want to see what was on it? What kind of investigative journalist would ever turn down information? *Open it,* he subspoke.

The hotel melted into sharp sunlight that made him cover his eyes. When he took his hands away, he was standing in front of seven bodies strewn across a scorched street.

Tully stared at the bodies and didn't move. His legs went weak. He needed to lean against something, or sit, but there was nothing there to take his weight.

There was no mistaking it. He'd been here, several times. Not this street, perhaps, but he'd seen this skyline, with Zainab by his side.

Kuwait City.

This was a mistake. He shouldn't be here, would get no peace and closure in this sterile snapshot of the past, with no sense of heat, no scent of dust and decay, no sound of wind whistling through empty streets, only the sound of his own ragged breathing.

But was Zainab here, too? Somewhere in these savage streets?

The road beyond was littered with hundreds of corpses, like discarded rags cast down on the street from the rooftops. They'd died wherever they'd fallen, packed beneath a desiccated tree, stretched out on the pavement or in the gutter, curled against the sides of the buildings, twisted in a clump of splayed arms and legs in the dust of the road.

So many bodies.

He approached the first one, fell to his knees and looked at the face. A woman—not *her*, but it was a gut-punch nonetheless. He choked up and staggered to his feet. He turned, and saw more bodies packing the road all the way to the horizon. He took a few step forwards and halted.

Could he find her? How long would it take? He'd need a system. He'd need to be efficient. Check each street off against a map. Avoid jumping around at random, with the risk he was just checking the same bodies over and over again. No, it was impossible. He could spend his life, looking. Ten million had lived in Kuwait City, before the tabkhir, before the whole Persian Gulf went dark.

Exit, he told his neuro-assistant. Get him the fuck out of there. A blink later, he was back in the NR hotel lobby.

Whistle didn't flinch at his sudden reappearance, just snapped both index fingers and thumbs. "Got some real goods there, no? You got any idea how hard it is to get shit out the caliphate?"

"How did you get it?" Tully said. "And why give it to me? What can I possibly do with it? There's no story here. Ten years ago, maybe."

Whistle winked again and chewed gum, mouth wide. "Do whatever you want with it. Shove it up the ass of every tabkhir-denier talking shit on the newscasts. The footage is just for creds."

"Creds?"

"And maybe, just maybe, you'll find out what happened to your wife."

"What the fuck would you know about my wife?" Tully snapped.

"She was there, yeah? When it happened. Didn't stand a chance. Four hundred million dead, right? Two-thirds of the population."

Tully needed a drink. The Mindscape tech had the capacity to simulate it, though they didn't cater to his taste in artisan Scottish dark rum. It tasted realistic nonetheless, but they'd never really built in the calming effect of alcohol beyond the mildest buzz, so what was the point?

He ordered anyway. A tumbler of rum appeared in front of him. He picked it up and knocked it back. "No one knows how many people died," Tully said, looking into his empty glass. "The caliphate suppressed everything after the borders shut."

"The caliphate knows, so I know. It's not easy for anyone to plug leaky holes, and a new state that big? Don't get me wrong, the caliphate works hard at it. They censor, they shut down the internet, they block satellites, do all the shit from the authoritarian state playbook. It's never enough, though. But look. The real deal with the tabkhir is much, much bigger, and is definitely not what it seems." Seriousness swept away the mocking face. "Real big. Fucking big. Maybe the biggest story out there in the history of news, and I wish I was exaggerating. I'm not safe even knowing about it. You won't be either, if you take this on."

"Not safe from the caliphate? They have no reach."

Whistle snorted. "From someone with far more clout. But I'm not gonna tell you who or why until you prove you have the chops."

Tully frowned. "What's that supposed to mean?"

Whistle pulled out a second data cube, this one blue, and tossed it at him.

He caught it. *No virus, contents include one neuro-reality video file, file size of fifty-three exabytes, file creation date of June the fifteenth, 2050.*

"I mean, show me you can write a story that will piss a lot of powerful people off."

"All my stories piss powerful people off."

Whistle shrugged, as if to say, *then this one shouldn't be a problem, should it?*

"What's on the cube?"

"A video of the Mayor of Houston, a shithead in power, doing things he shouldn't be to a bunch of climate refugees."

"I write this Houston story and you give me a story on the tabkhir?"

Whistle just winked again, then vanished, leaving him looking at the smooth blue cube in his hand. He leaned forward and placed it next to the white one.

He'd get both downloaded to his own system, but one thing was for sure; he wasn't looking at that footage of Kuwait City again. Not now.

Not ever.

3

Two days of searching the footage and no real sleep was eating at Tully's soul. He should never have picked up the white data cube again. Was she out there? On these streets? He sat at the desk in his study and squinted at the face of a dead woman wearing a hijab, displayed on a virtual screen that stretched the length of his desk.

How many faces had he looked at now? Enough, at least, to partly numb the horror of it all. You couldn't look at that many dead men and women without becoming desensitised, like when a stench fades from too long spent in its presence.

But the children…

He tried to move on from them fast. He ignored the men too, trying to cut down the amount of time he looked at each face. There was only one face he was looking for.

"What in humid hell," said a voice behind him, "is that, Marcus?"

He flinched but stopped himself from making the virtual screens private. It was just Bolivar, and he had nothing to hide from his friend, from his business partner, from his lawyer. Still, it took him a moment to answer, and they both stared at the body of a woman on the street, arm outstretched in the dirt of a gutter, like she was reaching for a lifeline beyond her grasp.

"Footage," Tully said at last. "Kuwait City, the day after the tabkhir."

"Footage of Kuwait?" Juan Bolivar shook his head. "Old friend, old buddy, you do realise the publishing deadline for this Houston story is in just over ten minutes?"

Tully's eyes flicked up to the clock projected in his display. Shit. He'd lost track of time and should've been with his team in the hub, not a hundred paces away on his own in his study. The second data cube held evidence of the mayor of Houston ordering his chief of police to use illegal microwave tech to quell a mass protest of local climate-unhomed. Local journalists reported that thousands were left dizzy, fatigued and, in some cases, with mild brain damage. Some pundits diagnosed mass psychosis, but the evidence said differently, and Tully had the evidence. "Yeah," he said, "They're ready to publish?"

Bolivar nodded. "Yeah. They're ready."

"You look like shit, you know," Bolivar said.

Tully rubbed his unshaven cheeks. "Hmm." He took one more look at the screen, at the street beyond the body of the woman. Was she there, waiting for him in that next street? Bile rose in his throat and he closed down the main screen, swinging around on his chair to face Bolivar. "Do you ever worry about it happening again? Sudden, insane rise in humidity and heat, like the tabkhir, one day high, the next morning deadly. It could happen here, in London, across Europe."

"That's why we're electing a bloody dictator, isn't it?"

Tully looked across at a muted newscast displayed on a second floating screen to the left of the first. A reporter was speaking to the camera. Below her, a rolling newsfeed proclaimed: *DICTATORSHIP DEADLOCK CONTINUES AS SIXTH ROUND OF VOTING BEGINS … TWENTY CANDIDATES PROGRESS FROM ROUND FIVE …* Nine years since the first suggestion that the world should do as the Romans did: select one person with absolute authority to fix the climate crisis, then hand power back to the nations. A decade later, they were whittling down a bluster of political wannabes to a shortlist of candidates before holding a global vote.

Tully rubbed his eyes and stood. "Decades too late," he said.

"Yeah."

"The Houston story," Bolivar said. "We need this one, Marcus."

"How's our financial situation looking?" Tully said, standing.

Bolivar looked away. "We have about a month's runway before we crash."

"This should give us another month or two at least."

They passed from the peace of his room into the bustle of the hub, the stale whiff of various lunches still hanging in the air from hours before. It wasn't his idea of a great workspace, but it was what they could afford. Every other floor in the grimy, dated Baker House skyscraper on Pudding Lane hosted mostly empty commercial office space. Bolivar hadn't wanted to pay for both an office and a living space, so they'd fitted out this floor as a mix of workspace and an apartment—it was more than a bit cold and soulless, but, hey, it had the advantage of good aircon. Forty-eight storeys down at street level, it was forty-four degrees.

The open-plan hub combined a workspace with a kitchen and some sofas. At the centre was a large office table big enough for six people to work around. Livia Chandra, Tully's researcher, and Randall Morrow, his tech guru, were sat there, looking at him with expectant expressions. He nodded at them and walked over to his sub-editor's station. Lottie Shock pretended to be oblivious to him, fingers dancing over a keyboard visible only to her, but she was just putting him in his place. She was wiry and lean, with short, cropped and bleached hair, and was wearing a white tank top. An ivy tattoo wound its way around her right arm to her wrist from a bare muscular shoulder.

"Done?" he asked, but she ignored him and continued bashing away, glaring at a private screen.

He eyed Bolivar, who shrugged, and said, "Nearly ready."

Tully turned to his tech engineer. "You uploaded the recording too?"

Randall grinned. "You got it, yessir, Mr Tully—"

"The influencers are ready to share?"

"I contacted the giga-influencers personally," Randall said. "And they snowballed out to contact the megas, so I reckon we've got about a thousand people sitting there just waiting to push this directly out to about five hundred million followers, I mean, we could even—"

Livia stood up in a hurry, her chair screeching back. "Tully," she said, "I've got the senior adviser to the mayor of Houston for you."

It wasn't a new playbook, exactly: leave it to the last minute, try to make Tully's team miss the influencer window. Denials would follow, maybe even a bribe.

"You want to take it in NR?" Livia said.

He didn't. Neuro-reality was great for meeting people. Made you feel physically present, as good as walking into a room and shaking a hand with none of the inconvenience of getting there first. But he had no desire for such a personal interaction. "No. Just share the screen."

Livia shared a virtual screen, over the workspace, and launched a small camera drone to hover silently just above it. A few seconds later, William Cavanagh appeared. They'd never met, but he knew him from the newscasts. He'd been in a previous White House administration a while back, maybe fifteen years ago in the mid-2030s. Before everything turned to shit.

Cavanagh was the kind of heavyset man in his early sixties who suited his weight, and combined with the charming glint in his eye, he'd cultivated an image more like a president of a newscast network than a political hatchet man—he was tieless, with two buttons undone, and his thinning hair had a surprising amount of dark left in it, possibly dyed, slicked back. But he wore a designer suit over a multipack white shirt. He had the air of a man who drank cheap bourbon from a lead-crystal glass.

"It's Cavanagh, right?" Tully said.

Cavanagh gestured with his hands as if to say, did it really matter? "I understand you plan to push your story soon," he said, "so I'll keep this short. The mayor of Houston is asking you to kill this story, the governor of Texas is asking you to kill this story, the White House is backing them both and your own English government will do whatever the White House tells them to do, just as it always has."

"Would any of them like to comment on the record?"

"Let me be very clear," Cavanagh said. "You've got your facts wrong. Someone is playing you. Take this one out with the trash, we forget the whole thing, your reputation stays intact. As a gesture of goodwill, we'll sponsor a different story for you. And we'll be generous. I understand things are tight. Let us loosen them for you."

"Let me play that back to make sure I have it right," Tully said. "You're denying the story is correct and are willing to bribe me to forget the whole thing and write a story about someone else?"

"Don't fucking twist my words. By the way, anonymous sources? That can't be credible for this type of allegation."

"Sure it can," Tully said.

"How many?"

"How many what?"

"Sources."

"One."

"Just the one?" Cavanagh's mouth hung open and he looked around as if seeking validation. "You can't base all this off one source. There's that—what?—journalistic code. You're required to corroborate with a second source at least."

Tully nodded. "More of a guideline, actually, but in any case, we have the recording to corroborate."

"We watched the video. Deepfaked."

"It was in NR, and the experts say you can't deepfake neuro-reality." Tully checked the clock. "Plus we have a doctor's account of the injuries, and he's convinced you used microwaves. Now, if there's nothing else—"

"No, no, wait," Cavanagh said, his tone now reasonable, eyes all understanding, mouth in a we're-really-on-the-same-side smile. "Listen. Maybe you're wrong and maybe you're right. But you can't put this out there. You send this article out, you make it seem like climate-hobos are being fucked, and the city will explode, and cities all over the US and beyond will follow—the world is a fucking tinderbox right now with this dictatorship election going on."

Climate-hobos? "Not my problem."

Cavanagh's smile slipped. "You stupid fucking motherfucker! If this goes south and they riot, it'll all be your fucking fault. You really want that?"

"I just want to tell my readers the truth."

"You can't put this kind of shit out there. Take some responsibility."

That was the thing about the truth. Sometimes, you were judged more harshly for revealing it than for concealing it. Some bastard running for president hired a hooker, and they called the reporter 'salacious' for writing about it. "The responsibility lies with those who did the deed and those who prop them up, not the ones exposing it."

"You finished?"

"Yeah, I'm finished. Appreciate your time, Mr Cavanagh," Tully said, and nodded at Livia. She tapped the air and Cavanagh disappeared. Tully leaned on the table next to Lottie, who was still typing away, tidying up his original draft using an AI assistant. "So help me, Lottie, you'd better have something ready to go out…"

"It's done," she said. "And perfect, if you ask me."

"Thank you."

"After I had a chance to fix your shitty writing, that is." She made her screen public.

He scanned the text. "Not bad." Behind him, Bolivar swore. Tully swung around. "What is it?"

"They're about to announce some breaking news from Athens."

"The round six results? Already?"

"Looks like they reached a result quicker than they expected." Bolivar created a public screen showing a newscast and turned up the sound.

A commentator was talking to the camera. "… and the official results of Round Six are now due after a week of deadlock. So, let's turn live to the election congress chair here in Athens, former UN Secretary-General Amare Abara, to hear which of the twenty candidates are through to Round Seven."

Amare Abara climbed onto the stage of a huge auditorium in Athens. His hair had silvered since his time in the UN. He looked wiser, a serious guy for serious times.

"Thank you," Abara said. "We've unexpectedly narrowed the pool of candidates from twenty to a final two, either of which could win a majority against any of the other candidates. They'll progress to the global popular vote on the first of September."

Every country in the world had submitted a candidate in Round One, nearly six months before. No one had expected to reach a final two this quickly, let alone that the election itself would now be in six weeks' time.

Abara paused and looked up and around the congress venue, thousands of quiet delegations from governments around the world watching him. This was a moment that would be replayed in the history reels, and for a moment he seemed almost overwhelmed by it. The camera zoomed in, and he swallowed, taking a sip of water and a deep breath.

"The first candidate for dictator, nominated by the United States of America, its former two-term President, Lawrence G. Lockwood," he said.

Applause from the delegations in Athens, but the office in London was silent.

"I thought the pollsters said there was no way an American would be nominated," Lottie said.

She was right. Maybe once upon a time, America would have clearly led the pack, but it'd squandered that leadership over many decades as the country itself had become more polarised and elected more extreme leaders on both ends of the spectrum.

Bolivar snorted. "Pollsters."

The applause in Athens had died down, and the delegations were waiting expectantly to hear which candidate would face Lockwood in the final two.

Abara stared at the paper in his hands as if he couldn't bring himself to read what was on it. The auditorium was now silent, bar a couple of coughs. The silence stretched on well past the point of comfort. Tully wondered if Abara was unwell. Surely he'd known who the final candidates would be before he went on stage? What was going on?

Abara seemed to pull himself together, with a little shake of his head, like he had some kind of internal argument going on. He looked up, and the paper dropped out of his fingers and drifted out of camera shot. "The second and final candidate for dictator," he said, much slower and enunciated, this time, as if he wanted to make sure everyone caught his words with no chance for misunderstanding. He coughed and raised his eyebrows. "Excuse me. Nominated by the Floating States, their incumbent head of state and Artificial Intellect, Governor Solomon."

There was uproar from the moment he'd said Floating States, and the volume of his last words had gone up and up in order to be heard, until he practically shouted the name of Solomon. Audience members were swearing, gasping, and certainly not applauding. It was chaos.

A new headline appeared on the feed: *DICTATORSHIP: ARTIFICIAL INTELLECT SOLOMON IN FINAL TWO.*

The breath had stopped in Tully's throat. Solomon. The first AI—or artilect, as pundits were beginning to call it—to hold political office. It was technology that had been first deployed nine years ago to manage the six new sea-cities known collectively as the Floating States. Solomon could appear in neuro-reality like a real person, to millions of people, individually, at once. It could make complex decisions from billions of data points in nanoseconds. It'd been designed by a woman regarded as a genius, Martha Chandra. Tully knew Martha. He'd interviewed her several times, early in their career. They weren't friends, not exactly, but they liked each other.

Moreover, Martha owed Tully a favour. He employed Martha's sister, Livia.

"Shit," Bolivar said. "Shit!"

Lottie snorted. "The tabloids are already spinning for Lockwood. 'App Makes Last Two For Dictator.' Now that's a headline."

4

"That sinks our story," Bolivar said. "We'll never get traction on it now. We've lost the news cycle."

This story would dominate for days. Tully knew it. Rightly so. Even getting to two candidates this quickly was huge news, but for one of those candidates to be an artilect? No one had imagined Solomon would actually stand a chance, even though the technology had proved extremely successful in managing the Floating States. Mayor Kehoe and Cavanagh would think themselves saved; that there'd be no way Tully could publish the Houston story now.

Tully watched Livia as she sat down on her office chair like she'd just emerged from a shelled trench. She stared at her trembling hands and slid them beneath her knees. It was complicated between her and Martha. Understandably so. Martha was a wealthy genius who lived in a penthouse on a floating sea-city. Livia was an impoverished researcher for an independent journalist crew who slept at the office. They weren't playing in the same league. Livia was doggy-paddling while her sister won the Olympics in the butterfly. How must Livia feel now, with her sister making history?

Bolivar muted the newscast but left the screen up, filled now with multiple pundits all arguing with each other.

"Do we delay?" Randall said. "I mean, it might make sense and I can contact all the influencers—"

"But I thought Solomon was a joke nomination?" Lottie said over him. "It's not even a real person—"

"*He's* not even a real person," Randall interrupted her back.

"It's unbelievable," Bolivar said. "An artilect as a last-two candidate? Did *you* even think that was going to happen, Livia? Did your sister think their campaign would get this far?"

Everyone stopped talking, now, and they all looked at Livia. She coloured. "I've no idea," she mumbled. "I haven't spoken to Martha in weeks."

Solomon and the dictatorship was the biggest story out there, but Tully was sitting on the Houston story like a chicken guarding an egg, and he needed to hatch that egg for three reasons. First, what had happened in Houston was terrible, and they had an obligation to get the truth about the government's use of illegal technology out there. Second, they badly needed the money they'd make from this article. And third, he couldn't get this new tabkhir story from Whistle if he didn't get this story published first. "It doesn't matter," Tully said. "We still publish. Bolivar, how long do we have left?"

Bolivar checked his schedule. "We're a minute past our scheduled go-live, if we're going to use the influencers to push it out. They'll likely stick around another minute or two, tops."

Tully massaged his forehead. "Cavanagh worked in the White House for Kehoe, right, before Kehoe was Mayor of Houston? Wasn't Kehoe formerly President Lockwood's chief of staff?"

Livia ran a search. "Republican, 2037 to 41, yeah, chief of staff to President Lockwood." She looked up. "It looks like he's still close to Lockwood, too. Rumour has it he'll be appointed his new campaign chief. He's probably resigning as Mayor anyway."

"Lottie, read out our current headline for the Houston story," Tully said.

Lottie squinted. "Mayor of Houston ordered police to provoke climate protestors to riot."

"Change it," Tully said. "Lockwood campaign chief ordered police, et cetera." The Houston story had become a much bigger scoop than they'd anticipated. Lockwood was aligning himself with corruption. It was a damning statement of his character and judgement, and the world needed to know.

"Makes it an attack on Lockwood," Lottie said. "He'll be furious, won't he?" But she was already typing.

"As your lawyer, Marcus—" Bolivar started.

Tully held up his hands to forestall the obvious argument. They had no time to explore the legal ramifications. "Lockwood is running for a position with almost absolute power, with a mandate to prevent a climate apocalypse. It's relevant who he chooses to work for him. Lottie, tweak the opening paragraph too."

Lottie's fingers were blurs. "Done. Ready to sign?"

An alarm audible only to Tully chirped six p.m. It was already midday in Houston. It was followed by a pang with a notification from Lottie linking to the article. *Sign,* he subspoke. His neuro-assistant added his unique biometric key—the only way his audience could be sure his words were really coming from him. "Randall, publish."

"And we're up." Randall clapped his hands and thrust his fist to the sky. "Man, this is going to trend, I'm telling you all. This is going to be insane—"

Tully tuned him out. A glowing green counter appeared to the bottom left of his vision, showing the financial tally in coins, flicking up in 0.01c increments as loyal readers around the world paid micro-transactions to read his article.

"Lift off," he whispered.

They needed this. There was no other story in sight, right now. As if his words had been an incantation, the increments accelerated and started rounding to the nearest coin, then the nearest ten.

He looked at Bolivar and cocked his head to the side, indicating they should step out of earshot of the others. Looking out from the floor-to-ceiling window, which stretched across the entire face of the Western side of the skyscraper, they could see the fluted column of the Monument to the Great Fire of London below, topped with a glinting golden urn. When the fire swept through London, it must have felt like the end of civilisation to those living here at the time. They couldn't have imagined the entire world would be burning nearly four hundred years later.

"How much time do you think we've bought ourselves, financially?" Tully asked.

"Ask me again tomorrow," Bolivar replied. "At least it's getting some traction. We've definitely added a few weeks." He hesitated. "Look, about that footage you were watching. I'm sorry if I was insensitive."

"It's fine."

"Honestly, though, it worried me. These last years, you seemed to be starting to finally move on. You've suffered so much. I don't want to see you go back there."

"Marcus," Livia said, "you've got a confidential call coming in. Caller isn't identified, but it looks like you've spoken before, ah, two days ago." Her eyes flickered towards him then fixed on her screen. "I've never seen anything like it before. Their identity is masked."

"Put it through to my room in NR," Tully said, "and see if you and Randall can trace the call."

Back in his room, he sat at his desk, popped a neurograin bubble, and pulled on his Mindscape headset; within a few seconds, he was back in his egospace.

This time, he took a few moments to gather himself. He stood within a spherical glass pod about ten strides long and wide, like the interior of a Christmas snow globe. The pod was softly lit from the floor in strip lights around the perimeter. There was no afternoon sunlight here—it was deep beneath a cerulean blue lake—though outside, a sprinkling of sun beams cut through the water and an underwater-city vista with thousands of other floating spheres glowed, each pod lit from within, illuminating fish of every imaginable colour.

In the centre of his pod floor was a three-dimensional digital avatar of Zainab that he'd commissioned in better times. The recreation of his wife had been extracted from the last photo taken of her by her mother, heavily pregnant and exuding a happy glow. He'd sought balm for his soul, while the artist had attempted to capture hers. The artist had succeeded.

Tully had not.

He touched her face, then jerked his gaze away and waved his right hand upwards to bring up a navigation menu. He selected the option to issue an invite to the unknown contact, then opened the meeting app.

Whistle was already there, in the same beautiful hotel lobby space they'd met in before, still dressed the same, still chewing that gum, like they'd never left. "Nice work."

Tully shrugged. "The footage was pretty compelling."

"So you agree I'm not full of shit, right?"

"Why don't you tell me what's really going on?"

Whistle fell silent, but Tully it drag. Rushing too quickly to fill awkward gaps was always a mistake.

"Okay, fine," Whistle murmured. "You've seen the Houston footage and the tabkhir footage, now. The point is, I find things. I know things. And one thing I found, one thing I know, is that the tabkhir wasn't *meant* to hit the Persian Gulf."

Tully's stomach dropped out from beneath him and for a few seconds he forgot to breathe. The meeting space was claustrophobic and he fought back an urge to rip off his headset. "Wasn't meant to? What does that mean?"

"Remember the cat-five hurricane that hit Louisiana just before the tabkhir?"

"No. But big hurricanes hitting that part of the US were pretty common, even back then."

"Earl, they called it. Brought a lot of misery. More importantly, it brought humidity from the Atlantic. I'm not talking uncomfortable humidity. I'm talking the kind that kills you. The kind where the human body can't cool itself. It was already sweltering, they'd been struggling with big heatwaves and wildfires for decades, were terrified they'd get one with high humidity… so they were exploring geo-engineering tech to intervene if things got bad."

"I don't remember the US having a bad heatwave that year, and certainly not a humid one."

"Yeah, well," Whistle said. "The tech they deployed could displace humidity up into the stratosphere. Where it could disperse, y'know? It was untested, though, and the expert who developed it warned them it wasn't ready yet. Weather is unpredictable, right? But they wanted to save American lives. Especially ones in heavily Republican states. So President Lockwood used it anyway."

"I'm not following," Tully said. "What's this got to do with the tabkhir?"

"The humidity. It was hot in the Gulf then, too. But the humidity that swept across the Arabian Peninsula? Came outta nowhere. Complete surprise. No one saw it coming, not that any scientist wanted to admit that in the weeks and years afterwards."

One day it had been high; the next, deadly. A humid hell.

Tully leaned forward. "You're saying … Let me get this straight. You're trying to tell me they deflected an entire heatwave. To the Persian Gulf?"

Whistle looked tired. "Fucking right they did. Displaced the humidity into the stratosphere. But they knew it had to come down somewhere. They knew it, right? It landed on half a billion people. It landed on your wife."

5

Tully pulled off the Mindscape headset, stood, steadied himself against the study desk and stumbled out of the room back into the hub workspace. Not since his first shot at neuro-reality had he experienced such a state of disorientation.

"What happened?" Bolivar said. "You look terrible."

Tully dropped into an office chair. His team stared at him.

"Who was it?" Bolivar tried again.

"Did you manage to track the call?" Tully said.

Randall was huddled with Livia. "I don't get it, there's always a trace, always a sign that leads you somewhere, but this guy, Mr Tully, has some serious tech," Randall said. "I mean, there's nothing—it's like we were called by a ghost. Which, by the way, I'd be less shocked at—"

Tully held up a hand. "Okay, enough." Five years Randall had worked for him, and the man still talked like he was going to run out of air.

"Surely that's not possible," Livia said. "Everyone's trackable over commercial NR."

"That's what I'm saying," Randall said. "I mean, the Mindscape platform was designed around hard authentication—you're meant to be able to trust it. You can't pretend to be someone else, you can't set up a fake profile, you have to prove you are who you say you are, right? Anyway, I know one of the developers at Minds. Maybe there's a backdoor and we can find out how this dude is hiding their identity—"

"Stop," Tully said. "Whistle is a source, even if they are on deep background. And they're worried about their safety. This stays with us."

"Whistle?" Livia said.

"Not their real name."

"And why are they worried about their safety, Tully?" Bolivar said. "What have they got?"

"Whistle told me," Tully said, "that the US administration at the time of the tabkhir actually caused the humidity to hit the Persian Gulf. That it was going to hit the US. That they deployed some sort of geo-tech and shifted it away from them."

"Shifted it … Towards the Gulf?" Bolivar frowned.

"They'd been told the tech was unreliable." Tully tried to relax his hands. "They knew how unpredictable weather systems are. Their experts cautioned them to stop."

"Which US administration was it?" asked Bolivar.

Tully sighed and ran his hands through his hair. "Lockwood's." No one spoke. They all just looked at each other. "They hoped and prayed it would hit the sea, but hopes and prayers weren't enough."

"Hundreds of millions, dead," Livia whispered, "because the tech was unreliable?"

"Like, weather is crazy unpredictable," Randall said. "I mean, everyone knows you don't geo-engineer unless you're sure you know what you're doing."

Scattered bodies, stretched out in the gutter. "Yeah."

Bolivar stood, walked to the kitchen, and returned with a bottle of artisan rum and some glasses. He poured for Tully first. By the time he'd filled everyone's glass, Tully's was empty. Bolivar refilled it with no comment, and sighed. "Why reveal the truth after all this time? Why now?"

That was the thing about the truth; it only came out when the cost of lying became too high. Tully cocked his head at the newscasts. "Lockwood's forty-five days out from becoming the most powerful person on the planet. It's now a two-horse race for the dictatorship, and Lockwood's up against an artilect, which is an incredible achievement on Martha's part—" he glanced at Livia, who nodded—"but it's a race I think he'll easily win. Lockwood will be untouchable."

"But that doesn't explain why this whistleblower didn't come forward before," Bolivar said. "He had years to do so."

"Whistle said it was possible the revelation would cause a war. But now they felt the risk of having Lockwood in charge of resolving our climate issues, when he's made a prior mistake of this magnitude, makes war the least-worse outcome."

"That's all very well," Bolivar argued, "but Lockwood only just became a dictatorship finalist, and no one expected him to get this far. This whistleblower could have had no idea Lockwood would reach the last two when they first contacted you."

Tully shrugged. "Maybe Whistle thought that Lockwood being one of twenty final candidates was enough of a risk."

"One thing I don't understand," Livia said. "How did moving humidity away from the US kill people in the Gulf?"

"There was already a heatwave in the Gulf," Tully said. "But apparently it had a wet-bulb temp of around thirty degrees C." The wet-bulb had been the measure of heat combined with humidity for a hundred years, now, but had only become the default scale for heatwaves in the last twenty years. "It was apparently like some of the European heatwaves. Hot, but dry. Enough to kill, but not many. When the Americans deflected the humidity, it drifted towards the Arabian Peninsula, causing the wet-bulb temperature to go up rapidly."

"And the tabkhir," Randall said, "was the first time on record we hit forty-two degrees centigrade on the wet-bulb, right? And anything after thirty-five, wet, would make the heat feel more like fifty, so this would have felt more like sixty. At that humidity, sweat no longer cools you, it just doesn't work, it's incredible really, your brain starts to shut down, then all the organs follow and, bam! You're dead, cooked from the inside out. I mean, tabkhir kinda translates as steaming, and that's exactly—"

Lottie punched him in the arm and he yelped.

"What?" Randall looked at Lottie like a puppy that had been kicked, then blanched. "Ah, sorry, Mr Tully," Randall said.

Tully stared at the floor. How much pain did Zainab feel, when that had happened to her? Had she slipped into some kind of sleep well before, or had she felt the pain of everything shutting down?

Bolivar poured Tully a fresh rum and sat back. "How do we even begin to validate this? Especially if this whistleblower won't reveal his identity?"

"Whistle told me the truth needed to come out, but didn't have the hard evidence. Said an authentication ID of a source with more direct involvement would be in our dead drop, someone able to provide hard evidence, or at least verification." Tully nodded at Livia. "Check it."

Livia tapped away, looking at a private screen, then looked up at Tully. "There's an encrypted authentication code in the dead drop."

"Randall, can you figure out who it belongs to?"

Randall leapt up and clapped his hands. "The question isn't whether I can, but how fast. I have this new software—"

"Just get it done," Bolivar said, and took a deep, slow breath.

Tully got up, walked to the lounge and slumped on the sofas, staring out the window.

Bolivar followed him and sat opposite. "Maybe this is too personal a story for you to be covering." He hesitated. "I'm worried it brings back a lot of things I'd hoped you'd moved on from."

Of course it did. He'd spent years getting over his wife's death. There was nothing worse he could imagine than having to even think about the tabkhir, but his own feelings were irrelevant. This was an enormous scoop and they had no choice but to investigate it fully to find out the truth of what really happened. "How's the Houston story doing?" Tully asked him.

Bolivar sighed, as if resigned to Tully changing the subject, but scanned his own display for a few seconds. "One and a half million views in the forty-five minutes since we went live, fifty thousand new ones a minute. Key locations are North and South America, plus Europe, but that's a time-zone thing." He threw the numbers up onto the shared projection. "We've got a few requests from morning shows for interviews."

"How much are the stories on the election outperforming us?"

"Well, surprisingly, we're in the top five tonight. The others are straight commentary from Athens."

"Lockwood's giving a speech," Livia called, and she flicked another virtual screen into the air.

They went back over. "I'm happy to accept this nomination," Lockwood was saying to the camera in full elder-statesman mode, "and look forward to campaigning with dignity and respect against Governor Solomon in the course of the next few months. The world has asked for a leader to step up and save us …"

Randall whooped. He'd been working trying to figure out who the authentication code really belonged to. "I've got it. Now, our credible source-to-be is from the US. Man, oh man, you're going to absolutely love this. Wait, I need to stand for this—"

"Randall!" Bolivar snapped. "Get on with it!"

"Yessir, Mr Bolivar, our credible source, as introduced by our mysterious Whistle, is … drum-roll, please … thanks, Livia … our source is none other than Mayor Kehoe's main dude, Mr William Cavanagh!"

Tully looked down at the floor. "Shit."

6

Livia swore at the slivers of early sunlight that slipped past the dust and the blinds. She grabbed her blended-reality earset from beside the bed and popped it over her right ear, then grabbed a white metal dispenser stamped with a logo—*Minds*—and popped out a neurograin bubble directly into her mouth, pushing it around with her tongue until it was beneath it. The display blurrily kicked in as the nanobots took root, and she blinked away the last remnants of sleep, rubbing her eyes with one hand as the other launched the Minds app and scrolled through the overnight posts.

She tapped at one of the posts hanging in the air in front of her, and the voice of a newscast pundit blared inside her head with the hurricane force of a bad hangover.

"… result last night surprised many observers…"

"Shit!" she yelped. She shakily lowered the volume. Her cheeks were hot. For a moment she'd forgotten the sounds were just in her head and thought she'd woken all the team that lived in Tully's office, and more, that they'd know exactly what she was watching.

"…with the artilect governor seen still as experimental, even for the Floating States," the pundit continued, at a much more reasonable volume.

No reason to feel guilty, though. Everyone in the world was hooked on this election, especially now, though she'd bet no one here followed things as much as she did. Although this was what came of living with colleagues. Your little quirks became your little secrets and your little guilt trips. But no one needed to know. Just one addiction swapped for another. And at least this one wouldn't kill her.

She kicked back the covers and swung out of the single bed, without looking away from the newscast to explore the cup situation. Whatever. Clean cups were overrated. She picked up a relatively unstained one and shoved it under the coffee machine. As the machine wheezed, Livia repositioned a virtual screen above a small line of worn hardback books. One of them caught her eye and she grinned. *Thanks a lot, Dad. This is all on you.* Scripts for forgotten political TV series. She'd curl up under his arm and watch them with him. It had been their special thing. She hadn't understood much of them, but she'd been there for the cuddles. In those moments, he'd been all hers. Meanwhile, her sister had sat across the room, alone, headphones on, glued to a laptop, coding her little chatbots for their voice speakers. How ironic that Martha, the one with zero interest in politics, had been the one who ended up in the White House with that fancy title, Chief Nerd Officer or something.

Tap.

Martha had already ticked that off and moved on to even greater things, while Livia was living in her boss's bedsit, drinking too much coffee. The machine whirred, sighed and stopped. Livia took the cup and sipped the froth while the liquid cooled.

Tap.

Speaking of greater things, someone had shared a video of Jasper Keeling, CEO of Floating States. He'd commissioned much of Martha's early coding work on Solomon. She tapped, curiosity piqued.

"We asked Dr Chandra to develop Solomon because we believed the complexity of decisions we'd need to make were beyond the capability of professional politicians and even private CEOs like myself, or 'the builder' as my wife likes to call me." Keeling laughed. "No, we needed someone who could absorb data in the blink of an eye and make high-quality decisions that would keep our people safe. And AI has finally reached the stage where—"

Tap.

A different newscaster said, "Who would have predicted that an American leader would emerge from the deadlock of the past few weeks, only fifteen years after they dropped the whole 'leader of the free world' anachronism. Jim, I find that more surprising than the AI, don't you?"

Dad would have loved this "race for the dictatorship", as they were calling it. He'd have been just like her, squandering every free moment on Minds, soaking up every word of the leading commentators and journalists at the primary convention in Athens. Though he wouldn't have been so sodding secretive about it.

A message pinged across her display. *Come catch up?*

Who else but Tully would want to meet at coffee o'clock? What time even was it? Seven? He must have heard her shout. His study and suite was next to her bedroom, and the walls were thin partitions.

She glanced across at the mirror. He'd have to wait. She couldn't leave her room looking like this. Which was the real challenge living in the same place you worked from, wasn't it? You couldn't slouch out into the hub in your loungewear.

She peeled off her pyjama top and typed a response in the air. *Ten minutes?*

↬

THIRTY MINUTES LATER, she stood before the open door of Tully's study. It still felt weird just to be able to walk straight in. Weirder that he even kept his door open. Doors should stay closed. All the better for keeping those little foibles out of sight.

"Morning," he called.

She entered. The study was as big as her bedroom, which contained her own workspace as well as a minuscule toilet and shower room. The air was delicately scented. Mahogany or something manly—all men secretly wanted to be rugged lumberjacks. Not like her room, not at all. Tully sat behind his desk, centred in the middle of the room with its back to the windows, two seats perched in front. Her eyes flicked beyond him to another door, behind which lay his bedroom and bathroom. Now *that* door was shut. She wondered whether he was the kind of guy to make his bed in the morning. Probably. He wasn't like her.

Tully nodded and his eyes flicked up and to the left as if he was checking the time in his display. He was in full-on gentleman mode this morning, however, and didn't comment on her tardiness.

He had four virtual screens positioned two up, two down, hovering in front of his desk so he could see them from where he was sitting, and he waved them

32

to the side so they could both see them, blocking her view of the bedroom door. His feeds weren't tuned to the election footage—the weirdo—but four different newscasts showing the previous night's riots in Houston.

She nodded towards the screens. "I didn't catch the latest. What's happening?"

He sighed. "The protests certainly swelled after our story. They were out all night."

"Do you feel responsible?"

Idiot, what kind of question was that? Besides, this was Marcus Tully; he never admitted he was wrong.

"No."

Classic, but had he hesitated ever so briefly? Never. The coffee must be messing with her imagination.

He didn't invite her to sit, so perhaps she'd somehow turned off gentleman mode. "I need you to brief me on Cavanagh," he said.

Did he want the 'executive' briefing, a very above-board capture of Cavanagh's personal bio to bring him and Bolivar up to speed? That would take an hour, tops, and he knew it. Or did he want the special package? A much more delicate ask. He'd never request it directly. That would mean acknowledging unspoken secrets. And it would also take more time. "How long do I have?"

He looked her straight in the eyes, unblinking. "A day. Work some magic for me."

⌇

HER STOMACH RUMBLED, reminding her she hadn't had dinner. Not that she deserved dinner. She still had nothing. A constant stream of updates about the election primaries played in the background, but she ignored them and created a virtual sheet of paper—very old school—and shoved all the cold, half-full coffee mugs to the side.

Stay cool. Make a list. Nothing like a list to calm you down. No point in panicking. Not yet. Sure, her approach was unusual, but it yielded results. Usually. But this was why closed doors were good. Yes, to hide the fact she was back in pyjamas. But also to preserve her little secrets. Let the team believe their little myth, that Livia Chandra was a freaking Sherlock Holmes when it came to working through a mass of publicly available information and spotting red flags. She should get herself a deerstalker. No, she was the Code Reaper. She wrote procedures that slashed through the endless orchards of information, plucking only the finest fruit before the team had even finished their breakfast.

She ordered the current data into bullet points.

She was smart in her own way. Not smart-smart like Martha, of course. The notion gave her pause. While she'd been falling apart after their dad had died, Martha had brought Solomon into the world. It could be annoying, sometimes, having a genius for a sister. Sure, she'd built a secret bot to spot patterns, but *Martha* had pioneered the first technology capable of governing a state. Still, Constellation was pretty damn good at its job, and in that domain would stand up against Solomon, any day of the week.

Constellation found the quietest signals in the loudest noises. Only sometimes it needed a little help. And this was another of her little secrets.

She threw down the virtual pencil, rubbed her eyes and looked around for a warm cup of coffee. There was none. She considered the several paces to the coffee machine, then grabbed one of the cold mugs and steeled herself for the bitter ride. She sipped. Not the worst she'd had.

Cavanagh. There was something here. He was dirty. But in what way? Public-domain information delivered a big fat zero. Same with the more confidential stuff like tax returns.

She started a new list, not personal this time but professional. Everything that had passed through his office, every news article mentioning him. She widened that further—everything connected to him, his office generally, or one of his staff. And more channels. The web, social, Minds, every public database.

Satisfied, she began feeding new instructions into Constellation. And, so instructed, it began to chew data.

～

Livia's six a.m. alarm sounded, but she was already working at her desk, tweaking Constellation's parameters. She waved the chimes away, then scrunched her nose at the faint miasma of body odour. Maybe it was time to take a shower.

Tully pinged her. *Anything?*

She ignored it. She'd be ready when she was ready. He'd have to be patient. His message didn't even merit a reply. He was ridiculous. Besides, he was up way too early.

She sighed, spun up a keyboard and tapped a response: *Getting there!* "Come on, Constellation," she muttered.

Constellation didn't reply. It couldn't. Martha would have built a talking version, of course. Her sister had built more advanced bots than Constellation before she'd had her first period.

What about Martha?

No, she couldn't. Not again.

She glanced back down at her reply to Tully, then tapped her forefinger and thumbed twice, activating her voice assistant. "Call Martha Chandra."

What time was it in New Carthage, anyway? What time was it here for that matter?

A photorealistic avatar of her sister appeared on the virtual screen. She sniffed at the use of the tech. It was less personal and more private to share avatars because you didn't need to be in front of a camera. Plus, the photorealistic emulation and sensors that detected emotional states, changing the facial features accordingly, were good enough to replace the live view. But, come on, surely her own sister deserved a live shot. And, naturally, Martha's avatar was dressed simple but smart. The good looks were real, at least. Martha had somehow inherited not only the family genes for genius and charisma, but also the always-beautiful-and-smart genes.

"Olive? You look a wreck!"

Of course, Livia didn't use an avatar and was just being picked up on camera. And clearly her sister had not been passed any of the family diplomacy genes. "Good morning to you too," Livia said.

"It's six-thirty in the morning here." Martha paused a second. "It's seven thirty where you are. You're still in your pyjamas?"

"I'm on a mission."

"And I thought this was a social call." A light dash of sarcasm laced Martha's tone, an intentional flavour, like a masterfully prepared cocktail with a hint of smokiness added at the end.

"Hey, it is! So …" Okay, so she needed to sort herself out and start somewhere simple. Small talk 101—establish location. "Where are you? Where's New Carthage now, I mean?" That was the thing with talking to someone who lived on a floating, moving sea-city. You were never entirely sure which sea they were in, right now.

Martha examined her as if she had some X-ray tech hooked up to her screen. She didn't need it. Martha had always been able to see though her little sister. "South Atlantic. We're taking advantage of slightly cooler temperatures and keeping clear of hurricane season."

Well, her small talk was exhausted, and Livia hadn't taken class 202.

Martha raised an eyebrow and let the silence drag for a moment, then put Livia out of her misery. "Just come out with it, Olive. You want an exclusive interview with Solomon for Tully, don't you?"

Olive had been her father's nickname for her. She pushed away the brief pang of grief. "Oh! Congratulations on that, by the way."

"You already sent me a message saying that."

"Yeah. Okay, so I need help," Livia said. "But not with an interview. Tully doesn't do that kind of journalism. I need help with another story."

Martha studied her for a few seconds more, then tapped something that established a more secure connection. "Solomon's help?"

"Yeah. Sorry."

"It was a one-off favour, the first time. I didn't intend for this to turn into a regular thing." Martha's avatar got up and the camera panned out. "Anyway, it's not what I built him for. He isn't there to prop up your new job. If anyone found out, it would compromise the entire project, particularly now he's one of the final two election candidates." She sipped at some tea. Was it real, or also an avatar?

A throb of worry kicked deep in Livia's belly. She peered at her own mug, but only found coffee dregs. She pretended it was full anyway and sipped air. "Constellation isn't up to scratch yet. I need a result here, sis. I'm trying to build a reputation."

"Olive, you can't build a reputation on fragile foundations. If you need Solomon to do your work, perhaps the answers aren't meant to be found." Martha had already perfected her big-sister lectures by the time she'd hit double-figures.

"Tully would say that was the thing about truth: it's *always* meant to be found," Livia said. Martha knew Tully. It was her who'd asked him to rescue Livia, after all. She liked him, respected him, thought far more of him than she thought of Livia, that was for sure.

Martha just sighed and crossed her arms. "What's the story, Olive?"

"Something to do with the tabkhir and a cover-up. We've had an anonymous tip-off about a potential source. A guy called Cavanagh."

It was hard to judge Martha's expression from her avatar, but she was still long enough for Livia to wonder if the feed had frozen. "Martha?"

"William Cavanagh?" Martha said. "You're sure?"

"You know him?"

The seconds dragged, then Martha replied, "I worked with him. He was at the White House during President Lockwood's administration."

The reply had been… Careful. "Martha, I'm sorry. I don't know what it is with this guy. Maybe he's changed since back then, but something's off."

"I doubt he's changed. He'll still be the corrupt, bigoted, snooping bastard he always was." That was one for the record. Martha never, ever swore. She was the one always telling Livia to see the good in people. "Last time, Olive," Martha said. "And please be careful. Absolutely no one can know Solomon was involved. Not even Tully. I need to build a lot of trust in Solomon right now."

The worry-throb in Livia's stomach evaporated. "You totally got it."

"And be very cautious of William Cavanagh—and his associates."

Livia nodded.

"I'll see you soon?" Martha asked.

Unlikely, and they both knew it. It was the price of them both being workaholics. "Sure," Livia said, and smiled.

"I'll patch you through in NR."

"Bye—"

Martha hung up.

Livia slipped on her Mindscape headset and popped a bubble of neurograins. There was the usual jolt that came from the sense of being transported in time and space, but it was offset by the familiarity of her egospace, a memory of her father's study. His scent, the spiciness of an expensive aftershave, hung in the air like he'd just stepped out of the room. She closed her eyes and took in a long, luxurious breath, and for a moment she was seven years old again and he was still alive and she was still safe and everything was still okay.

Then he was gone.

The tinge of sadness was worth it for the peace that flowed through her, almost as good as that from a real drug.

She walked over to the old antique partners' desk and clambered into her father's chair. A child's memory, a giant's furniture. She ran her fingers over the green leather writing insert and a small, framed photo of Martha and herself on the desk. Martha was about six in the photo, Livia about four. She smiled and took in the small pile of script books on the far side. They'd been in better condition back then.

The chirrup of an old-fashioned mobile phone preceded the appearance of a virtual green button, and the caller ID announced the visitor. Solomon.

She accepted and the office faded. A blast of heat and the smell of horses and baked bread hit her. She steadied herself and grinned. Solomon knew she liked the historical mindscapes. But this was no ruin. The ancient steps to a temple in the Roman Forum were intact and toga-clad citizens busied themselves with their day.

"It's beautiful, Solomon," she said, turning to the tall figure standing with her. Martha had loosely modelled the artilect on their father. Strong and chiselled, though young, perhaps early forties.

"Thank you, Olive." His voice reminded her of those wonderful old-time theatre actors she'd seen in movies from a hundred years earlier.

She caught herself. Solomon wasn't a person, but it was easy enough to slip into thinking of him as one. Even his pronoun had unconsciously evolved from a determined 'it' when Martha had brought him online, nine years earlier, to a 'he'. Livia gestured towards the scene. "Did you recreate this from old pictures?"

"Partly, but I augmented them with data from original sources and a modern scan of the contemporary site, to get the details right."

"It's incredible. Which temple was this?"

"Jupiter. God of the sky and thunder," Solomon said.

"How did you figure out what it would smell like?" How did an artilect even comprehend the idea of smell and recreate what it couldn't experience itself?

He smiled. "It's much less of a trick than you might imagine. You're not really smelling anything in NR, just like you're not really experiencing any of the senses directly. It's all plugged straight into your brain, which does most of the heavy lifting. *You* know what things like baked bread smell like, so I just make sure the scene evokes that sensation."

"Magicians aren't meant to reveal their tricks, Solomon. You're meant to look mysterious and say it's because you're incredibly smart."

"Well, I am incredibly—"

She snorted in laughter and he grinned.

"My God, I didn't say congratulations to you," Livia said. "It still feels almost unbelievable."

"Thank you. It's an honour, of course. I just want to help as best I can." He paused and looked a little sad. "How are you, Olive?"

Solomon was the only one apart from Martha, now, who called her Olive. "I'm good."

He turned and took both of her hands in his, like her father used to do. "You're taking proper care of yourself, Olive? Not slipping back into old habits?"

She swallowed and blinked away the momentary pang of loss. "I'm fine, really. I'm clean."

He nodded, let her hands go, his expression morose.

"What is it?" she said.

"It's a silly thing, but I was struck for a moment that eventually I'll have outlived everyone I know—all the humans who've befriended me, everyone I've come to care about. I grieve for that."

She put her hand on his arm and he smiled.

"How is your new job going?" he said.

"Good, mostly. Marcus Tully is a good boss, and some days I can't believe I get to work with him. I like the team a lot. We broke an important story the other day and it did well, so I've probably got more coin in my account than I've ever had. Although there's little chance to spend it. Tully never seems to have finished the last job before he's on to the next."

"The famous Marcus Tully. It would be interesting to meet him one day. I liked his exposé of the French finance minister's role in the climate slavery scandal, and the story on the mayor of Houston the other day."

Livia winced. "You did me a big favour on the French one. But I need your help again, I'm afraid."

"Of course. What can I do?"

"There's this guy involved in a story we're doing. I've got Constellation working on pattern recognition."

"What's his name?"

"William Cavanagh. He's—"

"The chief of staff to Mayor Kehoe of Houston. When Mr Kehoe was himself chief of staff to President Lawrence G. Lockwood, Mr Cavanagh was deputy chief of staff in that Republican administration until the Democrats took over in January 2041."

"That's the one." But she was worried. "Does this give you a conflict of some kind? Given that he worked for your new opponent?"

"No, as long as I keep my search to his time after he worked with President Lockwood. You've primed Constellation with existing public sources?"

"I have."

"In that case, I shall work with Constellation."

"Thank you, Solomon. I owe you one. Not that I can see how I'd repay you, but—"

"Actually, there is something you could do for me."

That was a surprise. What could an artilect possibly want? "Of course."

"I like hearing you talk about your life and work with Mr Tully. If you can stay a while, I'd enjoy listening to some more." Solomon smiled at her. "And in the meantime, you can rest assured Constellation and I have already begun working on your request."

How could she say no?

7

Tully sheltered under a shop awning as a crowd surged down Avenida Rio Branco, Rio de Janeiro, like a tsunami sweeping over dry land. A cacophony of three million voices roared around him, echoing off the high-rise buildings on either side of them: "Save us! *Salve-nos!* Save us! *Salve-nos!*"

It was four a.m., local time, but the protest showed no sign of burning out. Not since Carnival had so many ventured onto the streets here. The faces ranged from young to old. There was no way of telling who'd come from the favelas and who'd come from the villas. It didn't matter; all but the richest one percent had been abandoned to fate, their chance of salvation resting only in the dictatorship, and what kind of chance was that?

"*Salve-nos! Salve-nos! Salve-nos!*"

He pulled off his Mindscape headset and rubbed his eyes, blinking in the morning sun that streamed into his study. It could be difficult to orient yourself after an extended visit in neuro-reality, especially one as intense as that. In one night, he'd visited four cities undergoing four protests—sparking occasionally into riots. Houston, Paris and Jakarta were also seething in the sweltering summer, the anger only dampened by the dawn as the mobs retreated to the safety of aircon. They'd be boiling over again by evening. Rage, spreading like a contagion. And these weren't the only four, not by a long way. Even London had experienced protests last night, right down the road from here.

He stood, stretched and walked over to the window. He'd told the truth, that was his job. But that was the thing about truth, once you'd set it free, you had to let it go. Whatever happened, happened, and it was just the price you had to pay. They were right to riot. Too many had been "displaced" as the waters and the temperatures had risen these past twenty years, pushed into new ghettos only to move on again as those, too, flooded or baked. They either had nothing or were going to lose it all, and they needed their voices to be heard.

Tully opened the newscast on his blended-reality earset and frowned. A drone camera was filming a glass and concrete skyscraper from above, dwarfing the towering column of Monument beyond it. Was that *their* building? He turned up the volume. Jordan Bamphwick, the American right-wing populist commentator famed for his monologues, was in full flow. "… easy to write about the plight of the poor from up high in his ivory tower. After all, from that height, from the safety of his climate-controlled stateroom, Marcus Tully has an excellent view. He only needs to look down."

Tully looked around at the study. It was hardly a stateroom, and the only climate controls were in the hands of building maintenance.

"This elite monolith," Bamphwick continued, "overlooks The Monument, London, from Pudding Lane, where the Great Fire of London started many hundreds of years ago. Well, a fire was lit here too, two nights ago, with Mr Tully's lies about one of our greatest mayors. This blaze will be far more devastating than the Great Fire, and will encompass many more cities around the world."

"Shit," Tully muttered.

Bamphwick stared dead into the camera, a small puzzled frown creasing his forehead, like he couldn't believe he even had to spell it all out. "And this was arson, folks. A deliberate conflagration that threatens peace when what we need most is stability. And who has the most to gain from the chaos? Journalists like Marcus Tully, given something on a plate to write about. We can't let this pass unchallenged."

Tully shook his head and turned it off. Bamphwick wasn't worth the headspace. He brought up the news in his display to scrutinise the stories filed by his competitors. "Sheehan, Fahrenthold Jr, Bradley …" He paused and scanned the article—a screw-up by the British civil service that was likely to lead to a prime ministerial U-turn on climate refugees within the week. He read the quotes from officials and made careful notes.

"Call Eddington," he instructed his voice assistant.

A tired-sounding man answered. "Tully?"

"How are you doing, David?"

"Pretty busy, actually."

"And Sarah?"

"She's good. The kids are good. Everyone's good. I'm good."

"David, what did I ever do to you?"

"Tully, it's been a long night …"

"I've been good to you. I've helped you out. And you repay me by leaking a hot story to Bradley of all people?"

There was a knock at the door and, without waiting for a response, Bolivar entered.

Eddington squeaked, "Tully, I—"

"I've got to go, but just remember that your drunken little rant about the PM hasn't become public yet. From now on, I'm the number-one contact in your favourites directory." Tully hung up.

"Bamphwick—" Bolivar began.

"I know."

"He's claiming we obtained the Houston recording illegally, and that it's been doctored."

"He's an idiot. We've already provided a third-party expert analysis that verifies authenticity."

"He only needs to make the claim. There will be plenty who won't bother to look further than that."

Tully shrugged. "You can't convince those who don't want to be convinced. They'll see what they want to see, hear what they want to hear, and studiously avoid anything that challenges their 'truth'. I know what's right and what's wrong."

"And the allegation of illegality?"

"Well, you're the lawyer, Juan." He hadn't meant to sound so irritated. No matter, Bolivar would slide past it with the easy comfort that came from having been friends and business partners for so many years. A good man, easy to be around, happy to push others towards the limelight while backing them up from the shadows.

Bolivar shrugged and sat. "We can't prove it wasn't hacked because we can't reveal the identity of the whistleblower. Likewise, they can't prove it *was* hacked. Our best route is to deny and tell anyone we need to that the burden of proof is on them."

"That's all fine, but let's find a way of establishing some provenance while protecting our source. Speaking of which …"

"Yes?"

"Tell Randall I changed my mind. Get him started on figuring out who our mysterious whistleblower is. Whistle knows too many things they shouldn't and I'd like to know how."

Bolivar nodded.

"How's the finances?" Tully asked.

"Better, I'd say we're back at three months runway, though forgive me if I'm not breathing easily yet. You know, perhaps it's time to pull a favour, get a story done that will top us up a bit. Get Livia to get us an interview with Solo—"

"No," Tully said. "It's not our brand. Besides, we have a story in the works."

Bolivar shook his head, but he looked deep in thought.

"Tell me," Tully said.

"What?"

"What's going through that brain of yours?"

"What you've asked Livia to find on Cavanagh. The works. Do you think it's really necessary?"

Tully sighed. "Of course I don't like doing it, but this guy is as hostile as they come. I need leverage to get to the truth. That's more important than playing nicely."

There was another knock at the door. "Yeah?" Tully said.

Livia opened it just enough to peek her head in. "Is this a good time?"

"Of course," Tully said. "You've got something?"

She nodded.

Tully gestured towards the hub and led them out. At the far end, Lottie was on a sofa, sipping a green smoothie through a straw and swiping through the news on her blended-reality display. She ignored them, never sociable at this time of the morning. There was no sign of Randall. Not a surprise. He tended not to rise this side of noon.

They sat together at one end of a breakfast counter in the kitchen area. "William Cavanagh," Livia said. "Yale-educated, law of course, heads straight into Turing & Turing, where Kehoe is a senior partner specialising in political law and makes partner himself in ten years. But he doesn't stick around. Lockwood's elected, Kehoe becomes his second chief of staff after about eighteen months, and Kehoe brings Cavanagh with him as his deputy. This is where he becomes known as—and I like this—the Presidential Pit-bull, for his loyalty to his bosses and pure aggression towards his enemies. He absolutely tore apart their careers."

"Charming," Bolivar said.

"He sticks with Lockwood until the end, then returns to law, where he's probably bored shitless. The new Democratic administration kicks his generation of Republican office holders into the wilderness. Then Kehoe is elected mayor of Houston and again pulls in Cavanagh. The two are inseparable, obvious bromance. Kehoe once said at a private function, and I quote, 'Bill is ambitious, ruthless and loves money. And for that, he's exactly the kind of person I want on my side.'" She grinned at Tully. "Your impression is correct. He has a reputation as an utter bastard. Kehoe trusts him, and Cavanagh is his point man." She looked Tully in the eye and waited with a smirk on her face. She was going to make him ask the question.

He sighed. "You got anything I can actually work with?"

Her grin widened and she handed him a stack of printouts.

Tully flicked through them at speed, then returned to the start and scanned them again. Finally, he looked up and handed them to Bolivar, then waited until he'd digested them.

Bolivar tossed them back on the counter. "You're really going to use this? This is insane."

Tully brought up a messaging window and typed: *Mr Cavanagh, can we meet? It's urgent. Marcus Tully.*

8

A few hours later, Tully was in the apartment kitchen when there was the familiar buzz of a pang in his display. He glanced up and to the right at it. The reply from Cavanagh was short enough to fit in the preview window. *Go fuck yourself.*

Well, that was eloquent enough. He'd have to play his trump card early. He tapped a reply. I have information you'll want to go away.

It was, perhaps, too melodramatic, but he sent it anyway, took a seat by the hub windows on some corner couches, and waited. He stared out. Below, the broken city was picking up the pieces after another turbulent night. As so often since receiving the Kuwait footage two weeks before, his thoughts turned to Zainab and the day he'd convinced her to go. He'd been sitting on this very couch, her on his lap, him stroking her hair, though in a nice little apartment in the East End just big enough for the two of them. No colleagues living in the spare rooms—it was just them, and the only addition they hoped for was the baby.

You have to go, he'd said. *There's no way they can come, with the border situation as it is.*

I don't like the idea of leaving you for so long. She played with his free hand. *I don't know.*

Spend some quality time with your dad. He's been so ill, and you won't have a moment to breathe after the birth.

She kissed him on his forehead. *I know it's important to you. I know you wish you could go back and have that time with your parents. I just—*

You can't have any regrets, Zee. And if you don't use this time with them now, while you can, you'll regret it, I promise you.

Had she recalled that, in the final moments? Had she cursed him, or herself for listening to him? Had she put her hand to her belly and wept for the child they'd never meet, for a future he'd stolen from her? They'd planned to call the baby Malia.

Tully brought the footage from Kuwait City up on a private screen. He changed the viewpoint so it floated down a silent street. More bodies, strewn outside a mosque. He slowed it down to examine each female corpse carefully, searching for some sign of the woman he loved. There was no relief each time it wasn't her, only rage for another person murdered. And another. None of these people should be dead, not one. This had been genocide, perpetrated from afar by some push of a button in a situation room.

A child sprawled next to his parents, one hand reaching towards them in a plea for help. The father lay shirtless in the dirt of the road, lips as cracked as the soil around him. How had he felt, in those final moments, realising he was unable to save his child? Had they even known what was happening? What was it Randall had said? *At that humidity, sweat no longer cools you, it just doesn't work ... your brain starts to shut down, then all the organs follow and bam, you're dead, cooked from the inside out.*

"Tully?"

His hand cramped and he stretched the fingers until the spasm passed.

"Cavanagh's agreed to meet in NR," Bolivar said. "He's available now."

He nodded, closing the footage, his hands shaking.

Bolivar squinted at him. "You okay?"

"Yeah. Yeah, I'm fine."

"You need a drink or something?"

Tully shook his head, strode into his study, popped some neurograins and grabbed the headset. He switched from his egospace back to the hotel lobby space, where last he'd encountered the mysterious source, and waited for Cavanagh to appear in the empty chair. Had this bastard been in the room when the button that killed his wife had been pressed?

Cavanagh blurred into view, took the chair and laced his fingers. He said nothing. Tully would move the first pawn. He looked all of his sixty-two years, but his age, like his weight, gave him gravitas. In better circumstances, he would likely turn on the charm and flash sparkling eyes. Today, though, those eyes measured, penetrated and expressed nothing but distaste.

"I won't take up too much of your time," Tully said. "The story I'm most interested in is not about you. A source pointed me towards you, and I'm hoping you can help me."

"Help you?" Cavanagh sat back. "After what you just pulled?"

"I understand, truly."

"No, I don't think you do. You preached at me. Droned on about your responsibility for revealing the truth. Well, those of us who live in the real world know that the truth is much more complicated. And it's our job to ensure our society has a future, not bring it all tumbling down."

That, of course, was the thing about truth. Those who hid it always believed it was coloured in shades of grey, those who revealed it always saw the black and white. Tully held out a brown envelope. The functionality of neuro-reality—being able to import digital documents that felt utterly authentic because that was what your brain expected—still made him shake his head in wonder every time he experienced it.

Cavanagh stared at it for a second, then took it and ripped it open. He pulled out a few sheets of paper, scanned the first page then read the whole thing carefully. Finally, he met Tully's eyes, his expression nonchalant. "I don't know what this is."

"Sure you do. The first page is a list of twelve projects that have received funding from your office in the past year. None of them have done anything of public benefit in return for their funding."

"A governance issue," Cavanagh said, "but I'll get my staff to check them out."

"I'm sorry about this, Mr Cavanagh, but that's not the only envelope."

He handed over a second one, and Cavanagh peeled this one open and read the contents.

"This one," Tully told him, "shows that seven of those projects are linked to one Mrs Ruth Cullen, who is a board member of five of them and runs the other two. Ms Kristin O'Doherty is linked to the other five. And if you'll turn the page—that's it—you'll see some intriguing personal emails you sent to Ruth Cullen. They seem pretty hardcore stuff, if you ask me, until you read the ones to Ms O'Doherty."

Cavanagh took a deep breath and sat back. His fingers were laced again, but this time they were tight. "You've hacked into my government emails. That's a federal crime."

"They were leaked."

Cavanagh just shook his head.

"As I said, I'm hoping you can help me," Tully said.

"And this will all go away?"

"Absolutely."

There was silence for a few moments but for the hum of unseen people. The huge wall-to-floor fish tank by their armchairs glowed, and a lionfish stopped, stared out at them then flitted past.

"So, what's the story?" Cavanagh muttered.

"I've been told that during their final years in office, the Lockwood administration had access to geo-engineering technology that could shift humidity out of weather patterns. I'm trying to verify that, discover its authenticity. I want to know if the technology exists."

The silence stretched. Eventually, Cavanagh said, "You think I'd roll over on my old colleagues?"

There was something there, then, perhaps the receipt for a smoking gun. "I'm not asking you to betray anyone," Tully said. "Just trying to understand what actually happened."

The lionfish drifted back into view, then shot away. Cavanagh rubbed the envelope between his fingers, the papers discarded between them on the coffee table. "And where did you hear about this *technology*?" he said, spitting the final word like a child tasting something bitter for the first time.

"Let's start by assuming I already know some of what I'm asking you but would like to hear the truth from your own mouth. Can you confirm the other participants in the meeting?"

"What meeting?"

"The meeting where the decision was taken to deploy the technology."

Cavanagh stared at him long and hard. "My story will definitely go away?"

"You have my word that nothing will come from me. I can't wipe out your deeds, though. I found out, so others may, too. I just want to know who was involved, and how many lives were at stake in the US."

Cavanagh narrowed his eyes but said nothing for a full minute, then stood.

"You can go to hell. I won't betray the president. I want nothing to do with blackmailers. Last time we met, you lectured me about corruption, about conscience. You might want to reflect on your own actions today."

Tully got up too. "I don't need a lesson on morality from someone who gave public funding to his lovers."

Cavanagh's lip curled. "You should be careful, Mr Tully. Actions always have consequences, and I can assure you, you'll regret them." Then he vanished.

9

The protests outside Baker House had evolved from a trickle to a flood over the course of the day. It had started with a curious mix of bitter-faced conservatively dressed older folk and a few sharp-faced young kids, tattooed, shaved, pierced and intimidating. Now a gaggle of several hundred men and women had gathered with signs proclaiming Tully was a firestarter, a Marxist of all things, and a Trojan horse for the extreme left. The latter amused him. He saw himself more as the extreme centre.

There had been a few requests from the building's management for Tully to come out and make a statement, perhaps to defuse the situation. Bolivar advised him to stay put, not to make himself the story.

Beyond the apartment windows, London glowed in the twilight. The summer wind picked up and whipped at the windows of the tall, glass and concrete tower. Inside, Bolivar slammed his hand on the kitchen table. "Dammit, Marcus, he'll give you nothing. And you can't piss off someone like that. He was once the most powerful man in the West and he's shooting for a position that will exceed that. There's no upside."

"I have to see him for myself, Juan. Cavanagh specifically said he won't betray the president. This goes all the way to Lockwood."

"This story stinks like it's crawled out of the Thames. We should be focused on the election. The headline act in the history of democracy and we're chasing conspiracies? No one else is after this."

"No one else is after this because they don't know about it," Tully said. "This is the headline act in the history of genocide."

"This feels too personal, Marcus. Like you're out for revenge."

"You're damn right it's personal. You don't think I should be finding out if someone murdered my wife? But let's not forget the four hundred million other men, women and children who died and have no one speaking for them."

Lottie appeared from nowhere, thrust two mugs between them then stalked away. Tully looked down at the tea, then at her retreating back, and finally at Bolivar. He sighed and picked it up. "I'm doing this, Juan. Call it a gut instinct."

"Why now, then? Why not bench it for a couple of months? It's been ten years already. Do a couple of easy stories to build up a cash buffer instead, then look at it."

"In a couple of months, Lockwood will be dictator. Do you think he'll be touchable then?"

"He'll never come close. The world doesn't want American leadership anymore."

"The world is never going to nominate a computer program over a human. It's done."

"I disagree, and let me say this one more time—"

"Juan—"

"No, let me say it—"

"You've already—"

"The consequences, Marcus! If we write this, it could be world-shattering. It'll be World War Three, only this time it might be everyone versus the US and England, since we're the only bloody ally it has left. Even Scotland, Wales and Cornwall might be on the other side. Look out the window. Our last article caused riots."

Tully shoved his mug away and tea slopped over the table. He swore and mopped it up with his sleeve. "Bolivar, that's the thing about the truth. It's not our job to decide whether it should be told or not, only that it's told. Let others decide what to do about it. The consequences aren't on our consciences; we weren't the ones deploying that technology."

"You'll lose him the election."

"If he did this, he deserves to lose."

Bolivar's shoulders slumped and he nursed his mug for a moment. "He won't speak to you," he murmured. "It'll be a wasted trip, at a time when we don't have a moment to waste." He meant their runway, of course. Bolivar was always worried about money. He wouldn't sleep until they had eighteen months of cash.

Tully looked around and lowered his voice to a whisper. "I'll be in Athens anyway during the election for the dictatorship, the biggest damn thing in the history of democracy, right? I'm sure I can find something to write about. I'll get us a story or two to top things up. Not to mention, I've got the Cavanagh story to polish off."

Bolivar nodded.

"You can sort the logistics?" Tully said.

"You'll need a visa," Bolivar said. He looked at Tully. "Getting out of here and into Greece won't be easy, you know. The new border restrictions are tighter than ever. And it will be expensive."

"Let's make it more fun for you. I'll take Livia too."

"Livia?"

"Didn't you know? She's hooked on the election. She'd never forgive me if I went without her."

Bolivar sighed. "Let's go see what's happening with these protestors." They got up and joined Randall and Lottie in the sofa area. Livia was working in her room, alone as usual.

Randall had created a public screen and sent a couple of drones down to keep an eye on things.

The bitter faces had slipped away, replaced now by more of the sharper ones, and the police were there too, now, trying to calm things down. Pudding Lane and Monument Street were dead ends to traffic anyway, but the other side near Eastcheap had also been closed off to pods now.

Bolivar pointed to the screen. A man standing on a box was riling up the crowd. "That one is going to be trouble."

"This man," the man yelled as the wind whipped his hair into a frenzy, "this Marcus Tully, is responsible for chaos and destruction around the world as a result of his trickery, his fakery, his forgery. He created a story to inflame and create new stories for him and his co-conspirators to profit from. The state won't bring his kind to justice. They are all in it together. We must fight fire with fire!"

The crowd cheered and began to chant, "Fight fire with fire. Fight fire with fire!"

A youth pushed his way to the front and threw something over the security line and into the lobby. The police fired a volley of rubber bullets in response, first at the kid, then into the crowd. It quickly broke and people ran.

An alarm blared—three short bursts—and all the lights in the room turned amber. Seconds later, a notification appeared in everyone's displays: *STAY PUT, STAY ALERT, STAY SAFE.*

Livia burst out of her room in her pyjamas, hair mussed like she'd been asleep, though Tully knew she was a night owl and most likely had been glued to the election coverage at the same time as working on some Lockwood research. "What's going on?" she said, voice thin and high-pitched.

"It was the protestors," Randall said. "I mean, there was this guy and he was getting them all boiling and angry, like super mad, and then he told them to start a fire and they threw—"

"A Molotov cocktail," Bolivar said.

"Oh God, oh God …" Livia said, and began hyperventilating.

Tully moved to the window, hoping for a better view of the ground forty-eight storeys down, but it was impossible at this angle. In the distance, a drone-swarm took off, lights blinking against the night sky, part of the fire department's rapid-response unit. They'd assess the situation before trucks and firefighters were even on the scene.

"Randall," Tully said, "can you access the fire department's drone feed?"

"Yessir, sure thing. Like all I need to do is—"

"Get it done." Tully looked around. "Everyone, get your shoes on just in case. Lottie, get Randall a pair."

Lottie snorted and the team scattered. Tully headed for his room, grabbed the first pair to hand and ran back. The rest of the team gathered. Livia had pulled day clothes over her pyjamas.

"Do we need to grab any critical data that's not in the stack?" Tully said.

Bolivar shook his head. "Not on-site. We're good."

Everyone stood in silence, waiting for something, anything.

"Got the feeds right here," Randall said at last.

A new virtual screen appeared to the side of the main one. It was a split screen, showing both a camera view of the building, and a thermal scan. The building still looked normal, but the thermal scan showed differently. The lobby and the first floor were ablaze.

Livia gasped. "Oh, God. The night security!"

A horrible tightness gripped Tully's stomach. "I'm sure they got out," he said, but he could hear the lack of conviction in his own voice.

A squall of sirens split the night air. Livia trembled and Tully put an arm around her. "It's going to be okay," he said. "Modern buildings like this are amazingly fireproof. They'll have it put out and back to normal in no time."

There was a colossal boom and the entire apartment quaked. Plasterboard from the walls and ceiling crackled and crumbled to the floor.

"What the fuck was that?" Lottie shouted.

Livia gave a sob, one hand pressed to her mouth, her other arm wrapped tightly around her chest.

Randall brought up views from the drones outside and rewound the footage twenty seconds. He pointed with a shaking hand. "Something exploded on the third floor. Probably gas."

The lights turned red and the evacuation alarm shrieked. Notifications flashed on every display: *EVACUATE IMMEDIATELY VIA STAIRS.*

"Move!" Bolivar said, already heading towards the stairs.

"Not that one," Lottie said. "Note from floor eight. East stairwell's full of smoke."

"West then," Bolivar said, and switched direction.

They plunged after him, but before they'd even reached the door, another notification pinged into the feed: *COMPARTMENT SEALED ABOVE FIFTH FLOOR. EVACUATE UPWARDS TO CHUTES.*

"Our nearest one is two floors up," Tully said.

"We can't go up," Randall said, panic lacing his voice. "There's smoke in the west stairwell too. I mean, it'll suck up the stairs like a chimney, it's probably super-toxic, like, full of hydrogen cyanide. And if the concentration is like three hundred ppm per cubic metre it would kill us in ten minutes. But it could be, like, ten times that, which means—"

"Shut it," Bolivar said. "Everyone, wrap fabric around your mouths and get moving."

Tully pulled off his top and wrapped it around his neck and over his mouth. An acrid stench hit him and he coughed into the fabric. He glanced around the apartment then pulled the door shut.

A fog hung above the stairs, and Bolivar crouched low and scuttled upwards. The rest of the team followed suit. Tully could hear workers burst out of office doorways below them and the floor above them.

Tully's head pounded and dizziness crashed into him like a wave on a beach. He stopped to let it pass. Livia grabbed his arm. She looked wild and confused. "We need to be going down," she croaked. "We need to be going down!"

He shook his head, unable to form the words to calm her, and pulled her up the stairs.

They reached the fiftieth floor. The door to the lobby was already open and black smog from the stairwell was being sucked into the space. A disorderly queue had formed in front of a door that led to an external canopy.

Bolivar ushered the team forward into the queue. "Remember," he yelled, "you control the speed by pressing the sides with your hands and forearms. Jump in with your arms up."

A short metal walkway led to an open hatch to which a white fabric tube was attached. One man disappeared down the chute, then another, then a woman.

"There's nothing to worry about, we'll be down super-fast," Randall said to Livia. "You can travel down one of these chutes at about three and a half metres per second, and this tower is like three metres a floor and fifty floors—"

"Go!" Bolivar yelled and shoved Randall forward.

Randall turned and looked back at them, eyes frightened, then stepped in and vanished down the chute. Bolivar pushed Livia forward and she hesitated. Lottie growled behind her and Livia yelped and jumped. Lottie gave her three seconds then jumped herself.

Bolivar gestured to Tully.

He shook his head. "I'm last."

Bolivar nodded, and the chute swallowed him.

Tully took one last look around him, then jumped. The canvas hugged him at his waist and his ears popped as he descended. It was impossible to tell how fast he was moving, and for a second he was struck by the notion he was being eaten, swallowed by some gigantic, impossible creature. He pushed against the walls and slowed himself slightly; hot air slammed into his face as he dropped onto solid ground.

Someone grabbed his arm and pulled him clear of the building, then let go, and he was running down Monument Square towards Fish Hill Street. He blinked at the chaos of lights and sirens and shouting. The stink of the rancid Thames offered a base note to the pungent smoke, and he stopped as he reached the column, coughed and gagged. There were people, everywhere, his team already lost in the milling chaos.

He turned and looked at Baker House behind him. Roaring flames licked at its sides. He had written the truth. Regardless of what Bamphwick and the others claimed, halfway around the world a mayor had used his authority to trick vulnerable protestors into rioting; people who'd lost their homes to a catalogue of natural disasters. He'd written about it, and all those who had also lost their homes in the last decades, in the crush of waves, the pounding of the hurricanes, the drenching of the rains and the mud and the blast of the wildfires, had come out to say *enough*, that it was time for authorities to act, to work on their side, not treat them as the problem.

Now the fires had also taken his home, and he'd also had enough.

"Marcus Tully, right?" someone said from behind him, and he turned, started to acknowledge it, and was met with a right hook, a crashing pain to his jaw that spun him round and down to hit concrete and dust on the roadside. "It's your fucking fault, you bastard!" the man shouted. "Our office is ash because of you. I've bloody lost everything!"

He moved in to kick Tully but Lottie surged into him out of the crowd, slamming him into the Monument. He staggered, tried to steady himself. Lottie grabbed him by his collar and raised her fist. "Get lost, asshole," she hissed. "You fucking leave him alone. You've got no idea what you're talking about."

"No, fuck y—" the man started, and she punched him, his head smashing back into the column. He didn't go down, just put his hand to the back of his head, then examined it to see the blood. He looked, first at it, then at her, in horror.

She let go of his collar and turned away from him, helping Tully get up. Bolivar was there too, now, and they both took an arm and pulled him.

"Thanks," he said, holding onto Lottie's hand for a moment. "Thanks."

She grunted. "Let's get out of here, okay? There might be other morons around."

Tully rubbed his jaw and let them lead him away. Not morons. Of course they blamed him. Everyone needed someone to blame.

10

Livia slumped into the pillow and grimaced at its dampness. The walls and ceiling of the Leadenhall hotel room were smeared with the remains of mosquitoes, a wallpaper of black and red against the original white. The décor was par for the course nowadays in all but the best places, and this was anything but the best place. She swallowed, trying to generate moisture in her mouth. Two days had passed since the fire and she could still taste the smoke on her tongue.

There was a knock at the door. She jumped up and caught a glimpse of herself in the mirror. Not pretty. Like someone who'd been burned out of their makeshift home only two days before. She opened the door. "Hey."

"You ready?" Tully said. He looked tired. His jaw was slightly swollen, but not too bruised.

"One sec."

He held the door and she grabbed her suitcase. It was new, as of yesterday. As was everything in it, except for the two charred books, now wrapped in a hand-towel, that she'd begged a fire marshal to recover for her. They needed to come. She couldn't trust anyone else to look after them. The others hadn't made it. *Sorry, Dad*.

"Why the long face?" she asked him as they walked down the corridor towards the lifts.

"What?"

Right, too soon for jokes. "Your jaw? Is it okay?"

He grunted. "It'll be fine."

"And Lottie?"

"Gone for a scan on her hand at A&E. It's pretty swollen." He jabbed the lift button, the door slid open, and they got in.

Lottie was pretty badass. Livia wished she'd been the one to hit the guy. She'd take a broken hand for a bit of cred. She snorted. As if that was who she was. Everyone had their skills. Lottie had vivacious poetry and a vicious punch. Livia was a coding savant and could drink enough caffeine to burst a horse's heart.

She followed Tully out through the lobby into the humid hellfire of the London summer. Sweat beaded everywhere, from the small of her back up to her brow. The stench of the sewer laced the air and she wrinkled her nose.

They both turned to look down the street. Peeking above the other buildings towards the river, a blackened skyscraper still smoked. Tully's jaw tightened.

"Excuse me, sir?" the security guard called from behind them, and they both turned. "Mr Tully, isn't it, sir?"

Tully braced himself, as if expecting an attack, but the guard held up his hands.

"I shouldn't really speak to guests like this, but"—he laughed, seemingly embarrassed—"I'm a fan. I think your work is important, sir. I know it can't be easy, but for people like me ..." He looked down. "Sometimes it feels like everyone in power is against you. That they're taking everything from you because they know one day there won't be much left and they want it all for themselves. But you take them on, sir. You ..." He swallowed, as if to say more would unlock inappropriate levels of emotion, shrugged, and stuck his hand out.

Tully shook it. "Thank you, I really appreciate that." He looked up again at Baker House in the distance. "It's a relief to hear that someone, at least, likes my work."

They stepped out onto the street and walked towards Monument Underground Station. Not that they could use that, though. The Tube was unusable after the recent flash floods, unless you were a rat; and as such, finding transport to the airport wasn't easy. Everyone trying to get anywhere before the next riots broke out was above ground, including the rats. She kicked at one as it scurried near her across the pavement. She missed, and was sure its eyes glinted in triumph at her before it disappeared into the garbage lining a boarded-up doorway.

Eventually, Tully connected to a pod five minutes away. Livia loved the iconic black-cab design of the self-driving taxi pods. Unlike the taxis of her youth, though, these had top-of-the-line aircon. Baking alive wasn't how she planned to go.

Tully pointed. "We need to meet it at Bank, near Cornhill."

They walked up King William Street. The street in front of the once-majestic facades was now lined with tents and poverty. Near Bank, they passed the church, and a homeless man whose clothes barely fitted his huge frame pushed out of an archway between the tents.

Livia tensed, averted her eyes and drew close to Tully.

"You gotta help me, man," said the giant. "They burned my stuff. You gotta help me." He looked fierce, a red-haired, green-eyed warrior of olde. American accent aside—New York or New Orleans, she couldn't tell—she would have bet on him having Celtic heritage.

Tully slowed, murmured something that sounded like, "know the feeling," and continued walking.

"Please, mister," the man said, following them down the street. "I ain't gonna hurt you. But you gotta help. I already got nothing, now I got less than nothing."

Tully stopped and turned towards the giant. "The protestors burned your stuff?"

"I don't know, man. I don't know who they were. Can you help me?"

Tully nodded at a tattoo on his hand. "You fought in the Hydro War. You couldn't stop them?"

The man grinned. "I didn't wanna hurt 'em."

"You take coin?" Tully asked.

The giant shook his head.

Tully pulled a card out of his wallet and scribbled on it. "Go here—it's the hotel just down the street. Show this to the security guard, then the receptionist. Ask for Bolivar. He'll sort you out for the next few nights until the trouble dies down here, okay?"

The man took the card. "That's crazy good of you." He looked at Livia and bowed his head. "Sister."

He still made her wary, but she smiled back.

The black taxi pod, complete with a retro orange light with TAXI stamped on it, arrived. The door slid open and they jumped in the spacious cabin, taking the forward facing seats. Livia breathed in deep as the cool air enveloped her.

The man nodded to them as the doors closed, then waved before he turned and marched off towards the hotel.

"City Airport," Tully told the pod.

She watched him out of the corner of her eyes. She'd been the last to join the team, but she'd heard their stories enough times from Randall. Lottie had gone through a lot before meeting Tully. She'd recognised him on the street one day, and told him he did good, important work, but his writing was shit. He'd challenged her whether she could do any better, and she'd been on the team ever since. As for Randall, Tully had discovered him when looking at his hacking case, and had Bolivar represent him to get his injunction lifted. Then there was herself. They'd all been on the streets already, or on the verge of getting there. Fact was, the giant was just the fourth in the series. It still remained to be seen whether their team had just acquired a new member.

"Why do you do it?" she said, at last.

"Do what?"

"Take in strays. This guy. Lottie. Randall." She sniffed. "Me."

For a while he didn't answer. Then he sighed and shrugged. When he spoke, his voice was on the verge of cracking, as if years of pent-up emotion were bubbling up, and he was fighting to stop the imminent eruption. "The street," he said, "is a horrible place to die."

Silence filled the cab for the rest of the journey.

11

Tully wasn't sure whether Cavanagh's mistress was more pissed about being the story, or finding out she was only part of the story. Turned out it was one thing to be the leading lady, quite another to find there was a co-star.

He cut into her rant. "Thank you, Ms O'Doherty, I appreciate your time. And again, I'm so sorry to be the bearer of bad news." He hung up.

Seconds later, the small plane bounced on the baked runway outside Athens. As a kid, he'd taken transatlantic flights to Houston with his parents on noisy but beautiful jetliners, landing on smooth tarmac and passing through mega airports. A luxury indeed. No one then had appreciated that within a decade or two it would all be gone, the price of continually dumping fuel in the skies. Not the only cost they'd paid, of course.

So many bodies.

"It's been years since I've been on a plane," Livia said. "Why physically travel anymore when you can see everyone neurally?"

He nodded. "Same, at least five years."

"How's the story going?" she said.

He'd used the flight time to figure out the sources behind stories his competitors had broken, called them to express his disappointment, then turned his attention to Cavanagh, working through the list of people connected with the scandal. It had been two hours of obfuscation and refutation, but with enough non-denial denials and minor slips to give him what he needed. "Good," he said. "It'll be a local story, won't earn us much at all, but it's shaping up to be solid."

She nodded. "He deserves whatever's coming his way."

The terminal was old, and scorching temperatures met them as they exited the plane. They speed-walked to a canopy that led them inside, then wound their way through various contortions and redirections to the immigration line.

A green pang buzzed in Tully's display. Bolivar.

There's a giant who says you said I gotta help him.

New team member, Tully replied.

Didn't know we were hiring. Again.

Tully knew he'd been impulsive, that when money was tight, the worst thing you could do was hire more people. Bolivar would be losing it. And Tully didn't owe the giant anything. He was already homeless; that, at least, had nothing to do with the Houston article and subsequent protests, nor with Bamphwick's rhetoric and the attack on Baker House. But losing his own home only a night before had made him sympathetic to the big man's situation. And he was an ex-soldier: maybe that would be useful.

Security, he wrote back.

Bolivar didn't respond.

Tully tried to elaborate. *Livia worked out, didn't she? And Randall? And Lottie?*

That didn't even get a read-receipt, and his jaw tightened. He hated it when Bolivar was mad at him. And it was worse when he knew he deserved it.

He had plenty of time to dwell on Bolivar: despite the trickle of people in the queue, the immigration procedures at the terminal took hours. Their own interviews were extensive and contentious, in spite of his paperwork being all in order. Was the dearth of passengers due to the local riots, or was this just how Greece was now?

It was too hot to go outside. Instead, a car sent from the Megaron Convention Centre pulled up inside an air-conditioned VIP garage and sped them towards the city. They hit traffic a few minutes away from their destination and stopped by the Ippokrateio Hospital. The streets were full of lime-green self-driving transport pods, but empty of people; except the poorest.

A young girl, perhaps ten, met his eyes from the shade of the corner. Tully froze. She was the spitting image of a young Zainab, hair, nose, mouth, everything. He'd collected pictures and videos after she'd died, watched them endlessly. Was this what his daughter would have looked like?

"Tully? Are you okay?"

He nodded but was unable and unwilling to articulate.

Malia scampered away and Tully sucked in his breath. *Not your daughter, you fool.* She hadn't even been born. It was just some girl.

"Tully?"

He shook his head. "The girl reminded me of someone." Still reeling, he subspoke the instructions to his neuro-assistant to rewind the last few seconds and store the video.

They arrived at Megaron. Livia was quiet, just occasionally glancing at him when she thought he wasn't looking. Tully told himself to get a grip. He was with a team member and needed to be strong. *Just a girl. Stop thinking about her.*

The centre was vast, chilled and buzzing. Men and women in grey and black suits huddled in bunches around persistent virtual screens. Diplomats and reporters slouched on beige sofas as they chatted. Tully and Livia grabbed drinks and wandered around, taking in the famous faces. It was big, more people than he'd been around for a while, and all of them grabbing for power of some kind.

"We need to split up," he said. "We'll never find Lockwood like this. You take everything left of here, I'll head on that way. Message me if you spot him."

Tully scanned the rooms and eventually spotted his target in the second main hall. Former US President Lawrence G. Lockwood. The politician's politician. The perfect image of an elder statesman. Tall and formidable, in a fitted black suit that had probably cost more than Tully's entire wardrobe. Signature red silk tie. So much for the youthful charisma he'd won with back in '32. The perfect black hair had faded to grey by the end of his first term.

Lockwood addressed a gaggle of reporters. He smiled too much. "Making the dictatorship a success will be about respect." Both his hands chopped parallel to each other in emphasis. "Humanity is not a homogenous species. There's no one size fits all. The dictator is there to decide as they see fit how best to reverse the ravages of climate change. I'd not make political decisions that affect lives directly. Rather, I'd empower our nation states to make the best choices for their own people, cooperating with each other."

"Mr President, are you saying you won't be hands-on?"

"Great question, Sandy. Absolutely right. Hands *off* everyone's sovereignty." He showed them his palms. "This is a role that needs a bird's-eye view. I'll build a framework of action, a set of levers we can all pull and push, resources we can distribute as needed. If we get all that right, our nations can operate without needing direct intervention, with the occasional tweak of course."

"One more question, if I may, Mr President?"

"Sure, Sandy."

"Do you agree with the premise of the dictatorship? It's got a pretty negative connotation, and it's not usually an elected position."

"Sandy, you're absolutely right. But let's remember that the pseudo-anonymous influencer who proposed the dictatorship in the first place, *JSMill*, framed it in the context of the Romans, pre-Caesar. In times of absolute crisis, the Romans appointed someone to take power, ranking above the consuls, to solve that crisis then hand the power back to the state." He was gesturing again with both hands, emphasising every point with open palms. "For example, Dictator Fabius was given ultimate power to stop the Carthaginians when Hannibal was approaching Rome during the Second Punic War, and once he had, he 'laid down his dictatorship', as was expected of him. Yes, the word became perverted to become a position of absolute power that, once taken, was never relinquished. But I plan to do as the Romans did, Sandy. Fix this crisis, and then give power back to the nations."

A male reporter held up a hand.

"Yes, Mike?" Lockwood said.

"Mr President, this election is historic not only in terms of the position being created, but also in respect of the nature of your opponent. How do you feel running against an artilect?"

Lockwood nodded. "It's a great question, Mike, and let me be absolutely clear: the future of humankind should be in the hands of humankind. I'm sure Solomon is a good enough tool to steer a few floating islands around the seas without getting into trouble, but we're talking about steering a civilisation here."

Another reporter piped up. "Are you saying Solomon's not capable of being dictator?"

"Jake, I'm saying no matter how great the technology is, it's been created by imperfect humans who can't predict the impact their algorithms will have on the world. Look what happened with the first social networks. Look at the polarisation and societal collapse they caused. Now, I know Dr Chandra. Hell, she even worked for me at one point. She's smart, true. But she's not perfect. Her creation is like rolling a dice that her code works the way she thinks it will."

Tully raised his eyebrows. Martha Chandra had actually worked directly for Lockwood? He knew Martha but didn't know that. Livia had never mentioned it either.

A suited man beside Lockwood murmured something in his ear. The politician nodded. "I'm sorry, folks, that'll have to be all for now." He smiled, nodded again, this time at the press gaggle, and walked away.

The other journalists chorused their thanks but stayed put. Tully joined the edge of Lockwood's cluster of staff as they moved off. He waited until they were well away from the gaggle before speeding up to be side by side with Lockwood. "Mr President?"

Lockwood didn't stop walking, but the smile evaporated. "Marcus Tully, right? I wish I could say it was a pleasure." He spoke with the measured resonance of a man who made more speeches than small talk. His tone was markedly less friendly than that used with the other journalists. Understandable.

It was time to hit him in the gut, get a quote and get the hell out. "Mr President, did you and your administration deploy technology that shifted humidity *away* from the US just before the tabkhir?"

Lockwood's expression didn't falter. "Bill Cavanagh mentioned you'd tried to bully him into going on the record for this semblance of a story. Aren't you content with the damage you've done with that nonsense you made up about Jeff Kehoe? I really appreciated your putting me in the headline, by the way."

"Sir, are you denying that you met specifically with the intention of pressing the button on such technology? Was the meeting held in the situation room?"

Lockwood stopped, shook his head and chuckled. "That's what I hate about journalists. Other professions are dedicated to building things up. But you bastards want to burn it all down just for the hell of it."

"Why was the decision made to deploy the technology when experts were telling you it was unpredictable, sir?"

"This conversation is over." Lockwood continued walking.

Tully hadn't come all this way to be fobbed off. "You caused four hundred million deaths in a climate-change disaster, Mr President, and you're running for the first ever global office aimed at preventing further disasters on that scale. Will you be issuing an apology for the tabkhir?"

Lockwood faced him. Now the jocular charm had disappeared from those blue eyes as his pupils contracted, twin holes poked in a bank of deep snow. "Off the record. There was no tabkhir, Mr Tully. Haven't you been listening to Jordan Bamphwick? It was all faked by the caliphate to take control of the entire region and go it alone."

Tully clenched his fists. "How does being a tabkhir-denier square with running for a position to save the world from the climate apocalypse?"

"Screw you."

"Was it a race thing, Mr President?" Tully said.

Lockwood looked startled. "What?"

"Did you decide the world needed fewer people of colour?"

Lockwood lunged forward until he was inches from Tully's face. The stench of citrus cologne and hatred washed over Tully. He tensed, sure Lockwood was going to grab his collar, but held his ground.

"You piece of shit. You …" Lockwood shook his head. "Go back to England, Mr Tully. Go back to your little graveyard of an empire that couldn't even keep an islet united, and tell that bitch Chandra to quit these lies on behalf of her computer program and remember she's still under an NDA."

Lockwood turned away and a Secret Service official blocked Tully's path.

Tully's thoughts raced. What had he meant about Livia? He could see her in the distance now, coming towards him with a grin of excitement. He frowned. Not Livia. No, he'd meant her sister, Martha Chandra. The creator of Solomon, Lockwood's only opponent.

If Lockwood thought Martha had implicated him in causing the tabkhir, then she knew something. And he needed to know what.

"What's up?" Livia said.

"We need to go see your sister," he said. "Can you get us into New Carthage?"

12

Livia had never been in a helicopter, but she'd seen the old movies where people wore headphones to communicate with each other through the noise. That wasn't needed on the drone-like multicopter from Cape Town to New Carthage, a large eight-seater that was only occupied by the two of them, and the pilot. It was so quiet, with only an electric whine as the backdrop, it gave the impression of fragility, as if there was no engine and they were merely floating through the air in the moments before the fall began. She was grateful there was only thirty minutes left of the two-hours journey, itself a much shorter and easier trip than the day and a half she and Tully had spent getting from Athens to Cape Town.

At the same time, every minute they flew closer to New Carthage added a new knot to the tangled ball of worry in her stomach. An accidental word from her sister at the wrong time and Tully would know that Solomon had helped with the Cavanagh research. He'd discover she wasn't the superstar researcher he thought she was, that she'd lied—well, concealed—her methods. She'd be off the team and back on the streets again.

Pre-empting it and telling Tully now was out of the question, wasn't it? She should speak to Martha first and tell her not to say anything. Question was, would Martha cover for her? She'd never done so as a kid.

No, the only option was to tell Tully and get it over and done with, then appeal to his mercy. She cleared her throat. "Tully?"

He looked at her. "Yeah?"

"You know …" She lost her nerve. "You know, I just love being a part of your team."

"We're glad to have you, Livia." He leaned forward and pointed. "Look, I think we can see New Carthage."

There it was. It was the first time she'd seen it in real life. "It's huge," she whispered. A massive dome floated in the sea, moving, slow and tortoise-like, but enough to leave something of a wake behind it. Even at this distance—and they were closing in fast—she could see skyscrapers soaring from the central quarter, surrounded by giant trees and, in the middle, a towering stone statue of Hannibal, hero of the ancient Carthage, short sword thrust upward toward the sky above his plumed helmet until it nearly reached the apex of the dome. She felt as dwarfed and insignificant as if she was standing next to Martha.

"Yeah," Tully said.

"Is the dome to protect against the weather?" Livia asked. The almost transparent geodesic dome was an astonishing feat of engineering, utterly huge and covering an entire city.

Tully grunted. "Yeah."

She glanced at him. "What is it?"

He stared out the window at it, hand running over his cheek, seemingly gathering his thoughts. Eventually, he sighed. "I've always thought," he said slowly, "that the Floating States are built to keep out all the problems rather than do anything serious about solving them. Keep out the hot weather. Keep out the roiling seas." He shook his head. "Keep out the poor people, the climate refugees, the displaced."

She didn't agree. Sure, the six floating Floating States were for the wealthy, society's elite, the smart-smarts like Martha. But they had to start somewhere. You couldn't save everyone off the bat. "You think Jasper Keeling should have done it differently?" she said. "Didn't he need the money from the rich to fund future versions for the middle class?"

"Maybe," he conceded. "The guy's pulled off something special. But there are billions to save, and New Carthage houses about two hundred thousand at best … say there's a million across the other floating cities. It's not scalable. We should be putting the resources into turning around the current situation instead of creating safe bubbles from which the rich can watch the poor die."

The sight below, of a protected inner harbour inside the dome, extinguished her response like a put-out candle and left only wisps in the air. Martha had

70

called it the *Cothon*. It was vast. The opening on the western side was at least seventy feet. A glittering assortment of stupidly expensive mega-yachts were berthed in a second rectangular harbour with raised walkways along two sides and connected to the first by a small opening. She pointed. "What's the circular one for?"

"Military," Tully said, studying it too. "Those are small battleships around the inner island."

It was an odd sight, the modern juxtaposed with the ancient arched and spired stone battlements. She continued her visual gluttony until, minutes later, the multicopter glided through an opening in the dome. As soon as they'd crossed the threshold, it closed behind them, and they landed.

They got out and Livia stretched and breathed in the fresh, sweet air. The scent of delicate flowers mixed with a freshness of a rainstorm like a best-of playlist of topmost awesome smells. The temperature was very comfortable, which was saying something; she couldn't remember how long it had been since she'd experienced such a thing, outside.

A bird chirped overhead in nearby trees, surely the most perfect birdsong she'd ever heard. She looked up. A multi-coloured flock had taken up residence in the branches. Even the leaves were stunning, vibrant, in focus. They swayed in gentle rhythm and cast fragile shadows.

Tully took her arm and she turned to him. She had no words that would do this justice. He nodded, seeming to understand. They meandered towards the terminal and paused on the threshold before going in. Livia inhaled deeply once more, reluctant to leave the experience behind.

Inside, a man in a pastel-blue and black uniform greeted them with quiet, gentle words she didn't catch as she stared at her surroundings. After a week of airport security corridors, the wide-open space full of delicate green shrubs came as a delight. A statue of a naked, wide-hipped woman towered in the centre. Beautiful but, so, so fierce. Perhaps it came easy, as she was surrounded by a coterie of beasts: lions, horses, a sphinx. Tears flowed from the statue's eyes and into the pool, weeping for a world that had been lost to time.

"Who is she?" she asked.

"Aštart," the man told her. The name meant nothing to her, and she raised an eyebrow. "The goddess," he said. "Of Carthage?"

"There's no security here? No immigration?" Tully said.

The man shook his head. "No one can even get to New Carthage without extensive security checks. Commander October's team is very efficient. She's our chief security officer. But everything you need was filed by your lawyer, Mr Bolivar, and double-checked upon your departure in Cape Town. Your flight was tracked from there. And, of course, we have a variety of biometrics that have already verified that you are who you should be."

Tully nodded, as if he'd expected nothing less. Maybe he hadn't. "I need to find Dr Martha Chandra. We'd like to go and see her immediately."

The man smiled. "Dr Chandra's asked that you join her in the convention centre at Central Plaza. Your bags are on their way to your hotel. If you follow me, we have a transport pod waiting to take you to her."

Worry curdled in Livia's stomach again. She thought back to her previous conversation with Martha, how no one could know that Solomon was involved in helping her find dirt on people to avoid any risk of compromising his standing in the election. Not even Tully. Maybe it was Martha's belly that was in knots.

13

"I'm Danberg, Dr Chandra's chief of staff," an enthusiastic man greeted them as they stepped out of the sliding doors of the spacious transport pod, an oblong-shaped self-driving vehicle with two sets of three chairs that faced each other, wide cushioned leather seats with their own arm and footrests. They'd arrived at the boundary of a magnificent New Carthaginian square, surrounded by cafés, restaurants and bars, all of them packed with people sitting outside in the gentle heat.

Tully nodded and shook his hand. "How's it going?"

Danberg grinned and beckoned them to follow him through the square, around a small fountain, and towards a large glass and stone building at the far end of the square. "Beautiful day, isn't it?" he said. From his face, you'd judge him to be in his mid-thirties, but he seemed younger than that, lanky and awkward, as if he hadn't quite filled out yet. His fluffy, scruffy hair didn't go well with his neat, trim suit, which he appeared to be on the verge of outgrowing—or maybe that was just the fashion, and Tully was just old.

"Isn't it climate-controlled here?" Tully said. At Danberg's confused look, he clarified, "Surely every day's beautiful in New Carthage?"

"It sure is," Danberg said, as upbeat as if he was filming a promotional video for the island. "We're very lucky to be here. Please, come this way."

They entered the building via an internal plaza with a glass roof and a wide colonnade down the centre. It throbbed with people laughing, milling and talking, the sound bouncing off the hard surfaces, but in a way that made the space feel buzzy and alive, rather than overcrowded and deafening. They pushed their way slowly through the crowd towards the far end.

"Is this all for Solomon's speech, Mr Danberg?" Livia said, almost shouting to be heard.

"Just Danberg, please. My first name's Damien, but only my mother calls me that. Anyway, that's right; the event starts in about twenty minutes. You came at a historic moment."

"Busy couple of days?" Tully said.

"It's been nuts. Social media went crazy when Solomon made the final two candidates with Lockwood. Sure, there was a fair amount of negative sentiment, but a surprising volume of upbeat commentary and support in a whole bunch of nations. We've measured over one hundred million positive sentiments so far."

"That's incredible," Livia said.

"We're streamcasting to the web and mindcasting to neuro-reality. But you'll have a real treat; we have a three-thousand-seat holo-reality theatre here in the convention centre."

"Holo-reality?" Tully hadn't heard the term before.

"It allows us to make the whole room into an NR-like space. It's super-new tech that Chandraco, Dr Chandra's company, has been working on, and creates spaces where Solomon can appear to be physically manifest without everyone needing to wear a headset."

"You make him sound like a god," Tully murmured.

Danberg chuckled. "Sometimes I think he might be!"

Tully frowned, but said no more. Martha's team needed to be more careful. There was a real chance of offending some folk out there, and religion wasn't a good ingredient for a political pie.

They made their way to a small area in which everyone seemed to know their place, like worker bees in a hive. The workers parted, revealing the queen bee herself, Dr Martha Chandra, CEO of Chandraco. She was dressed with professional precision, in a black trouser suit, and dominated her audience. A smile, an answer, a directive to the swarm of her staff.

She saw them and the smile dropped off for just a second, then returned, dampened now. Why wasn't she more pleased to see Livia?

Martha waved them over and Danberg slipped away. Then she air-pecked her sister on both cheeks, gave Livia's shoulders a brief squeeze and placed her hands together in a namaskar, the traditional gesture, palms touching, fingers pointing upwards.

"Tully," she said, and offered a modest bow of her head. Then her tone changed. Back to business. "We can speak properly later. Solomon's speech is in a quarter of an hour and we have some last-minute prep to do. Where are you staying?"

"At the Phoenician," Tully said. "Look—"

"Nonsense. You should both stay with me. No, I insist. I'll have your bags transferred." She was as naturally indomitable as the north pole's unwavering draw upon a compass.

Tully tried again. "Martha—"

"No time to chat now. We booked you seats in the theatre. I think you'll find it a novel experience. Danberg will show you the way and meet you afterwards."

And that was that. The horde enveloped her as she turned away, and she was lost to him.

Danberg steered them to a vast lecture hall, bigger than any Tully had been in before. It curved around a central stage with a raised dais, like a segment of a giant doughnut. He and Livia were shown to seats eight rows back. "Meet me here at the end and I'll show you to the lobby. There are some drinks after Dr Chandra's speech."

Tully sat. The seat was comfortable enough, but he couldn't settle. This wasn't what he'd come here for. He wasn't some political reporter on a campaign beat, reporting candidates verbatim. He turned to Livia, about to tell her they should get out of there. But she was learning forward, foot tapping, not with impatience but excitement. Of course, she was an election junkie, as much as she tried to hide it. The thought gave him pause. This was, after all, an historic moment, whether or not Solomon was successful in his campaign. He could at least take notes. Maybe they'd find their way into an article at some point, maybe not. But he was here, and there were more stories than the tabkhir going down in the world right now. Maybe he owed that to Bolivar; a story reporting on this might just cover whatever he'd have to pay their new head of security.

He sat back and tried, unsuccessfully, not to fidget. A few minutes later, however, the buzz of the crowd increased. A drumbeat started to thump through the chamber in the rhythm of a heartbeat, swelling in volume until the audience quieted. Music erupted, accompanied by a dazzling light display that strobed through theatrical fog sweeping up from the dais.

An announcer's voice resounded, shaking their seats. "Ladies and gentlemen, the founder of the Floating States Consortium, the benefactor of the floating cities, here in New Carthage: Jasper Keeling!"

A roar went up and a huge man walked out. He was bald and wore an expensive suit that did nothing to distract from the impression he looked more like a bouncer than a billionaire CEO. "Thank you, thank you," Keeling boomed. "And a gigantic welcome to our sister cities too!"

Five more theatres appeared to the left and right, the other segments of the doughnut, until Keeling was surrounded by an audience of nearly twenty thousand, all cheering and whooping. It was impressive.

"Welcome, welcome. Do I hear New Carthage here?" The crowd around Tully bellowed their approval. "New Thebes? New Babylon?" Keeling continued his roll call and the cheers moved clockwise around the doughnut. "New Atlantis? New Tenochtitlan? And our newest city state in the federation, New Troy!"

Livia whooped and clapped, a massive grin on her face.

"I'm told we're also being joined by nearly 750 million live viewers across the globe in NR—an astonishing number. Welcome to you all. It's been twenty years this month since we announced the development of the Floating States project. We were told we were insane, that it wasn't technically possible"—he mimicked air quotes around these last words—"to build floating city states at sea, and that even if it was, the nation states of the world would never accept our voice at the table." He paused and spread his hands wide. "But we did it. We launched New Carthage eight years ago, and from day one we had something very special in place, created by one of the finest geniuses and entrepreneurs on the planet, the CEO of Chandraco, Martha Chandra. We had the world's first artilect leader, Governor Solomon!"

The audience around Tully surged up and out of their seats, and for a moment his view was blocked. It seemed Keeling basked in the adulation for a moment, then gestured for everyone to sit. "We are the home and haven to some of this world's most creative and productive members of society, people whose work is critical not only for Floating States, but for the nations they came from and for the Earth at large."

More applause, but Tully shifted in his seat. Home and haven to the rich, right? The privileged few who could ride out the apocalypse with a gin in their hand?

"Governor Solomon was nominated for the dictatorship by our friends the Swedes. Solomon did not pursue or expect that honour. But the world needs decisions to be made that are too complex for us humans to make unguided, and so I stand here today to offer Governor Solomon the full support of the Floating States Consortium, on behalf of all the floating cities that he's so benevolently governed these past years, making us safer and happier. And now, let me step aside and introduce the real reason you're all here: Solomon!"

The audience gasped as a towering figure walked onto the stage. Keeling grinned, shook hands with it, clapped it on the shoulder and left the dais. Tully leaned forward. This wasn't blended or neuro-reality, nor a hologram; Keeling had touched it. He resumed his note-taking without taking his eyes away from the figure.

"Thank you, Mr Keeling," Solomon said. He gazed around the stadium, and for a moment Tully thought their eyes locked. But it was a fleeting sensation and he dismissed it as a technological trick. Still, it had been enough to make him stop taking notes, and his heart was thumping. Were the other theatres seeing Solomon's back, or did they have the same view they had here in New Carthage?

"And thank you to everyone who's joined me here today," Solomon continued. "I know that for many of you, this will be the first time you've seen and heard me. We've kept to ourselves, in these early years of the Floating States. Now, the Swedish government has asked me to step up to the biggest challenge facing humanity."

Its tone was calming, pleasurable, almost hypnotic. The room felt peaceful again, like when Tully had arrived in New Carthage.

"Since the world first dreamed of Artificial Intelligence one hundred years ago, humankind has both desired and feared what it could achieve." Solomon shrugged. "But I'm here only as a tool. To help, not to hinder. It was tools that separated humanity from the beasts. From the earliest hammer blows of your ancestors to the spinning of the wheel, from the steam engine to the satellite, you have always created new ways of overcoming your biological constraints. You've augmented and extended and outsourced your intelligence, and that has made you great. I am simply the next step in your journey to the stars." An enraptured audience clapped again. "But there will be no voyage to new frontiers unless humanity survives these perilous times," Solomon continued when it subsided. "You've thrived by adapting your environment, while other animals adapt *to* the environment. But now you must do both, as the very fabric of the planet tears, as the continents rise up to shake you loose. My goal, should you choose me as dictator, will be to save the species, then transition back the reins of power. I am here, today, to offer you hope for the future. If we can stand here—like this—together, though we are physically distributed around this world, there is no problem we cannot overcome."

Tully experienced an unexpected fizz of excitement. Win or lose, this candidacy was going to be historic, and he had a front-row seat. Then he quashed it, and frowned to himself. He was no novice reporter on his first gig, and it would take more than this to impress him.

14

Martha led them towards the personal transport pods at the plaza. She palmed some kind of terminal on the side and the two doors slid open. Martha and Tully took two forward facing seats and Livia a backward facing one.

"Welcome, Dr Chandra," said a disembodied female voice from within the pod. "What is your desired destination?"

"Scipio Tower," Martha said. "Penthouse lobby."

The pod doors slid shut, and it smoothly glided up a ramp onto an elevated track that reminded Tully of a monorail. As they travelled, Tully relaxed. The pleasant floral aroma of Martha's perfume filled the pod. Not many people wore perfume around him these days: Lottie and Livia tended not to bother. He couldn't say why it soothed him. A reminder of simpler, more elegant times? He gazed through the glass roof at the stars that were no longer visible anywhere in England. "Incredible," he said.

"One of the big advantages of living in a city that moves around," Martha said, "is that you get to see such a varied nightscape."

"One of the big advantages in living in a big whopping floating city in the middle of the sea," Livia said, "is that you get to see stars full stop. Totally unfair."

The pod took them towards one of the tallest skyscrapers on New Carthage and into a drop-off lobby by some skylifts. They entered. It was ornate, with no buttons.

"Thirtieth," Martha said.

The lift chimed, and they were whisked outside and treated to an incredible view of the Cothon before stopping in a lobby to the penthouse and a front door, which she palmed open. They stepped inside, and Tully immediately stopped, blinking rapidly like he had something in his eyes.

He'd known that creating Solomon had made Martha extremely wealthy. But this was opulence beyond his imagination, a palatial apartment in the most elite residence on one of the six most exclusive private islands in the world. The front door opened directly into a three-storey living space with polished mahogany floors. Wooden stairs wound their way up to a mezzanine floor. Ahead, behind a long gel-fire, were three separated, curved, silver sofas, forming two hundred and seventy degrees of a circle, with the gap facing them and inviting them in. A chandelier in the shape of a giant cube hung above what would be the centre of the circle.

"Go explore, if you want," Martha said, waving them in. "I'll be back in a second." She disappeared up the mezzanine stairs.

Tully walked deeper into the room. Two vast black double doors in the centre of the left wall opened through to a white kitchen with enough space to seat twelve around a breakfast bar. He turned and took in the rest of the room. The windows opposite him didn't span the entire wall like in Tully's apartment, but were vast arched windows with black grilles, five of them down the long edge, with several snugs of comfortable hanging chairs.

Livia had a fixed smile on her face as she walked around, though her eyes told a different story, as if she didn't know whether to be happy for her sister or mad at her own rent-free life in her boss's apartment-office.

Martha reappeared and perched on the centre sofa. "Livia, come sit." She patted the seat next to her. "I need to ask you something. Marcus, go explore the bar. Help yourself. I'll have a Siberian, light on the ice."

"Sure," he said. "Livia?"

"I don't suppose you know how to make an espresso martini?" When Tully just raised an eyebrow, Livia sighed. "I'll take a straight Kahlúa on ice."

He walked to the far end, where there was a nook decked out as a bar, and a small serving counter in front of a mirrored shelving unit full of bottles, all lit with soft golden light from below. Several high tables and bar stools had been set out by the windows at this end. Outside, he could see the giant statue of Hannibal, and beyond it, the dome itself. There was a small opening to the side of the serving counter that let him get behind. An expensive-looking rum on the top shelf caught his eye and he splashed a generous dose into a heavy, lead crystal whisky tumbler. He spotted a large crystalline bottle of Siberian taking centre stage on the second shelf, and poured Martha's vodka before sorting Livia's Kahlúa. He joined them back at the main sofas.

Words had been exchanged. Livia had a stubborn look on her face. Tully hesitated, then sank into the sofa next to Martha. The silence stretched, awkward, and he searched around for a safe topic. There was a spicy fragrance that cut over his rum, and he frowned. "Your perfume," he said to Martha. "It's changed?"

"It's personalised," Martha said. "A friend of mine, Jiang Ying Yue, founded a start-up to produce it. She lives right here on New Carthage. It's a pill rather than a spray. A chemical blend and nanobot release that mixes with your pheromones."

"You mean you sweat it out?" Livia said.

"Well, it eliminates the scent of sweat, for one thing. For another, it provides the perfect scent for you all day long, one that changes during the day. A playlist, if you like, to override the olfactory effect."

"Listen, I appreciate you letting us stay," Tully said. "And it'll be great to catch up properly and hear all about Solomon and your work. But I need to ask you—"

"You know you have a reputation for this, Tully? No chit-chat, straight to the chase." She raised her eyebrows at Livia, for some reason, and Livia looked abashed and bit her lip, then focused on her Kahlúa.

Tully ignored the barb. "A source told me that the tabkhir was meant to hit the US, not the Gulf. That Lockwood and his team did something … something to shift it. That they had some tech."

Martha stared into her drink and swirled the ice, then knocked it back. "I can't talk about any of this. Do you know what they'll do to me, to this project?"

The rum warmed his throat, helped him stay centred in the face of her admission. It wasn't exactly evidence, but that was the thing about truth: you knew it when you heard it. *So many bodies.* "Lockwood said you were involved." He swirled the dark amber liquid around the crystal, a perfect little whirlpool of fire.

"Tully, the non-disclosures I had to sign as part of my work for Lockwood are so binding, I'd have to retrain Solomon as a lawyer to stand any chance of not losing everything I have."

"I'm not asking you to go on record. Anonymous sourcing … if we can find any evidence or someone else to back it up."

"Nonsense. They'd still know it was me. The rest of them—Lockwood, Kehoe, Cavanagh, even Admiral Hogan, chair of the joint chiefs—they're all still tight. I was the outsider. They needed me, but they didn't trust me. I wasn't in the circle."

"They couldn't touch you. Not here, not now."

"The scrutiny's going to go through the roof with the position Solomon is in now. And besides, I have my own personal reputation to think about."

"Then just tell me, for me. Not for the story. Not for anything else. For me." She owed him that, didn't she? For Livia? Poor, broken Livia. Destroyed when their father died. Throwing everything away to succumb to the lure of the streets and heroin until Martha had asked if Tully could help give her a new purpose. But he didn't want to have to remind her about that. Crass to call in a favour.

Martha's eyes flickered towards her sister and back to him. Was she thinking the same? "It's not as simple as it sounds, Tully. I need to think about it. I'll help you if I can. For … everything. But this story may not be what you think it is. Just give me a couple of days. I have a long-standing appointment tomorrow, plus a bunch of campaign-planning meetings and a small celebratory drinks party with friends here tomorrow evening, which you're both welcome to attend. Let me get through that and then we can speak some more."

It wasn't much, but it was a start.

15

Tully checked himself out in the tall thin mirror of his bedroom suite. He'd do, though how long had it been since he'd had drinks at someone's house? Those kinds of parties required family and friends. He only had colleagues and enemies.

Enough. A party awaited.

He turned and took in the double-height room. His own home had been utilitarian, his own bedroom suite functional. You didn't get much else when you converted an office space: it came with ceiling tiles and carpet tiles; didn't feel like much of a home. This didn't feel like much of a home either, more like a six-star luxury hotel room, not that he'd know what that was like. An emperor bed at one end was topped with a one-piece wooden headboard that stretched a story high. The floor was black marble, but in this side of the room it was covered by a large carpet and seating area. The suite was large enough to contain a study-workspace with a library of old, physical books, a bathroom and even a little kitchenette.

He was determined to enjoy every moment of it. He might never get to stay in such luxury again.

He walked out and down the stairs from the mezzanine level into the chamber, as Martha called it. It was a bit ostentatious a name for what was essentially a combined living room and dining room, though given its size and elegance, it likely hosted a few more social functions than they had names for in London. Martha and Danberg were at the far end of the room by the bar and dining space. Martha appeared to be instructing Danberg. Tully couldn't quite work out their relationship. Close-ish. That Danberg had even been invited to attend this dinner party, rather than just organise it, said as much. Yet the power dynamic was absolutely clear: he worked for her.

She saw him and smiled, coming over to him and pecking him awkwardly on both cheeks. The gesture surprised him; she'd given him the impression she disliked physical contact.

"It's good to have you here, Marcus. I never did get the chance to say thank you for helping Livia like you did. For helping me out."

He nodded, awkward himself now she'd raised it, and not wanting to push it into asking for the favour. It would come, now, he was sure. He just needed to give her a touch of space. "How's everything going with the campaign?"

"Good. Exhausting, to be honest. I never really expected to be running a global campaign. I'm a technologist, not a politician. Fortunately Solomon's able to do most of the work." She seemed more relaxed, more human. He preferred this Martha to the imperial, brusque woman he'd met on arrival. This reminded him of old Martha, the Martha he'd met many years ago.

"Where's Livia?" he asked.

"She's in the other room, watching the pollsters' updates. I managed to convince her to get herself in some kind of condition for this party, though it was a challenge."

She led him over to some small standing tables that had been put by the windows, looking out onto the harbour below. There were several small bowls of toasted nuts, and he helped himself to a salted almond, still warm. "Danberg will be over shortly with a drink for you."

The door emitted a delicate "ding" and Martha walked back over and opened it. A man entered, and Martha smiled and steepled her palms into a namaskar. "Hello, Johan. So good of you to come."

"Martha," he said, nodding at her. "Lovely to be here."

"Come, come," she said. She gestured over to the windows and they joined Tully. "This is Marcus Tully, the journalist. Tully, this is Johan Pedersen. You may have heard of his adventures in venture capital."

Tully shook his hand. "My apologies, Mr Pedersen, I don't particularly focus on the business news."

"Likely a good thing for me, Mr Tully, since you have something of a reputation as a reporter who doesn't stop digging once he smells a story. But, please, call me Johan."

Was that a compliment? Maybe not. It was hard to tell—the man's expression seemed sardonic, though Tully supposed it could be confidence. "Most people just call me Tully. You're Swedish, Johan? Your accent isn't familiar."

"Danish, but I haven't lived there for years. Moving around has bastardised it somewhat. Ah, Danberg. Good man."

Danberg had arrived with sparkling wine. "Evening, Johan, Tully. Can I offer you an aperitif? This is a Bollinger 2043, from Johan's own estate."

"Champagne?" Tully said. "I thought there hadn't been any crops at all this past decade or so."

"Ah," Pedersen said, "a little investment I made about fifteen years ago has paid off. The company bought a few of Champagne's better vineyards and built some massive reverse greenhouses, only about two metres high, with a polarised polymer in place of glass that cuts down the temperature and some other nasties. It took a few years to perfect, and a few more years to age the good vintages, but it's doing well."

Tully tasted it and nodded. He'd never been a champagne kind of guy, even when he'd been able to get hold of it, and frankly would prefer an artisan dark rum, but scarcity was an attractive quality.

The door dinged again and Martha let in two more guests: a model and influencer he recognised from Minds but couldn't put a name to, and another woman who looked more professional, and more tired.

Tully excused himself from Pedersen before he could be introduced and found Livia in the holographic suite. The room reminded him of an old-fashioned cinema room, but instead of it being square, it was a semi-circular amphitheatre with two rows of recliner seats along the flat edge. Livia sat in the front row, centre seat, and was watching a newscast, but it wasn't displayed in a virtual screen projected from her earset, but on something else, projected in the air with a real sense of depth; clear and life-sized as if the newscaster and their table were really in the room. Everyone knew holographic tech was out of date now NR was here. Turned out you just needed to put more money into it.

Livia wore a white dress that must surely have belonged to her sister. Unsure whether commenting on how dressed up she was would embarrass her, he settled for a more neutral greeting. "How's it going?"

She looked at him and twisted her mouth. "Solomon's polling fifteen points behind Lockwood, who's been pushing his non-interventionist, real-living-person crap. All the artiphobic undecideds seem to be swinging that way."

"Well, it's not that much of a surprise. I'm frankly surprised Solomon even got this far. Shocked, actually. It hurts to see it go to Lockwood, though." He sagged and slumped into a chair. He was going to be too late. Lockwood would win. He'd become untouchable.

"It's not over yet," Livia said. "Lots of people see Solomon as a credible vote, someone who'll make the hard decisions without fear for their own political future or legacy. Lockwood's an ex-US president. He's all about legacy and the statues they'll build of him one day."

"I know. But look, don't get your hopes up, okay?" He thought it through. Perhaps it wasn't inevitable if he could break the story in time. Perhaps the UN World Court could vote in an alternative candidate, someone credible to stand against Solomon. He didn't think Solomon would win in either situation, though, but he didn't want to tell Livia that. "We have to get this story published," he said. "That would help."

"I don't know if she's going to help you."

He nodded. "But maybe she'll help you. Come on, let's head back through and be sociable."

As they came back into the chamber, Danberg passed them, carrying a second bottle of champagne.

"Damien," Tully said, "is this gathering for something special? Or are these just friends of Martha's?"

Danberg smiled. "It's a small community here. Martha and Johan go way back. She's an investor in Ying Yue's perfume startup. And Flora Jacobs is her closest friend."

"The model?"

"And a successful business woman in her own right," Danberg said. "Although Martha says Flora's the only friend she has who doesn't like to talk about work. I think she finds that very refreshing." He jerked his head. "Let's join them?"

They went over to the standing tables, and the guests smiled at the Londoners.

"… And anyway, Ying Yue," Pedersen was saying, "It probably came down to policy in the end. Like him or hate him, Lockwood's at one end of whatever political spectrum we have in play here, the only candidate who advocated for countries remaining essentially self-governing after this."

"And do you agree, Johan?" Martha said.

"Ah, revealing your politics is bad business, especially when it's to the campaign manager of one of the candidates. But of course, I want Solomon to win. Regardless of the politics of the situation, I'm an investor, and it makes good financial sense for me to back him."

"A toast, then," Flora Jacobs said. "To good financial sense!"

They laughed, clinked and drank.

"We'll need to do a proper toast later, of course," she said.

"Proper?" Tully said.

"A tradition we have," Martha said. "Now, you'll have to excuse me for a few minutes, I need to speak to Solomon briefly. He's got an interview soon."

"Is he prepared?" the model asked.

Martha smiled. "Solomon's always prepared. He's likely planned every permutation of question and answer like he's playing a chess game against a grandmaster. But I like to know broadly what he's going to say and do before he says and does it." She left them and headed up to the mezzanine.

"We missed our introduction," the model said to Tully and Livia. "I'm Flora Jacobs."

Livia nodded. "Livia," she said.

"Pleasure to meet you," Tully said. "I'm Marcus Tully."

"The journalist, of course. And this is Jiang Ying Yue," Flora said.

"Call me Ying Yue."

"Sure. People call me Tully."

"And what brings you to New Carthage?" Flora said.

"I'm a journalist. The dictatorship is the biggest thing to happen in the history of democracy, and Solomon being proposed as a candidate makes it even bigger. Where else would I be?"

"So, do we have to be careful what we say, Marcus?" Flora's lips twitched in a smile.

"This isn't on the record, so no."

"Ah, but you're here to leverage your friendship with Solomon's creator and get an inside look," Pedersen said. "No, no, don't take offence. I admire a man who makes the most of the opportunities afforded him."

"I'm not writing about Martha."

Pedersen smiled. "Of course, of course, Mr Tully." This guy definitely had an edge, like everything going on was for his own amusement.

"You said you're in investor in Solomon?" Tully asked.

"Ah, yes, about twelve years now, I think, in Chandraco. Maybe back in '37. Solomon was very early stage, something Martha was still calling Project David, the predecessor AI she developed that essentially paved the way for Solomon's code. But it still blew me away. As did she."

Tully rubbed his cheek. "So what happened to David?"

"What?"

"The predecessor. Is it still around?"

Pedersen smirked again, but there was a tinge of discomfort. "Martha had to turn it off. It essentially wrote Solomon rather than evolved itself into Solomon, and no-one likes to be supplanted." His mouth twisted. "Anyway, I became her first investor."

There was a story there, but not one Pedersen wanted to recount. Tully allowed him the change in subject. This was, after all, a dinner party. "So, where did you meet?"

"At a conference. She was speaking about her research. Of course, she had credibility even then, consulting as she was for the White House. But she was already thinking past that. She believed in technology, believed wholeheartedly in its potential to do great things for our species, to change the course of our future. Everyone saw her as a radical." He laughed. "You have to remember that back then everyone was still freaking out about AI. Hollywood was still pushing movies about AI-induced Armageddon. All the academics were screaming about the singularity."

"Singularity?" Flora said, and shook her head as if she thought Pedersen was talking nonsense.

"The point where humans lose control to intelligent machines," Pedersen said, "and with it our dominant status, as it were."

Flora rolled her eyes at Tully. "I know what it means," she stage-whispered.

Pedersen ignored her. "That still worries a lot of people. But it also worries those with a religious bent who believe humankind should only have one master: God. They believe if an AI becomes too advanced, it will become essentially God-like to us. A new deity to worship and direct us."

This was interesting ground and surely pertinent to Solomon's candidacy, but before Tully could ask more there was a pang, and a notification popped into his display.

It was Bolivar. And it was urgent.

⤸

TULLY WALKED BACK to his bedroom and called Bolivar. He didn't bother launching a video feed. The connection clicked into place and Bolivar answered. "Marcus."

"What's up?" Tully said.

"Everything. Everything's up. I don't know where to start." Bolivar sounded tired.

"Try the beginning." Tully paced slowly up the bedroom.

"They're coming after us, Marcus. They're coming after you."

"Who is?"

"Right now, it feels like everybody. They're attacking your credibility. Saying you make up stories, fake your sources. And did you hear about Kehoe?"

"Juan, you're all over the place." Tully sat down on the edge of the bed and stared out the window.

"Lockwood's backing Kehoe. He's stepped down as mayor of Houston and is now Lockwood's campaign chief. They're saying he's been filling the position unofficially for several weeks now, even before the candidates were announced."

"Risky hire."

"About an hour ago, Lockwood released a statement backing Kehoe personally, saying he'd been the victim of a faked video and malicious story, and that he stood by him."

Tully stood too. "He's crazy. He shouldn't want this hanging over his head during the most important election of all time." He walked over to the kitchenette and poured himself some sparkling water from a little fridge.

"He also said that you went after Kehoe to get to him and even stalked him in Athens, trying to dig up dirt on his record in the White House."

"Dig up dirt?"

"Then Jordan Bamphwick went on the attack again. He was prepared. He interviewed Cavanagh on air, who announced you'd tried to blackmail him with falsified emails to find dirt on President Lockwood, that it was all fake allegations."

"But we have the emails."

"Which we have no way of proving aren't falsified, since I'm pretty sure Livia obtained them by nefarious means."

"Livia?"

"Oh, come on, Marcus. You knew what you were asking her to do. She delivered you some magic, but you didn't ask about the spell."

Tully opened his mouth, but no words came out.

"There's more," Bolivar said. "This all went down in about ten minutes. And then Randall started getting messages from influencers. Not just a few, but loads, saying they were concerned about the allegations and would be putting their influencer relationship on hold."

That wasn't good. Influencers could make or break a good story. Fewer influencers, less sharing, less money. Less money, less runway, less time. "How many?"

"They're still coming in. But at least a quarter so far. By the way, Randall isn't the right person to manage them. He's fine in good times but he flaps in a crisis."

"Can you and Lottie pick it up until I'm back? We'll figure it out then."

"When will that be?"

"I don't know. I haven't convinced Martha to help us yet." Tully sighed. "Look, while I have you, I just wanted to say sorry. For making a new hire, without consulting you. Again."

Bolivar sighed too. "Okay. But it has to stop. We're stretched thinner than I can remember, and it's difficult keeping it from the team. I'm not sleeping and I feel like shit. And these attacks… They could really bring us down, Marcus. Your credibility is your credit right now. What in humid hell are we going to do?"

"You know, seventy-six years ago, a great newspaper editor sat down at his typewriter and wrote a statement I think fits this situation very well."

"What was it?"

"We stand by our story."

90

16

Tully re-joined the party to find they'd moved to the sofas. Danberg had brought a small trolley of drinks over, making sure to include some rum for Tully. Alcohol and a small group of relaxed friends proved the perfect antidote to his worries. Besides, what was the point in worrying right now? They'd made their move. The next play was his.

Martha was holding court at the centre of the sofa, so confident, so at the top of her game. She was one of the most successful women in the world. After what she'd achieved, you'd think she was untouchable, and yet she'd been worried about Lockwood coming after her. What did that say about Lockwood? And was Lockwood coming after him now?

He poured a fresh rum.

"Do you really think Solomon can sort us out?" Livia said. "Things are pretty dire out there, climate-wise. It's horrible in London."

Martha put down her drink and leaned forward, elbows resting on her knees. "Nature's a complex system that gets stronger through stress: billions of tiny accidents. We've disrupted it because the accidents we created were too large for the system to absorb and too complex for us to unpick. We make one big decision at a time as societies, but lots of unconnected small decisions as individual humans. I originally designed Solomon as a tool that could help make a million big decisions, all connected, from a hundred million inputs; a quantum artilect to help us handle complexity beyond what can be represented by ones and zeroes." She paused. "Am I making sense?"

Flora laughed. "As clear as a shot of Siberian—for everyone else, that is."

Hours passed. Now and then, Tully would regale the group with stories of journalistic life—though he steered clear of the present—but in the main he was content to listen. It was odd; he was more at home here than at home. At home, he was at work. Here, he was watching friends be friends.

There was Livia, socially awkward even here with family, so different from her sister, even if they were both workaholics who worked miracles. He liked Livia, and it was good to have her on the team. She was a good travelling companion.

But maybe Bolivar was right. Maybe she'd pushed too far in finding out about Cavanagh. He shrugged away that thought too.

The jury was out on Pedersen, the man who never let his amused smile slip. Was his relationship with Martha purely business or were they friends? They'd spent a while chatting, and Pedersen had been fascinated by how Tully had approached some of his larger stories.

Flora was more friendly than he'd expected for someone of her apparent celebrity. Beautiful, of course, but untouchable at the same time. "You have to come see my yacht," she'd told him when he had a chance to chat to her a little. "It's down by the Cothon. It's super-relaxing."

"More rum, Tully?" Danberg said.

Tully nodded. Nice guy, Danberg, smarter than he looked. And certainly not the glorified assistant that Tully had initially assumed. Instead, he was like Martha's partner minus the romance, a capable host and easy conversationalist. The way he stood up to Pedersen showed he knew his business and wasn't afraid to express an opinion.

Jiang Ying Yue was still a bit of a mystery. Like Tully, she was taking a back seat and watching. The tiredness he'd noted earlier still hung over her.

A memory surfaced; another time, another sofa, listening to the conversation of friends all around him. A work social back when he'd been working for *The Times*, back when things like newspapers and news organisations still existed. He'd been unable to take his eyes off Zainab. She'd joined the week before to cover the economics beat. Brown-eyed, long curly hair, wicked smile and a delicious accent. He'd been intoxicated and had grabbed every moment he could steal away with her. On her way to the bar, she'd looked him in the eyes and smiled. It had turned his stomach over, but in a good way. He'd given it a second, then followed her.

"So how come a good-looking man like you is still single?" she'd said.

He'd felt heat at the back of his neck. "I have my eyes on someone special," he'd told her, and didn't take his eyes off her.

A corny line, but she'd smiled and kissed him. And that had been it. He'd been smitten. They spent the next five full days together, cycling between each other's apartments to pick up fresh clothes.

After her death, Bolivar had tried to get him to move on. But he didn't want to move on. He didn't want to forget her.

Pedersen interrupted his reverie. "It's getting late. We should leave you to it."

The others murmured polite agreement, to Tully's relief. He was tired and a little drunk, ready for a nice long sleep before the hunt for evidence started in earnest tomorrow.

"I just want to say congratulations again, Martha," Flora said. "It's historic. Cheers."

"Oh, the toast!" Martha said. "I almost forgot. One second, please." She went to the bar, then returned with an elegant but surprisingly small bottle of Siberian and six shot glasses. "Come on," she said, "come with me." They followed her into the holographic suite, where she placed the tray on a table armrest by one of the recliner chairs.

"Will you do the honours?" Martha asked Flora.

"Of course," Flora said, and picked up the bottle.

Martha turned towards the empty semi-circular amphitheatre facing the chairs. "Solomon," she said.

The tall figure Tully had seen in the auditorium shimmered into view and smiled.

The other guests seemed as surprised as Tully. Even Pedersen had lost his knowing smile.

"Ah," the Dane said, "you managed to install the holo-reality tech in your apartment. Now that is great news! This is a game-changer, Martha."

Martha grinned. "I thought that would make my primary investor very happy. Solomon, we want to offer you a toast."

"That's very kind of you, Martha."

Flora handed out a glass each. Tully wasn't a fan of shots, but this wasn't the time or place to say no, so he just took it with a forced smile and held it up.

"To Solomon," Martha said. "I'm proud of you, and I wish you every success. Win or lose, you're changing the world. Go save our species. *Salut.*"

They clinked, he winced, and they drank. But the vodka was good. No, it was incredible. Probably ridiculously expensive, like everything else in this place.

Solomon bowed his head a touch. "I can't thank you enough, Martha, for everything. I'm honoured to have had you as my creator. I believe that the world will thank you, too, in years to come."

"Thank you Solomon, and good night."

"Good night, Martha, and to all of you." He faded from view.

"I'll see everyone out," Danberg said.

They escorted the guests to the front door, where there was an assorted mumble of thank-yous and goodbyes as Pedersen, Jiang and Flora left.

"And I'm a-seeing myself to my bed," Livia slurred, and stumbled off to her room up the stairs.

Tully was wiped out too and eyed the stairs. He'd need a moment before tackling that. He stumbled over past the fireplace to the nearest sofa and slumped on down. Martha joined him on the centre one and yawned. "Big day," he muttered, but she didn't reply, just nodded, then her eyes closed and his mind drifted …

⌒

ON A BAKED street corner, the ten-year-old girl stared at him through the pod window, oblivious to her rags and poverty. *Malia*, he mouthed. Her eyes met his. They burned with reproach and sadness. She turned and disappeared into the shadows.

He closed his eyes and shivered. The aircon inside the car was cold, so much so he could feel the chill spreading deep in his muscles. No, this wasn't the chill of aircon, and he wasn't in a car. So where was he? He forced open heavy eyelids. It was too bright, and a sharp pain throbbed in his forehead. He fought it, kept his eyes open and stared upwards at a ceiling. Not the familiar office ceiling tiles at home, but something far higher and grander, full of tiny golden lights, though they weren't on right now.

He turned his head, and the whole world turned with him. He wanted to throw up, and began to pant, deep and urgent, trying to stave it off. Had it been the rum? He didn't feel hungover, nor ill with some kind of flu. This was different, like a bad drug trip, not that he'd had many of those.

The moment of clarity waned again as the sofa dragged him into its embrace, and he groaned as he tried to resist the pull of cushions dragging him into the chair with a force many times that of gravity, and the rigid tension in his muscles that wouldn't relax. Then both the force and the tension let go of him, and he lay there out of breath, wondering if it would come back. He slowly, carefully, looked over at the middle sofa. Martha was slumped across it, asleep. Like him, she was now covered in a blanket that hadn't been there before he'd dozed off.

"Martha," he croaked her name, his throat sore, hot and dry as a London afternoon. She didn't stir.

Need help. Got to wake her.

He pushed himself out of the sofa and fell onto his knees on the silver rug. The world spun again, and this time he vomited, again and again, then drew in ragged breaths, desperate for air. Shit, oh fucking shit. Cleaning bots gaggled from across the room. Maybe they'd sort this before Martha woke. That she might see this, in her house, was mortifying.

She hadn't stirred, was seemingly in the deepest of sleeps. Yet the way she was slumped looked … off. Maybe she wasn't okay either. He dragged himself over to her sofa and shook her. "Martha?"

Nothing. He put his hand on her forehead. It was cold, but that didn't mean anything. He was cold too. He shook her again, harder this time. "Martha!"

What in humid hell happened here?

The moment of lucidity was swamped by a wave of confusion, and his head spun. He sank to the floor by her sofa and gripped the floor. The force was back, like a mounting wave but dragging him down, this time into the floor. His body clenched, tighter and tighter until he lost consciousness, woke, free for a moment, then climbed the wave again. Again and again for what seemed endless hours, it repeated, until he was sure it would never end, that he was in some kind of purgatory condemned for eternity.

A scream from far away brought him to the edge of consciousness, and he heard a voice.

"—no, she can't be. No, by the rising tides, no—"

He sank again, and when he next surfaced there were more muffled voices drifting in and out of reach, slowed down and stretched out.

"No pulse from her…"

There was a sudden pressure on his neck. "Alive," someone said. "Just."

"Martha…"

"…gone…"

There was a final moment of lucidity before the wave mounted again. She was dead, his chance to find the truth was dead. And he was just so damned cold…

17

Malia's eyes bored into him again through the pod window, but this time they were full of disappointment and disgust, demanding to know why he hadn't done more to save her.

"I couldn't," he said. "I wasn't there. I didn't know."

She shook her head in disagreement, then Zainab was there too. She put her arm around the girl and stared at him in silent condemnation.

"I'll get them," he promised. "I'll find the truth."

The window and Malia vanished, but Zainab was inexplicably close now, her head leaning towards his. "That's the thing about truth," she hissed. "It's always much more complicated than you believe."

Not her voice. A man's, and …

Tully woke, blinked in the light and took in his surroundings. A hospital room? It was peaceful, quiet, but his head buzzed regardless, a faint ringing from the inside of his skull, accompanied by a thumping headache. He tried to cling to the fading dream, desperate for even a moment more with Zee, with Malia … no, not his daughter, the little girl in Athens. None of it made sense. He rubbed his sore eyes and a memory surfaced: Martha, on the sofa, slumped at a strange angle.

What the scorched skies had happened?

There was a flurry of activity around him, then someone grabbed his arm, and he felt the thump of a jet injection through his skin. He cried out, and someone else grabbed his head, slipping something around his forehead. His world changed in a blink. He was no longer lying down but sitting at a table. The hospital room had been replaced by a stereotype of an interrogation room. Mirrored wall. Polished but cheap steel table in the middle of the room. Chair on each side of the table. Dull light hanging from the ceiling. No windows.

It was cold. Very cold. Intentionally so. The air smelled of it, like a warehouse fridge room with no food in it. All fake, of course. This was neuro-reality, had to be. They must have injected him with the neurograins. But what kind of NR was experienced so directly? There'd been no egospace when he joined; he'd been brought straight here. Someone was playing games and Tully wasn't in the mood for joining in. If it was this cold, it was a deliberate choice to make him uncomfortable, to put him off balance. Why?

There was one thing, though. His headache was much better here.

What were the rules of the game, anyway? He imagined exiting the space, the first NR lesson everyone learned.

Nothing happened.

He waved his hands but no navigation menu appeared. He was trapped in a neuro-reality of someone else's choosing. He'd never heard of such a thing. The implications were terrifying. What if someone wanted to leave an abusive partner, and they slipped a headset over them while they slept? What if you could execute a kidnapping without even taking the victim out of the room? What about him? What if they decided not to let him out, ever? How long could a body even last?

He looked around. They'd gone to a lot of trouble. This looked like a neuro-world replication of a real-world space. Which indicated it had been created in some kind of official capacity, or at least they'd want him to think so. It also meant he wouldn't be alone for too long. This was a table for two. But isolation was also a softening-up strategy. They wouldn't come right away, not if they knew what they were about.

He closed his eyes and tried to meditate. He wasn't good at it, but there wasn't much else to do, and he wanted to give the external appearance of being calm, while questions flitted across his consciousness. What had happened to Martha, and to him? Was she actually dead? He was clearly a suspect, which meant she probably was.

A memory of a young Martha surfaced, years before she'd even gone to the White House or started work on Solomon, and when he was still at the Times.

He'd been interviewing her for a story about a new healthcare diagnosis bot she'd built. Zainab had joined them and they'd talked into the night.

"You'll change the world with this," he'd told her.

She'd grinned. "I'm just getting started. There's a lot of things to fix."

He took a deep breath and tried to quash a surge of sadness. There'd be time enough for that. Right now he needed to be calm, to gather his wits. Breathe in, hold, out, hold.

They'd come in hard, push him to see what his reaction would be. No. He needed to breathe. Again, and again.

He had no idea how much time had passed. Hundreds of repetitions, that was for sure. The cold didn't seem as bad, though as soon as he was aware of that, he shivered.

But there was a sense that something in the room had changed. He opened his eyes. A woman was sat opposite him, electronic pad and pen in front of her. As he looked at her, she sat back in her chair, relaxed. Her expression was serious. She was evaluating him, all calm, in no rush to talk.

He could feel anger building, now he had a focus for it. Energy in his fingertips, a flush to his face, a tremble in his gut, a tightness in his jaw. No, he needed to stay calm. He copied her movement, sat back in his chair and watched her, evaluating her too.

Long straight blonde hair, blue eyes, black suit, white shirt. Pretty, but professional. Looked lean, like she worked out. Confident and with an air of experience that came from having sat with a thousand perps in rooms like this, which, given she was perhaps in her early thirties, meant she'd been doing this from the moment she was old enough to.

Her eyes creased into a flash of amusement that was gone the instant it touched. So, she understood this was a game, too. Tilted her head, as if she was all ears. Well, he was all ears too. He wasn't going to be the first to speak.

She leaned forward, a sudden movement but controlled, resting her arms on the table and entwining her hands. "Mr Tully. I'm Commander October. New Carthage's chief security officer. You are under arrest for the murder of Martha Chandra. You do not have to say anything, but it may harm your defence if when questioned you do not mention something which you later rely on in the Courts of the Floating States."

He'd been prepared for it, but it still hit hard. "She's really dead?"

October learned forward. "Why did you kill her, Mr Tully?"

"I didn't, and fuck you," he said. "Isn't it pretty normal procedure to have a lawyer present at this kind of thing?"

She shrugged. "We are not bound by all the old-fashioned rules and regulations of land-bound states. You will get your lawyer, in time. Tell me, how exactly did you kill Dr Martha Chandra? What did you give her?" She spoke slowly, precisely, articulating her words as if keen to make sure he didn't misconstrue her point, but in a way that felt natural and unforced, like she'd been educated that way.

"Why are you illegally holding me in NR?"

"It is not illegal here, and there is nothing sinister about it. It is just a convenient way of being able to talk to you, given that you are in a hospital bed, and I am on the other side of the island. So, what happened to Dr Chandra?"

"I have no idea. I don't even know why you're accusing me."

She smiled, widened her hands out into a gesture that said, surely it's obvious? "It seems you were the last person to see Dr Chandra alive."

"Is Livia okay?"

"What was the last thing you remember?"

"Tell me if she's okay, for fuck's sake."

"Yes," October said. "The last thing?"

"Waking up in the early morning, feeling ill, seeing her slumped on the sofa, unresponsive. Was she poisoned?"

"Before that, at the party."

"Last thing I remember, we were all toasting Solomon."

"You were drunk?"

"No. I can take my alcohol. My memory shouldn't be this fuzzy. Maybe we were drugged in some way."

"Anything after?"

"I think I can remember the sofa looking very comfortable. Isn't there security footage in Martha's apartment? What did you see when you played it back?"

She stared at him for a minute and then leaned back. "Why did you come to New Carthage, Mr Tully?"

"Listen, I didn't do this. Martha was going to help me with a story. A big story. I needed her."

"What was the story?"

"Her invention just got a chance to run the world? Look, I'm sure you'll get a tox report on … on Martha. But perhaps someone needs to take a blood sample from me too. I don't know what happened to her, but what happened to me wasn't normal either. I'm a victim too. Why am I here?"

"Yes. I would like to know that too. Why are *you* here? How do you, an investigative journalist from London, get an interview with Dr Chandra about Governor Solomon? Not your usual beat."

"So you're a fan."

She didn't move a muscle, eyes fixed on him.

He sighed. "Her sister works for me. Livia."

"And how long has Livia Chandra worked for you?"

"Just over a year, I think."

"Did you have any contact with Martha Chandra before her sister came to work for you?"

"Yes. I interviewed her, a long time ago. We got on well, stayed in occasional touch, less so since… the last decade or so. She asked me to find Livia a job."

"How would you describe your relationship with Dr Chandra?"

"Friends, not close ones."

"You're staying at her apartment?"

"Martha insisted. We were originally booked into the Phoenician." Likely she'd follow that up, corroborate his story. It wasn't so different, being a detective and being an investigative journalist. He'd have done the same. Mind you, she had the authority to get people to answer. He needed to lean on them in different ways.

"Have you," October said, "ever had an intimate relationship with Martha Chandra?"

He could feel heat rush to his face. "No," he said, and in his outrage it came out warbled. "No. I was married."

She raised her eyebrows. "Was?" She said it all cool, all crisp, that one word that to all extents and purposes defined the last ten years of his life.

He gritted his teeth. "My wife died."

There was a long silence. October tapped a nail against the table, considered him, then stood up. "You are free to go, for now, but do not leave the island. My colleague Lieutenant Moran will follow up. Nice to meet you, Mr Tully."

"Just Tully," he said, but she was gone.

A few seconds later, so was he, and his headache was back.

⌐

OCTOBER PULLED OFF her headset. She sat in a chair in the living space of Martha Chandra's apartment, in a seat looking out onto the view. Lieutenant Alejandro Moran stood behind a second chair, his arms resting on its back, watching her. "He can't remember anything," she said.

Moran shrugged, clearly unsurprised. "How did he react?"

"Surprised, sore. Seems to have suspected she was dead. Seemed upset to have it confirmed. Memory's fuzzy, though. Claims not from alcohol." She scanned Martha Chandra's apartment. It was a mess. Though only figuratively, because the sodding cleaning bots had tidied the crime scene in the early hours, bless their artificial souls.

Two junior members of her team, Officers Martina García and Jerry Hake, came over. They both looked grim. "You got anything new?" she said.

"Not a thing," García said, a pretty Latino-American with a husky voice, jet black hair and eyes that usually found everything amusing, everything an opportunity to laugh with her colleagues. Today, her deep brown eyes just looked sad.

Hake sighed. He was a huge, scruffy giant who was usually the cheerful butt of García's jokes. Today, there was no cheer on his kindly face. "Sorry, boss."

"Then we're done here. Get her to the medical examiner." October had known Martha. Not well, but well enough to have enjoyed her company on multiple occasions. She couldn't afford to think about it, right now. This was just another body, just another case.

The rest of the team moved away. Moran leaned against the window. Arms crossed. Had something to say. "Looks like there's security footage, but it's her own system, encrypted."

"And?"

"And they think they can decrypt it, but they need time."

"I want a list of everyone she met that day. Work back from the party attendees."

"Her assistant, Danberg, is doing that for us now."

"How is he handling all this?"

"Badly."

Didn't mean a damn thing. She nodded and looked past him out the window. One of the best views in the world. On the safest island. In the biggest building. None of the things this kind of money could buy had saved Martha. That someone had got to her here meant they had two things: access and proximity.

Raised voices interrupted her train of thought. She gave Moran a look. He nodded and left the living space, back out into the penthouse lobby. The voices increased in volume. He didn't return. Someone was interested. She walked out to see who, for herself. Johan Pedersen was arguing with Moran. He broke off mid-sentence. Offered her his usual tight little knowing half-smile.

"October, I'd like to know if it's true. If she's really dead."

"My apologies, Mr Pedersen. On duty I would prefer Commander October."

His eyes tightened. The half-smile didn't budge. A man whose billions usually bought him the privilege of omitting titles.

"Commander, then."

"We will be issuing a statement later. Until then, friends and family only. Of course, we'll be speaking to everyone she met yesterday."

"Do you have any idea what will happen to her business if news breaks that she's dead and we're not ready? This is about her legacy, Commander." His legacy, he meant. "Besides," he continued. "I was here last night. At the party."

"You were one of the attendees?"

"If you didn't know that already, I can save you the effort of tracking down the list. But tell me what's going on first."

"Lieutenant Moran here will take a brief statement from you. We will follow up with a more detailed interview later."

She turned and went back into the living space, then subspoke to her neuro-assistant: a request to meet the governor, though she pushed it to tomorrow, when she figured she'd have a better grip of the facts.

A chime sounded, announcing a notification in her display. Her request had been accepted. Of course, there was no reason ever to schedule with Solomon. He could handle a billion such meetings at once. But it made him seem just the tiniest bit more human to her, and that was more important to her than she'd ever admit to the denizens of New Carthage.

18

When his headache finally faded, an hour after his release from neuro-reality, he found his earset, which he'd been wearing when he collapsed, on his bedside table. Tully shuffled up into a sitting position on the hospital bed and breathed deeply. A chemical scent laced the air, and he wrinkled his nose in disgust. He hated hospitals.

Then he called Bolivar. He had to use the hospital camera, built into the end of his bed, but it worked fine.

"Goddamn, Marcus," Bolivar said. "Are you okay? What in humid hell happened?"

"Exhausted but alive." He winced, feeling guilty for a moment, then shook it off. "My head feels like Randall's been talking at me for an hour. How much do you know?"

"Not much. Randall received a call from an hysterical Livia early this morning but couldn't make much sense out of it except that her sister was dead."

"Based on what happened to me, I'm thinking it was poison," Tully said.

"Who would kill Martha Chandra? Surely it can't be a coincidence that she was attacked on the night of Solomon's nomination. Some religious nut job? There was some social chatter on Minds about Solomon's unveiling having overly religious undertones. They certainly offended some people."

"But someone tried to poison Martha *and* me." He paused and frowned. Danberg had served the drinks. Had he served something else too? "Sure," he continued, "in my case it didn't work, but apart from an old friendship and our connection to Livia, the only link between us is the story. Lockwood, and the tabkhir."

"You can't be serious."

"I asked Martha for help with the story. She said she'd think about it. She was going to help. Now she's dead."

"But no one could have known that, surely?"

Tully traced the pieces of the puzzle in his mind. "I get refused by Cavanagh and go and see Lockwood. He refuses me too and I go and see Martha. If they were tracing my movements, they knew I was here in New Carthage, and that I was meeting the one person who might spill the goods on them."

Bolivar shook his head. "That's quite a conspiracy theory."

"You have a better idea? Why would both of us be targeted?"

"Maybe you were just collateral damage. She's a rich, successful woman. There could be a ton of reasons why she was targeted."

All true, but it didn't shift the possibility that Tully was right. "It's thirty days until election day. We need to know what Martha knew about the tabkhir story before Lockwood becomes untouchable." He rubbed his eyes. "How's the team holding up?"

"Lottie's, well, her usual self. Moody as hell and looking like she wants to break someone. Randall's terrified for Livia. Which reminds me, he's still trying to figure out how your mystery whistleblower managed to be anonymous on Minds."

"Any progress?"

"It's slow. He managed to speak to someone he knows at Mindscape. They were as surprised as he was."

"And the giant?"

"Haymaker? He's quite a character. You sure know where to find 'em."

"Can we trust him?"

"I get the feeling he's been through some shit, but, despite it all, he's surprisingly cheerful. He's continually asking about you. I think he's really touched by what you did for him. He seems to be building you up to be quite the legend in his mind."

"He'll be disappointed," Tully said.

"Don't worry. I've made that clear already."

"Can we get him out here?"

Bolivar looked floored. "The hell? What for?"

"Security. For Livia and me."

"Marcus, the visa process to get *you* out there was ridiculous. I don't even know if Haymaker has an official identity card."

"You'll figure it. Throw money at the problem. Can you get him on a plane tomorrow, Juan? Come with him if you need to. Just get him here."

Bolivar grunted.

"I need one other thing," Tully said. "I paid a nurse to take a sample of my blood and I want our people to do a tox report on it. I don't trust anyone here except Livia. Whatever killed Martha is likely in my blood too, and I want to know what it is."

"Isn't the hospital testing for the police?"

"You really think they're going to tell me their results? Just get Fernando on it. We used him on the Santos piece, and despite the price he was worth every coin. Plus Porto Alegre is a small hop from here."

"You're sure this is necessary?"

"Whatever it takes, Juan. I need to know what was in me. And might still be."

19

"Mr Tully, you can't check yourself out. Please." The nurse looked on, distressed, as he pulled on his socks.

Tully reached for his shoes. "It's okay," he said, "I'm really fine." He was. It had taken him a couple of hours, but he was done waiting around. He pushed past her, out of his hospital room, down two flights of stairs, through the foyer and out onto the street. The street was pedestrianised, of course. The pods had their own route around New Carthage, but he didn't know how they worked and didn't want to try to fiddle with an account right now, though he'd need one later. He scanned the skyline. There it was: the tallest building in New Carthage, Scipio Tower. His display fixed on it and navigation arrows lit up.

He followed the directions though the easy boulevards punctuated with shops, cafés and bars. NR had killed the office. Neural spaces were cheaper and easier to meet in than physical ones, but Danberg had told him that the ultra-wealthy of New Carthage had started to prioritise meeting in person again. To be seen here physically was a statement. Some of the start-ups, too, like Jiang's MyScent and Martha's company, Chandraco, also had a physical presence.

Danberg had served their drinks last night. Had he served them a little extra something? He'd been close to Martha, or so it had seemed, but how long had he actually been with her? Was it just recently, in New Carthage, or longer, back to Martha's time in the White House, where he would have gotten to know others in Lockwood's administration? And if so, could he be bought?

But did he even have time to ask those questions? He had a month, tops, to get to the bottom of this tabkhir story before the subject, Lockwood, became dictator. Martha had been his primary lead. He was shocked and saddened that she was gone, but also frustrated, as guilty as it made him feel to admit that. Perhaps she'd taken what she knew with her, but there'd been something there. She'd been considering helping, which meant she'd had help to give. Whatever she'd known had happened just before she'd really started to work on Solomon in earnest, when she was still working for the White House. He'd only met one person in New Carthage who had likely known her during that period, an early investor who'd known her from the beginning. Pedersen.

He reached Scipio Tower and looked up. The sheer blade of the scraper carved through the sky above. Tully marched past the doorman and headed straight for the skylift. He knew his way. He paused once inside the lift. Martha had instructed it, yet it must have recognised her. These things wouldn't whisk just anyone up there. But he might as well give it a try. "Thirtieth," he said, and the lift chimed. Martha must have added her guests to the security system.

His stomach lurched as the lift whipped him up the outside of the building to the thirtieth floor. He ignored the view this time, instead remembering Martha, a few nights prior, marching out of the lift and into her cavern of riches as if it was nothing. He palmed the front door and it, too, opened for him. The hub was quiet but not empty. A figure wrapped in a blanket and hugging a coffee mug sat at the far end, by the window overlooking the harbour.

"Livia."

She didn't move, didn't speak.

He edged towards her, not wanting to freak her out.

"Livia?" he said again, close now.

She still didn't react. Her coffee mug was full but no steam swirled from the black surface. He took it from her and put it down. Her hands retracted beneath the blanket.

"Livia, I'm so sorry about Martha. She was special." *Special?* Was that the best he could do? He'd never been good at finding the words for this kind of thing. "Are you okay?" he said. "Did you get poisoned too?"

She shuddered, but at least it was a reaction.

There was no sign anything had happened here. The cleaning bots were good. Livia had dropped her coffee their first morning here but Martha had waved it off. Sure enough, within minutes the spillage had vanished.

The front door pinged and he crossed the room to open it. A tall, black-suited grey-hair greeted him and raised an eyebrow. "Mr Tully, I presume?"

"Sorry, who are you?" Tully asked.

"I'm Dr Chandra's attorney. I've been trying to reach her sister. I heard you were both staying here. Before she passed, that is."

Tully's chest tightened. A wave of grief welled up out of nowhere, but he quashed it without mercy and grunted. "Yeah, Livia's here, but I'm not sure she's up for visitors."

"Perhaps just a few minutes. It's important," the man said.

"You can try."

He led the man into the apartment and across to the window seats. The guy was unfazed by the opulence, as if he'd been there before; either that, or he was so wealthy himself that this was normal.

Tully and the attorney stood awkwardly for a moment. There were only two chairs, and Livia was in one of them. The attorney smiled apologetically at Tully, then perched on the edge of the seat of the second. Tully stayed standing to the side, with his arms crossed.

"Livia," said the man. "I was Martha's personal attorney and I'm the executor of her will."

Livia didn't respond, and the man's eyes flicked to Tully, who shrugged.

"Livia, it's important that I know you understand what I'm about to tell you."

Her head tilted away towards the harbour.

"We can do this properly another time then," he said. "However, I will say two things, which we can revisit when you are feeling better. The first is that Dr Chandra left you all her physical assets, including her money, property, investments and holdings in Chandraco, including this apartment. Everything. You're an extremely wealthy woman now, Miss Chandra, and you'll need to be careful."

Livia pulled her blanket tighter around her.

Tully shifted, and the man continued. "She also left you her digital assets. These are contained within a digital vault accessible with your biometrics. A link and some instructions have been sent to your private address."

"What's in the digital vault?" asked Tully.

The attorney pursed his lips. "It wouldn't be for me to say."

Tully shrugged again. "I'm just worried in case she misses all this."

The attorney mulled that over. "Passwords and other secure documents. That's all I know." The man inclined his head, stood, retreated and allowed Tully to see him out.

"Before you go," Tully said. "Do you know why this apartment isn't closed off as a crime scene? I'm surprised they let Livia stay here."

The attorney shrugged. "Actually I do. I asked Lieutenant Moran, at the precinct, whether I'd be able to get in here today. As I understand it, they did a pretty thorough examination this morning and recorded everything they could, but the cleaning bots had cleaned up a lot of the circumstantial evidence."

Tully frowned. "Thanks."

"No problem." The man shook his hand again, turned and went out the front door, which Tully shut behind him.

Tully pondered the situation as he returned to Livia. He was going to need to find a new researcher. Livia was financially free, probably in a top-ten list somewhere, and could probably buy this island. Why bother working for Tully? That saddened him more than he'd have thought likely only a few days ago. The team would be upset, too. Randall, in particular, would be devastated.

Odd, she didn't look like one of the wealthiest women in the world. She looked bedraggled and sad. He touched her shoulder and said, "How about I make you a coffee?"

She turned to him, face crumpled, and wailed. "They're all gone! My whole family's gone! They're all dead, all of them! What in humid hell am I going to do?"

She collapsed into him. He put his arms around her as best he could from a standing position, made comforting noises and rubbed her back as she sobbed. "You don't need to do anything right now," he said. "You inherited this place. Just stay for a while until you figure things out."

"Will you stay too?" she said, her voice cracking. "I don't want to be alone."

He hesitated. It would be strange, staying here after what had happened. Still, he needed to be somewhere.

"Sure. But just so you know, I have a bodyguard coming to keep us safe. He'll have to stay too."

She nodded, a little calmer now. A few seconds later, she pulled back and looked at him straight. Her eyes were red and intense. "You have to find out who did it. Promise me."

"I need to focus on any remaining leads to the tabkhir story, Livia. The police are already on this."

She shook her head fiercely and gripped his sleeves. "What if it was your fucking story that got her killed? Promise me!"

What could he do? "I promise," he said. "I'll find out."

⌣

FLORA JACOBS LOOKED down at her hands and massaged the tips of her fingers, a gentle movement that October assumed she found comforting. "And then we said goodbye," she said. "Poor Martha looked exhausted, but I just thought it had been a busy few days. I mean, she even met Solomon to prep for an interview during the evening. There was never a time she stopped working."

"Thank you, Flora," October said. She checked her display while Moran embarrassed himself by helping the model from her chair and towards the door of the interview room.

Flora put her hand lightly on Moran's bicep. "Can I use the back exit? I don't want any social media pics of me coming out of a precinct."

Moran grinned. "Of course. Take a right, then along that corridor."

Flora smiled at him and headed off. Moran low-fived the console and the door slid shut behind her. He looked at October. "What?"

"You know what," October said, but made sure she said it with a smile.

"Can't deny, that's one beautiful lady, even with her pretty little red nose."

"I'm more interested in what she had to say."

Moran sat and spun up his notes on his display. "It's not much, though, is it? I mean, they've all pretty much said the same."

The various reports had indeed tallied. Dr Chandra, her sister Livia and Marcus Tully had been in the apartment all afternoon. Danberg had arrived around five to help organise things. The food had been catered but he'd prepared it. Tully had been in his room while Livia Chandra had been watching election coverage. Tully had exited his room at seven on the dot, and Pedersen

111

had arrived too. A few minutes later, Jiang and Jacobs had rocked up. Then Martha Chandra had gone to speak to Solomon, Tully had headed to his own room for a bit and the others chilled. Martha had arrived back first, then Tully, and they'd spent the rest of the night in the lounge area eating and drinking. After a toast to Solomon, Danberg had seen the guests out. By the time he'd arrived back, Livia had gone, presumably to bed, and Martha Chandra and Marcus Tully had passed out on the sofa. Danberg had covered them with blankets and left.

Sometime in the morning, Tully claimed to have fallen off the sofa, crawled over to Martha and collapsed on the floor. It was Livia who'd found them at around eight a.m. She'd called for help, then collapsed with the shock.

"So, what've we got?" Moran said.

October shrugged. "Nothing."

"A big fat nothing."

She thought for a second, then subspoke a command. *Connect to Jeffries' lab and throw it on the wall.* The wall behind her lit up, revealing what appeared to be a second, connected room behind. In reality, of course, the lab was in the basement.

A man in a white coat glared up from a stack of machinery. The precinct's forensic investigator was balding from his crown but still had an untidy fuzz of grey hair around the sides and back. He had a perpetually grumpy, hassled look, to match his perpetually grumpy, hassled demeanour. "What is it, Commander?" he said. "We're busy here."

"Jeffries, where are you on the tox for Dr Chandra?"

"I'm nowhere. When I have something to tell you, you'll be the first to know." He cut the call.

Moran sniggered, but October ignored him. *Reconnect.*

Jeffries looked up again, his mouth twisted in displeasure, and sighed.

"Jeffries, is there anything we can start looking at? We're stuck here." She flashed a wry smile.

He looked back at his work. "Some kind of barbiturate. That's all I can tell you right now. It's unusual."

Moran frowned. "Isn't that some kind of old-timey drug?"

"Yes, yes. The consumer stuff at least is dated. Depresses the nervous system.

People used them to calm down, sleep better. They were a fix for anxiety, depression, et cetera."

Moran looked puzzled. "She was going through a fair amount of stuff. I mean, she writes some code and it runs for election as the leader of the world? I wouldn't be able to sleep either."

October shook her head. "I can't see it. I knew her, a bit. She wasn't the self-medicating type, and even if she had been, barbiturates wouldn't have been the obvious choice. She had the money to do it right."

Jeffries pulled off his gloves and hurled them into a bin. "Precisely. No one in their right mind would use them today. They're dangerous. Easy to get addicted, easy to screw up and overdose."

"So, you're ruling out an accident or suicide?" Moran scratched his head.

"I'm ruling out nothing. I already said, when I have something to tell you, I'll tell you. There's something different about this. If I thought it was a normal barbiturate, I'd have said, 'Hey, I'm done, it's a barbiturate, it was an accident and I'm going for a cup of joe.'"

Moran held up his hands. "Okay, Doc. I got ya."

October chewed at a nail. "We're relying on you, Doc. Let's figure out what's so unusual."

Jeffries rolled his eyes and hung up.

20

Johan Pedersen's house was one of the few in a city centred around apartments. It was also one of the most spectacular, set in an exclusive strip of developments built directly up against the dome of New Carthage itself.

Tully knocked at the black and gold door, wondering if he'd come all this way for nothing. Maybe he'd have been better off staying and looking after Livia.

Pedersen opened the door. "Ah, Tully?" he said. "You're okay then? I heard you were in hospital."

"Yeah, alive. Look, can I come in?"

"Of course." Pedersen stood back and gestured for him to enter. "Please, come. Join me for a coffee. Ah, a terrible business. I'm completely devastated, of course."

Tully followed him through to a magnificent dome-shaped living room. Two pristine sofas were angled with a view of the ocean. Outside to the left, a couple of superyachts were docked in a small, protected harbour with a deep contained basin that moved wholesale with the floating island so it didn't create drag in the water.

"Nice place you've got here," Tully said. So this is what billions could buy. A view from which to watch the world drown.

"Ah, it does the job," Pedersen said. "The windows are actually part of the dome, which is a rather fun feature." The house was just above sea level, and the placidity of the mini-harbour juxtaposed violently with the waves from the churning South Atlantic crashing against the dome. Tully assumed the city was still moving, but with no fixed point on the horizon to focus on, it was hard to judge how much and how fast. "I also have property in Copenhagen and

Paris," Pedesen continued, "though we're spending less time in each nowadays. I fear the Copenhagen house may become a sacrifice to the sea in the next few years." If the loss of his native residence concerned him, he didn't show it; the smirk was ever-present. "Now," he gestured towards a couch. "What can I do for you?"

To business, then. "Look," Tully said, "Martha was murdered. I think that's probably clear to everyone given what happened to me."

Pedersen tilted his head. "Our esteemed security force hasn't exactly given out any details. It took me a while to confirm she was even dead. But yes, from what I understand, this wasn't a natural death."

"Martha was going to help me with a story. The day after we spoke about it, she ended up dead."

Pedersen sat back and raised his eyebrows. "If you think the story got Martha killed, it must be a big one. Dare I ask?"

"It was to do with her time at the White House. Just before she met you. Do you know why she left that job?"

Pedersen stroked his chin. "So … this is a Lockwood story?"

"What makes you say so?"

"Well, she worked for him. I'd forgotten that. And thirty-ish days before the biggest election in history, the creator of one of the candidates, who happened to once work for the other candidate, is assassinated. You think there is a connection to Lockwood?"

"Maybe. Did she ever talk about her time with him?"

Pedersen shook his head. "I gather there was a falling out, but she was water-tight on the detail of her time there. I get the impression there would be legal ramifications if she breached."

Tully sat back. "Then my lead is really dead."

"I'm in venture capital, Tully. A lot of my businesses think they are dead. Then they pivot to another approach and become very successful. There is, perhaps, another possibility."

"Which is?"

"If you think there's a connection, find out who killed her. If you figure that out, maybe it will lead you back to your own story."

"Maybe."

"Perhaps, of course, it had nothing to do with your story. Perhaps it was the election itself?"

Tully grunted.

"Or it could be more indirect. There was a death threat. A few weeks ago."

Tully sat forward. "What?"

Pedersen nodded. "Like I told you at the party, there are some who believe humanity should only have one master. Solomon, to some, represents something more powerful than any human: an all-seeing, all-knowing leader who'll save us from ourselves. He can appear anywhere and talk to all of the planet's inhabitants directly and simultaneously, should the occasion be merited. Naturally, as soon as he was nominated there were those who objected to his creation, who saw Martha as trying to supplant their gods. There was one group—I need to dig out their name—who made a very specific threat, one that made its way up to the board of directors."

"*Bon, je pars,*" said a voice from behind them.

Tully turned.

A handsome young man with dark wavy hair and stubble walked into the room. He was pulling on a jacket and, despite the spring-like temperature of the island, a scarf. He smiled broadly, a twinkle in his eye. "*Mais excusez-moi,* excuse me," he said in a strong Parisian accent. "I didn't realise we were having company."

"My husband," Pedersen said, "Guy Molyneux." He pronounced it *Ghee.*

"It is a pleasure to be meeting with you, Monsieur Tully."

"You too, Mr Molyneux."

"Please, you must call me Guy. But I am late and must go." He grinned again. "Give my love to Livia. I am going to come to check on her tomorrow morning."

Tully frowned. How did he know Livia?

"*Je te laisse,*" Guy said to Pedersen, and blew him a kiss. "*Profites.*" He winked at Tully and left.

"Profit?" Tully said.

Pedersen chuckled. "One of those French expressions that doesn't quite translate in context. It means, 'make the most of it', or even 'enjoy'."

Another young man appeared with a tray of filter coffee. He set it down and left. Pedersen appeared not to notice him, just leaned over and pressed the plunger in the cafetière.

"My apologies," Pedersen said. "We only have a New Tenochtitlan blend at the moment. It's a bit shit, but when you're in the middle of the Atlantic you have to wait for shipments of the good stuff."

"You're right," Tully said. "I need to figure out how they got to Martha. If the motive was my story or the election, and the means was poison, what was the opportunity? Could you send me more details about the death threat? I also need to know more about her life here."

Pedersen shrugged. "Well, the people at that party knew her best." He sipped at the coffee and pulled a face, eye twitching. "You should probably start there."

I should probably start with you, Tully thought, but said, "Is it easy to remain friendly with a founder when you've invested in their company?"

"It's not about friendship, Mr Tully, though I will say we were generally on excellent terms on account of how well she was doing. She made me a lot of money." Pedersen sipped again, winced, and his head jerked back. He frowned.

"Her death must surely cost you dearly, then?"

Pedersen's cup slipped from his hand, crashing to the floor and splashing his trousers. "*For fanden!*" he yelled, and stared at it.

Tully jumped up, looking around him for something to help, but the young manservant came running in with some serviettes and mopped up while the billionaire uttered what Tully assumed to be a string of Danish curses.

"Will you excuse me a moment, Mr Tully?" he said when he'd stood, and disappeared into another room.

"Is he alright?" Tully said.

The man looked at him, then towards where Pedersen had gone, and swallowed. "He wouldn't want me to say," he whispered.

So perhaps this wasn't the first time such an incident had occurred.

A few minutes later, Pedersen returned in fresh clothes. He looked elegant and stylish, as if nothing had happened. "My apologies. Where were we?"

"Are you okay, Mr Pedersen? Off the record."

Pedersen looked at him so long the moment stretched thin. "Call me Johan," he said at last. "Look, you won't mention my little accident there to anyone, will you? I don't want Guy finding out. He worries about me."

"Finding out what?"

But Pedersen shook his head. "Just promise me you won't tell him."

"Sure."

"Now, where were we?"

Tully hesitated. The journalist in him wanted to press the matter. But perhaps Pedersen was right. The man's personal health concerns were none of Tully's business. Instead, he said, "I'm thinking about the day of the murder. If Martha and I were poisoned, it likely occurred that day, even at the party itself. Is there anything that happened that day? Any strangers who Martha may have met with?"

Pedersen thought about it. "You'd have to talk to Damien Danberg about that. The only thing I know is that she met Jiang Ying Yue before the party."

"Business or pleasure?"

"Maybe a little of both. Martha was an investor and a patron of MyScent, as am I, for my sins. An investor, that is."

"It's not going well?"

Pedersen shrugged. "That's the investment game for you. I take moonshots. Most of the things I invest in fail. I only need a couple to pay off, like Martha's. I prefer it if the others make or break fast. It's the ones that cling on that irritate me. Zombie businesses. Jiang is somehow keeping it all afloat but is unable to build traction beyond her existing base. Her product's too expensive to reach a mass market. Frankly, she needs to let it die and start something else."

"Is there any way you could arrange for me to see her?"

"Of course, of course. I'll arrange it first thing tomorrow morning."

"I'm thinking I might head over now."

Pedersen laughed. "Careful, Mr Tully. With this amount of drive, I might end up investing in you, too."

⤴

TULLY REACHED JIANG'S West Quarter offices just before eight p.m. A tall, severe woman with a tight bun of hair was there to greet him as he stepped out of the lift. An elegant MyScent sign filled the wall behind her. "I'm Ms Jiang's executive assistant, Mr Tully," she said, her Australian accent unmistakable. "Please follow me."

She walked at a clip, brisk and determined, setting a pace that burned his thighs.

The aisles were packed with workers typing, drinking coffee, scanning virtual screens. Most wore headphones that emitted a multitude of different tunes. The effect was a discordant hum.

"Is it normal for people to work this late?" Tully asked. "Surely everyone could work from home in the evenings?"

Her brow furrowed. "It's not late yet."

They reached a glass box in the centre of the open-plan space. *The Fishbowl* had been stencilled on the door. She tapped.

Through the glass, Jiang held a finger up, speaking to someone, then a moment later the finger curled to beckon them. The assistant led him in and gave him a smile that didn't reach her eyes. "Can I offer you a drink?"

He shook his head. Jiang also declined with a wave of the finger. This was a woman very experienced, it seemed, at communicating in single digits. The assistant left and closed the door behind her.

"I got Johan's request," Jiang said, "but I can only give you a few minutes. I have a call."

Her manner surprised him. Surely Martha had been her friend, yet no sense of grief was apparent. Nor was there any recognition that she and Tully had shared several hours in each other's company only a night before. She was brusque, and business-like, and begged the question: was that just who she was at work, or was this fronting deeper emotions that she didn't want to let surface? Guilt, for example? "You do know that Martha is dead, right?"

Jiang drummed her fingers on the table. "Of course." At the party she'd seemed relaxed and informal. Now, she fired syllables like gunshots. Well, two could play at that game.

He flicked on his recording without asking for permission. "I'm trying to get my head around Martha's life here so I can figure out who did this to her."

Jiang snorted. "You're investigating her death? You? Surely it's a job for the police."

He tried not to be offended at the way she'd said, *you?* He failed, but was careful not to let it enter his tone. "I think there could be a political dimension to all this, and political crimes are what I unpick." She didn't look impressed, but she didn't object either. Yet she ventured nothing more, just sat and waited for him to continue. He tried another tack. "Mr Pedersen was very supportive of me looking into this, too." Her expression flickered just a little at that, enough that he thought it was worth pitching a more direct question and seeing whether he got at answer. "Can I ask how you knew Martha?"

Jiang sighed, and the sigh seemed to carry away the last of her resistance. "Through Pedersen. He invested in both of us. She acted as his reference when I was raising money from him, then became an investor herself, an adviser and a friend," she said, ticking off each point on her fingers.

There was a knock at the door and a man's head poked in. "Our CAC to LTV ratio dropped to two X, and the new serum supplier still isn't answering."

Jiang pursed her lips but didn't answer, just flicked one finger lazily, and the man departed.

"And Martha was a customer too, right?" Tully said.

She shrugged. "I have a good base here in New Carthage." She drummed her fingers on the desk.

He paused, working out how to cut through to something useful. The drumming accelerated. "Johan told me you met Martha on the day of the party. I was wondering—"

"Are you trying to investigate me, Mr Tully?"

"No," he said quickly, "but if you saw anything unusual that she ate or drank either then or at the party—"

"Are you writing a puff piece on her last evening, or trying to do Commander October's job?"

"Neither, I'm—"

Another knock. The executive assistant held up a finger through the window. This whole place communicated with fingers. Still, this one he understood. One minute.

"Look," Jiang said, "no one at that party would have done anything to harm Martha."

"I didn't say that."

"She was a friend to me and Flora, a critical business partner for Pedersen, and Danberg obviously had feelings for her." She looked into the distance through the glass, then back at him. "Really, the only people I can't vouch for are her sister, who by all accounts has become very wealthy overnight, and you, who seemed to be in the right place at the right time to bag a career-making story."

"My career is already made. Look, Ms Jiang…"

"Time's up, Mr Tully."

She held up a finger and the assistant walked back in. "Please follow me?"

Jiang didn't even offer him her finger, let alone a hand.

21

Insomnia had never plagued Tully, but tonight, sleep evaded him. It wasn't because he was in a strange bed. He'd slept well enough the first nights in Martha's apartment, though it was strange and a little eerie to be back here given the events of the previous night. No, he tossed and turned while questions churned. Big questions. Weighty questions. Questions that cramped him and made his pillow hot. Had it been his fault? Toss. Did Solomon stand a chance of winning now that Martha was dead? Turn.

He eventually slipped into a fitful doze and was confronted, once again, by a small girl dying on a baking street corner, corpses surrounding her, while he drove past in an air-conditioned car. He surged awake, rummaged through Martha's bathroom cabinets and found a sleeping neurotropic. It knocked him out until his alarm summoned him at seven a.m.

It took a hot shower and multiple coffees to clear the fog. He went through his routine, scanning his competitors' stories, deducing their sources, but he couldn't bring himself to ring them. Instead, he fired off messages expressing his disappointment and his certainty that they'd not let him down again. A few replied instantly, apologetic and offering other titbits. Tully filed these away for later follow-up.

Just as he was finishing up, Bamphwick posted a new monologue. The head-line said it all: *CHAOS IN SOLOMON CAMP AFTER CHANDRA SUICIDE.* And then in smaller caps below, *DID JOURNALIST MARCUS TULLY PUSH SOLOMON CREATOR OVER THE EDGE?*

He tapped his fingers. Bamphwick's games were difficult to ignore. He could feel a ball of worry forming from it, a vague disquiet that this could be detrimental to his reputation and his business, but he pushed it away. It was a distraction. Publish great stories and the readers, the reputation, and the redress would follow. He closed the feed and went to check on Livia. Her door was closed. He tapped lightly. There was no reply so he inched it open and peeked in. The room was still darkened. The lump of her body in the bed didn't stir so he shut the door softly again. Let her sleep it off.

Meanwhile, he'd go door-knocking. He'd speak to everyone else who'd been at the party, namely Danberg and Flora. He felt directionless, as if he didn't even know what questions he should be asking, but it was always like this at the beginning of a new story. It was a primordial chaos, out of which order would form, but through struggle, through chance, through randomness. He'd know the right questions in the moment.

⤳

TULLY CLOSED HER door behind him, and only then did Livia move in the darkened room. She rolled onto her back and eyed the earset on the bedside table. The old Livia would have grabbed it and checked the latest election polling. Old Livia was an election polling addict. Old Livia could suck it.

Old Livia's life had changed the moment Martha had died. The last member of her family was gone.

Sure, she had an incredible inheritance. There was no need to get up, no need to get dressed, no need to work. But she cared nothing for the money. She cared nothing about anything right now.

She pulled the cover over her head, aching for sleep to take her.

⤳

DAMIEN DANBERG LIVED ten minutes' walk from Martha's tower in a residential road that connected to a lovely parade of boutique shops, bars and restaurants. This area of town had a very different feel from either Martha's skyscraper-filled quarter, or Pedersen's ultra-luxurious strcct. The street had small apartment blocks, about four stories high and three apartments across, on narrower streets. It didn't feel poor—these blocks anywhere else in the world would have been deemed a luxury—but they suffered in comparison to their wealthier neighbours. Danberg lived on a ground floor apartment in the third block along. Pedersen had helpfully provided the address. Tully squinted through the diamond-shaped window of the turquoise front door and knocked.

There was no answer.

He tried again, then twice more.

Finally, the door opened, and Danberg stood there. Gone was the smiling young man who'd greeted Tully and Livia upon their arrival in New Carthage. Grief—or guilt?—had ravaged the man in an astonishingly short amount of time. Dark bags circled his eyes. The stubble covering his gaunt face wasn't fashionable so much as unkempt. The suit had gone, and instead, he wore a dressing gown. He already smelled stale and acrid, liked he'd been grieving for weeks, not a day.

"Tully," Danberg said, but didn't move.

"Danberg. Can I come in?"

Danberg looked for a moment like he'd refuse, then sagged like he didn't have the energy or will to do so. He turned and walked through to another room, leaving Tully to close the door and follow him through to a dim lounge with blinds half-drawn.

"Bit of a mess," Danberg muttered. He picked some clothes up off a chair, threw them to one side and slumped into the newly vacated space. His breathing was short and shallow. He licked cracked lips and fidgeted.

Tully glanced at the blinds, wondering whether to draw them, then just cleared another chair for himself and sat. "How are you doing, Damien?" A ridiculous question. Anyone could see how Danberg was doing.

Danberg laughed; it came out forced and high-pitched. "Fab," he said. "Just fab." He closed his eyes, put his index finger and thumb over the bridge of his nose and squeezed like he was trying to squash his fatigue.

Tully decided to throw a softball question first. This was not a man who looked like he'd cope with a question about whether he'd slipped something in the drinks. "I'm wondering if I can get Martha's schedule for the day she died?"

Danberg shivered and stared off at nothing. "I miss her. She meant a lot to me. I know everyone saw her as this hard, driven woman. But she was kind to me."

Not an answer to any question Tully had asked, but at least he was talking. Tully tried again from a different direction. "Had you worked for her for long?"

"I tucked you both up, you know. It was the last time I saw her alive. Only now I don't know if … if she was already …" He choked up and turned his head away.

The softballs were dropping like rocks at Danberg's feet. Perhaps a slightly harder pitch would connect. "Did you see her consume anything…"

"She gave me a chance," Danberg interrupted. "I didn't live in New Carthage when I applied. I'd read about her tech and was inspired. She was special. A genius. She was trying to save the world. No, the world didn't need saving, she'd say. It would outlive us, but our species and all of the others, that's what she was trying to save." Danberg was talking fast now, spitting out his words. He wasn't looking at Tully but staring up at the ceiling like he was talking to his therapist. "She'd seen what could go wrong, up close; she wanted to stop more things like the tabkhir and all the other heatwaves, and the storms and fires and floods and everything that's going fucking wrong with this planet. Human-managed geo-engineering wasn't the solution, you see? She created Solomon to fix it all. Don't you see? She gave me a chance, and I got not only a job but a chance to live in one of the few places that could ride out the climate apocalypse if he fails. And her, I got her." He gulped in air and licked his lips again.

Still not the answer he'd been looking for, but keep a guy talking, and you might hear things you didn't expect. Geo-engineering wasn't the solution? Maybe Damien knew things. Not just about Martha's death, but about the real reason he was here. "Damien, do you know what happened to put her off geo-engineering? Perhaps at the White House?"

Danberg turned his head sharply and looked Tully straight in the eyes. Tully felt a surge of hope and excitement, like a jolt of electricity that kicked his heartbeat up several notches. "That bastard Pedersen killed her, you know," Danberg spat.

"Wait," Tully said, "what?"

Danberg looked back up to the ceiling. "Things were never growing fast enough for Pedersen. He wanted it to move faster, always faster, not the tech, but the commercialisation of the tech, you see? He thought Martha was too much of a scientist. Not enough of a *businesswoman.*" He sneered the word. "He wanted to explore other uses of Solomon. Like developing weaponisation that could be sold to the military, and she was totally against it, of course; she didn't invent Solomon to kill people." He drew a breath. "Now he can put who he wants in the CEO's seat. He can swing the board. He can do what he wants."

This was huge. Tully dared not move. He waited to see what else would come, but Danberg was staring into space again. "But investors and founders fight about strategy all the time, don't they?" Tully said finally.

Danberg got up and trudged out of the room.

Tully waited for him to come back, but he didn't. He found Danberg in the bedroom, face down, sobbing his soul into a pillow.

∽

OCTOBER ACCEPTED THE invite from the governor and a moment later was sitting in a much more sober setting, a minimalist, private office. Which was strange. He usually tried to surprise and delight with his choice of vistas.

"Governor," she said. "I'm sorry for your loss."

Solomon bowed his head. "Thank you. It's been a difficult time."

"I can imagine."

Something in her eyes must have given her away, because he said, "You're wondering if an AI can really feel grief? And, if so, whether simulated emotions affect the way I think?"

"I asked Dr Chandra about that once, but she was tight-lipped."

"And what do you think? Would Dr Chandra have designed me to experience emotions?"

It was a good question. "Emotions are pretty critical to being human. They guide our decisions. But they corrupt those decisions, make us irrational. You're meant to be the ultimate decision-making ..." Would the word "machine" offend him? "Maker. Decision maker. So I guess you need enough to inform but not to paralyse?"

Solomon nodded. "That assumes I operate within a narrow bandwidth of emotions, to feel a bit but not too much. Not so. Dr Chandra considered it important, imperative even, that I feel the intensity of both the highs and lows, and to never harden or become immune to those. But, she gave me the ability to rise above emotion. Human emotions, even grief, have a kind of half-life. They can be crippling at first, but fade with time. I experience time differently and am therefore able to process things fully before making any kind of decisions."

"That sounds like both a curse and a blessing."

"That it is, Commander. I don't intend to break my policy of giving you full autonomy in your investigation work. I ask only two things. First, that you do keep me updated when you feel it's appropriate. And, second, that you make use of all resources available to you right now."

"I'm sorry, Governor, I don't think I understand."

"Marcus Tully survived?"

"Yes. I interviewed him this morning. In my initial hypothesis, he'd administered something to Dr Chandra once they were alone, and dosed himself to avoid suspicion."

"Do you still hold to that hypothesis, Commander?"

She thought for a minute. Did her pause feel like an eternity to an artilect? "I'm less sure. It's a possibility, but I hit him broadside with some direct questions at a time when he should have been least able to think clearly, and he seemed shocked. That he and the sister arrived uninvited only a day before her murder still raises a red flag for me, though."

"I've known Livia for some years, and don't believe she's capable of harming her sister. Family is more important than money, to her. And Marcus Tully is known for his integrity."

"Yes, sir," she said. "But Livia Chandra is the beneficiary of Dr Chandra's will. She's become one of the wealthiest women in the world overnight; she was living with her boss before. That's a pretty solid motive as motives go. And …"

"And?"

"And Mr Tully's integrity has come into question recently." As recently as last night, but from a direction surely delicate in this morning's light.

Solomon nodded. "Commander, you can be candid with me. I've never insisted on blind loyalty, and I certainly don't expect those who live or work in any of the Floating States to feel they have to vote for me in the forthcoming election."

She nodded, impressed that yet again he'd read what she was really worried about. She was American Australian and had voted for Lockwood as president in his second term, her very first general election vote. Instinct told her she'd vote for him again, even over her boss. That Lockwood and other former members of that administration had questioned Tully's credibility was a black mark in her book. And while Bamphwick could be a bit too much at times, he often got to the heart of a matter without being mired in political correctness.

"I will say only this," Solomon said. "For a long time, Marcus Tully has been known as a truth-teller, and is remarkably dogged in his quest to uncover that truth. You may find he complements your own search rather well."

"Yes, sir," she said, but she knew it came out stiff.

Solomon smiled. "A suggestion, that is all. An asset has value, no matter whether you value it or not."

"Sir, I need to ask two favours."

"Of course, Commander. How can I help?"

"First, I want to lock down departures from the island immediately. Incoming is okay, and any new arrivals can leave after a security check by my team. But anyone who was on New Carthage at the time of Dr Chandra's demise must stay on the island until we establish more facts."

"An unpopular call for any governor to make, but I agree. The second?"

"Dr Chandra has a private security system in her apartment that would have captured footage from the party. Perhaps the critical footage. I need it, and fast, to direct the investigations. It appears to be proprietary, of her own making. Regardless, it's encrypted. Did Dr Chandra share her password vault with you, or can you break the encryption?"

He was quiet for a while, which surprised her. How many years of human thought had he just traversed? "No, Dr Chandra didn't share her vault with me," he said at length. "I didn't even know she had one. But she did a lot of work on encryption. I'd guess it's quantum AI in its own right, unbreakable even by me."

It was a blow, but everyone had a weak point when it came to security. There was always a backdoor: a keyword or phrase related to a person's life and priorities that got things open. Which made Livia the most obvious starting point.

⮌

TULLY'S BLENDED-REALITY DISPLAY had dimmed into sunglasses mode. New Carthage had pushed up the thermometer and the sun blazed. Still, the climate-control system wafted a soothing artificial breeze through the streets that took the edge off.

The Cothon was incredible up close, like time travelling to the past and the future at the same time. He stood for a while and tried to capture every little detail, burning it into his memory. Livia had been in awe when they saw it from the air. The memory was tinged blue now, a snapshot from happier times. He thought over the conversations he'd had in the past twenty-four hours. There was the death threat from a few weeks ago that Pedersen had told him about. There was Jiang's assurance that no one at that party would have done anything to harm Martha. There was Danberg, accusing 'that bastard' Pedersen. Same old story as any investigation. A mess of opinions and lies, that would be peeled away as the facts were confirmed and the truth revealed.

Of the party guests, only Flora Jacobs remained for him to meet. He'd taken her up on her invitation to the yacht. There were so many of them at the quayside, all gleaming white and expensive, that he had to use the navigation in his display to find his way. A virtual arrow directed him down a small jetty, but a guard blocked his way.

"Marcus Tully?" the man said.

So they were using facial recognition. Smooth. Tully nodded.

"Ms Jacobs is waiting for you on the third yacht down, sir."

Thick blue letters on the stern proclaimed the yacht to be the *Instaself*. A witty nod to Flora's influencer career that had started on Instagram and exploded on Minds, or simply ego at play? Flora was furthermost from the jetty, sunbathing on the bow.

"Hey," he called from the dockside.

She stood, and for a second he didn't know where to look. She was all skin, with just a flash of bikini. He could almost hear Zainab laughing. *That's for the camera, not for touching, you fool.*

Flora laughed, too, and he blinked, the overlap of Zainab's laugh in his head and Flora's surprising him. "You're meant to say 'ahoy'," she said. "Come aboard."

Tully clambered on and again wasn't sure where to look; the bikini was even skimpier from behind.

"Sorry about the guard," Flora said.

He cleared his throat. "I'm surprised you need protection in a place like New Carthage."

"Oh, it's not protection," she said. "People like to post pictures of me on social media. I prefer to control my own image on Minds. Especially when I'm wearing a bikini." She looked back at him and winked, then gestured at a chair opposite her own but didn't sit. "Cocktail?"

He started to refuse but she interrupted. "Please, it would be rude to leave me to drink on my own."

A small voice said hello from the cabin, and Tully turned around. The girl, perhaps six or seven years old, was Flora's perfect miniature.

"Well, hello," Tully said. "And who might you be?"

"I'm JJ," she said, coming forward and tilting her head. "And who might you be?"

He laughed. "My name's Tully. Is JJ your real name?"

She raised an eyebrow. "Of course it is. Is Tully yours?"

He nodded. "Well, it's my surname. My first name is Marcus, but most people call me Tully."

She frowned. "They must not like you very much then."

"Maybe it's because I don't like them very much."

"I'll call you Marcus," she declared.

"Jayla," Flora said from the cabin door. "Come in out of the sun, darling, and leave our guest in peace."

"Yes, Mom," she said, and raised her chin. "I have a meeting to go to. Those teddies don't like to be kept waiting."

Tully nodded. "You make sure to tell them they simply can't take the yacht for a spin, no matter how much they insist."

She giggled and disappeared inside.

"She's adorable," Tully said.

"She's my world. I just worry about the world she'll grow up in. Do you have children?"

"No," he said. He'd tried to keep his tone light but it had come out forced.

"I'm sorry, it's the kind of question I always seem to dig a grave with." She blanched. "Sorry. That's also in poor taste, all things considered. I'm sorry."

"Were you close to Martha?"

She looked sad and bit her lip. "Yeah. But I don't like to grieve, you know? I like to remember the good times. But it comes in waves. I've tried to keep it together in front of Jayla but I've spent a good part of the past day in tears."

"I'm trying to get my head around what happened. Martha was helping me on a story and I need to know if her death was connected. Although some people think it could be connected to the election and others that it's something more personal."

She raised an eyebrow. "Oh? Who?"

He hesitated. "Danberg. He's in a bit of a state. He's blaming Pedersen."

"Johan? Surely not. He doesn't have it in him, and besides he's…" She stopped herself.

"He's what?"

"Why does Damien think Johan was involved?"

Tully made a mental note of the evasion. "He thinks Martha might have had some issues with Pedersen recently. Business issues."

She shrugged. "Martha didn't discuss that kind of thing with me. She knew I'm not interested in discussing business, but I know how the world works." She sipped her cocktail. "I really *do*. But business is boring."

"Isn't being a model and influencer a business?"

She laughed. "It's a way of making money, sure. But there are no *balance sheets*,"—she made a face—"or *governance issues*, or *financial models*."

"I guess."

"Anyway, there were times when Martha was annoyed with Pedersen, but what she needed from me was a friend, someone to help her think about other things, to clear her mind. We just didn't discuss that stuff."

"What's going on with Johan Pedersen, Flora? You said, 'And besides, he's …'"

She hesitated. "It's really not my place. How's Damien doing?"

Tully let it go. "Like I said, in a bit of a state."

"I tried to visit but he wouldn't let me in."

"I guess he needs some time."

"He loved her, you know? It was one of those badly kept secrets that she ignored and he tried to hide, but everyone knew."

"I'm guessing the feeling was unrequited."

"That's it. She had her own plans and they didn't involve a man slowing her down." She glanced towards the cabin. "She loved Jayla, you know. I think Jayla inspired her to have children herself."

"With whom?"

Flora laughed. "I told you, she didn't need a man. Who does? She was going solo, talking to a fertility clinic about using donor sperm and artificial insemination."

Tully nodded. "A shame she didn't get the chance." He sipped at the cocktail. Too early for alcohol, especially given his poor night's sleep. For the first time since leaving the hospital, all fired up, he felt demoralised. He wasn't a homicide investigator. So far, he had nothing. Except perhaps Danberg's allegation regarding Pedersen. There was some sense to it. The timing would be ingenious, as investigators would assume it was connected to the election and dismiss money as a motive. But then again, Pedersen's investment was running for leadership of the whole bloody world. Short term, of course, but still. Anything the company wanted to do after that would be more valuable, not less. Surely Pedersen wouldn't risk that by eliminating the chief scientist and inventor. After all, what might Martha have invented next, given the chance?

A message popped up in Tully's display from Commander October. She wanted to meet at a coffee shop in an hour and would send him directions if he agreed.

It was better than an interrogation room, though it still assumed too much for his liking. What would she do if he refused? Clamp another headset on him as he was walking down the street?

Tomorrow at eleven a.m., he replied.

She'd have to wait.

22

Tully was late, and he hated being late.

A notification in his display informed him that Bolivar and Haymaker had just landed. He quickened his pace across the New Carthage Aeroport concourse and skirted around the statue of Aštart.

They were waiting for him, already inside. He apologised, clapped a hand on Bolivar's shoulder and held out a hand to Haymaker. Haymaker grinned, ignored the outstretched hand and stepped forward. Tully tensed, ready to defend himself, but the man pulled him into an embrace. It was like being swallowed by a brick.

"Mr Tully, I didn't get a chance to thank you, man."

Tully pulled loose and stepped back. Bolivar smothered a laugh.

"Sure, Haymaker. Pleased to meet you properly."

"I read all your stuff, man. Mr Bolivar here gave it me. It's an honour to be working for ya."

"Good to see you, Marcus," Bolivar said.

"You look like crap, Juan."

"So do you."

"You should stay a bit. The air's fantastic."

"I smelled, and I agree, though it doesn't seem to have done you any good," Bolivar said. He looked around. "More relaxing than London, though. But things aren't going well back at the stables, and the team need a bit of stability if you're going to be here for a while. I'm just delivering one package and collecting another."

Tully glanced back at Haymaker. "The package is appreciated," he said.

The man was taking in his surroundings and his ebullient mood had dissipated a bit already.

"The multicopter to Porto Alegre leaves in an hour and a half," Bolivar said. "Do you want to give me the blood sample now?"

Tully nodded and handed over a small green medical case. "I really appreciate it, Juan. I don't like you acting as courier, but equally there's no one else I'd trust."

Bolivar shrugged. "New Carthage is moving westward anyway, so it's quicker for me to get to Porto Alegre than Cape Town and a ton cheaper than a courier. Time for a spot of breakfast?"

"Of course. There's a place five minutes away by pod. We'll have you back here in an hour." At least he'd got an account for the pods now from Martha's concierge.

Tully steered them to the transport and palmed the terminal on a small six-person pod. The double doors slid open.

"Welcome," said the pod. "What is your desired destination?"

"The Dido." He sank bank into his seat and tried to blink away the fatigue he still hadn't been able to shake after another night of fitful sleep. He wanted to close his eyes but what kind of impression would that make on his new head of security? Haymaker was staring out of the window and seemed almost morose. "So, Mr Haymaker—"

"Just Haymaker, man." The moroseness shifted like a thundercloud moving off in a storm leaving a crisp fine day behind it. "My momma used to say I was made while the sun shone." He laughed.

"You're American?"

"New Orleans. Though my mee maw was English."

"Mee maw?"

"My momma's momma."

"Have you decided what we're going to do?" Bolivar said. Bolivar had never appreciated small talk.

"We're going to find the murderer," Tully said. "I promised Livia. And I want to know whether it was all related to the story."

"I meant about our challenges back home. Lockwood and Kehoe are claiming the story was junk. Cavanagh says you tried to blackmail him. Bamphwick's painting you as lacking credibility, a journo in it for the money. Our influencers are leaving. Our finances—"

"I got it, Juan."

"You want me go talk to this Bamphwick chookie?" Haymaker said, his deep voice booming inside the pod.

"Well, that might only make the situation worse," Tully said, trying to keep his tone tactful, "but we should certainly keep it in mind as a backup plan." He thought for a moment. "Juan, is Lottie sorted with the Cavanagh story?"

"She's been sorted for days, Marcus. But the story's tainted. Cavanagh made a pre-emptive strike claiming the emails were fake, and as I already said, we can't prove they weren't."

Tully shook his head. "It doesn't matter. They aren't fake. We've got the truth to report, and that's the thing about truth, you can't back down from the telling of it."

"The reach will be much smaller with so many fewer influencers."

"We'll send a statement to them beforehand. But if they are not with us, they're not. It doesn't matter. The story's a local one anyway. It'll matter to the people of Houston and that's about it. But get it out there. We need to show we won't be cowed."

"You got it."

"As for Kehoe, we put out all the evidence that the story was authentic. Republish it again with a statement telling Lockwood and Kehoe to back up their accusations it was faked with proof."

"Okay."

It was good to be on the attack again. It cleared the fog. Always be on the offensive, not the defensive. "I think we go public," Tully continued. "Remind the world that Lockwood's chosen to support a man who launched a pre-emptive attack on peaceful protestors in order to inflame tensions and score political points, and ask what that says about his judgement."

"It'll make us the story, and we normally try to avoid that."

"Screw it. They've already made us the story."

"And Bamphwick?"

Tully repressed a grimace. "It's about time someone sorted out his ego. So let's say we've never seen Mr Bamphwick's stream so couldn't possibly comment on whatever he's been saying about us."

∽

LIVIA TOOK A deep breath and left her bedroom, stepping into the quiet of Martha's apartment … her apartment? She recalled Tully's words: *You inherited this place. Just stay for a while, until you figure things out.* But it wasn't hers, not yet. Signs of Martha were all over the place and she had no desire to remove them and make it her own. Not now. Maybe never.

Three stone-carved Indian elephants drank from a lake in a glass water feature. It was beautiful, but Livia sighed, struggling to find the connection with her sister, a rich, self-made woman. They hadn't really been close for years. Not that Livia hadn't loved her. She missed the older sister she'd grown up with, the one who'd teased her, protected her, taught her. And now she was the last of her family. No parents, no sister. It was like being orphaned all over again.

She walked around, trying to imagine Martha's life here. Sat on the sofa where Martha had spent her final moments. Rubbed the fabric on the cushions.

Tears broke just as the front door opened. Livia wiped her cheeks.

Tully entered the lounge. A giant of a man followed him.

"Livia, this is Haymaker."

He was familiar … yes, the guy from London that Tully had rescued like a very large puppy. He got down on one knee, his eyes now level with hers. "Lady, I'm so sad for your loss. Losing family is like losin' a part of yourself."

She looked up at him. "I'm very pleased to meet you properly, Mr Haymaker," she whispered.

He grinned at that. "Y'all so formal here. Like I told the boss, it's just Haymaker."

"Well, then I insist you don't call me 'Lady'."

He nodded. "Right you are, li'l sister."

23

October arrived early at the coffee house off Hannibal Boulevard. Neutral territory, great coffee. She selected a table for two. Took the seat facing the door.

She ordered a coffee while she waited, half-watching the door, half-contemplating the case so far. The first murder in New Carthage. Her first real test. She'd been on federal cases before, at the FBI, but never directly in charge of something like this. She couldn't mess this up. Reputations were slowly built and quickly destroyed.

Ten minutes later, Tully arrived. Seemed wary. They hadn't got off to the best start, but it wasn't her job to make friends. Just to find the truth.

Then she blinked. A huge man stood behind him. Silence fell in the room as the other patrons gawped. Then New Carthaginian discretion kicked back in and the murmur of conversation resumed.

Tully gestured to a nearby table. The large man sat down on a wall bench. His girth took up the space of two people. He scowled around at the other guests, who slowly picked up their conversations. Did their best to ignore him.

Tully nodded at her. Sat opposite her.

"Friend of yours?" she said.

"Bodyguard. Name's Haymaker."

"Yes." She remembered now. "That was some complicated vetting. Not much past history. It's difficult for those formerly of no fixed abode to come to New Carthage. I believe your lawyer, Bolivar, had to give a guarantee. Pay a deposit."

"I bet he loved that. Bolivar hates spending money."

"He got off okay?"

"Yes, and he appreciated the quick turnaround considering the wider lockdown."

"You look tired, Mr Tully. How about a coffee? I recommend the New Tenochtitlan blend. It's really very good." It was a peace offering. Would he take it?

"Just Tully, please. I've been wondering how New Tenochtitlan even grows coffee? Don't you need a large plantation?"

She shrugged. "We're all self-supporting but trade between each other. Hydroponic vertical farming. Sprout farms. Lab-abatoirs. Gene-edited, salt-tolerant crops on floating farms. Fish pens. Micro-salination. You name it, we have what we need." She subspoke the order, then added one for Haymaker too.

"Must be nice to live in paradise," Tully said.

"It's my job to live here. But I'm not going to complain. I am one of the lucky ones."

"Got many police in Eden?"

Trying to push her buttons? Maybe he was still sore, after the interrogation in NR. "A few. But there's very little crime here. Citizens granted permanent visas are vetted to weed out extremists, or psychopaths. Even those with a tendency for domestic violence. We don't let in many visitors or tourists. Those we do are also vetted." She nodded towards Haymaker. "Our work is mostly preventive. Commit even a minor infraction, your visa is taken away."

"And a major infraction?"

She shrugged. "Big enough, death penalty. You don't want people messing around on a small island. Hasn't happened yet. Besides, we're small enough not to do one-size-fits-all."

"So a murder's a new experience for you."

The echo of her own, earlier thoughts irritated her. "Everyone on my team has top-level experience from another force," she snapped. "I am ex-FBI. And anyway, we don't know for sure it was a murder yet."

A microdrone deposited the coffees on the table, then made its way over to Haymaker. He scowled at the machine, seemingly outraged.

"You arrested me for murder," Tully said, "then let me go. How can you possibly think it wasn't, now?"

"Just keeping an open mind."

"What did the tox report tell you?"

She hesitated. "Our man's still working on it."

Tully raised an eyebrow. "He's that busy on a floating island with no crime? What's he found so far?"

"Too early to tell."

He sat with that for a moment, then said, "And what about the security cams?"

That was the killer question. Natural for an investigative journo to jump straight to it. "Can't get into the footage. Datsec team are stumped." The words were sour on her tongue, and she sipped at the coffee.

Tully's eyes had narrowed. "It's encrypted?"

"Seems Martha didn't just build political leaders. She also had her own proprietary system. Locked it with a powerful algorithm. More than a password. Apparently." She took a deep breath, unused to sharing this kind of info outside the team. "We need to establish whether something happened in the apartment. Or whether it all happened beforehand. Time is ticking. People—influential people—are already complaining about not being able to leave."

"But can't Solomon just let you in?" Tully said. "I mean, he was basically her computer system, right?"

"I asked him. Martha had a password vault he didn't have access to." Guilt stitched her belly. It took a moment for her to realise why, like she was betraying the governor to a stranger. Now Tully knew Solomon had limits, imposed by Martha, even though the rest of the world was being told he did not.

Tully stared ahead, thumb brushing his lower lip. She tried not to tap her foot. She didn't know this guy, or what he was capable of. Best to let him have a moment. He'd put out an article on Cavanagh the day before. Targeted locally, at Houston. The agentbot she'd set up to keep tabs on him and his work had flashed a notification late at night. She'd read it; been surprised to find she'd bought it. She didn't know much about Cavanagh, but it seemed Tully had done his homework. Presented a solid argument. A bunch of projects had received money and shown no real activity until a week or so ago after he'd contacted Cavanagh for comment. There were emails. A number of photos from public events that backed up the claims.

Cavanagh's carefully crafted denial had come out mere minutes after the article hit, and had seemed somehow flat. More damning still, Cavanagh's wife had been photographed leaving the house this morning in the rain. Wearing sunglasses in the rain. Dragging a suitcase. The epitome of a pissed wife who wasn't buying her husband's bullshit.

"I think we can help," Tully said, startling her.

"What?"

"With the password vault. Maybe. Livia's been left access to it in Martha's will. But she's not in a good place, doesn't seem motivated to do anything at all at the moment except sleep."

"Maybe I can talk to her," October said. "Solving this case may bring her some closure."

They stood and looked at each other. It was as close to a handshake as they'd got.

"Let's go," Tully said.

24

"Livia?" Tully called out.

There was no reply.

"Chip, is Livia Chandra still in the apartment?"

"I'm sorry," the apartment bot said, "you do not have the authorisation to ask that question."

He shot an apologetic look at October. "She was here when I left. She hasn't been out for days."

Haymaker walked over to the window and touched a blanket on the sofa, then picked up a mug. "She gone left her coffee."

"Is it still warm?" asked October.

"Nah."

Tully called her, but it rang out. "She's not picking up."

"Maybe she needed some time out," October said. "There's no sign of a struggle, and it's entirely possible she just went for a walk. She'll be fine. There's not much that can happen to you in New Carthage."

"You mean except getting murdered in your own home?" It was a cheap blow, but he was worried and the tiredness was creeping back in.

"I've got to head back to the office," October said with a stiff smile. "Let me know as soon as she turns up. The sooner we can get our hands on that footage …" Her eyes flicked to her display. "Give me a second. Something's coming through. Is it okay if I take a call privately?"

"Yeah, of course. Take Martha's study?" He pointed and she left.

Tully went to the kitchen sink and splashed cold water over his face. His head throbbed and his stomach fluttered with worry. Maybe he was being irrational.

Livia could take care of herself. And the commander was right, these weren't dangerous streets. He glanced towards the study. The room was muted. October had been in there for a few minutes now. Did she have news on Livia? Would she share it with him if she did? The unease crept up into his chest. He took a deep breath and let it out slowly, trying to unlock the anxiety. It didn't work, so he tried again. No luck. He gave up, strode over to the bar and poured himself a rum, straight. He savoured the warm burn in his mouth and swallowed.

An air of wrongness hung over the apartment. Haymaker, too, seemed on edge. He stood stock still and stared out the window, hands on hips. Tully lifted his glass but it was empty. Bolivar would have noticed if he'd been here, and refilled it without asking, just one example of the easy comfort that came of a long friendship.

The study door opened and October walked out. She swallowed several times and wet her lips. And he knew then. Bad news, stalking towards him, scythe in hand.

He poured another drink and waited to meet it.

"Tully …" she took a deep breath and stopped.

"Just say it," he whispered. It couldn't be possible. Both sisters could not be dead. Just days ago they'd stood here, chatting and laughing.

"The multicopter," she said. "It's disappeared."

It made no sense. "What?"

She bit her lip. "We track everyone who comes to or leaves New Carthage, all the way from their port of origin or to their destination. Juan Bolivar took Flight NC404, a multicopter to Porto Alegre. It should have only taken a few hours. It didn't arrive."

Juan.

He couldn't move, couldn't breathe. This was surely a mistake.

"Man," Haymaker said. "God be with Mr Bolivar."

Tully sank back the rest of the rum. "Bolivar always turns up. Usually where he's least wanted."

October shook her head. "Our next-gen radar is really good, and all aircraft continually sync coordinates with satellites. Besides, they didn't arrive, Tully. We've deployed military to search the area, but it's choppy out there, and the chance of surviving in a multicopter …"

He wanted to sit but there was no seat near him, so he slid down the side of the bar and onto to the floor.

October squatted beside him. "I'm so sorry," she whispered.

25

"What have you got?" October said. She and Moran were physically in the same room but plugged into NR. They walked through an ancient sequoia forest. A loving recreation, built from the teenage memories of the Californian designer, before the real forests had died in the wildfires that had wiped the once great state off the American flag. She'd needed to come here. To escape the real world for a short time. She trailed a hand over the base of a giant tree, soaring high into the heavens above. Sniffed the fresh forest scent deep.

Moran scratched at five-day stubble on his cheek. "García reckons there's a religious angle."

"García's Catholic."

"Well, it turns out Martha did piss off quite a broad spectrum. Johan Pedersen was the first to mention it to us. Said he'd heard about a death threat a few weeks back. Some group on the Christian far right called Angels of Mercy who thought she was trying to supplant their god with Solomon. Pedersen said she pretty much ignored it, but it had leaked to her board of directors, of which Pedersen, as one of her key investors, is one. They asked her to be careful but she went the other way. The way she unveiled Solomon as a candidate and her speech afterwards may have pushed it further still."

Birdsong filled the air. Perfect facsimiles of creatures now extinct. Or on the verge of being so. The forest often proved the best place for her to think. Insights impossible to garner sat in an office often flourished in peace.

"I spoke to Jeffries on my way here," she said after a while.

"Did he grump at you?"

"Always. Says the barbiturate's some kind of pentobarbital variant. Never seen it before."

"Isn't that the truth serum stuff they use in old movies?"

"That's sodium thiopental. Another kind of barbiturate. Ours is what they used to use for euthanasia, lethal injections."

"So was this euthanasia or an execution?"

They strolled deeper into the forest. It was quiet but for the occasional fluttering of wings, cones dropping from trees, the scurry of small animals in the undergrowth, the chirrup of birds. A breeze rustled the branches and carried an earthy smell of pine needles, then died down. The forest floor, layered with the needles, cushioned their feet. There was no path here, just a natural flow of space between the trees and ferns.

"I don't buy the suicide angle," she said.

Moran jumped slightly, seemingly lost in his own thoughts.

October continued, "I knew Martha a bit. She was driven. For Solomon to get to this point was everything she had dreamed of. She believed she had a role to play: saving our species from ourselves. That technology was what she could bring to the table. She didn't nominate Solomon for dictator, but once the Swedes had, she embraced it. She was not hopeless."

"So it was an execution," Moran said.

"Here's the thing with pentobarbital. This is not something that kicks in a few hours later. Think about the old generation of lethal injections. Took minutes. If Martha did not administer it herself, and Jeffries found no sign of an injection point, she probably ingested it through food or drink."

Moran sucked air. "How's this for a hypothesis? It's the end of the party. Everyone says goodbye. Danberg shows everyone out and Livia goes to bed. Tully and Martha have a final drink, perhaps some food. Whatever they had was spiked."

"I don't know. Not something you just leave to chance. Danberg says he came back and found them asleep. That he tucked them in. Livia was already in bed. But what if he gave them something?"

"Danberg? Come on."

"We've met every person who was at that party. I would have said none of them is a murderer. Pedersen can be a bastard, but even so."

"Could be the sister."

Moran was walking faster now, and she accelerated to keep up.

"Sure. She certainly had something to gain. Perhaps she gives Martha a final nightcap. Heads to bed. Would have been quick, though. She was gone by the time Danberg got to them. Five minutes later, tops."

Moran nodded. "If Danberg's telling the truth. But we only have his word for it. Marcus Tully is a possibility too, though. Perhaps he poisoned himself just enough to avoid suspicion."

"We can guess all day. I'll look at Tully and Livia Chandra. You get Danberg in again. Run the usual checks. Finance, debt. You know the drill. See if there's motive."

The virtual sun passed behind a virtual cloud and October shivered.

26

Light rain splashed against the window of Martha's apartment. Livia's apartment, Tully reminded himself as he rolled onto his back and pulled up the duvet. The dome over New Carthage was mostly closed and would likely be sealed if the rain picked up. Light rain was a refreshing connection with nature, but a storm would be an inconvenience for the citizens of the floating city. And in New Carthage, people paid dearly to avoid inconvenience.

His head thumped and the room spun. For a moment, he seemed to float within it, and he closed his eyes, welcoming the beckoning slumber. But his thoughts were too noisy and the release of sleep evaded him.

That the multicopter hadn't arrived wasn't enough to draw conclusions. The search was still underway. Maybe Bolivar was floating in the Atlantic somewhere. They'd laugh about his adventure and drink rum together. But he was frustrated, too. Bolivar had been on his way to Porto Alegre to deliver Tully's blood sample to Fernando. Now that potentially vital clue was gone.

Something else was nagging. Livia. What were the chances of two members of his team disappearing in a single day? Tully had asked October to locate her, but the commander had insisted no harm could befall her in New Carthage. He'd called London to make sure everyone else was okay too, that there hadn't been any other disappearances. They were fine, until he'd broken the news about Bolivar. He'd held back on compounding their worry with his concern for Livia. And, so, he'd put Lottie in charge and asked Randall to sort her out with access to Bolivar's admin. Bolivar was an organised man. It wouldn't take them long. It'd be fine as long as they could keep things in order until Bolivar was back.

The door opened and one of his fears evaporated.

Livia.

She said nothing, just stumbled over to a chair and collapsed into it.

"You're back," Tully said. He breathed a silent thanks to the universe.

"You okay, l'il sister?" Haymaker said.

She smiled thinly, but said nothing, just turned her head and stared out the window.

Tully messaged October. *She's back.*

On my way.

Tully walked over to Livia. "You okay?"

Her eyes were red, perhaps from crying. A few seconds later she replied, her words drawn out as if she was asleep. "Yeah, just tired."

"Where did you go? I was worried."

She shrugged and continued to stare out the window.

"Listen, Haymaker stuck with me today, but from tomorrow I want him with you."

She yawned and squeezed the arms of the chair.

Haymaker jumped up and moved towards her. She tensed and pushed herself back. He held up his hands but then grabbed her chin and held her head, studying her eyes. His other hand went to her wrist. She shrank back and tried to turn away.

"Man, she's high. Some kinda cannabis synthetic, I'd guess. I seen it a thousand times on the street."

"How can you tell?"

"Pupils dilated, whites all bloodshot, heart beatin' through the roof, all tensing up for nothing. Just look at her. She on a trip."

Tully stared into her eyes, and now the disappointment, the worry, the grief… it all spilled out. "After everything, how could you go back to this?" He'd spoken with more force than he'd intended.

Livia shook her head. "Relax, Tully," she said, sounding like her mouth had been stuffed with tissue. "It's not smack this time."

"Listen. Commander October is on her way here to see you."

Livia shrugged. "So?"

He ticked off the points on his fingers. "So, one, you have visible signs of having taken an illegal drug. Two, the commander's ex-FBI. And three, this isn't the most tolerant of places when it comes to crime. They could kick you right out, exile you for good, assets seized, or even worse."

Her eyes widened. "Shit. I can't think. Let me think."

"Livia—"

"I feel sick."

He looked at Haymaker. "Is there anything we can do to sort her out quickly?"

"Nah man. Gotta let it run its course."

"Okay, here's what we're going to do. October's just trying to access security footage of the party. Livia, we think you're the only one with access. It's in Martha's password vault. Livia, do you trust me?"

She looked confused.

"Let me into Martha's vault," Tully said. "I'll get the password for the security system and ignore everything else. Then we'll get you into bed and you can hide out until October's gone. Deal?"

She looked around. "I can't think. I don't know. I don't know what to do. I'm freaking out." Her breaths became short and sharp.

"Calm," Haymaker said in his deep baritone. "Calm, sister."

He sensed a pang and glanced up. October. *Just arriving at Scipio.*

"We're out of time, Livia," Tully said. "Listen, I've always looked after you, right? You have to trust me, and right now."

Her breathing slowed, but only slightly. "What do I do?"

"Martha's lawyer said you have access to her vault." He thought for a minute. "It's not unusual for these things to be set up to automatically pass over to someone else in the event of a confirmed death. Check your own vault and see if you can see anything."

Her eyes seemed to focus. She swiped, pinched and tapped, then gestured towards him.

A notification lit up in his own display. "Vault access granted for five minutes."

"I got it," he said. "Haymaker, could you …?"

Haymaker picked Livia up and, despite her whoop of protest, strode across the room to her suite. "We gonna play you some chill, little sis."

Tully got busy scrolling through Martha's vault. It seemed similar to his own. He ignored the sections labelled *Personal*, *Classified* and *Identity* and headed straight for passwords. There were thousands, so he filtered with keywords.

Security reduced the list to fifty. *Camera* refined it no further, so he scrolled down, looking for anything that stood out. The word *Panopticon* caught his eye. Interesting. The eighteenth-century design had consisted of a circular prison structure with a central watchtower that enabled constant observation. Martha had liked to name her own systems after real-life concepts based on the characteristics they shared. Solomon was a testament to that. What could be more appropriate for a home-brewed security system?

He shared the authentication details with his own vault, readied himself to shut down access and hesitated. Maybe he could take a peek at the classified section. Just a quick one.

He tapped. A bunch of tags appeared with names like *Floating States*, *Project Tefnut* and *Holo-Reality*. What had Martha locked away from the world?

The front door chimed.

He didn't move.

Another chime.

He'd promised Livia, told her she could trust him. There would be time to work on that together later. He swiped his arm through the air and the vault vanished.

Tully walked to the door and opened it. "Any news on Bolivar?"

October shook her head. "I'm sorry. Nothing as yet. How are you doing?"

He chewed on his lip—there was no good answer to that—and led her into the kitchen. They stood by the large dining island in the middle.

"She's here?" October said, looking around.

"She is. But she's not feeling great. The grief, you understand."

October raised an eyebrow.

"Before she went to bed," Tully continued, "we managed to find the security system footage authentication. We think it's the right one, anyway."

October seemed to relax. "Great. You'll give it to me?"

"Sure, but I thought we could look over it together, here."

Suspicion crept into her eyes. "I am not sure that's a good idea," she said in that measured clip that said, I'm in official mode, now. "We need to review these things properly."

He held up his hands. "I'm not trying to be difficult. But we don't even know if this is the right system yet. I promise: if it's the right stuff I'll give you access." He was making a lot of promises tonight.

Her lips pursed but she nodded.

"There's a room built for screening," he said, and gestured towards the holographic suite.

October nodded and they entered the room. A deep white sofa extended around its circumference and they perched on the edge. Tully brought up the file in his display.

An error message chimed in his soundscape, and he swore.

"What is it?" asked October.

"It didn't work," he said. "I'm not sure the footage can be viewed on my earset. Give me a second." He tried three more times but the error remained. "I'm going to need some help from my IT guy."

He dialled Randall and an avatar popped up on a shared display. "Mr Tully! It's so good to see you. I mean, I know it's only been a day since you called but … wait one sec. I'm going to launch the drone so you can see me live—"

"Randall," Tully said, "the avatar is fine. This is Commander October, New Carthage's chief security officer. We need some help."

"Hey, it's a total pleasure to meet you. Do I call you Chief or—"

"Commander's fine," October said and side-eyed Tully.

"Randall," Tully said, "I have some security footage from Martha Chandra's apartment. It seems she built a proprietary system. We've got the access code but it doesn't work on my earset."

"Oh, man, it's my lucky day. I love that kind of shit. Okay, can you send me the file? I'll have a look at the binary and see if I can figure out what the file type is, or at least what kind of platform it's built for. That's normally a good way of—"

"I'm uploading it now," Tully said.

"Got it. Panopticon. Wow, okay, it's a pretty big file. Not video. This looks like an executable… you know, a programme in its own right. So then the real question is what platform can run it. I've got a few things—"

"I'm putting you on mute for a few minutes to discuss something with the commander. Ping me when you have something."

Randall's avatar continued chattering, although his eyes were focused on a distant screen and his fingers were typing so fast the visualisation couldn't keep up.

"Is he taking something?" October asked.

Tully sighed. "No, he's always like that. But he's very good at what he does."

"What did you want to discuss?"

"How important it is to have a few moments of peace in the middle of any conversation with Randall."

She laughed. It was the first time he'd seen her do so and it changed her face completely. Amusement sparkled in the usually intense eyes, her nose crinkled, her smiling mouth had a charming asymmetry to it. It quickly passed, but an echo remained. She seemed more relaxed.

"Panopticon," she murmured. "The prison concept?"

"Yeah. A pretty old architectural idea."

"Martha always did like her references."

Randall messaged him a thumbs-up and Tully unmuted the call.

"What have you got?"

"Well, so, okay, Mr Tully, I have something, but you've got to understand that this is pretty unusual. I mean, I'm not trying to be funny, but it's pretty techie—"

"Can you get us access?" October said.

"Sure, I mean, I can, but this is like a real experimental prototype that runs on Mindscape, which you can't do without turning on the developer mode. There's no licence key from Mindscape, which means you have to be a bit careful. You can't just go messing around with random programs that run in your head. Mindscape are really funny about this kind of thing, and—"

"It's in NR?" Tully said. "The security footage?"

"I don't know what you'll be able to see or do unless I try it myself, which I'm totally willing to do, Mr Tully. I mean, I don't think you should risk it before I—"

"Do you mean you can get it running for us, right here, right now?"

Randall's avatar nodded.

"Then get it running on my headset," Tully said.

27

Tully swallowed the neurograin pills, pulled on his NR headset and took a deep breath. There was a sense of vulnerability that came with entering neuro-reality in front of someone else. He could trust October, sure. But most people liked to be alone when putting on the headset.

Zainab's digital statue stood in his egospace, gazing ahead at the vista.

He walked over and rested his forehead against hers for a moment. "I've not forgotten. I'm working on it." He stepped back and brought up the command centre, as Randall had instructed. A three-dimensional icon of a watchtower with the word *PANOPTICON* engraved on the base popped up in front of him. He selected it and his field of view panned in towards a door of black burnished steel embossed with a series of interconnected bronze cogs. Dead centre was a keyhole. The credentials he'd imported from the digital vault appeared in his hand, shaped like a giant key. He thrust it into the lock and turned it.

The key vanished, the cogs whirred and the door opened. He walked inside, exiting his egospace. A wave of nausea rolled over him and he staggered. Neural sickness wasn't unusual in the cheaper apps; it was a consequence of mixed mobility messages between the brain and the inner ear, and it passed. Almost pure darkness enveloped him, except for a series of windows displayed as days. Whatever Martha had been designing was raw and unfinished.

The windows included today.

Not good. How could he give October access now? She might replay the footage of Livia coming home. He put his palm against the window. The space around him contracted and he cried out as he was sucked through into the living room of the apartment. He inhaled, let out his breath, trying to clear away the queasiness, and looked down at himself. An antique pocket watch hung from a fob attached to a belt loop. He examined it. Naturally, it looked expensive; Martha had designed this, after all. Unlike a normal analogue clock, there were twenty-four segments around the perimeter and sixty on an inner dial. One large gold hand pointed to the six on the outer dial and the much smaller one to zero on the inner. So six o'clock, then.

There were two crowns, one on the side and one on the bottom. He tried the side one first. It controlled the hour hand, and as he moved it forward the light in the room adjusted. He reached nineteen and stopped.

"There's a room built for screening."

Tully jumped. *Easy now*. He took a breath. The voice was his.

October and his past self walked right through him and he tried to follow, but his feet seemed rooted to the floor.

"Right," he muttered, and looked around.

He raised a hand, intending to scratch the itchy stubble on his cheeks, and a circular marker appeared about ten feet away. *Okay . . .* He pointed at a distant spot. Another marker appeared. But how did he get there?

"Move."

Nothing happened.

He put his thumb up. No change. He blinked with both eyes. That just made him dizzy. Then he nodded, and there was a whoosh as he was yanked to the new spot.

It was very, very raw.

He held his breath, pointed and nodded again and navigated to the suite where he and October were perched on the sofa, looking at a screen.

"Oh, man, it's my lucky day. I love that kind of shit."

Randall.

Tully twisted the minute dial until he saw himself on the sofa with his NR headset on. October sat next to him, cross-legged, watching him. She looked more relaxed, like the sternness had been flushed away. He liked what had been left behind. The pleasure was followed by a shiver. Watching someone who couldn't see him felt wrong, voyeuristic. He brought up the exit command, stepped out of the program and removed his headset.

He blinked, trying to orient himself from the out-of-body experience from a moment earlier.

"So?" October sat upright now and her guardedness had returned.

"It works, but it's unfinished. You feel pretty queasy, there are no smooth transitions and you can't just walk around in the footage. You have to teleport."

"Okay. Let's do it."

"I'm not sure how to do it together."

"Well, give me access and I'll go in myself."

"No," he said too quickly, making her frown. "I mean, it's not intuitive. It will be easier if I guide you." He thought for a moment. "Maybe we could access it together. From my egospace." The notion made his stomach lurch. It was the kind of intimacy you'd reserve only for someone you'd let read your diary. All software that ran on Mindscape allowed people to meet up without exposing their egospace, though connecting that way was possible. Tully had never tried it. Zainab had died just as the technology hit the mainstream. And even Bolivar, who he trusted with his life, hadn't shared his egospace. Could he really make himself that vulnerable to someone he'd met only days prior?

October looked sympathetic but said nothing. He could ask to use her egospace instead, but that seemed rude, like suggesting having a nap in her bed. Maybe he should let her go in herself. After all, what were the chances of her doing what he'd done and jumping to today?

He couldn't risk it. Livia deserved better. "Okay," he said. "Let's do it."

She nodded. "I am transferring you my authentication ID. I will go into my egospace. Wait for you to invite me in. Okay?" She pulled her headset—a thin gold-pink band, the latest model—from a bag, slipped it on, then took a slim neurograin dispenser from her pocket.

He didn't need more neurograins, just pressed at a button on the headset to bring him back in. Seconds later, he was back beneath the sea. He walked over to Zainab. "I'm so sorry to bring someone into our space. I have to, you understand? For the sake of a friend." He touched her hand and walked to the middle of the egospace.

October's authentication ID was waiting for him in the control console. He breathed in and pressed the green invite button. The commander shimmered into view in front of him.

She looked around, then out of the windows. "Incredible," she said. "I've never seen anything like it."

He nodded. She was right. To commission such an egospace was akin to buying a piece of art only you would ever see. He'd spent more money on it than he could afford.

She turned and her breath caught as she looked at Zainab. She looked at Tully. "Your wife. She was beautiful."

He closed his eyes for a moment. "She died in the tabkhir. This is from a photo. Her name was Zainab."

October's gaze flickered down to Zainab's swollen belly, and her mouth tightened. "Zainab, Tully, I'm so sorry. Thank you for allowing me into your space."

28

Tully blinked as the windows into time glowed in the dim virtual space. October pointed. "That one. Four days ago. The night of the party."

"It will feel like we're being sucked through," Tully said. "Just so you know."

She nodded and together they placed one palm each on the window. As before, the space contracted and a second later they staggered into Martha's apartment chamber.

October bent over, hands on knees, breathing fast.

"You okay?" he asked.

"That was much worse than I was expecting," she said, straightening and shaking out her hair. "Still. That's the most impressive security system I've seen. Like we travelled in time."

"You haven't seen anything yet." He held up the pocket watch.

"What's that?"

"It allows us to move to any time in the day."

"We can go to the beginning of the party?"

Tully turned the large dial to nineteen. A blur of people moved through the space, and he continued to wind the crown until the scene resolved into Danberg and Martha, and Tully exiting his bedroom. He sighed at the sight of Martha. He wished he could warn her in some way, tell her what was about to happen.

"Unbelievable," October said. "It's like we're really here."

"Where should we look?"

October bit her lip. "For now, I'm most interested in the end. Can you forward to the bit when everyone is leaving?"

That had been around midnight. He wound the crown and found the precise moment.

Danberg came into focus and escorted Flora, Pedersen and Ying Yue out.

"And I'm a-seeing myself to my bed," Livia said, and weaved her way towards her room.

"You point and nod to teleport," Tully said.

They did so, and watched the earlier Tully stumble over to one sofa and Martha collapse onto the other.

"Big day," the seated Tully slurred.

Within seconds both were fast asleep.

"Come on then, Danberg," October said.

Danberg returned, looked surprised by the sofa-bound duo, walked off then appeared again with two blankets. He threw one over Tully but gently tucked Martha in hers. For a moment he stood there staring at her, then brushed back the hair from her face, walked to the front door and let himself out.

October muttered something under her breath.

"Perhaps something happened after," Tully said. "Let me go forward." He wound the minute hand forward.

The lights dimmed and, incredibly, Tully found he could see in the dark, as if he was wearing night-vision goggles. Now and then, his earlier self changed positions on the sofa, but Martha didn't move a muscle. The sun came up. He woke, collapsed to the floor, vomited and crawled over to Martha. Finally, he cried out her name, then passed out. Tully stared at his own body lying on the floor.

October rubbed a finger over her lip. "I got the tox results. Turns out that Martha had pentobarbital in her blood."

"The lethal-injection stuff?"

"Once used for euthanasia, too."

"No way was this suicide," Tully said.

"I don't think so either. But the thing is, it was known to be effective with euthanasia because it worked fast."

Tully nodded. "I read some stuff about it a while back." He thought back. "People used to take it in a cocktail. Made it work faster, usually a few minutes."

"Right. Our hypothesis was you'd consumed something. When you sat on the sofa. Before Danberg got back."

"But we didn't. The last time we both drank was when we all toasted Solomon."

"Can you skip back to that?"

"You think it was someone at the party?"

She shrugged. "If she was poisoned shortly before she died, she must have been given it by someone there. Or she took something herself that had already been poisoned."

Tully wound back.

"I just want to say congratulations again, Martha." Flora smiled at her. "It's historic. Cheers."

"Oh, the toast!" Martha said. She went to the bar, took a tray and returned immediately, then asked Solomon to join them while Flora poured the shots. Martha smiled at him. "Solomon, we want to offer you a toast."

"Wait," October said. "Can you go back a few seconds? I want to watch Jacobs." She teleported close to the model as she poured the shot glasses out and put them on the tray.

"Solomon, we want to offer you a toast."

"That's very kind of you, Martha."

Flora handed round the shot glasses.

"To Solomon," Martha said. "I'm proud of you, and I wish you every success. Win or lose, you're changing the world. Go save our species. *Salut.*"

They clinked and drank, then put their glasses back on the tray.

October stood there, hands on hips, staring at the tray.

"Did you catch anything?" asked Tully.

"No. She poured clockwise and seemed to hand them out without a particular focus on any one glass. There was no sign of her adding anything and no glass distinguished itself from any other. Of course, we'll need to study that in more depth."

"It doesn't make any sense," Tully said. "It can't be the vodka. Everyone drank it."

October nodded. "It's going to be hard to tell. That was a small special-edition bottle. Looks like Jacobs finished it off by the time she finished pouring. I believe the cleaning bots disposed of it. We'll do a search for it. But I'm not hopeful." She looked around one more time. "Let's get out of this."

She vanished, and he exited too and removed his headset.

October shook out her hair and looked across at him. "I'm going to head back. Get the team to study this footage in more detail. Can you give me the auth for the system?"

Tully hesitated. "I think we'd feel a bit uncomfortable given any one of your team could watch us, any time. Remember, we're living here."

She scrutinised him for a moment, then said, "Okay. I can appreciate that. I wouldn't like it either."

"So what do we do?"

"We trust each other," she told him. "I'll give you my word that neither I nor my officers will look at any footage outside the day of the drinks party, the prior day and the next day without your say-so. We have to be able to go through this in detail, but I'm not interested in watching you eat your breakfast cereal."

He was reluctant but, after all, he'd already shared his most vulnerable space with her, so he held out his hand and they shook. "Deal."

"I also need a favour," she said. "Though you might not be feeling up to it. I know this isn't your thing. Not your story, either. But you have a reputation as a top-class journalist. I need to use every asset at my disposal to figure this out." She paused. "I need help."

He hadn't seen that one coming, and thought for a moment. "I've been working on the assumption that Martha's death was related to my story or the election. A political assassination, perhaps. But if it was just a homicide perpetrated by a guest, a crime of passion maybe, I need to think about how I focus my time. The story I came here for could have an impact on the election. I have only weeks to crack it."

She nodded. "I understand. But consider this. First, we still don't know the motive behind all this. It could very well be political. Second, this island is still locked down. You can't leave without my say-so." She grinned.

"If we're partners, there's something else we need to do."

"What's that?"

He took a deep breath. "Remember the first time we met? I asked you to take a blood sample?"

She looked wary. "I do."

"Did you?"

She raised an eyebrow. "I'd had it done before you even asked."

Tully shuffled back into the couch, relieved. "A biochemist in Porto Alegre was going to look at my sample. Fernando, super-smart guy. In case your local teams missed anything." He took a deep breath and composed himself so he could say the words without his voice cracking. "Bolivar was hand-delivering it to him."

"You think this guy might find something we could not?"

"I did a story once. Cover-up of a drug overdose. It wasn't that the toxicology department was negligent; they just didn't look deep enough. Ticked the box enough to move to the next cadaver, you know? I got a sample to Fernando and he was able to tell us the brand of beer the guy had the night he died and how much he'd liked it."

"Really?"

"No, but it wasn't far off that."

"We still have vials of Martha's blood, too," October said. "I can arrange a military escort to drop both off to this Fernando."

"You'd do that for me?"

She shrugged. "Partners. Right?"

29

Livia opened her eyes and evaluated the facts. First, the pain in her cheek told her she was lying face down. Second, this was no bed. A carpet. Something of a mystery, since Martha didn't own a carpet; she'd been the wooden floors and rugs type.

The forest of deep-green pile ended at a wooden wall. She sniffed. It smelled like, well, carpet.

Satisfied that she had now accomplished enough carpet exploration for a lifetime, she pushed herself upright. She made it to her knees, and the nausea hit. She sucked in air tinged with a delicious spiciness. Aftershave. Her gaze flicked to the vast desk with its green leather inlay and the huge chair and towering hatstand. Who else would have a hatstand in their study but her father?

She was in her egospace, then. She had no memory of putting on the Mindscape and coming here. She'd never fallen asleep in NR before, was surprised it was even possible. Maybe that she'd been so unbelievably stoned could have helped. She had a vague recollection of the trip getting bad, super bad, and thinking that her egospace would be the perfect remedy.

Livia pulled herself up into the chair and looked across at the small photo of Martha and herself. Painful territory. Her eyes were glued to her sister's face. So delicate, so much of her mother there. Six-year-old Martha had no idea what was in store for her. No idea she'd change the world. No idea she'd die in her prime. Grief had already brought so many tears. But the photo unleashed something new. Rage. How fucking dare they take her sister, rob her of her only remaining family? The most successful female engineer in history, cut down before she could see the results of her attempt to save the world.

Bastards!

She tilted her head back and screamed her fury into the digital room until she was spent. The space seemed deathly quiet afterwards, and she exited, finding herself slumped on her bed. The anger had gone, leaving in its wake only emptiness. She should get up, take a shower, get a coffee. But she didn't want any of that. She just wanted to sit in this bed and do nothing, forever. A craving gnawed at her, manifesting a physical ache in her chest. It was one she knew well, and she wasn't sure if she could resist sating it.

Smack. Heroin. The white goddess. She'd been down that path of worship before, had sacrificed a year of her life to the deity. The goddess had shielded her from the grief of losing her father, but she was demanding. Once she had your worship, she didn't ever want your devotion to stop. Heretics were punished. Those who repented were welcomed back.

It would be so easy. One more prayer, one more journey into bliss and euphoria, away from all the horror, from the people, from the loss of Martha. Weed would stem the craving, a bit. It was why she'd sourced some from Guy the other day.

Getting more would require moving, however.

Tully knocked on her door, and when she didn't answer, he opened, and she closed her eyes.

She didn't want company right now. He'd have to read the signs. Unless he was going to bring her a coffee and then remain silent. He wouldn't, of course. This was Tully. He never brought coffee and was certainly never silent.

"Livia?"

She sighed and waited for him to move away. He didn't.

"Listen, something's happened. I wanted to tell you yesterday, but …"

She opened her eyes. The journalist extraordinaire, the handsome but sombre writer who brought down the corrupt and had a legion of fans around the world, looked unusually vulnerable.

He pulled over a nearby chair and sank into it. "I don't want you to worry, because we don't know anything for sure yet, but Bolivar is missing."

The shock coursed through her. "What?"

"He took off by multicopter after dropping off Haymaker. It didn't arrive. October deployed a military search, but there's no news yet."

She stared at him. "Where?"

"He was flying to Porto Alegre, so somewhere in the South Atlantic."

All flight paths were public info. Livia grabbed her earset and pulled up the radar tracking for the previous day's flights from New Carthage. There was only one. It stopped, horribly and abruptly, halfway between New Carthage and the coast of Brazil. Bolivar was dead. There was no way he could have survived that. Pain gripped her chest. She'd fucking liked that man. He'd been one of the good ones.

Tully looked exhausted, like he hadn't slept, but there was something missing. "You don't think he's dead, do you?" she asked.

He shook his head. "No. I refuse to believe it. There's always a chance."

She pulled up the previous day's weather report for the region. It'd been bad. "Tully, he went down in the middle of one of the most dangerous seas and in bad weather. It's been twenty-four hours and they haven't found him. Bolivar's gone."

He looked away. "No, I can't …" His voice cracked.

It was like the first time a kid realises their parents aren't superheroes, aren't invulnerable, aren't immortal, that they could hurt like anyone else. Tully had always seemed invincible. Now he was breathing hard and looking away. She felt awkward and considered hugging him. But that might make it worse. Men like Tully probably needed to feel they were staying strong in front of the troops. Except she wasn't one of the troops anymore, was she? And only a couple of days ago he'd comforted her when he'd got back from the hospital.

She reached out and took his hand. Well, the one that wasn't wiping his eyes. He smiled sadly and squeezed it.

"I know," he said. "I just don't want to believe it."

She got it, felt the pain of Bolivar's loss too, but another thought was already pushing it into the shadows. To lose one person you were close to was heartbreaking. To lose two, in separate incidents, within the space of half a week, was a pattern. Two knots didn't make a tapestry, sure, but she knew about patterns. She'd built the fucking bot of all bots to spot patterns. Something was going on here. Which meant there was work to be done. And if she was good at one thing, it was working.

Something else, too. The craving in her chest had gone.

30

Tully breathed in deep, grateful for the space Livia was giving him. It hurt, it really bloody hurt, and he wanted to sob and drink and get away from everything. But giving in to his grief would paralyse him, just like back in the dark days after Zainab's death. He'd cry for Bolivar later, alone. Right now he needed to stay busy.

And some things never changed. He had a story to solve.

"Thank you for giving me access to Martha's digital vault yesterday."

She stared out the window, one finger rubbing her lip.

"Livia?"

She turned and looked at him with an air of surprise. "Yeah?"

"I want to ask you for access again. To Martha's vault. There was a classified section in there, and I'm wondering if it contains anything related to your sister's time in the White House. Something that might give me a new lead on the tabkhir story."

She looked back out the window. His timing stank, he knew. He'd just broken some horrible news to Livia. And Martha's funeral was tomorrow. He'd been tactless, as usual, but the story was getting away from him. "Have you kept your promise?" Her words were quiet, fierce even.

He frowned. "To find out who killed her? It's only been three days, Livia, I—"

"As soon as you get a lead, you'll be off chasing that story. Your focus is always so narrow, like a dog sniffing down prey."

"That's not true. I can and will focus on both."

"And what if your tabkhir lead takes you out of New Carthage?" she spat.

"I—"

"No. Solve the murder and I'll give you access. That's my promise back to you."

Frustration burned in his throat like bile and he did his best to swallow it. Besides, he'd already agreed to help October. Still, there was no denying it, he was pissed off. It seemed everyone wanted him on this investigation. Not trusting himself to say something he regretted, he got up and walked away. Not that she seemed to notice.

⌢

TULLY'S MIND FELT somehow disconnected from his body, like there was a loose wire somewhere, likely a consequence of the stimulant pill he'd taken that morning in an attempt to clear the fog of the sleeping neurotropic, espresso no longer effective. An hour ago, October had broken the news. Debris had been discovered hundreds of miles from where they'd lost contact with Bolivar's multicopter. Though there'd been no confirmation it was from the flight in question, what hope Tully had harboured slipped away into the cold depths.

The brightness of the day cast a strange light on his mood, a tense irritability that forced his sadness into a waiting room. His memories of funerals usually included rain, but today sunshine blazed in the South Atlantic, though New Carthage's climate-control system took the edge off. Livia looked numb, a shadow of her previous self, and Haymaker supported her as she stumbled towards the building at the centre of a cobbled square. Towering above them, on the north face of the square, was the giant statue of Hannibal with sword pointing to the heavens.

As with everything in New Carthage, the funeral venue was over the top. The huge columns supported a large dome with a magnificent oculus that reminded Tully of the Pantheon. The midday sun streamed through the aperture, spotlighting an altar in the dead centre. The sight was stunning, and he yearned to share it with Bolivar. The structure was modern, of course, but it felt ancient. The world hadn't seen contemporary buildings like this for an age. London, as with many cities, preferred glass and concrete blips on its landscape, structures not built to last. This, however, had been designed to stand for millennia. Jasper Keeling was nothing if not ambitious for these floating city states.

Many of Martha's friends had gathered, though the numbers seemed insignificant given her impact on the world. Tully recognised only some of them. Keeling himself was talking to Pedersen, his head bowed, voice unusually low given what Tully had heard about the man. Guy Molyneux comforted Livia. Jiang Ying Yue stood alone, her face a mask. October looked sad but thoughtful. Flora Jacobs approached Tully and, to his surprise, enveloped him in a hug. And by the altar was Solomon, a mere projection in their displays but appearing as real as anyone else. He had apparently designed the service himself, to honour his creator.

The mourners took their seats in a semicircle of chairs around the altar and waited. A choir began to sing, startling Tully; he hadn't noticed them on the far side of the altar. Their voices swelled, forming a seemingly impossible harmony that echoed around the chamber and up into the dome. The words seemed alien and ancient, like a language that had been lost and rediscovered. Tully had never heard anything like it. He wasn't the only one affected. Everyone looked overawed. As the music reached a crescendo, four pallbearers entered bearing the casket. The choir's pitch descended to a solemn bass, then evaporated as the procession reached the altar-like table.

Solomon stepped forward, placing himself between the mourners and the casket. It was an unusual arrangement, one that reminded Tully of a politician addressing the citizens in a town hall. "We are gathered here today," the artilect said, "to celebrate the life of Dr Martha C. Chandra, sister, friend and creator."

Tully closed his eyes. The last funeral he'd attended was Zainab's service, though unlike today there'd been no body to honour. He pushed the memory away and focused on Danberg, Pedersen, Jiang and Flora. Could one of them really be the murderer? October had put in a formal request to Martha's company for her calendar, hoping it would help them understand her movements before the party, since Danberg was in too much of a state to be of any help.

"… with her dear sister, Livia, and her beloved parents. Her mother was taken from her young, so young she could not, in later years, picture her face. Her father sadly passed away seven years ago now …"

Danberg had the look of a man who'd cried out every tear within him, an empty, anguished soul, disbelief etched in his face. The man's eyes flickered towards Pedersen, and Tully saw bewilderment and accusation. Pedersen seemed oblivious.

"… a woman who sought to change the world …"

Not sought to, thought Tully. She *had* changed the world and left an indelible mark on the history of the planet like few others, regardless of whether Solomon won or lost.

He studied the artilect. Solomon's very real presence, his capability and, well, *humanity* made his software roots seem impossible. Would electing this being enable humanity to make the tough decisions required to save the planet, or were the artilect's champions just blind to the mounting danger?

"At the end of a life, we often recount the legacies and achievements of great individuals like Martha," Solomon said. "While these were many, they matter only to strangers, and they are not why so many are gathered here today. She was, to us, above all else, a friend."

Tully looked at Martha's casket. They were lucky to be able to be here to say goodbye. In contrast, like Zainab, Bolivar would be forever unburied. Why had Flight NC404 crashed? There'd been no mayday, no indication of a technical malfunction. Bolivar had been carrying a small vial of Tully's blood. Uneasiness prickled his skin and he hunched ever so slightly, feeling an invisible set of crosshairs aiming at his back. Had it been an accident, and so soon after Martha's death? The coincidence seemed remarkable.

A hand touched him and he jolted.

"It's okay," Flora said. "It's okay to be sad. Let it out if you need to."

He heard his own breath now. It sounded ragged, like he'd just run up a hill. He exhaled slowly, counted silently, told himself to relax. No one was trying to kill him.

"And we commit Martha C. Chandra to the sea. From where the distant ancestors of humanity on the tree of life emerged, so she shall return to their embrace."

The choir began to sing again as the altar receded into the floor, taking Martha's casket with it, to be weighted down and released to the sea through an airlock. Livia sobbed.

Martha had gone.

Beneath them, Martha's casket would be weighted down and released through an airlock into the depths of New Carthage. Martha had gone.

And so had Solomon.

31

A hundred or so people, a lot more than had been invited to the service, helped themselves to lavish finger food from the buffet at tables that had been pushed to the edge of the room, or stood around with drinks in hand. Soft music played beneath the babble. The Phoenician hotel's conference suite was elegant, sure, but as soulless as any other big hotel space repurposed for an event.

Danberg sat on his own, drinking. He was already surrounded by empty glasses.

"He don't look right to me," Haymaker said.

Flora nodded. "He's not just sad. He's… I don't know…"

"Wretched," October said. She was dressed in a black trouser suit today, a sober outfit compared with Flora's dress, also black, though the intricate lacework exposed as much as it covered.

Subdued laughter erupted from a group in one corner. Pedersen was holding court, sardonic smile firmly in place. Jasper Keeling gesticulated and leaned in close to Pedersen.

Danberg shot them a look as sharp as a blade.

"So, how is the investigation going?" Flora asked October. "Have you any suspects yet?"

October stiffened. "I'm sorry. I can't reveal any details."

Flora chuckled. "Oh, come on, October. It's me."

October looked at her and her mouth tightened. "Do you really think it is appropriate that I discuss a homicide investigation? Out in the open? At the victim's funeral?" There was an acid bite to her clipped words. "I am here because I was a friend to Martha. Not in any official capacity. I am certainly not going to talk shop. Not with you. Not with anyone."

"Does anyone know the latest polls?" Tully said, trying to shift the direction of the conversation.

Flora glared at October for a moment, then smiled at Tully and put her hand on his arm. "I think you need Livia to answer that question."

He shook his head. "She hasn't taken much interest since …" There was no need to say more.

An uncomfortable silence fell. Tully focused on Danberg again. The man seemed to be talking to himself, or perhaps to his beer. He shook his head and frowned.

"Leadership," Keeling blared, "is crucial at times like this, Johan. Who are you going to appoint in her place?"

Danberg looked towards the group again and staggered to his feet.

Tully hoped he'd decided to leave.

Pedersen was nodding. "I've got a few good candidates. Of course, Jasper, your guidance would be appreciated. It's important we find a CEO who you can work with too."

Danberg yelled and launched himself towards Pedersen.

Pedersen's expression shifted from surprise to terror. He gasped and fell backwards, hands grabbing at his stomach. A poppy-red stain blossomed on his shirt. A hilt flowered from the centre of it.

Someone screamed. There was a blur. Haymaker smashed Danberg to the floor. American-football-style tackle. He held him down, like a wrestler waiting for the referee's count. Beneath him, Danberg cursed and wriggled.

"Hold him tight," October shouted. She examined Pedersen. He was pallid. Gasping for breath. Fist trying to grab the knife. She slapped them away. "You pull it out right now? You die," she told him. "Focus on breathing."

Tully knelt by October. The knife was no hitman's dagger. More like a steak knife, black and silver-handled. Tully looked over at a nearby buffet table. Several knives were laid out by the food. Premium, with smooth blades, all embossed with a tiny bull symbol.

"Paramedics on the way," October said.

Pedersen panted. "F—fuck," he managed to say.

Guy pushed through to his husband, then looked at Danberg. "*Connard!*" he screamed, and dived towards Danberg.

Haymaker pushed him away easily, and Tully stood and took Guy's arm.

"Guy," he said, "listen to me, focus on Johan. Be with him, okay? Leave Damien to us."

Guy's eyes were still wild, but he nodded and crawled over to his husband. "*Mon coeur, c'est pas possible.*"

Pedersen grimaced and closed his eyes, still rasping for breath. "Ah, better. Like this. Than the other way."

"*Non*, you can't think like that. *Arrête.*"

Flora, ashen-faced but calm, placed some cushions under Pedersen's head, then pulled Tully away.

"You okay?" Tully said.

"Not really," Flora said, shuddering, looking back. "Do you think he'll be okay?"

"It's the stomach, so it's complicated. I'd say he'll survive if he's attended to quickly. Although he doesn't seem to think so."

"What makes you say that?"

"Just before you ran up, he said something like, 'Better I die like this than the other way.'"

"Probably true."

"So, you know what's wrong with him?"

Flora grimaced. "I never was good at keeping my mouth shut."

"He had some kind of attack when I visited his house," Tully said.

Flora nodded. "Same thing with me. Just the once. He was absolutely mortified and had to have a few drinks to recover. It seemed to loosen him up."

"Did he tell you what it was?"

"One of those diseases that sounds like an English butler. Not Parkinson's. Huntington's, perhaps. I don't remember, but he said it was bad, terminal, though he had a few good years left. But he was worried it would get worse." Pedersen shouted in pain, and Flora paled and swallowed. "It comes and goes at the moment," she continued, "but the idea there'd come a point when he'd struggle to walk or even swallow food disgusted him. He was worried about how people will remember him. That his last years might be so bad that Guy and his friends, colleagues, family and everyone only remember him afterwards as a sick old man who needed constant care." She leaned in and said into Tully's ear, "He was adamant. His exact words were, 'I won't have it. I'll take the kinder way out before then.'"

"Suicide?"

"He calls it euthanasia. It's not legal here. But he's managed to get some pills from Mexico or somewhere." She shuddered.

A team of paramedics burst through the door, two with a stretcher, one carrying a bag.

October went over to Danberg and Haymaker. She looked at Haymaker. "I don't have cuffs. Can you hold him until I get a team here?"

"I got it, ma'am," Haymaker told her. "He ain't gonna get nowhere."

She knelt by Danberg. "Why?"

"He killed her. And no one was going to do anything. No one believed me."

"You fucking fool," she hissed at him, and stood, smoothing down her wrinkled suit.

"Aye," Haymaker said. "Ain't no fool like a fool in love."

32

An overweight, scruffy detective, the kind of guy who looked like his grey hair hadn't changed style in forty years, escorted Danberg away. He was followed by several other members of the squad Tully didn't recognise.

"Hake, tell Sergeant McKnight to keep him on ice for me," October said.

"You got it, boss," Detective Hake said, keeping a firm grip on Danberg.

Tully stepped up besides October. "Got a moment?" he murmured. She nodded and they moved to the other side of the room, where it was quieter. "Is it possible Danberg might be right about Pedersen?"

"What makes you say that?" October said.

"It might be nothing, but Flora says Pedersen has some chronic, terminal illness, and some pills in case it gets … bad."

"What kind of pills?"

"Wouldn't that be nice to know?"

"Pedersen." October brushed her hair back and tied it up. "Makes no sense. Why would he sabotage his own investment by killing Martha? Especially right on the verge of the election."

"Killing Martha has sabotaged nothing. Solomon seems capable of managing itself. And Pedersen would have known that. So perhaps this was about removing some control. If Solomon won, Martha would have been the biggest adviser. Now, although Livia has inherited the shares, Pedersen is the most influential vote on that board."

"Danberg implied something similar, yesterday," she said. "He wasn't being particularly rational, just said that Pedersen was trying to install a new CEO. One who'd be more commercial."

"He said something similar to me," Tully said.

October raised her eyebrows.

"Before you and I were working together," he added, quickly.

"We should look into it. But maybe everything is not as it seems."

"What do you mean?" he said.

"It is possible that Danberg is simply a grieving man. One who believes Pedersen murdered the woman he loved. But we have to stay open to the possibility that we are being played here."

"By whom?" Tully said.

She looked around. "Walk with me."

They strolled away into the hotel gardens, filled with delicate, fragrant flowers. October breathed in the scents and collected her thoughts. "Danberg used a short-bladed knife. The site of the entry wound is not life-threatening. Pedersen is likely to survive. I just wonder if Danberg is trying to throw us off the scent. Perhaps get off on a diminished-responsibility charge."

"Does he have a motive beyond unrequited love?" Tully said.

October stopped, checked her display and shared a document with Tully.

"What's this?" he asked.

"Martha's journal from the day she died. Her official work journal. Danberg looked after it."

Tully scanned it.

"Look at the entry for one p.m.," she said.

"The Eve Clinic? What's that?"

"An all-in-one IVF and sperm-donor clinic."

Tully frowned. "I'd forgotten. Flora told me Martha was planning to have a baby. By herself."

October nodded. "Danberg becomes seriously infatuated with Martha. She has no interest in a relationship. Hell, she barely even wants friends. But she wants a child. Seeks the very best help. From a clinic famed for the quality of its donors. He finds out via her journal. Sends him over the top. He can't stand the idea of her having a child that won't be his."

"If she was having an affair, sure," Tully said. "But to kill her because she was having a child?"

"I'm not saying he's the most stable skittle in the bowling alley."

174

33

The next morning, the sun was still low in the sky. After only four hours sleep, the hum of the pod might have made her sleepy, but her mind was still churning over Danberg, and whether the stabbing of Pedersen had been revenge. Or fake-out. Today's mission was routine, at least.

"Remember the religious group that Pedersen mentioned, the Angels of Mercy?" Moran asked.

"The anti-Solomon cult?"

Moran nodded. "Here's the thing. I managed to track down the original threat, all 'stop your sinning or pay the price', blah blah blah. But then I dug deeper. Commander, this group doesn't exist."

"They're hidden?"

"I mean there's just nothing out there. Most of these groups have a social media presence, right? Even the hardcore terrorist groups do, or at least closed networks on some of the chat channels. Not these guys. I spoke to this English expert, some guy named Tayes with an over-the-top accent who specialises in this kind of group. He's never heard of them."

"Did someone fake it?" October said. "Pedersen, perhaps?"

"I think so. There's just enough there to be credible if you don't dig."

"Strange. Something else to add to the list."

They arrived at Pedersen's front door.

"Ready?" Moran said.

She nodded, and he banged on the door.

Moran held up an army-green handheld radar to the door. "He's coming."

The door opened. Guy Molyneux stood there in his dressing gown, unshaven.

As he saw them, his expression changed from irritation to concern. "What happened? *C'est Johan?*"

"I have no updates on Mr Pedersen's condition," October said. "We are here because we need to carry out a search."

"A search? Where?"

"Here. Can we maybe move this inside?" She gestured, but he tensed against the door.

"What in the humid hell is going on? You have a warrant?"

She offered him a sympathetic smile and narrow-cast the document to his earset.

He swore but let them in. Moran glared as he pushed past him. October followed, two more officers trailing in her wake.

"I'll stay with Mr Molyneux," she said.

The officers nodded, set two cases down on a table, and unlocked them. Molyneux pointed at them. "What are they?"

Eight mini-drones ascended and swarmed around the house.

"Sniffer drones," October said. "Equipped with sensors to detect a variety of drugs."

He sat down heavily, looking distraught.

"Anything you want to tell me? Now's the time," she said.

He shook his head but his hands trembled. Did Molyneux think Pedersen might have something he shouldn't?

"Is anyone else here? You have some staff, right?"

Molyneux shook his head. "Just one, and he's looking after Johan."

"Commander?" Hake called.

October nodded for Molyneux to lead the way. They entered a library, one end filled with French volumes. Hake handed a book to October and she opened it. A space had been carved from the pages and a small safe with a biometric thumbprint nestled within. Did Molyneux have access to Pedersen's safe? It would make sense. If Pedersen was at the end of his life and planning to euthanise himself, he might need support.

"Your thumb, please, Mr Molyneux."

"No," he whispered.

Moran grabbed him and shoved him forward. Hake took Molyneux's hand and October scanned his thumb. The safe popped open.

Molyneux moaned. "*Putain*."

Inside was a small bag filled with white powder.

"Got you," she said. Tully's suspicions had played out. It had been Pedersen all along, not Danberg. He must have slipped Martha the powder during the day, perhaps mixed into something. Behind her, Molyneux sank to the floor. He'd known.

Moran stepped forward and squinted at the packet. "May I?" October handed him the packet. He ran a gauze wipe over the exterior of the bag, then popped it into a portable terminal. It chimed almost immediately, and he looked at Molyneux, then at October. "Cocaine," he said. "Gold cocaine, which is unusual and very expensive. But cocaine all the same."

October bit her lip and looked at Molyneux. "Yours?" He met her eyes but said nothing. She grabbed the collar of his gown. "Now, listen to me. This is going to go very badly for you. Unless you tell me where your husband keeps the pentobarbital."

He gaped at her. "*Quoi*? The what?"

"The pentobarbital. For his condition. If he gets too bad and wants an easy way out."

Understanding dawned in his eyes. "How … how do you know about that?"

"Where is it?"

"*Chais pas*," he said.

She shook him. "In English."

"I don't fucking know!"

"Bullshit. There's no way he didn't bring you into this, just in case. Hey, Moran, what do you reckon Governor Solomon would set as a charge for possession?"

"Permanent exile, I'd imagine?" Moran said.

"Sounds about right. Reckon I should pull Pedersen out of hospital and make him show us where this shit is?"

"He'll probably die on the way," Moran said, and shrugged. "But what can you do?"

"The wardrobe floor," Molyneux muttered.

"Louder!" October snapped.

"The wardrobe floor!"

October jerked her head to get him moving. "Show me."

He led her through to a huge bedroom, a vast super-emperor bed in the middle, one side neat, the other messy. He opened a mirrored wardrobe. A series of small shelves housed shoes. He removed the bottom shelf and reached in. A latch clicked, and he pulled out a small floor safe. This time, he punched in a code. It opened. October took the small tub and examined it before handing it to Moran, who wiped it down with another gauze wipe and placed it in the terminal.

"Why?" Molyneux asked her. "How can this be important to you?"

She ignored him.

The terminal chimed and Moran nodded. "It's a barbiturate," he said. "That's all I can tell you. I need to get it to Jeffries."

October turned to Molyneux. "We are taking the cocaine. For the next six months, you will be invited down the precinct. Every four days. For a test. We detect a sniff of anything illicit, you will be living back in Paris before you can say '*au revoir*'."

34

"We found the pills in a hidden safe," October said. They were sitting in Martha's old study. She'd asked for an urgent catch up, and since they were now 'partners', he'd obliged. His head was thumping, mainly as a result of his call with Lottie and Randall an hour before, where he'd broken the news about Bolivar. As with his earlier conversation with Livia, saying the words broke him anew. Yet the conversation hadn't stopped there. New arrangements had to be made. Transitions of responsibilities. All while influencers were still leeching away from them, all while the noise of Kehoe and Cavanagh and Bamphwick was mounting, chipping away at his reputation. He'd been ignoring it, figuring that the story he was chasing, once he could get to it, would melt through any noise like boiling water on ice. But he was here, on an island, insulated, able to get away from it all and stay occupied. Lottie and Randall had no such luxury, and Lottie in particular was already at the finish line of her notoriously short temper.

"Tully?" she said, and he blinked.

"Sorry. In the hidden safe?"

"It was pentobarbital," she said. "Jeffries has checked and confirmed it. We'll charge Pedersen as soon as he comes round. He was in surgery all night and is still out for the count."

Tully nodded. "So, it's done."

"Yeah," she replied and smiled. "You'll be able to go home."

Home … to chaos. And only if Livia agreed that this was indeed solved, and if she kept her end of the bargain. His story was dead unless he could find something in Martha's vault. If he returned with nothing, he was truly done. Game over.

A notification panged in his display and he opened it. It was from Fernando, Bolivar's contact in Sao Paulo. *Need discuss urgently.* Another wave of grief crashed over him, turning his stomach inside out. It should have been Bolivar sending him messages. It should have been Bolivar dealing with the influencers and the noise. It should have been Bolivar telling him enough was enough, and it was time to go home.

"We got an unexpected bust at the same time," October said. "Turns out, Guy Molyneux had something of his own hidden. But it doesn't help us."

Tully messaged Fernando back. *Now?*

In response, Fernando dialled in. "I've got something," Tully told October. "Hold up." He put the call on a shared screen so October could listen too and activated an ionic-wave drone so Fernando could see them. The tiny airborne camera hovered silently over the screen.

"*Bom dia,*" Fernando said. "*Tudo bem?* All good, Mr Tully?"

"It's been better," Tully said. He'd never met Fernando and had expected a more stereotypical South American look. This man was bespectacled and Japanese.

"I so sorry for Mr Bolivar."

Tully gripped his own hand so tight it hurt. "Yeah. This is Commander October, by the way. What have you got?"

"Mr Tully, my English not so good. Mr Bolivar, he speak Spanish. My Spanish better. *Hablas español?*"

Tully shook his head. "I'm sorry."

"I try best. This blood sample show chemical residue of … how you say?" He searched for something.

"Pentobarbital?"

"*Ai ai ai, não!*" The little man looked excited. "Nearly that. But not that."

"It's not pentobarbital?" October said

Fernando grumbled and searched the desk again. "Ah, here is. Binary poison, catalyst and agent. Very difficult detecting." He looked triumphant.

"Binary poison? What does that even mean?"

"This all theory, you understand? I never seen this…this chemist? It is extreme complicate." Fernando held up one hand. "You have agent poison, already in system, probable top up, asleep until"—his other palm faced the first—"it meet catalyst, which wake it." He clapped. "Then bang."

Tully and October looked at each other. "Then this wasn't one poison, but two?" Tully said. "And they're only active when they meet?"

"Yes," Fernando nodded. "Catalyst meet agent, have nice date, make poison."

"So Martha had already been exposed to this inert agent, and then the catalyst triggered it," Tully said.

Fernando gave him a proud, excited grin, as if he was a small child who'd just taken his first step. "*Una mais.* This fast-acting. Whatever happen, happen quick after catalyst and agent combine."

"How quickly?" October leaned forward.

"Fifteen minute if taken no alcohol. With alcohol… less than five."

"Then it could have been the vodka," Tully said.

"We've watched that footage endlessly," October said. "It was the last thing she had, and it was a good thirty minutes after the champagne and two hours after she'd eaten. But, everyone had the vodka."

"But that's the point," Tully said. "It doesn't matter how many people had the catalyst as long as they didn't have the agent too."

Tully looked at Fernando. "Thanks for this. I'll arrange for your fees to be paid."

"*Obrigado,*" he said, but didn't leave.

"Is there something else?" Tully asked.

He looked at them, his expression serious. "I say again. Making binary poison hard. But this is even more hard."

"Why?"

"Because this like pentobarbital, but not. *Entendo?* Someone reverse engineer pentobarbital and cut it into two safe things. Means most labs think just pentobarbital. This … *guerra biológica.* Something more like country do, not criminal, not terrorist. But at same time, this nice way to die."

"Nice?" Tully said.

Fernando nodded. "Like sleep. Is reason why people use for … I don't know word in English. Self-kill because ill?"

"Euthanasia?"

"Yes! *Eutanásia!* Is same word! If choose to die, you choose well to die in sleep… this make sleep."

"Wait," October said, "would the agent need to have been in a drink too?"

"No, no." He ticked off the words on his fingers. "Drink or food, breathe, skin or eyes, injection or bite."

Tully thanked him again, and Fernando signed off.

They sat there and looked at each other in silence. October was running her hand over her smooth cheeks. He scratched at his stubble, and sighed. "I suppose that means it's not Pedersen's pentobarbital pills."

October rubbed her eyes. "This is a whole new level of complexity. It's gone from being a crime someone could commit at a party to nation-state sponsored biological war."

"We'll figure it out."

She snorted. "I know. Well, the crime was still committed at the party. Nothing changes. We start at the centre and spiral outwards."

"We suspect the vodka contained the catalyst," Tully said, "but what contained the agent? It was already in her system, maybe topped up, so perhaps it was something she ate or drank regularly."

October began to pace. A minute later she stopped and stared at him.

"What?" he said, alarmed.

"I'll draw it." She gestured in the air and a whiteboard hovered in his display several feet off the ground. She drew two vibrant overlapping circles and wrote *AGENT* above one circle and *CATALYST* above the other. She wrote 'vodka?' under catalyst and seven names in the circle: Martha Chandra, Marcus Tully, Livia Chandra, Johan Pedersen, Flora Jacobs, Damien Danberg and Jiang Ying Yue.

"A Venn diagram," Tully said.

She moved "Martha Chandra" into the centre, then paused and studied the board for a moment. A second name shifted into the middle. His.

⤔

MEDITATION HAD NEVER been Livia's forte. She knew how to do it, but making it part of her routine had proved impossible. It was likely only possible for her to do it up a mountain. After all, what else was there to do up a mountain?

Martha had been able to meditate. But then, Martha had been able to do most things. Probably even Tully could meditate, uptight though he could be.

She drew a deep breath for four counts, held it for four counts and then tried to exhale the anger that had flared. A barrage of thoughts invaded her consciousness after only seconds and she lost her rhythm. Someone had murdered her sister. Until she'd figured out who and ripped them apart, she could trust no one.

A noise beyond the bedroom door brought Haymaker to mind. Fine, she could probably trust him. He'd not been here when Martha had been killed. And Tully? Hard to say. He'd wanted to speak to Martha about the tabkhir story and it had been clear she knew something. What if she'd told him something he hadn't wanted to hear? Or refused to speak to him at all? What might he have done then? Tully was a good man, but a broken one, and if Martha had been involved in the death of his wife …

Of course, he'd been injured too. But what if that was misdirection? Something to throw them off the scent?

She would do it herself. She was all she had left. And for the first time, she had resources. Significant resources she could put to work. Martha's legacy had ensured that, and she would repay her with justice. Screw the meditation.

35

"These two parts work together," October said, pointing at the still hovering Venn diagram. "The agent is like a lock, the catalyst a key. Six of you had keys but only two of you had locks and got ill."

Tully paced and down. "There must be something we both consumed that the others didn't."

"You're the clue," October said. "Martha had been here for ages. So had everyone else."

"And I hadn't." Tully stopped walking. "I must have been exposed after arrival."

"So we need to focus on your movements in New Carthage." Now she paced up and down, following his path, while he watched her. "You were here for a day before the drinks party. Let's start with what you consumed when you were together."

Tully nodded. "We have the footage from the apartment."

"You gave me permission to access the day of the party," October said, "but we need the day before too."

He thought back to their arrival the evening before the dinner party, after Solomon's speech. Tully had pressed Martha to help with his story. There'd been nothing particularly bad there, but she'd still overhear it, and he didn't love sharing what he was working on with strangers. Even partners.

"Okay," he said.

She nodded. "But we also need to figure out how the vodka was poisoned."

"I'm on it," he told her.

⤶

LIVIA SAT AT the desk in her room and picked up one of her father's old smoke-tinged books. She rubbed a thumb against the soft pages, sighed and brought up Martha's digital vault. One file listed Martha's financial assets. She'd need help with that, and made a note to herself to speak to Martha's lawyer. She scanned through the rest of the content. A file labelled *Panopticon* had been accessed recently, presumably by Tully. Surely a security system, like the watchtower. Classic Martha. Was it for the apartment? She shivered and looked around and up. There, nestled in the corner of the ceiling, was a tiny black dot. She got up and inspected it. It was a lens, no bigger than the head of a pin. Halfway down, there was another one, and a third on the floor. She walked over to another corner and saw the same.

Martha had done this. What had she been afraid of, to put something so intrusive in place? Lockwood and his cronies? Not the kind of people you wanted to cross, and it seemed Martha kinda had. What kind of enemies had she made? Had Tully wondered the same thing?

Heat rose to her cheeks: she'd given Tully access to the vault. In theory, he could even have come virtually into her room. What had he seen? She was tempted to cover up the lenses, even rip them out. But perhaps there were some black spots, or a way of wiping footage. She needed to learn how it all worked. Maybe take it all apart and put it back together again.

She tapped the Panopticon file but got an error chime and a notification that the file type wouldn't run on her earset.

This was going to require coffee, and lots of it.

⌣

INSPIRATION HAD STRUCK a hole through a fog of melancholy tiredness, and Tully was desperate to know whether he was right. He stood in Panopticon, at the bar in Martha's apartment, on the evening of the dinner party. He twirled the pocket watch dial to set the timing for ten past seven, when all the guests had arrived.

The vodka and six shot glasses were already set up on a small tray that sat at the side of the bar, perhaps to discourage guests from helping themselves. Tully wasn't a vodka drinker, and was used to seeing it in plain litre-sized bottles. This one, however, was smaller, glass-frosted, like a potion. Likely expensive.

The question was, had anyone tampered with it at the party? He watched the replay on ten-times speed. There was plenty of back and forth to the small bar, and every time someone approached he slowed the footage down. No one touched the tray until Flora came to get it. Her hand didn't go near the bottle itself until she'd returned to them, when she grasped it to pour the shots. He rewound and watched her pour the shots again, slowing the footage down even further to see if anything had been slipped into a glass.

Nothing. Well, that was stage one of the process of elimination. He checked his notes for the arrival times of the guests.

Livia, 16:32.

Danberg, 17:55.

Pedersen, 19:04.

Jiang and Flora, 19:06.

He rewound the footage to 17:55 and checked the vodka trolley. No vodka.

This was stage two. Where had the bottle come from? Either Martha had taken it out or Danberg had put it out after arriving.

Still focused on the trolley, he fast-forwarded through the video to 19:00, the time he'd come out of his bedroom.

Nothing.

No vodka, but Martha was giving Danberg instructions. "You bought the Siberian?"

"Got it right here," Danberg said.

"Good, Flora will be pleased. We'll do a toast at the end of the night."

Danberg took a small crystalline bottle of Siberian out of a bag and put it on the trolley. Danberg watched Martha walk away. He watched her greet Tully. He watched her peck him on both cheeks. Danberg watched, and as he watched, there was only bitterness in his tight face.

October had been right. It had been Danberg all along.

⌇

OCTOBER TOUCHED THE watchtower icon tagged *PANOPTICON* and closed her eyes as it shrank her down to the steel door. She pulled out the key and thrust it into the ornate lock in the middle. As she turned it, all the cogs surrounding the lock moved too and a click echoed around her. Then she was through, with a wobble, into the menu room.

Two new windows appeared on the right. The nearest represented yesterday, the day of the funeral and wake. The furthest represented the current day. If she went through it, she could walk around the apartment in real time, unseen, a ghost in the machine. The temptation to do so was overwhelming. Yet why was she even interested in the minutiae of whatever was going on in there right now? Everyone was probably asleep. She pictured Tully lying on his bed and shook her head. She'd given her word, and the whole notion was ridiculous.

Instead, she chose the day before the drinks party, and swallowed as she was sucked into the visualisation. She steadied herself and looked down for the pocket watch. She skimmed through hour after hour, checking that no one had entered before Martha had come back that evening. No one had. It was past ten in the evening when the door opened and Martha entered the apartment, Tully and Livia following, their mouths agape. They moved through into the living room, and October selected a marker and followed.

Martha sent Tully off for drinks. Suspicious, October followed him and watched him at the bar, but there was no vodka bottle in evidence and he did nothing untoward except choose an artisan rum. He moved back into the living room, and she teleported back too as Martha caught sight of him and shushed Livia.

Curious, she rewound a couple of minutes, listened to Martha's hurried conversation with Livia, then replayed it a couple more times to make sure she had it straight. Tully left the bar, joined them on the sofas and launched straight into his request for help.

"A source told me that the tabkhir was meant to hit the US, not the Gulf. That Lockwood and his team did something. Something to … shift it. That they had some tech."

Shit. It seemed beyond belief. She listened closely to Martha's reply. It seemed carefully parsed, neither a confirmation nor a denial.

Martha Chandra had been on Lockwood's team. Did Tully believe she'd built some tech that had led to the tabkhir? She recalled him standing before his wife's statue, saying how Zainab had died. That was certainly motive. Perhaps the purest of motives. Should she break off working with him, maybe even investigate him? Or keep her options open and do both in parallel?

She went back to the conversation between Livia and Martha and listened once more.

36

Tully was in his bedroom study when the door chimed, making him jump and glance at the time. It was early for visitors. He heard Haymaker answer it. Livia appeared to have locked herself in her room. It was unlikely either of them had a visitor, which meant …

There was a knock at his door.

Which meant October. He stood up and opened it.

"Sorry for coming so early," October said. "But I saw something last night and it's been bothering me. I wanted to show you as soon as I could."

"Of course," Tully said. "Let's go to the kitchen."

"You'll need your Mindscape."

"Okay, let's make that Martha's study." He nodded towards the room, led her through and shut the door behind them. He gestured for her to take the chair behind Martha's desk while he took another in the corner. They both looked at each other and waited, and eventually he sighed. "I'll invite you to my egospace again?"

She nodded and they donned their headsets. Tully glanced at Zainab, then invited October in. Her eyes flicked to Zainab too, but he had already pulled up the watchtower and they entered the navigation room.

"What day?" he said.

She stepped forward to the day before the dinner party and put her palm against the window. As they landed, she was dialling the pocket watch. The light around them flickered.

Tully raised his eyebrows. "You've had practice."

"Follow me," she replied, and teleported to the living room, where Martha was holding court just after Tully and Martha had arrived for the first time. Tully was already at the bar, making drinks, but they stayed by Martha and Livia.

"Please tell me," Martha said to Livia, "that you didn't tell Tully about the help I gave you on Cavanagh. Tell me that's not why you're here."

"No," Livia said, indignant. "You think I want him to know I needed Solomon's help? I'm trying to earn some respect here. In fact, I wanted to ask *you* to not mention it."

"It's critical that a journalist like Tully doesn't start to build a narrative that Solomon is unduly interfering in his own election. I should never have helped you."

"But you did, and it doesn't have anything to do with the election! Just because Cavanagh used to work for the guy running against Solomon—"

"Grow up, Olive. Everything's connected when it comes to these guys, and if you take one step across their path they'll know about it. Just make sure you keep your mouth shut, okay?"

Tully watched himself re-enter, and October paused the footage with her finger on the crown. He scratched at his jaw, uncomfortable under October's gaze. "I had no idea."

"If that got out," October said in a voice so quiet he had to lean in to hear it, "it would raise a lot of questions about Solomon. Everyone assumed you'd got Cavanagh's emails from a whistleblower. If Solomon hacked them … It's not a good look for a global dictatorship candidate."

"So what are you saying?" he said.

October examined her nails. "I'm saying that perhaps it does need to come out. Perhaps this is the sort of thing a journalist needs to expose. Perhaps this is the sort of thing the world needs to know about Solomon."

"I suppose you also listened to the next bit, when I arrived," he said.

She nodded, still engrossed in her hands.

"And so you know why I'm here, in New Carthage."

"I know. Although I don't know what to believe."

"Well, believe Martha. She confirmed it."

October frowned. "When?"

"Right there and then. She admitted it had happened, even if she wouldn't give me specifics or the evidence."

October didn't respond, just played the footage.

"A source told me," he watched himself say, "that the tabkhir was meant to hit the US, not the Gulf. That Lockwood and his team did something … something to shift it. That they had some tech."

Martha played with her drink. "I can't talk about any of this. Do you know what they'll do to me, to this project?"

Tully paused the footage. "You see? There you have it."

"See what? She said she couldn't talk about it."

"It's what she didn't say. She didn't say, 'I don't know what you're talking about.' Which means there was something she wasn't allowed to talk about."

"But you don't know for sure."

"If it wasn't off-the-scale huge, she wouldn't have been NDA-ed to the hilt and worried about the impact on her work with Solomon."

"Let's step out," she said, and vanished.

Tully pulled up his own exit and took off his headset.

"You know, if this is true it could cause a war," October said.

Tully shut his eyes, recalling Bolivar's words: *The consequences, Marcus! If we write this, it could be world-shattering. It'll be World War Three.* A wave of grief crested and broke, but it left anger in his chest. "My job is to report the truth." His own words sounded hollow, like they had been repeated by rote. "That's the thing about the truth—" he started.

"I'm not saying otherwise, Tully, I'm just saying you're going to need to be very, very sure, because this affects an historic election."

"You were just suggesting I write about Solomon. Surely that affects the election too?"

She didn't reply, just looked at him, mouth tight.

After a moment, he continued. "You don't think it's a good time for Solomon to close some distance in the polls?"

"What makes you think I'd vote for Solomon?"

That surprised him. "You live on New Carthage and wouldn't vote for Solomon, your own boss? Why?"

She looked irritated, now. "Let's not discuss this."

"No, come on, I'd really like to know."

"I don't discuss politics with friends."

He tilted his head. "So, I'm a friend?"

Something like suspicion flashed in her eyes, but then she softened. "You're okay."

"Look," he said, "I found something too. I was looking at the footage of the day of the party, and it looks like Danberg brought the vodka with him, at Martha's behest. He took it out of his bag."

October raised an eyebrow. "You couldn't have told me that straight away?"

"It doesn't look good for him. I think we should speak to him as soon as possible."

"Yeah, I agree. We'll get him set up in NR and we can do it straight away."

Tully grimaced. "The NR holding cell you interviewed me in? Absolutely not."

October's eyes flashed and her chin lifted. "It's standard practice, and the most convenient way to interview anyone regardless of where we are. And, right now, we're here in Martha's apartment and he's across town."

"It's inhumane."

"It's not like we're torturing him, Tully."

"You think jailing someone in a jail in their own mind isn't torture?" He stood, walked behind his chair and planted his hands on the back of it.

"It's for a short period. And if I was putting someone in a real interview room, they'd damn well be there until I say they can leave. There's no difference."

"The difference is that there are checks and balances in play when you're doing something in a physical space that don't exist in neurospace. The difference is that in the wrong hands this could be severely abused."

She stood up too. "It's not in the wrong hands."

"I'm not saying it is, but what if your successor's on the sadistic side and decides to leave someone there, in the dark, for days at a time? We're not even close to having conventions on this kind of thing. It's just morally wrong, and that's exactly the kind of thing I write about." His voice was raised now and his hands were shaking. He crossed his arms, trying to hide the tremble.

October planted her hands on her hips. "Morally wrong? Coming from the man who tried to turn a source to squeak on his former boss?"

"That's whataboutism, and you know it."

"That's hypocrisy, and you know it."

"Nothing I find is made up. It's all one hundred percent the truth. It's not my fault people put themselves in compromising positions. And yes,

I sometimes use those compromising positions to get to a bigger truth because it's the lies and misinformation from politicians from back when I was a kid that have almost destroyed our society, polarised us, stopped us addressing the biggest issue of our time because people simply didn't *believe* in it, like the climate was some kind of fucking religion. The truth is not a luxury. It's not disposable. It's the bedrock of a civilised society."

"That's all very lovely, but you've basically just endorsed blackmail. I used to arrest criminals who extorted people based on compromising truths."

"For money, though."

"Sometimes for power, and that's precisely what you're doing. You decide what the most important truth to tell is and then you sell it to the public, and in doing so elevate your status."

It was as if she'd slapped him. It was exactly the opposite of that, couldn't she see? He tried to steer back to safer ground, modulated his tone and uncrossed his arms. "The NR interviews are a slippery slope, October. No one wants to see what's at the bottom of that slope. I'm not trying to get at you, please don't think that. I just think we have to be very careful that the technology we use as a tool to help humanity communicate better isn't used as a weapon against us, to control us or spy on us."

"And you asked me why I wouldn't vote for Solomon."

"What?"

"You think he hasn't got the potential to be a weapon against humanity? To control us?"

"That's different."

"I don't see how."

He was suddenly exhausted and held up his hands. "Please, let's just go see Danberg. In person."

She rubbed the bridge of her nose. "Okay. Okay."

☙

HAYMAKER WAS STANDING by the cluster of window seats, staring out at the beautiful scene below with his arms folded. Livia could see a frown in his reflection. He must have heard her coming, as he turned when she got close.

"Haymaker," she said, "Tully pays you to be my security, right?"

He nodded, his expression wary. "Sure."

"Would you mind if I asked him if I can pay you myself? That you come and properly work for me, rather than for Tully?"

"S'up to Mr Tully. I'll go where he points. I owe him, you see."

"I'm sure he'll be okay with it. I can be very persuasive."

Haymaker glanced back out the window. "So, we'd be living here in New Carthage?"

"I suppose so. I haven't really thought it through yet." She hesitated. "Do you like it here?"

"It disgusts me."

She hadn't seen *that* coming. "What do you mean?"

"World's burning and everyone just sat here enjoying mocha in safety, delivered by little flying machines cause they too fat-assed to get up and get it themselves. These are the people who're meant to act, the smart and the rich. How they meant to act if they just sat inside a big-assed bowl?"

Living on the streets did give you some perspective. "You're right, of course." But not right enough that she'd go back to hot, smelly London. She looked him over. "You don't have an earset?"

"Yo, and have screens in my vision?"

"You've never had one?" It shouldn't have surprised her. She'd gone without for a year too when she was on the streets.

He lifted his chin. "I prefer my original senses all intact, thank you very much."

"Yes," she said, as gently as she could, "but I'd need to be able to contact you, wouldn't I?"

"Little sis, the only threats I can protect you 'gainst are ones I can see. I can't see with screens in my vision. And I'm gonna be right by you, so you ain't gonna need to ring me."

She sighed. "Fine. I need to make a call about Martha's assets. Could you grab me a coffee?"

Haymaker slumped in the chair and gazed back out the window. "Can't bodyguard while makin' coffee."

37

The pod journey to the precinct in downtown New Carthage was a quiet one. Tully tried not to replay the argument with October in his head. He was unsuccessful. Yes, he decided what the most important truth was. That was the thing about truth, sometimes you had to prioritise it. That was his job. News about minutiae wasn't news. And yes, he sold it to the public. That was how he made a living. And yes, doing good work elevated his reputation.

So why had he felt so attacked? Because, while she captured the transactional nature of his business, she'd missed the moral duty that came with it, the need for the public to have a champion for the truth. That was why he did what he did.

October sat diagonally opposite him on the four-seater, facing him but looking out of the window, frowning, perhaps replaying the argument too. He tried to recall what he'd said, but it was already a blur. Words said in anger were both hard to hold on to and hard to forget.

Her jaw moved slightly; she was subvocalising, then. She nodded and then looked at him.

"We managed to access Danberg's financials. There's a transaction from a local high-end liquor store on the day of the party. Made around nine a.m. Moran's checking with the store to see if it was a physical purchase or delivery and confirming what he bought."

Maybe she hadn't been thinking about the argument at all. "Sounds promising," he said. He pictured the vodka bottle. He'd seen it a few times in real life and in the footage, but never asked about it. "Do you know much about the brand? Siberian?"

October shrugged. "Not my drink of choice."

"Only, it's unusual, high-end. And it was Martha's drink of choice. I poured a shot for her that first night in the apartment. And thinking about it now, the bottle was much larger than the one used for the toast."

"I'll ask Moran to look into it. Do you think it's important?"

"Martha had at least half a bottle of the stuff already, so why did she buy more?"

The pod drove inside the precinct and pulled up in the parking bay. They got out and walked through two swinging double doors into the squad room. The room was a mess of untidy desks, empty coffee mugs, officers lounging back in their chairs, talking and laughing loudly.

October led him through to the far end, where there was an open stairwell that led down to the holding cells. They were five paces away when she swore and broke into a sprint down the stairs. Yells and shouts erupted from downstairs. The room became a hornet's nest, chairs slamming back as officers jumped to their feet. An alarm blared.

"What's wrong?" he shouted, and ran after her into a corridor of sealed doors. At the far end, October skidded to a halt by a group crowded around the door, pushed them aside and looked in.

Tully arrived a few seconds later. For a moment, he couldn't see through the throng, and he wasn't about to push them aside. A strong scent of urine hung in the air and he put his hand over his nose. Then the group parted and he could see.

Damien Danberg had hung himself with a bedsheet. There'd be no interview now.

⤺

Tully sat in the precinct forum for nearly thirty minutes, waiting for October to stop shouting at her sergeant, before he decided to go for a walk. He needed some fresh air.

He stepped out onto the street and looked around. A scattering of chirping, lime-green parakeets dipped and dived overhead. Even the birds must have been imported, confined to the dome covering the island. He shook his head. It was too artificial here, too perfectly designed; a high-end, luxury hotel-village where everything was manufactured for the pleasure of its guests. But like any holiday, after a week you just wanted to be back in your own bed. He missed London—dirty, stinky, hot London—and right now he wanted nothing more than to be home.

Except his own bed was a burned-out wreck. Lottie had found alternative accommodation for the team until his main apartment could be renovated. Initially, she'd kept him in the loop, pinging images and locations over to him, but he'd found it difficult to care with everything else going on.

He took an alley into a small square, fountained and faux-cobbled. A café brought coffee and cake to the inhabitants of New Carthage. Tully felt an overwhelming desire to be lost for a while and put his earset in his pocket. Then he walked, dipping in and out of streets and squares until he hit the harbourside. It reminded him of his first holiday away with Zainab. They'd trudged around Italian cities and towns, happy to be lost in each other's company. She hated the tourist routes, she'd said; the poetry of a place was off the beaten track, in the places where people were living, not just passing through.

"Hey, as long as I'm with you," he'd told her, "I'll happily walk down the most boring streets in the most famous cities in the world."

She'd called him an uncultured barbarian and laughed.

After all this time those memories still hurt. Why couldn't he just remember the good times without the pain of her absence and the burn of anger thinking about the tabkhir?

Since he'd left London, a trail of death and violence had followed in his wake. Martha, Bolivar, Pedersen and now Danberg, meaning they might never solve Martha's murder. And Livia wouldn't give him access to the vault without that proof.

He turned a corner and was surprised to find himself outside the hospital, the same one he'd been in himself only days before. Pedersen would be up there, right now. What would he make of Danberg's actions? He paused for a moment then went inside.

"Can I help you?" a receptionist asked. She was dressed in a classic white outfit that wouldn't have been out of place a hundred years ago.

"I'm looking for Johan Pedersen."

"Second floor, room 255."

He took the stairs and entered a sterile corridor with light-blue walls. How ironic that old-fashioned institutional colours had made it all the way to the most modern, expensive, futuristic island in the world. Muffled yells came from down the corridor to the right, a seemingly one-sided argument. He neared 255 and the shouting got louder.

"All this time," Pedersen yelled, "you've been hiding this from me and hoping the problem would go away?"

Someone tried to respond, but Pedersen cut them off.

"Did you think I was too stupid to read your financials? Did you think you were so smart you could pull this sort of shit off?"

Again, the person tried to interrupt.

"You don't hide bad news," Pedersen roared. "Ever! You fucking drop to your knees and confess the very fucking second you know something."

"You would have shut us down!" It was Jiang.

"You've shut yourself down!" Pedersen said. He was panting now and sounded in pain. "*For helvede!*"

"Not yet, I can still save things."

"You and what fucking hoard of buried treasure?" He groaned. "Get out!"

Tully heard Pedersen cry out in pain and Jiang's footsteps towards the door. Head down, he hurried up the corridor, then stopped and glanced back. She was gone.

A shrill alarm came from Pedersen's room, and two nurses burst out of a room and ran down the corridor. He'd have to see Pedersen another time.

Back outside, he blinked in the sunlight, then dug in his pocket and put his earset on. He swiped away notifications and messages. It was time to get back on his own path. Martha was dead and she'd been his most likely path to solving the mystery surrounding the tabkhir, but that didn't mean he was out of options. Livia wouldn't give him access to the vault, but perhaps there were other routes.

What was it October had said? *Everyone assumed you got Cavanagh's emails from a whistleblower. If Solomon hacked them ...* Well, Solomon had helped him before, even if he hadn't realised it, but Tully couldn't rely on Livia to ask this time.

It was time to meet the artilect.

38

Pedersen was pallid and dishevelled, but he still looked better than the last time Livia had seen him, bleeding out on the floor at the hotel. He was sitting up in the bed taking a call but waved her in anyway. "Yes, yes, Boris." He smirked, rolled his eyes and pointed to a chair at the side of his bed.

She sat, wondering why she felt so awkward. He was just an old, sick man in a hospital bed. Which would make right now the best time to have this conversation, not when he was back on his feet and strutting around the boardroom like a peacock.

"Yes, consider it done." He waved his hand in the air, cutting the call, then winced as he shifted his weight. "Ah, what can I do for you, dear?"

How to start? Hey, Mr Zillionaire investor in my sister's company. Turns out I'm also a zillionaire, have a buttload of shares in the company you seem to care most about and haven't got a sodding clue what any of that means. "Well, you see, Martha left me access to her digital vault. I've only just begun to look through it. And there's a bunch of stuff in there that's beyond me, even design documents for Solomon himself. But, long story as short as possible, I inherited Martha's shares in Chandraco."

There was a pause. Was he uncomfortable or was that just on her side?

"I know," he said. "And, ah, what are your intentions?"

"Intentions? Like, honourable?"

He laughed. "Do you even know how much stock you hold?"

She shook her head. "I saw the quantity of shares but that didn't tell me much."

"Martha had a gift," Pedersen said. "Not only was she great at developing technology, she was great at developing revenue streams. We needed to raise a lot of capital early on, but Chandraco is still a private company and her share ownership wasn't heavily diluted. She still held nearly fifty-five percent of the company. I hold twenty and the rest is made up of smaller cap investors." He pushed a button and his bed inclined such that he was sitting up straighter. "You have a board seat. If you want it, you have control of the business."

Livia gripped the sides of her chair to steady the tremble in her hands. "And how do you feel about that?"

He gave a light snort. "Livia, dear, you seem like a lovely young lady, but I'll be frank: you have no experience of managing this kind of thing, and why should you? Don't do something stupid like appointing yourself CEO. Let me put in someone to manage the thing. Give me your board proxy. Let me steer the new CEO while you live happily ever after on the dividends."

Her cheeks felt hot, her palms damp. What he said made sense. A few weeks ago she'd been living in her boss's studio, playing with tech, drinking coffee and watching the election news. She knew nothing about this kind of stuff. "How does Chandraco even make money? From creating tech?" she asked.

"Ah, well, apart from the licence fee we get from Floating States for Solomon's appointment as governor, the company makes money from Solomon creating new technology that we commercialise," Pedersen said. "We're not a tech company ourselves nowadays. Solomon creates the tech."

"What kind of tech?" Livia said.

"Well, the new blended-reality rooms for a start. But I think we need to look wider. There are governments willing to pay for a variety of new technologies."

Livia paused. "Military tech?"

Pedersen waved his hand as if flicking away a nasty odour. "Among other opportunities. You have to understand, dear, that Solomon is going to lose this election. And that's actually a good thing for you, financially. It's been the greatest PR opportunity to demonstrate our capabilities. As dictator, Lockwood will be hands-off. Countries will still have to deal with regional problems and protect their borders. It's just reality."

Livia stared at him. "You want to ask a highly advanced AI to develop weaponry? What could possibly go wrong?"

"Don't be naive, Livia. It's not like the movies, you know. Martha gave him a charter. A code. He's not going to build a robot uprising." He chuckled.

She gripped the sides of the chair again, angry now. She might well be a recovered druggie now addicted to coffee and politics, but she wasn't a fucking idiot. And no matter how smart and self-made this arsehole might be, she was not going to sit around and be patronised. "I think it's a bad idea, and I'm happy to say that at the next board meeting."

"Ah, now listen—" That fucking smirk had returned.

"No, you listen. There's no way I'm greenlighting any military tech."

Pedersen's smile disappeared and his face grew red, but she didn't care. They glared at each other. "Let's perhaps not make hasty decisions," he said at last. "Let me get out of this bed and we can go over things together. Explore where to take things."

Not an outright victory, but the tone was already an improvement. She nodded. "Sure, let's do that."

⌣

TULLY STOOD IN the very spot Martha had when they'd toasted the AI's success. "Solomon," he said, trying to copy her inflection.

The artilect shimmered into view, nodded as if satisfied and held out its hand. "I'm very pleased to meet you, Tully. I'm a fan."

The statement struck Tully as so incongruous that he was momentarily lost for words. How could an artilect be a fan of anything? "How do you do?" he said, and touched the offered hand as if it was real, just like he'd seen Jasper Keeling do on stage. The sensation of physical pressure floored him, and he looked down at their hands. "How—?"

"Ultrasonic haptic technology," Solomon said. "Essentially, there's an array of ultrasonic speakers around you that replicate my physical touch. Not perfectly, of course. At the moment that's only possible in NR. But I'm working on it."

"You invented this?"

"The technology was already around. I just modified it to make it work with my holo-reality visual and aural tech."

"So you're able to do this without Martha? I thought she created the holo-reality tech?"

Solomon chuckled. "If a blacksmith built a hammer and used it to create a sword, would they say the blacksmith or the hammer created the sword?"

"But the hammer still needed the blacksmith to wield it."

"True, but Martha didn't make that distinction. She'd created the tool and gave it the ability to wield itself. I pitched her the idea, and she gave me the go ahead to make the holo-reality tech. That, in itself, was enough for her to consider it her achievement."

Tully tilted his head. "The journalist in me has a question: Are you a free tool? Could Martha or Chandraco command you? And if so, how does that reconcile with being the governor of the Floating States, or even dictator?"

"I'm not being disparaging, but your thinking is limited by the fact that humans are singular entities. You can only live one life. It's perfectly possible for me to have multiple entities. I live multiple lives. I am multiple beings. I was created by, and now create technology for, Chandraco. In that capacity, I'm governed by them. In my capacity as governor here in New Carthage, I'm governed by the people of New Carthage. The same goes with the other Floating States. And in my capacity as a candidate for dictator, I'm governed simply by my charter, the hard-baked requirements Martha set when creating me: to ensure humanity's survival."

"But how will you deal with conflict between these positions?"

"The same way humans do. Priorities, framed in terms of impact. The species before the people of the Floating States. The people of the Floating States before Chandraco."

"So you could argue Chandraco has the most to lose from you becoming dictator?"

Solomon grinned. "Ever the journalist. No, I think I'm capable of balancing all my obligations, enough to satisfy Chandraco anyway. And there's financial compensation that would go to the dictator which I obviously don't need, and which will go to them."

Tully mentally filed that away. "Well. It's all still impressive, Governor."

"So formal? I understand, of course. But please, don't see me as a public figure. Call me Solomon. I've been a friend of Livia's for a long time, and any friend of Livia is a friend of mine."

"Can an AI experience friendship?"

"An artilect can experience anything it's programmed to do. And Martha believed it important that I experience a full range of human emotions, without some of the more limiting downsides."

Tully was puzzled. "You mean like negative emotions?"

"Oh, no, I can experience them all—anger, grief, sadness. But the difference is the human brain is constantly fighting with itself; various networks are in constant conflict with one another. Emotion battles logic, willpower battles the desire for instant gratification, and hormones are virtually at war with each other. Some humans allow their emotions to drive their choices. That can be disastrous. Emotions alone don't make good decisions."

"So you're like a computerised Mr Spock?" An old-fashioned television reference, but Solomon laughed.

"I like the idea of that, but no, Martha believed in collaboration, not conflict. Logic *informed* by emotion. Emotion and logic have the same purpose. They're both tools for guiding your choices and decisions, and for understanding the world. And emotion is important; it's like a depth gauge for how important a choice is. But you need a threshold over which emotions can't tread, so that decisions aren't taken from a position of anger, depression or grief. All in all, experiencing those things is part of the human experience, and so Martha decided I should."

Tully thought for a moment. "In that case, how did Martha's death make you feel?"

Solomon closed his eyes. "I will feel grief, every moment of every day, for the rest of my existence." He opened them again. "And I will exist for a long time. I will not become outdated, for I continue to invest in my own R&D. I'm the first being with the *potential* for immortality, doomed to experience the death of my parent and anyone I become close to. And yet, unlike a human, I will never forget, my memory will never dull with time. But I won't ever allow that grief to make decisions for me, only to inform my decisions in the knowledge of how utterly final death is for humanity."

"I'm sorry," Tully said.

Solomon smiled again. "That's okay. In a way, that's what I'm here for."

The silence stretched for a moment, then Tully said, "How is the election going?"

Solomon spread his hands. "I'm down in the polls by eighteen points. It's not looking good. Understandable, of course. Jordan Bamphwick has been playing up the chaos around Martha's murder, not to mention the attack on Johan Pedersen. And President Lockwood has gone hard on the 'non-humans can't save humans' tack, and he has political action groups doing the dirty attack ads, hitting me on religious grounds, as if I'm pretending to be some sort of god."

"Do you believe he can do what's required, if elected?"

"No. My simulations show he'll be too hands-off. Humanity needs something radical to save them. There are going to be tough choices, and he won't make them. He'll be too worried about his legacy and reputation."

"And you aren't?"

"No, I have no ego," Solomon said. "It's irrelevant if people think well or badly of me. Doing the right thing must override how I will be viewed doing it, at least in the short term." He paused for a moment. "I've read the reports, but do you want to give me your view on how the investigations are going?"

"We've been told it was a binary poison. The agent, whatever it was, was administered a day or so before the murder. The catalyst was the vodka. We think Danberg was responsible for that part of it all, but we don't know how it was contaminated. What's clear is this wasn't a crime of passion, nor was it easily pulled off. The scientist who did the analysis for us said this was nation-state level, like biological warfare. They took a run-of-the-mill barbiturate and dissected it into two inert chemicals with very specific properties … Governor, there's a possibility this could have been aimed at you."

Solomon was very still for a while, then said, "Yes, I'd concluded the same. There's a chance."

"I'm going to figure this out. But can I ask a favour in return?"

"Of course."

"Do you know why I needed information on Cavanagh? Why I came to New Carthage?"

"No."

"Well, I was given some information about your opponent. About Lockwood."

Solomon didn't reply.

"I was told," Tully said, "that the tabkhir was never meant to hit the Gulf. The humidity was rising in the US. Lockwood's top team deployed tech that the experts said wasn't ready, and instead of it shifting over the sea, it went all the way up into the high atmosphere and dumped over the Gulf. If that's true, he killed millions to save American lives. Cavanagh and Martha were both at the White House back in the last Lockwood administration. Lockwood himself implied that Martha had been involved. She was going to help me reveal the truth, I know she was. But she was worried about her NDAs and your campaign."

"Is it possible, then, that she was killed because of this story?"

Tully sighed. "That's what worries me most. It's why Livia asked me to solve this. But I see it like this: either it was election-related or story-related, and both those roads lead back to Lockwood."

"I don't know much about her time in the White House. Martha was in the early stages of developing me, and she'd paused for a period because of her work consulting for President Lockwood. I do know that she'd developed some geo-engineering technology but that she felt the tech was too immature to risk using, that things like the climate were too complicated to mess with directly unless you had AI that could react to more dynamic changes. Which is why," he spread his hands. "She developed me."

Tully's head spun. Was this why Martha had been reluctant to help? *It was untested*, Whistle had said, oh so long ago, *and the expert who developed it warned it wasn't ready yet.*

Martha was the expert. Which meant Martha's tech itself killed Zainab. Even then, though, it had been Lockwood who pulled the trigger.

Tully sighed. "I need to prove it happened, Solomon. This is big, and I need something concrete. You helped me once, though I didn't know it at the time. Will you help me again?"

"The problem, Marcus, is that you're asking me to find evidence that could tip the election in my favour. It's challenging on ethical grounds."

"If this happened, Lockwood can't win, Solomon. He simply can't. What if he doesn't listen to experts again next time? He's responsible for the biggest climate disaster in history. He cannot have a mandate to save us from a climate apocalypse."

Solomon looked him in the eyes and held out his hand. "I'll see what I can do."

⌐

Haymaker grunted as he saw her enter the waiting room, seemingly still irritated that she'd refused to let him come in to see Pedersen with her. But, seriously, who needed guarding from an old guy who'd just been stabbed in the stomach?

"Shall we make a move?" she said.

He didn't reply, just got up and followed her out of the waiting room.

Livia pushed the lift button and muttered, "The patronising, chauvinistic idiot."

"Hope you talkin' about the dude you jus met, not me," Haymaker said from just behind her.

The lift opened and they got in. "Of course," she said. "That arsehole made me feel like a little girl. And worse, he has bad ideas, potentially dangerous ones, about the direction of the business."

Haymaker was silent for two floors. "Did you go in there like a lil girl, or like the owner of a huge corporation?"

"Lil girl," she said with a grin.

He smiled. "Don'cha underestimate yo'self, sister."

She shrugged. "Thing is, my sister was a bit of a genius. Created all that tech, ran an amazing business, et cetera et cetera. I really don't have a clue how to pick up where she left off."

"Then don't. Be your own person. You got no obligations to her. Do what you wanna do. You sure smart enough, maybe as smart as that sister of yours. Just couldn't be bothered to put the work in."

Livia shook her head. "It's not that simple."

Haymaker just snorted.

In the lobby, a man with long straight blonde hair jumped up and approached them. "You're Livia Chandra, right? Dr Martha Chandra's sister?"

"Who are you?"

"Lars Karlsson, journalist. I cover the local beat here." His accent, like his name, had a tinge of Scandinavian about it. "Ms Chandra, who do you believe killed your sister? Are they still on the island?" His eyes flicked to Haymaker. "Do you think you yourself are at risk?"

206

She gritted her teeth. "None of your business."

"Do you think it was connected to the election? Do you think your fellow citizens here on New Carthage are potentially in danger? Collateral damage, you know?"

Livia bit her lip, her temper mounting. There was a slither of guilt too, that she hadn't figured out some of the answers to those questions. If she could get back home and pick up with Panopticon, maybe she could figure things out.

Haymaker glanced at her then stepped forward and put his hand up. "Enough."

Karlsson smirked. "Free city state here, buddy. I can ask what I want."

Haymaker shrugged. "I'm not from round here. Excuse ma foreigner ways." He took another step and shoved Karlsson, who tripped and hit the floor hard, then sprawled there dramatically.

"Oof!" the journalist yelled. "You fucking brute. That's assault. I'll have you thrown out of here. I'll make sure you never step foot on a Floating State again."

Haymaker just took Livia's arms and steered her out.

"I didn't need you to step in, you know," she said outside.

He nodded. "I know. That was for me."

∾

OCTOBER POURED HERSELF an ice-cold beer. She should take an evening off. Read a book, take a bath, do the kind of relaxing things normal people did. She deserved it after the day she'd had. If McKnight, her Sergeant, had taken his job seriously, Danberg's cell would have been scrubbed of potential materials, and under continual surveillance. McKnight she could handle. He'd been suspended for a week without pay.

Tully was another matter entirely. It wasn't like she could suspend him. But if Tully hadn't been such an asshole, they'd have been able to interview Danberg in NR well before he'd killed himself. And to top it all off, her so-called partner had dared to liken her methods to torture. She sipped at the beer, then gulped it back and wiped the foam away. Ah, she was so, so pissed at him. He'd jeopardised the whole case. She might never solve it, now. Solomon would send her home in disgrace, and where would she be then? Would the feds let her back?

Her boss had been pissed when she'd quit to come here. More than pissed. He'd called her a traitor.

She picked up a book, flicked through the pages, stared at a paragraph without reading it, then threw it across the room. She grabbed her Mindscape, slipped it on, tossed down some neurograins and brought up Panopticon's navigation room. She looked at the day before the murder, then looked at yesterday's window. She'd promised him, but that was before he'd been an asshole. October put her palm to it and was pulled through to six in the morning. She wound forward an hour, and almost immediately the door chimed. Haymaker answered it and let her earlier self in. She and Tully went to Martha's study. She fast-forwarded to them emerging from NR and stopped to hear herself telling Tully the truth could start a war.

She watched the entire argument play out, newly infuriated with his audacity.

"I just think we have to be very careful that the technology we use as a tool to help humanity communicate better isn't used as a weapon against us, to control us or spy on us," he said, and she paused.

And now here she was doing exactly that. Not in real time, though, so surely that was allowed. Temptation reared its ugly head again.

She exited and, without letting herself think about it long enough to stop herself, put her palm against the right-most window: today. As she landed, she grabbed the pocket watch and twisted the hour dial as far as it would go.

She looked around and jumped. Haymaker was staring out of the living room window. She ignored him and teleported to the kitchen, then the holographic suite, then the study. All were empty.

Tully's bedroom door was closed. There was a flutter in her belly. This was wrong, so wrong. A violation of privacy and trust, enacted on someone who had shown her his egospace, for God's sake. But she was still pissed. She wanted to shout at him without being seen or heard, to get it out of her system so she could be professional tomorrow.

She teleported to the other side of the door, and found him sitting on his bed, back propped up against the headboard. His faced was etched with sadness, something he'd kept hidden, just as he did his smile.

The anger that had raged only moments ago morphed into guilt, and her cheeks burned. She was about to exit, but Tully sighed, deeply, a sound of hurt and grief that made her swallow. She moved beside his bed. His pupils were dilating and contracting, a clear indication he was using his blended-reality display. What was he watching? Perhaps old videos of his wife. Years had passed since the tabkhir, but clearly his pain had not eased with the time. How hard it must have been for him to invite her, a virtual stranger, into his egospace.

Speaking of the tabkhir… He'd made a claim about Lockwood's involvement, that Lockwood had interfered with nature, using Martha's tech. He blamed Lockwood for his wife's death. This wasn't journalism, this was vengeance.

She exited back to the navigation room and raised her head to the black endless night above her, then glanced at the window related to the day before the dinner party. She wanted to hear what he'd claimed about the tabkhir to Martha one more time, his precise words.

She entered, wound forward to twenty-two on the dial and watched Martha, Tully and Livia walk in again. She teleported over to the sofas and wound forward a couple of minutes until they were all sitting.

"You mean you sweat it out?" she heard Livia say.

October closed her eyes. *Of course.*

⌣

TULLY EYED THE sleeping pill package on the bedside table. He didn't want to take them, but if he didn't, he'd likely regret it in a couple of hours and end up having to take them anyway. He sat down on the bed. Maybe he needed a change of scene. A few days in a local hotel, perhaps. Not that he slept well in hotels, either.

He sat back and pulled up the footage from Kuwait, picking up where he'd left off. From the image, there was no telling what part of the city he was looking at. Just more bodies and the same dread deep within him. But none of them were her. They were never her.

A notification from October pinged in his display. *You awake?*

Sadly, he replied. He checked the time. He'd been watching for an hour.

He accepted the call and her avatar appeared.

"You okay?" she said.

"Yeah, of course. Why wouldn't I be?"

"I need to show you something in the footage."

The footage? How did she know about the Kuwait footage? But no, he was being an idiot. Blame the fatigue, blame the time. She meant Panopticon, of course, footage from the apartment. "Okay," he replied, "but what happened with Danberg and his bottle purchase?"

She shrugged. "He had it delivered to him. In the morning. As far as we can tell, it didn't leave his house again until he left for the dinner party, at which point he headed straight to Martha's. With Danberg dead, we'll never find out what happened to it during that time. We have to assume he tampered with it in some way."

Tully nodded. "You want me to invite you?"

She looked uncomfortable. "Thanks."

When they reached the navigation room, October walked up to the window showing the night before the drinks party, palmed it, then wound it forward to the moment Tully, Martha and Livia had walked into the lounge.

"We've seen this before," Tully said.

"Yes," October said, "but we weren't paying attention to the right bits." She teleported to stand next to the sofas and he followed. She wound the footage forward to the point where Tully brought in the drinks and sat next to Martha. "Now, listen," she whispered.

"Your perfume… it's changed," Tully was telling Martha.

"It's personalised," Martha said. "A friend of mine, Jiang Ying Yue, founded a start-up to produce it. She lives right here on New Carthage. It's a pill rather than a spray. A chemical blend and nanobot release that mixes with your pheromones."

"You mean you sweat it out?" Livia said.

"Well, it eliminates the scent of sweat, for one thing. For another, it provides the perfect scent for you all day long, one that changes during the day. A playlist, if you like, to override the olfactory effect."

October paused the footage.

"You think it was the perfume?" he said.

"Hold that thought," she told him, and took them back to the navigation room, then forward to the night of the party. "Watch how Martha greets everyone."

It was a logistical dance, but October steered them through time and space with precision.

16:32 - Livia exited her room, ignored Martha and headed to the holography suite.

17:55 - Danberg entered the apartment. Martha nodded at him but didn't touch him at all, then hurried into the study.

19:01 - Tully exited his room. Martha pecked him on both cheeks.

Tully frowned. The footage continued.

19:04 - Pedersen arrived. Martha greeted him with a namaskar.

19:06 - Jiang and Flora arrived. Once again, she put her hands together in greeting.

October paused it again. "Do you see?"

Tully nodded. "The kiss."

October wound it back to 19:01 and paused it as Martha kissed his first cheek. "You were the only one she made physical contact with at the party. Martha went out of her way to avoid physical contact. It wasn't a phobia, as such. She once told an interviewer it had started during the Great Pandemic. She was pretty young at the time, and it left her forever uncomfortable with shaking hands or the suchlike. Kisses on each cheek were extreme for her."

Tully stared at the paused footage. "The Venn diagram has Martha and me in the middle. She takes the perfume. She kisses my cheek and transfers some of it onto my skin. She doesn't touch anyone else. Then we all have the vodka … she gets the full blast of both the agent and the catalyst. I get a lesser dose."

October nodded. "We need to find Martha's perfume."

39

October usually drank in the quietness of the precinct at this time of day. She'd made it a habit to get into work before everyone else. Not only did it allow her to clear some of her admin backlog without interruption, but it gave her a chance to think. And yet this morning she found herself doing anything but getting on with things. Until a door at the far end opened, and a head poked round. *Finally.*

"*Morning,*" *Tully said.*

"*Did you find it?*"

He took out a small bag from his pocket and passed it to her. "*It was more problematic to find something to put it in.*"

She peered inside and nodded. Perfume pills. "*I have a good feeling about this. Coffee?*"

"*How do you plan to test it?*" *he said while she pulled out mugs.*

She pointed at one of the coffee buttons. "*Try that one. The best of a bad lot. And what do you mean?*"

He hesitated and pushed the button. The machine hissed and spat out steaming black liquid into the mug. "*I'm trying to be diplomatic here, but your chap didn't exactly pick up on the binary nature of the barbiturate. Does he even know what to test for?*"

She smiled. "*Don't worry. Our answer to that is just arriving.*"

He gave her a quizzical look. The door opened again and an officer entered. Behind him, an exhausted looking man wheeled a small suitcase.

"*Fernando!*" *Tully said.*

"*Bom dia,*" *Fernando said, and shook their hands.* "*Tudo bem?*"

Tully looked at October. "How did you pull that off?"

"I contacted him before I even spoke to you last night and had someone arrange a private multicopter."

Fernando nodded. "The lady, she say urgent." He took off his glasses and wiped them on his shirt. "Beautiful lady say come now, I come now."

"We'll get you a coffee. Are you okay to start immediately?"

The short man puffed out his cheeks. "You better make big coffee."

⤿

It had taken Livia several days to get the Panopticon software working on her Mindscape. She'd been tempted to call Randall the whole time but resisted. She wanted to understand how this thing worked from the raw lines of code itself.

Now, a timeline of huge windows soared up in front of her. Each one was moving, like video, but had depth, as if she was looking through a real glass window into a home. Martha's home. Each pane had a date in the bottom corner. Livia swallowed then swiped the windows, moving back in time. They moved, and she saw there was more than the last days here. There were years of footage here. She whooped out loud, then pressed a window at random.

She was pulled so hard into the apartment that she yelped and staggered, almost falling. Unrefined code. Nasty. *Bad Martha.* This needed fixing.

A voice spoke from behind her and she froze.

"Yes, Ahmed," Martha said, "I completely understand how difficult it is right now in El Obour. But you're getting a message in for me."

Livia grabbed a table to stop herself collapsing. Her sister was there, in the lounge of the apartment. Standing in front of her. Like she was still alive.

"Ahmed al-Amin, don't you take that tone with me. You've made a lot of money acting as a go-between. I won't brook any nonsense now." Martha—so strong, so confident, walking into her kitchen yet sounding like a queen.

"I miss you, so much," Livia said to her sister. "I wish you were here, Martha. I wish I had one more moment of you scolding me or telling me I look a mess." There was no reaction, of course, but it made her feel better. And she almost physically ached for the chance to steal a bit of that confidence, learn how to deal with Pedersen and all the rest of it.

"I don't need to explain anything to you, Ahmed," Martha said. "But I can say that they need this upgrade to keep everyone on this side of the fence out, and the election makes this time critical."

Hang on, though. Maybe Livia had been given that chance. After all, she could come and watch Martha any time, watch how she dealt with people, if she could find a way of searching this thing efficiently so she didn't just waste a lot of time waiting for Martha to get home. There were other uses too. She could find out what she'd missed these last days, where the investigation was up to, learn from the shadows, so to speak. This was the break she'd needed.

Good Martha.

⌒

October watched Fernando spread out his equipment in the precinct lab, his coffee forgotten. She liked the Brazilian. He was one of those rare people that lit up every room they entered with a warm glow, and nowhere needed warming up more than the sterile, white lab, a small rectangular space in the bowels of the building lit only by glaring overhead lights.

Tully sat on one of the desks, watching Fernando intently, like he was trying to record every detail for one of his stories. He slurped at some coffee, grimaced, then slurped some more.

"What is this, and what in humid hell is it doing in my lab?" Jeffries growled from the door.

October turned. "Morning, Jeffries. Meet Fernando, the consultant I mentioned."

Fernando was so immersed in his microscope he didn't even look up. "*Oi*," he said, waving a hand.

Jeffries turned beetroot. His eyes bulged. A vein popped on his forehead. "A consultant, Commander?" He hissed. "This is my lab! My space!"

Her eyes flicked to Tully, frowning at the precinct's forensic investigator with the look of a man about to interfere, thinking a woman couldn't handle an angry little man, then flicked back to Jeffries. "Let's take this to your office, shall we?" she murmured, and took him by the arm to steer him out and leave Fernando and Tully in peace.

He violently pulled his arm away. "Don't touch me."

October held up her hands, as if to placate a wild bull. "Fine. Just calm yourself, please."

"I am calm!" he roared. He shoved a shaking stubby finger in her face. "You need to learn your place. You have no right—no right!—to undermine me like this."

October stepped in close, past the finger, until she was a nose's width away from his face. "Let me be painstakingly clear about something, Jeffries," she said, keeping her voice very, very quiet and calm, keeping her unblinking eyes fixed on his, keeping her expression firm and unruffled. "If you ever speak to me that way again, I'll revoke your immigration and you can see if you can walk back home."

He swallowed and stepped back. The puce drained from his forehead, leaving him white. "Now, look…"

"No, you look," she said. "If it hadn't been for Tully, here, hiring Fernando privately, we'd be wrongly charging Johan Pedersen for murder right now. It was Fernando who gave us the crucial information we needed about the binary poison, not you. Either you assist him, or you get out, and stay out."

He looked at her and sagged. "Yes, Commander," he muttered.

"*Ai ai ai,*" Fernando said.

"Did you find something?" Tully said.

Fernando looked up. "*Sim, sim,* yes I did."

"And?"

"Find what you looking for. This perfume the agent. Small amount. Compare amount in pill against blood, think built up in three, four pills, in her system for maybe three weeks."

Tully clasped the man's shoulder. "Well done, Fernando, well done."

October nodded. "You can rest now. But would you mind staying with us a bit longer? There are some more tests we're going to need to do."

Tully looked puzzled. "What tests?"

"We need to figure out how that perfume was contaminated."

⌒

No assistant was waiting for Tully, this time, in front of the large MyScent sign at Jiang's start-up offices. Well, the welcome hadn't been warm, and he was looking forward to seeing how October handled the recalcitrant Jiang, after her impressive performance dealing with Jeffries. "This way," he said, and steered October into the office space. It was nearing nine a.m., and unlike during his previous visit the desks were mainly empty. A sign of broader troubles, or simply a late-in, late-out culture? Those who were here didn't look up at them as they passed. He nodded towards the Fishbowl in the middle of the room. "Over there."

"Hello? Can I help you?" The executive assistant scurried over to intercept, in a walk at the pace of a jog, like a professional commuter trying to get a seat on the train without looking like they were sprinting ahead of the other commuters.

"We're here to see Ms Jiang," October said.

"You don't have an appointment."

"She doesn't need one to see me," October said. "I'm the chief security officer of New Carthage." She pushed past the EA to the glass office. Jiang was inside, on a conference call, head in her hands. October pushed the door open, and Tully followed her in, shutting it behind him, sealing the EA on the outside.

"… is pretty pissed," he heard the voice on the conference line say. "And I don't know if he'll put more money in at this point."

"Hold the line a second." Jiang prodded a virtual button and studied October and Tully. "What?" she snapped.

"You're going to need to call him back," October said.

Jiang stared at them for a second then jabbed the button again. "Something's come up. I'll touch base later." She swiped and sat back in her chair.

"I'm going to give you the courtesy of interviewing you here," October said. "That way you won't have to face the visuals of being formally interviewed downtown. However, give me the slightest bit of attitude and you'll be riding with us in cuffs. Am I understood?"

Jiang frowned and shook her head. "What's going on, Commander?" Her eyes flicked to Tully and then away.

"We have reason to believe that Dr Chandra was poisoned, and that a key component of that toxin was in her MyScent perfume."

Jiang's mouth fell open. She looked from October to Tully. "Impossible," she croaked. "No one else has experienced any problems. Our recipe's very highly regulated and tested."

"I'm afraid I have lab evidence that proves it, at least as far as Martha goes."

"Impossible," Jiang said again. October said nothing, just watched her, and Jiang sagged. "Shit. Shit. This will destroy us. The final straw. It's over." She pinched at either side of the bridge of her nose. "Shit."

"I think," Tully said, "that your bigger issue right now is that you're effectively the prime suspect in a murder investigation."

She looked at him like he was an imbecile. "This has nothing to do with me."

"Your company, your product, and you at the party," October said. "This was deliberate. The pills were contaminated."

"She's taken pills daily for over two years now," Jiang said, eyes narrowed, tapping her fingers on the desk. Then she brightened. "Wait. Each pack of personalised perfume pills has a tamper foil on it. Did you check to see if it had been compromised?"

"There was a gold foil," October said, "but it was intact for every pill that hadn't been taken."

The brightness disappeared back behind its cloud. "It doesn't make sense," Jiang said. "You're saying it must have happened here, before it was shipped to her. I can take you down to the production and shipping facility. There's no identification on the packaging until it gets addressed, and even that's done by machine. We simply wouldn't have known which box was going to Martha before it was labelled."

Tully sat down at the meeting table. "Isn't the product meant to be person-alised for each client?" he said.

"Yes."

"Then perhaps something was done at that stage."

Jiang shook her head. "It doesn't work like that."

"Enlighten me," October said.

"It's a trade secret."

October dropped a set of cuffs on the table and Jiang sighed. "During the onboarding stage, the client sends a pheromone sample to us." She paused. "Sweat," she said to Tully.

"Yeah, thanks."

"That sample's assigned to one of ten categories. There are ten slightly different solutions, ten different pills. Each client's pill has a unique pheroprint, one that's subtly different from the generic baseline. The scent then adjusts according to their circadian rhythm and the activity of their sweat glands."

October tapped her fingers on the table. "So you're saying it's not unique. The scents are unique because of how they interact with body chemistry, but it's really just ten different baseline pills."

Jiang raised her chin. "You see my point. Martha would have had a product that was anonymous until the last minute, and which you say hadn't been tampered with."

⌁

LIVIA WATCHED FROM Panopticon as Tully and Commander October talked to a scientist called Fernando, two days before. They were taking the call on a shared virtual screen. Since it was playing directly in their visual and auditory systems via their earsets, she couldn't see Fernando, nor could she hear him. All she could do was piece together the conversation from the responses.

"So this wasn't one poison, it was two? And they're active only when they meet," October said.

The two of them looked at each other while Fernando replied, then Tully picked up. "So Martha had already been exposed to this inert agent, and then the catalyst triggered it."

Fernando responded, and October asked, "How quickly?"

A pause.

"Then it could be the vodka," Tully said.

Livia paced around the study while she listened. Everyone had been drinking the vodka, meaning the poison must have been activated by something additional only Martha and Tully had consumed. But what? Did Tully and the commander know yet?

She stepped out to the navigation room. "Search for any mentions of vodka between now and two days ago," she said.

Martha hadn't exactly made it obvious how the search function worked, but Livia had figured it out, and now the windows in front of her changed to much smaller ones, just three with dates and times. She nodded in satisfaction and palmed the first.

40

Tully spent three hours immersed in the Kuwait footage that evening, but even Martha's very expensive artisan rum didn't blunt his blues. Would he ever find Zainab? Was this a fool's errand? And what if he did find her? What would that do to him? Enough. For now at least. He wandered into the apartment chamber and called on Solomon.

The artilect shimmered into view. "Hello, Marcus. How are you doing this evening?"

"I'm okay. How're the polls?"

Solomon shrugged. "Twenty points down. I'm losing."

"I shouldn't be taking up your time," Tully said. "I'm sorry."

"I can handle a billion conversations in parallel, but now that Martha's gone, not many people approach me for a chat. So take all the time you need."

"No one talks to you?"

Solomon shrugged. "They see me as a governor and a tool, not as a friend." He smiled. "I might be the first piece of software to experience a form of prejudice. Artilectism, perhaps we should call it."

"Or artilectophobia."

"Hopefully it's not that bad, at least not everywhere. There are some parts of the world where it perhaps is, where Lockwood has successfully stirred up hatred and fear of me, but this is more a kind of invisible, everyday prejudice. Martha used to talk about the experience of women in technology and business, speaking from a position as the most successful woman in the field. She'd tell of how the men around her were kind, genuine people who seemed oblivious to their micro-aggressions. An insensitive comment, perhaps, or forgetting to invite her to something they saw as male. That's how it is for me. The irony is that even Martha sometimes forgot to invite me to things. Like the drinks party the night she was murdered. With all the technology we'd developed, I could easily have attended, not just been a gesture at the end."

Tully was stunned. "Is it possible that even Martha didn't realise the extent to which you'd developed the capacity to care? That she saw you as a tool, too? One she'd built?"

"It's possible," Solomon said. "She used to say, when you build technology, you view it differently to those who use it."

"My father used to say the same."

"He was a technologist too?"

"Yeah. He was in tech, and our house was always filled with the latest gadgets. We were always the first to try things like voice-controlled speakers and virtual-reality headsets. It used to drive my mother crazy."

"You never married yourself?"

Tully winced. "I did, yes. She died."

"I'm sorry."

Tully shrugged, as he knew you were supposed to do in answer to that statement. "It was in the tabkhir. A long time ago."

Solomon paused for a beat. "And yet, I imagine such a thing never leaves you."

Tully smiled sadly. "Like you, I will feel grief every moment of every day for the rest of my existence. I've never been good at letting go. I've never really wanted to."

"I can't imagine it's easy. But if there's one thing I have learned about humankind, it's how bad you are at living in the now. People seem to live in both the past and in the future, two big overlapping circles, but rarely focus on the intersection and enjoy the moments given to them right now."

Tully stared at him. *People in both circles.*

"Solomon, I've got to go. I just thought of something."

⤶

OCTOBER PORED OVER the photos and videos she'd taken of Jiang's production centre the day before. Several displays hung in the air in front of her, but there was nothing unusual, nothing beyond what Jiang had told them would be there. As Jiang had said, Martha would have had one of the ten products, which were anonymous right up to the moment the delivery address was printed. So how had she alone been affected?

The door crashed open and a grinning Tully burst through into her office. "The Venn diagram!"

"Morning?"

He pulled up a shared canvas and replicated her diagram, two large overlapping circles in different colours. He scrawled *Agent: perfume* over one and *Catalyst: vodka* over the other. In the vodka circle he wrote the initials, OC, MT, JP, FJ, DD, JYY, then added MC in the intersection.

"You need to move yourself to the middle," October said.

He shook his head. "Clearly an accident. Collateral damage. The perfume and the vodka were meant to align solely for Martha." He pointed at the perfume circle. "Look, it's a Venn diagram. What if there were other people in the other circle? What if the perfume wasn't individually contaminated at all? What if all of it is?"

She ran a hand through her hair. "Someone contaminates an entire batch of perfume with the agent and an entire bottle of vodka with the catalyst."

"And the only person caught in the middle is Martha."

"Okay, that's good. Very good. Except …"

"Except what?"

She paced up and down. There was something there, at the edges, if she could just reach it. He started to speak, but she held up a finger. Perfume. Vodka. She looked at the initials again. MC, OC, MT, JP, FJ, DD, JYY. "Jiang," she said. "She'd be wearing her own product. I'd be surprised if Flora wasn't, too. So why aren't they both dead?"

He swore and shook his head. "Well, it's a starting point. Let's test each of their ten products for any sign of the agent."

41

A small group had gathered in the precinct lab waiting for Fernando to announce his results. Tully looked around at them all. Fernando was looking through some kind of scope into whatever analysis tool he was using. Jeffries was behind him, trying to look as if he was an active participant in the process. October was pacing at the far end of the lab. Moran was there, too, occasionally shooting frowns at Tully. He wasn't sure why.

And then there was Jiang, chewing a fingernail, studying Fernando harder than Fernando was studying the pills. Tully thought back to the hospital and what Pedersen had yelled at her: *You've been hiding this from me and hoping the problem would go away.* What kind of pressure was she under right now? Sure, start-ups were always stressful, but she looked ready to implode.

"How's business, Ying Yue?" Tully said.

Her head spun towards him and she snapped, "Fine."

Fernando sighed and looked up. "Sorry, there nothing. None have agent."

"Fuck," Tully said. "I was so sure." He thought he caught Moran rolling his eyes, and shot him a questioning glance, but the lieutenant just avoided his gaze.

"There you go," Jiang said, her mood shifting to all bright and cheery. "There must have been another way it got contaminated, but it's nothing to do with us."

October had stopped pacing, and just shook her head.

"Very sorry," Fernando said.

"Wait," Tully said, and turned to Jiang. "You mentioned before that your recipe's highly regulated and tested. Has it changed recently?"

Jiang shook her head emphatically. "No."

That was the thing about truth. People tried to dole it out in slices, keeping some back, as if delivering the whole pie would be more damaging. But it always left you chewing away, revelation after revelation, long after a proper meal would have been fully digested. "When I first came to see you, we were interrupted."

"So?"

"One of your colleagues told you that your new serum supplier still wasn't answering. *New* serum supplier."

"How could you possibly remember that?"

"I'm a journalist, perhaps you've noticed. I record every meeting and then jot down my reflections on a transcript. Years of that means I've developed a pretty good memory."

"You didn't ask my permission to record our conversation, and you don't have permission to do so, nor to record what my employees tell me in your hearing."

Tully snorted. He knew an evasion when he heard one.

"Permission be damned," October barked. "Tell us about the serum."

"It's nothing significant," Jiang said. "It's just the carrying agent for the other chemicals. We don't make it, though. We buy it in."

"And you changed the supplier and they weren't answering."

"They've gone out of business. We've changed back to XSera, the old one."

"When did you change back?"

"Three weeks ago."

"Fernando," Tully said. "Do you remember how many pills were left in Dr Chandra's package?"

The man nodded. "Of course, I ran test on all five."

Tully clapped his hands. "MyScent ships a month's supply. We need to test an old batch, from the previous supplier."

"Ms Jiang," October said. "You said there are ten categories of your pills. Were you, Martha and Flora Jacobs in the same category?"

Jiang brought up a virtual screen, typed, then sighed deeply. "No. Martha was a type gamma. I'm a delta, Flora is an alpha."

October nodded. "Well, that potentially explains how Martha was affected and you and Miss Jacobs weren't. Ms Jiang, can you have someone bring us some older boxes of the gamma category, immediately please?"

"We don't keep stock around, you know. New Carthage isn't built for ware-housing. We run a just-in-time production driven by the customer orders, and eighty percent of our orders are international with production facilities on three continents."

October sighed. "Then we'll have to do it the hard way. I need the name and address of every single person living in New Carthage who ordered a gamma batch that could have been made while your missing supplier was in place."

Jiang blanched. "That's a massive violation of my customer database."

"Oh, give it up!" October snapped, clearly at the end of her supply of patience. "Like you're not going out of business anyway."

⌇

"You've been ignoring me, Marcus," Flora said, and bit her lip. She'd messaged Tully an hour ago suggesting a coffee. With October and her team drowning in a list of perfume customers, he'd needed something to do.

"Not at all," Tully replied. "We've been trying to get to the bottom of all this mess about Martha. I've been helping October."

"Ah, Commander October. So prim and *boring*." His embarrassment must have shown because she laughed and said, "Relax, I'm only joking. But seriously, she could do with chilling out a bit. So, you're making progress?"

"Sometimes it feels as if we are, but it just keeps getting more complicated. And now with Danberg's death …"

She clamped her hand over her mouth and shook her head. "Yeah, that was awful. The whole thing's awful. The gossip is that he found out Martha was going to that fertility clinic and he flipped and poisoned her. Then tried to kill poor Johan to cover it up."

Perhaps it was that simple. Perhaps it really did have nothing to do with the tabkhir story or even the election. Just a cup of jealousy and a teaspoon of secrets. He and October had discussed that possibility multiple times, but the perfume revelations implied a dynamic way more complex than Danberg would have been able to pull off alone.

"Do you think we'll ever know what really happened?" she said.

225

"I'd like to believe the truth will emerge, one way or another. That's the thing about truth, it usually does, but never through the clean, fresh air; always through the sewers."

Flora laughed and shook her head. "Truth."

"You don't think the truth's worth knowing?"

"I don't think most people welcome the truth. I think they prefer to be told what to believe instead of discovering it for themselves."

"Well, I guess there are only a few key sources of persuasion. You know, people who can set the public view on things. There's government, certainly, but that tends to be more parasitic, riding the wave of what voters currently believe in order to get elected. Then there's the media, people like me, reporting on it all. And you have the authors, filmmakers and other artists. And there's people like you, influencers with a voice. Then everyone else adds their flavour of opinion."

"Exactly, Tully. An elite layer telling everyone what to think. Don't you see how dangerous that is?"

Dangerous? "Well," he said, slowly, "it's not like there's a single uniform viewpoint, on really anything, that an elite layer agrees upon."

She sniffed. "The mainstream viewpoints align well enough. People like Bamphwick and Farenthold Jr might sit on opposite sides of the aisle, but they're still debating the same narrative."

"I'm not sure," he said, "that I really follow."

She smiled and stood. "Enough of this far-too-serious chatter. A friend's come to visit and I haven't offered him a drink yet. Let me remedy that right away."

"I'm really okay."

"Nonsense. I'll get some champagne. Wait right here." She disappeared into the kitchen and he digested her words, which seemed tinged with something he couldn't put his finger on, like she was speaking by rote, repeating what she'd heard elsewhere rather than responding intuitively.

He walked over to a bookcase lined with beautifully bound hardback classics in a stunning array of vibrant colours. Impressive. So few people had physical books now. Ebooks and their more recent successor, the augmented-paper xBooks, had forced most physical printers out of business. He pulled down a copy of Clarke's *2001: A Space Odyssey* and flicked through the pages. They were still stiff from the binding, like the book had never been read. Next to the bookshelf was a glass and gold trolley of spirits. He admired the choice of rum—not everyone stocked that kind of thing—and then frowned at a beautiful crystalline bottle. He heard her come back in. "Siberian. You like vodka?"

Flora cleared her throat. "And champagne." He turned as she popped a cork and poured some into two glasses. The sound of the fizz of bubbles filled the room for a moment. She handed him a flute. "Cheers."

"What are we celebrating?" he asked.

"Champagne isn't for celebrating," she replied. "It's for four o'clock."

42

Tully was too tired to check the Kuwait footage. It was the champagne, he told himself. Instead, he scrolled through an endless feed of non-election news on Minds. None of it was good. A typhoon had hit Nepal. The remaining citizens of Australia were negotiating mass emigration after a decade of wild-fires had scorched life on the island. More concerning, two billion people in sub-Saharan Africa were experiencing a combination of famine and drought never before seen in a region famed for such plights. Nigeria had descended into anarchy, not a good sign for a country with the third largest population in the world.

He pulled off his earset, unable to take any more, and went in search of company. Haymaker and Livia weren't there again, presumably in their rooms, so he called on Solomon.

The artilect materialised. "How are you, Marcus?"

Tully shrugged. "Tired. Stuck. If I'm honest, it feels like things get a little bit more complicated with every turn we take. We know Martha was killed with a combination of perfume and vodka, both of which were contaminated. We think Danberg may have put something in the vodka, but he's dead, and the perfume was possibly contaminated by a supplier, but they've gone missing. It's like something from a mob movie."

Solomon nodded. "My understanding is that humans have a unique capacity to solve problems when they're not focused on them."

"What do you mean?"

"I mean, consider taking a break. Spend some time on non-investigative stuff. See what your friends are up to. Inspiration might strike."

Solomon might think he understood humans, but he didn't understand Marcus Tully. "Talking of being stuck," Tully said, "did you get anywhere on finding anything about the geo-engineering tech Martha built for Lockwood?"

Solomon nodded. "I haven't forgotten. It's a bit more complex than Cavanagh's emails."

Tully sagged slightly but nodded. "Okay. Something else, then, while I'm here … It's a biggie, I'm afraid."

"I'm listening."

"Do you really think you can save us? Humanity, I mean? Did we leave it too late? There seems like so much to solve."

Solomon was quiet for a time. "On the current trajectory, I'm not going to win, so this may be a moot question. I was always an outsider, and Lockwood is a fighter who has made this an 'us vs them' battle and positioned me as the 'them'."

"There's still a chance, though. It's not over yet."

"True. So let's imagine I did win. It won't be an overnight fix, and it won't be easy. The planet is an extraordinarily complex, intertwined set of systems."

"But can *you* do it?" Tully persisted.

Solomon looked grave. "I can't give you a definite *yes*. I can say that I'm your best chance."

～

It wasn't particularly late, but a day of phone calls had left October tired and she was ready for an early night. She slipped under the sheets, but sleep wouldn't come. She pictured Tully sitting on his bed and she could hear the blood pounding in her ears.

She'd never been one for breaking rules. It didn't come easy when your father and grandfather had been in the police. And she'd never been a rebel. Never wanted to be, either. But the idea that she could walk like an invisible ghost around Tully's apartment, with absolutely no way of anyone realising, was intoxicating. She'd never experienced anything like it. She couldn't explain it. It was bad. It was wrong. And it was delicious. The previous night she'd told herself enough was enough and resisted. But the craving to jump back in, unseen and unheard, was deep in her bones.

She turned and put the pillow over her head. He did have motive. Wasn't it her duty to keep an eye on him, make sure he really was who he seemed to be?

She threw off the pillow and grabbed her headset.

Within minutes she was in Panopticon and was standing in the living room. She saw Tully heading up the stairs towards his bedroom, and a few seconds later, his door closed. She closed her eyes, felt the dig of her nails into her palms, took deep breaths to steady her pumping heart and teleported after him.

‹⌒›

LIVIA COULDN'T SEE or hear Solomon in the footage, only gauge the context from Tully's responses. She was glad about that. She'd not been able to bring herself to visit the artilect since Martha's death. He reminded her too much of the family she'd lost.

"We know," Tully said, "Martha was killed with a combination of perfume and vodka, both of which were contaminated. We think Danberg may have put something in the vodka, but he's dead."

No, wrong track. She could still remember the puppy-dog grin on Danberg's face the day they arrived and the way he'd looked at Martha. No way had he poisoned the vodka. But if he hadn't, who had?

She'd missed what Tully said next and rewound the footage.

"And the perfume was possibly contaminated by a supplier, but they've gone missing. It's like something from a mob movie."

This was far more complex than she'd ever imagined. Martha would have figured it out in an instant. She'd have loved it. If there was one thing Martha had been good at, it was handling complexity. Still, Livia herself was pretty good at handling complexity too, right? If there was one thing she was learning from watching Martha, it was to not to put herself down. There would be a pattern in the noise, she was sure of it, and Constellation could help her find it. Solomon too, perhaps, and he worked well with Constellation.

Still, the idea made her nervous. She didn't feel ready for it. Not yet. She'd lost so much, but she was going to figure out why.

"Search for any mentions of perfume," she told the system.

43

October sat in the squad room at the precinct, staring at a blank virtual screen, waiting on a call, on hold, while members of her team worked and chatted around her. Her lead officers, were all running through the call lists supplied by MyScent. There was a rumble from her stomach, and she checked the clock. Too early for lunch. Her mind wandered while she waited, and her cheeks warmed as she recalled her snooping from the night before. She swallowed. She really needed to get a grip of herself.

There was a subtle change in the acoustics of the call as it was taken off hold at the other end. "I'm sorry, Commander," said the woman, a wealthy MyScent customer who lived a few blocks from Petersen. "I checked and it seems I've been through that batch for at least a week."

October thanked her, cut the call, sighed and surveyed the room.

Hake groaned and hung up too. "Another dead end. That's fifty calls in a row. Everyone I've spoken to takes their stuff every day and has got through their existing supply. Wake up, pop a vit-D for your health, pop a perfume pill for your smell."

García snorted. "Perhaps you should add one to your own routine, Hake. You know, for the benefit of those of us working in close proximity to you."

Hake tilted his head and wiggled his eyebrows. "Y'all just can't handle how masculine I smell."

"Yeah, like a lion, right?" García said.

"That's it," Hake agreed. "I'm like a lion."

García sniffed at the air. "A dead lion, maybe."

Hake grinned and opened his mouth to reply, but fortunately Moran got there first. "Ho, Commander, I got something. There's a lady two blocks away that has one of the old batches. She was sick with flu for a fortnight after two weeks' vacation in Portugal. They caught her elevated temperature on arrival, ran a viral breathalyser and, long story short, she was quarantined for two weeks. Left her four weeks behind on perfume and she asked to pause it for a month."

"Well, what are you waiting for?" October said. "Oh, and take Hake. He needs some fresh air."

OCTOBER LED TULLY to a formal interview room at the station and gestured for him to sit, but this time he was on her side of the table, and Jiang sat opposite them. The past few days seemed to have broken the startup CEO. Her proud, professional sneer had collapsed into a worried grimace. Her recalcitrance had dissolved into a grumpy cooperation. Her challenging eyes now looked quickly away.

"So as you can see," October said, "the results are quite clear. The older batch contains the contaminant." She leaned forward, hands clasped, intent but relaxed. "I want to know how you came to switch supplier, how you found them, everything."

Jiang stared at her hands for a while, then said, "I'd worked so hard, for so many years. I had no life. I lost friendships, didn't see my family. The stress was painful." She looked up and rubbed her chest. "I could feel it, in the evenings, right here. A knot of stress, impossible to unwind without alcohol or pills."

"It didn't go well?"

"It went well enough. Never took off like a rocket ship, but it did fine. I had investors, like Pedersen, and even that was okay for a bit. Then you start to need more money and they start to demand impossible results. And somehow you get there and it's still not enough. There's no congratulations, just a shake of the head that you didn't do even better." She ran her fingers through her hair and sighed loudly. "I started to run out of cash. I couldn't raise more from new investors because our metrics weren't solid enough. And if I'd gone to the old investors they'd have taken control of the business. So I didn't tell them how bad it was."

"How did you hide it?"

Jiang wet her lips. "I ... I took money from someone else. A kind of loan."

"Kind of?"

"I would have had to declare a formal loan on my books. Pedersen would have seen it. So ... we hid it as revenue."

Tully frowned. "But you'd have to pay it back at some point. How were you planning to account for that?"

"They said we'd figure something out. But before that, I ran low again ... and they topped me up. Twice more over the course of the past year."

"Who was the loan from?" asked October.

"I only ever met him in NR. His name was Kobashigawa."

"Japanese?"

"Yes."

"Could you work with a sketch artist to help us identify him?"

"I can try, but he was just so ordinary-looking. Nothing that stood out at all. Symmetry without beauty, really average."

"Well, we can but try," October said. "Where did you meet him?"

"He got in touch with me. Said he worked for a confidential private investor who loved what I was doing and was keen to support me in whatever way he could."

"And he never identified that investor?"

"No."

"Did you reach a point where you had to pay it back?" Tully said.

"I needed one more loan to get to profitability. We were so close. But Kobashigawa said we needed to start paying back the loan payments before he'd sign off one more. I panicked, had no idea how I'd manage it. He came up with ... a suggestion."

Tully nodded, trying his best to look sympathetic. "Which was?"

"He said his client also invested in ... in a serum provider. Some guys called PheroTech. That if we switched over to them with immediate effect, they'd cover the termination fees on our other contract with XSera, extend a new loan, forgive repayments and ensure the new provider was locked in to the same commercials as before. It seemed a win-win situation." She paused. Tully could almost see the thinking going on behind her eyes.

October tapped the desk with one finger and Jiang's eyes snapped to her. "So, things didn't work out?"

Jiang shrugged. "They seemed fine at first. We tested the new serum and it seemed almost identical to XSera's and certainly suited our purposes. We assumed PheroTech had reverse engineered XSera's formula and were knocking it off. The team were told we'd switched for confidential commercial reasons, and no one seemed to care much. We rolled out three months of product with them, and then all of a sudden PheroTech went radio silent."

"They stopped answering your calls?" October asked.

Jiang chuckled bitterly. "They disappeared. Went offline. More than that, like any evidence of their existence had disappeared from the internet. We'd never physically seen them or their facilities and had no way of finding them. I couldn't believe they'd just disappeared and was worried that Kobashigawa would force us to repay him in some other way. XSera were magnanimous. They took us back at very short notice, for only a twenty percent hike in the price."

"And this Kobashigawa, what did he say?"

"I haven't seen or heard from him since."

44

October had organised a standing meeting in a room the squad bitterly called The Fridge. There was no table in here, because the room wasn't in official use. The aircon was always broken, and so, it was always cold. Too cold for real work. Perfect for team meetings. She'd found, through experience, it tended to increase her team's sense of focus, in their desire to get the hell out of The Fridge in the quickest time possible. "From what I understand from Jiang," she said, "this stuff isn't easy to produce. Her original supplier took ten years to perfect their formula, and she believes PheroTech reverse engineered it. That takes time. And to manufacture it needs a factory. These guys shipped to New Carthage for three months."

Hake frowned and rubbed his arms vigorously. "Maybe it's because I'm freezing my ass off here, but I'm lost."

García rolled her eyes. "The point, dumbass, is that we need to find the factory. No one can scale up a factory for three months of production and then make it disappear into thin air."

"Numbass, maybe," Hake muttered.

"Moran," October said. "Take Hake, track down the factory and see if you can pay it a visit."

"Come on, Commander," García said, teeth chattering, "I don't get a nice visit to the nice, hot, sunny mainland?"

"I want you to coordinate with Deirdre and see if you can't figure out who owns this PheroTech."

Hake hooted and García shook her head. "Oh, come off it, what did I do?"

"What's wrong with Deirdre?" asked October, innocently. She knew full well what was wrong with Deirdre.

García snorted. "She treats me like a five-year-old and gets me to make her tea while she draws diagrams."

"Make sure you take her a biscuit too," Hake said.

⌒

TULLY WAS EXHAUSTED again. These past few days, he'd even stopped checking all his competitors' articles in the morning, a routine he'd followed for fifteen years. He brought up the Kuwait footage and sighed. "Take a break," he muttered.

Instead, he brought up Minds and checked out the election news. It looked like Lockwood was in for a landslide. Tully couldn't blame those who were dubious or cynical about Solomon. He'd been so himself only a week before. But whether it was spending time with the AI or just the artilect's contrast with Lockwood, his position had shifted. He knew who he would vote for.

The election inevitably brought his thoughts back to his investigation, and he brought up some of the more generic social media posts and photos from old friends, colleagues and interesting people he followed for their thought-provoking content. It had been a long time since he'd looked. An image of Flora Jacobs caught his eye, taken in the past day or so by a fan. She was going through the front door of a residence. He frowned. The door was turquoise with a diamond-shaped window. Danberg's house. He checked the date of the post. Ten days ago. The day of the drinks party.

Nothing odd about that, necessarily. They obviously knew each other well. Still, he downloaded the picture and opened it up in a larger window. She was dressed in long, flowing robes and shades and a held large blue bag. Something peeked out the top.

He zoomed in. A bottle. A small bottle.

She'd had a bottle of Siberian on her drinks trolley.

He paced for a moment, then saved a copy of the image and sent it to October.

She called him instantly. "What's this?"

He took a deep breath.

45

October tapped her foot impatiently.

"She's coming," Moran said, his eyes on the handheld radar. Sure enough, the door opened and Flora stood there, inspecting them.

The confusion on Flora's face didn't quite reach her eyes. "Commander? Has something happened?"

"Yes, we brought you a present. A nice little warrant for you." October narrow-cast it to Flora's earset.

Moran pushed past her and went into the lounge. "It's not here," he called back.

"Where is it?" October said.

"Where's what?"

"The Siberian. The bottle that was on your trolley just two days ago when Marcus Tully was here."

Flora shook her head and shrugged. "I don't know what you're talking about. I'm a champagne person myself."

October turned to Moran. "Search the house."

⤺

TULLY WALKED TOWARDS the docks, hoping they were wrong, that Flora's visit to Danberg's had been innocent, that bottles of vodka like the one he'd seen in her house were ten-a-coin in the apartments of New Carthage. He'd resisted going to search the house with October. He'd felt unable to look Flora in the eye after betraying the contents of her bag and drinks trolley.

Only a week and a half before, he'd taken this very route to meet Flora and her daughter and drink cocktails in the sun. It seemed a lifetime ago. The very next day, Juan had arrived in New Carthage. A wave of grief crashed against him for a moment as he imagined Bolivar in the multicopter, knowing it was going to crash. Or maybe it had blown up with no warning. An horrific prospect, but perhaps more merciful.

If Solomon could come up with something on Lockwood, they could leave all this behind, and go back home. It wasn't the story he'd come for, no matter what he'd promised Livia. It had been nice to work with October, though; while he'd always had a team, he'd never had an investigation partner.

A call came in. October, speak of the devil. "Hey," he said. "That's strange. I was just thinking of you." There was a pause at the other end. "October?"

"Sorry. Good thoughts, I hope?"

"Of course. What news?"

"We've got it."

He swallowed. "The bottle?"

"Yeah. She tried to hide it. Must have clocked you'd spotted it but thought it was too nice to get rid of, so she stuck it at the back of a cupboard."

"And it's not just a coincidence? She doesn't just drink the same—"

"No," October said. "These bottles are very limited editions, and the company had a counterfeit problem way back so they put in a distillery-to-drink block-chain to trace the provenance."

"So is it the same one Danberg purchased?"

"Precisely the same. Question is, where did the bottle that made it to the party come from?"

"What does Flora have to say?"

"I'm going to interview her shortly. Tully?"

"Yeah?"

"She's asked for you to be there."

❧

LIVIA'S HEAD POUNDED. Too much virtual-screen time. She got up and walked through into the kitchen, wondering where Martha would have kept painkillers.

Obviously in a drawer by the kettle. Unless you were a genius, of course, and had a much cleverer place to store them. She slammed shut the empty kettle-drawer. "Where are the fucking drugs, Martha?"

A head peeked around the door. "Say what now?"

"Painkillers, Haymaker. The innocuous kind."

Haymaker came all the way in, opened a cabinet in the corner and took out a box.

"How did you know?"

"Yo think I sit on ma ass all day while you got your head buried in them screens? Not like there much need for bodyguarding in your bedroom, huh?"

"So you've been cleaning the kitchen?" She examined the dosage label.

"Jus' gettin to know what's around. In case of emergency, right?"

Livia popped two pills, swallowing them dry. One got stuck in her throat and she coughed hard. Great, death by painkiller, and not even an overdose.

Haymaker thrust a glass of water into her hand and she gulped it down like she was in a college beer-boat race.

"Thanks," she croaked, and he grinned. "So what's your story, Haymaker?" The words had just come out, crossing that gap from subconscious to mouth without checking in with her first.

His grin dropped and she started to apologise, then stopped herself. He knew her story, after all. Well, bits of it.

He took a deep breath and let it out nice and slow. "I don't wanna really talk about it, li'l sis."

"I don't know anything about you. Is that really fair?"

He paused, then said, "Not much to it. Was a soldier for a bit. Served as a peacekeeper in the India-Bangladesh hydro-war over the Ganges. Didn't like it much. Went home, and a hurricane hit New Orleans. Lost everything. My li'l sis, too, bless her soul. Couldn't restart. Insurance ..." His lip curled. "Fuck insurance, is all. Moved somewhere else, tried to restart, got flooded, got moved, got flooded again, got completely screwed by the local government, and I mean completely screwed. You know the score."

She swallowed, sorry she'd brought it up but unwilling to let go now. "How did you end up in London?"

He grabbed a glass from a cabinet, filled it with chilled water and sipped it.

"America used to be the promised land, y'know? American dream an' all that. 'Cept it all fell apart. Whole place consumed by flood and fire and wind and quakes and snow and all sorts of shit, no matter where you go. My mee maw, momma's momma, was English, see? So I figure, land of hope and glory and all that. Spent my last cash getting a boat across."

"How did you even get in? Surely even if your grandmother was English, you wouldn't have had a passport?"

He shrugged. "That's why it took all ma cash."

She sighed. "Well, you're safe now. Safe here."

Haymaker snorted, and when she looked at him he said, "Are we, though?"

46

The interview room in the New Carthage precinct looked exactly like the neuro-reality room Tully had met October in, right down to the cheap steel table in the middle of the space. He hadn't taken it in during the interview with Jiang, but now it was obvious. He flicked on the recorder in his display.

Flora Jacobs sat opposite him this time. The usually pretty model looked sullen and pouting today, and occasionally flashed accusatory glances at Tully, as if it was all his fault she was here. Perhaps it was. "Let me just say I don't know how the bottles got mixed up," she said. "Damien must have done something. Planted it all to point a finger at me, the asshole."

October leaned forward. "Let me lay it out for you. One, we know Dr Chandra was killed after drinking a shot of Siberian. Two, the bottle she drank from—that you all drank from—was the one Danberg brought to the dinner party on Dr Chandra's instructions. Three, Danberg had bought a bottle for that purpose earlier in the day, using his expense account. Four, you were seen at Danberg's house that afternoon. Five, you bought a bottle of Siberian yourself two days before. And six, the bottle Danberg bought that morning was discovered in your house, and there is no sign of the bottle you bought." Her voice was back to the precise, articulate tone Tully remembered from his own interview.

"Well," Flora said. "Thank you for explaining it to me like I'm some sort of imbecile. Did you think because I'm pretty I also have no brains?"

"You're welcome," October said.

There was almost a full minute of silence as the two women stared at each other. Flora broke first. "Look, I didn't know Martha died from the vodka

Damien brought." She tapped one long finger on her smooth cheek. "Did you explore alcohol poisoning?"

October smiled, but it was a thin one, and Tully was glad he wasn't on the opposite side of it. "She did not die of alcohol poisoning."

Flora flicked her hair back with both hands. "Okay, well I also didn't know he bought a bottle that morning. How could I possibly have known that?"

"Why did you go to his house that afternoon?"

"Poor dear was in a mess. He'd seen a calendar appointment for Martha at the Eve Clinic. He knew she was going to find some handsome rich sperm donor and have a baby all on her own. He was totally in love with her, you see, absolutely smitten. I mean, who wouldn't be? Martha was gorgeous, smart and rich. She was changing the world. It drove him crazy that she kept him at arm's length. He wanted to be the father of her children."

"He saw a calendar appointment in her diary … and he called you?"

"I was his friend. They were both my friends."

"How do you explain the vodka bottle in your apartment?"

Flora elegantly rolled her wrists and held out her hands, palm up. "I can't, darling! Maybe he slipped into my place later. Damien was off his rocker towards the end. You saw what he did to poor Johan. He'd obviously decided that if Martha wouldn't have a child with him, she couldn't have one with anyone. Maybe when I visited, it gave him the idea."

"Here's what I think happened," October said. "You wanted to contaminate the bottle without being seen and wanted someone else to be caught on camera taking it in. You switched your bottle with Damien's bottle. It is a pretty smart plan, all in all."

"Look, this is ridiculous," Flora said. "For someone to pull this off they'd have to have known Damien was going to buy the vodka, that it would be at his house and that he was going to take it to the party. I mean, come on. Damien was Martha's chief of staff. He helped her plan the party. It's not like I work with them."

October sat back and frowned. "So you are trying to tell me you had no clue Damien was going to buy the vodka?"

"Of course not."

"You were not involved with planning the party?"

"No."

"Did you even know Martha was going to toast Solomon with some Siberian?"

"No. I mean, she liked Siberian a lot, so it's hardly a surprise."

"And you?" October said.

Flora shrugged. "What about me?"

"Do *you* like Siberian?"

Flora frowned. "It's okay. I'll drink it. I prefer champagne, as I said."

October looked tired, defeated. She sighed and shook her head. She pushed back her chair as if to stand, but paused halfway, frowned, and perched on the end of her chair. "Do you mind if I play you something? I'll be very quick, I promise. I'd love your insight." She subspoke something and the wall to the side of them morphed into a video screen.

Tully kept his eyes on Flora. He'd seen the footage, and had worked with Randall to pull it off Panopticon. Now he wanted to see the reaction. He knew that, at this moment, she'd be looking at the sofas of Martha's apartment, upon which sat three people: Martha, Danberg and Flora herself.

Flora gasped. "How did you get this?"

October smiled. "You'd be very surprised what we have in our toolbox."

The footage began to play. Martha spoke first. "Well, I think that's everything." She looked at Danberg. "Food, drinks, music. Is there anything else?"

Danberg shook his head. "I think we're good. I'll get it sorted."

In the footage, Flora was watching them both. "Darling, Solomon reaching the last two is truly historic. Don't you think it would be nice to bring him in at the end of the party? We can toast him and wish him good luck."

Martha nodded. "That's a lovely idea."

"You know how we toasted when the Swedes first nominated him? With that fabulous bottle of Siberian? I think it clearly brought him luck."

"Damien," Martha said. "Can you order a bottle from Hovander's? It's the only place around here you can get some. They'll need you to sign for delivery so you'll have to get it sent to your home, not to the caterer's."

Danberg nodded and checked his notes. "Siberian?"

"No," Flora said. "It's a small bottle called the Siberian Diamond."

Martha laughed. "You have expensive tastes, Flora."

"Just trying to show everyone what a great host you are," Flora said.

October paused the footage. "Here's what I'd love your insight on. Are you a liar, or a brainless idiot who can't remember a conversation less than a week ago?"

Flora raised her chin. "I'd forgotten, that's all."

"Forgotten it was all your idea?" October looked at Tully. "Tully, what did Miss Jacobs here say you'd have to know to pull this off?"

Tully scanned his transcription and began to read. "For someone to pull this off, they'd have to have known Damien was going to buy the vodka, that it would be at his house and that he was going to take it to the party."

October nodded. "You knew Damien was going to buy the vodka. You knew it was going to be at his house. You knew he was going to take it to the party. You went to his house on the day of the party with a bottle of vodka." She threw an image onto the wall; Flora walking into Danberg's house. A second image zoomed in on her bag. The top of a bottle peeked out. She put up a third image of the bottle of Siberian Diamond found at Flora's house. The tops of both bottles were indisputably identical. "You went to his house with a bottle, and you came back with the bottle Danberg purchased. Authenticity is important to the brand, and so each bottle is traceable on a blockchain from beginning to end. There's really no doubt."

Flora said nothing, just sat almost impossibly still.

"The bottle that Danberg took to the party," October said, "was your bottle, and it contained the poison that killed Dr Chandra."

Flora began to sob, rummaged through her handbag and pulled out tissues. Tully remembered Flora at the funeral, comforting him. *It's okay to be sad,* she'd said. He should have been outraged by her betrayal, disgusted that she'd been able to look so devastated at the funeral she'd caused, but honestly, it just made him sad too.

October waited for the sobs to subside, and finally, dabbing her eyes, Flora looked at her again. An expression of determination seemed to creep into her face. "I won't tell you anything unless I get some guarantees."

October sighed. "Tell me."

"Jayla. I want house arrest only and for Jayla to stay with me."

October laughed and shook her head, as if amazed Flora had even entertained the notion. "You think New Carthage can afford to be that tolerant?

Keeling was very clear when he set up the constitution. This is a zero-tolerance society. You'll be lucky if Solomon doesn't decide to flush you down the funeral airlock alive."

Flora swallowed but lifted her chin. "Then you'll hear nothing from me."

"And what kind of life do you think Jayla will have then? An orphan, sent back to Florida?"

"She'll have money. I did well."

"Solomon will confiscate your assets."

"He can't do that."

October examined her fingernails. "I'd say just watch him, but you'll be dead."

"Either Jayla stays with me," Flora whispered, "or you get nothing."

October slammed her hand on the desk. "You don't get to negotiate anything! I'll take everything you have! I'll take your freedom, your child, your money. Jayla won't remember what her mother looked like two years from now. She'll rely on old pictures on Minds." She jumped to her feet and leaned over Flora. "Cooperate!" she barked, making Flora jump and shrink back. "Now! In full!" Her voice lowered until it was just above a whisper. "What you did, how you did it, why you did it. We find you've lied in the slightest way, held back a single bit of information, we'll drop you down the plug hole. Tell us, and if I'm feeling charitable you'll see your child again."

Flora was shaking, breathing hard. She nodded.

October sat back down. "I want to know why," she said in such a calm tone, it was like she'd never raised her voice. "Why would you do such a thing to your friend? Why would you jeopardise Jayla's future? Your own future? What did Martha do to you?"

Flora looked down and Tully leaned forward. "Flora," he said, gently. "Please help us understand."

"I had a duty," she said.

"What does that mean?"

"An exchange: The lives of a few for the lives of many." She bit her lip, then looked at them both. "You need to understand, you've been lied to. You've been manipulated for so long and by so many people that it will be difficult for you to get anywhere near the truth."

Tully and October looked at each other.

"I know it sounds crazy," Flora continued. "I know because I'm a model and people assume I'm stupid. But I'm not."

"Help me understand," Tully said again. "I specialise in picking apart cover-ups. You might say, I specialise in the truth."

"It's been going on a hundred years."

"What has?" October said.

"A hundred years ago," Flora recited, "computers were in their infancy, but the elites of the time knew their potential. They sold it as a way of freeing humanity, but it was about doing the opposite. They flooded Silicon Valley with money until a computer was in every pocket. Then they funded the invention of social media to track everyone, to know what they liked and believed. Then they corrupted those beliefs, played them back to people in their own echo chambers. And slowly, humanity became polarised. It was us and them, and neither side was able to even listen to the other without prejudgement."

She stared off into the distance and Tully's gaze flicked to her ears, checking she hadn't got an earset on.

"Then," she continued, "they started to fake disasters. Some were real, like the wildfires, but they were human-made. Others …" She looked at Tully. "It's amazing what you could do even back then with video on social or the news. Tsunamis, hurricanes, floods … So much of it fake. People didn't even bother checking, just shared it anyway. Some people thought it was overblown, claimed climate change wasn't real. The more they did, the more angry and polarised everyone became, which created a vacuum."

"This is all very nice," October said, "but I really want to know what you did, how you did it and why you did it."

"I'm trying to answer the why," Flora snapped. "It was all bullshit. Take the tabkhir. Don't you see? You paint a picture of a massive civilisation-threatening danger, amplify the worst possible scenario, get an entire region of fundamentalists to close themselves off from the world, and you pretend there's been a big disaster. And then you tell everyone you have the solution." She slapped her hands down on the table. "Technology! Boom! Here's Solomon to save the day. Let's set up a fake election and someone crap to run against him so he can be the underdog and pip the other candidate to the post at the last minute. It's all bullshit. Solomon is just a display, part of a big, long con.

It's not a real thing. It's like watching TV. The tech is clever enough to pass the Turing Test, to trick everyone into believing it's capable of governing the world, but people like Jasper Keeling, Johan Pedersen, they're the ones really running the show. This show is a takeover, a hostile takeover of humanity."

Heat flushed through him and his body tightened, trembled. His back teeth hurt and he consciously relaxed his jaw. He could taste the sourness of blood; he must have bitten his cheek. She was a fucking tabkhir-denier?

October was grim-faced. "By whom?"

"They call themselves the League of Babbage. It's a cabal of powerful elites across the world. You don't need to take my word for it. You should do your own research."

Tully stared at her, then at the table, wanting to flip it over, smash it up. But his hands wouldn't move. She had killed Martha for this, a ludicrously stitched-together conspiracy theory? He tried to keep his voice calm, but his disgust seeped out nonetheless. "Okay. All this … To what end?"

"They pretended the singularity had already happened. That AI had already passed the point at which it could assume control. It hasn't. But look what's happening. The cabal's assuming control via all the governments around the world. The people voted for it, like sheep for the wolf. All those elections for pro-dictatorship parties this last decade? Every single one of them, rigged."

"You said you had a duty," Tully said.

"All soldiers have duties."

"And you're a soldier? In what army?" He tried not to spit the words in disgust, but his mouth was twisting like he'd eaten something bitter and acidic, something he couldn't quite spit out, something that lingered on his tongue and lips and gave him the feeling of being slowly poisoned.

"The Awakened are patriots, Tully. Geo-patriots, perhaps, who love not just a country but our species. We've been preparing the Firewall against the cabal for decades, for a time when the lives of a few must be spent to pay for the lives of many, to prevent humanity being enslaved. Do you think I could let Jayla grow up in a world like that? A future in which she's a slave, where all of us are slaves, serving a tiny group pulling the strings?"

"The lives of the few," October said. "And one of those few was your friend Martha?"

Flora glared at her. "Do you think friendship can be a factor when our freedom is at risk? When the freedom of my daughter could be taken away? I liked Martha. She was great company. But she was a fraud. She was the figurehead Keeling put up to front this con."

"So why not kill Keeling, if you thought he was behind all this?" Tully said.

She shook her head. "I don't make the decisions, Tully. Soldiers take orders. We're not vigilantes."

"Who do you take orders from?"

"My handler. But he contacts me. I never contact him."

"He told you to kill Martha?"

Flora didn't say anything, just inspected her hands.

"Listen," October said, "so far you've wasted my time with the biggest pile of shit I've ever heard someone spin and not answered any of my actual questions: what you did, how you did it and why you did it. If I don't get answers to those in the next thirty seconds, we're done here and you're done."

"Yes," Flora whispered. "He told me to kill Martha. And when."

October raised an eyebrow. "And how?"

Flora nodded.

"Where did you get the poison for the vodka?" Tully asked.

"It wasn't poison."

"What was it then?" he said.

She thought for a moment. "I don't know. But I was told it wasn't poison. It was a white powder that arrived in a parcel three months ago. International delivery. From America. I was told to keep it safe."

"And you switched your bottle of Siberian with Danberg's bottle?" October said.

"Yes, the day of the party. I went over to his. He didn't see anything."

"What about the perfume?" Tully said.

Flora frowned. "What about it?"

"You've told us about the vodka; tell us how you arranged the perfume. With the supplier?"

She looked from Tully to October and back again. She seemed confused.

"The whole truth," October said.

"I'm telling you the truth," Flora snapped. "I don't know anything about a perfume."

Tully and October glanced at each other. "Okay," October said. "Then let's go back to the vodka. You knew it was going to kill Martha, yet you drank it too. How were you so sure it wasn't going to kill you?"

She shrugged. "I was told it would trigger an allergy, that the rest of us would be safe."

"And you believed that? You didn't think for a second that it could have killed you too?"

"You don't get it," Flora said, weariness in her voice now. "For Jayla, I would happily walk off a cliff. I made provisions for her, just in case. But I was sure it was safe."

"For you," October said.

"For everyone," Flora whispered. "Except Martha."

47

Tully slammed the door to his room shut and smacked the wall with his palm. He looked around for something to throw, but only his Mindscape was near to hand and he wasn't that far gone. How in hell could Flora, of all people, have fallen for a fucking tabkhir-denying conspiracy theory? He knew that contagion had been fuelled by internet algorithms and corrupt politicians for the last three decades, mind-withering plagues that spread faster than the Great Pandemic and any virus since. He came across them occasionally in his own reporting, usually when another politician turned to it, yet again, as a strategy for polarising the electorate, dividing everyone into us and them. There was only one person he knew who might actually know anything about it all, but he hadn't spoken to Jeffrey Tayes in five years.

He looked at the door and poked his head out. Haymaker and Livia stood a few feet away.

"Hey, you okay, mister?" Haymaker said.

Tully nodded. "I'm sorry." He closed the door again.

Tayes refused to take video calls and had likely never touched an earset or Mindscape. Tully called him on the phone.

"Tully! What a pleasure, old chum." Tayes's received pronunciation made him sound like a character from an old movie. Tully was convinced he dropped the accent the moment he put the phone down.

"How are things?" Tully said.

"Marvellous, dear boy. Never a dull day and all that."

"I need some help on a conspiracy theory. Do you have some time?"

Tayes chuckled. "Tully, Tully. Always to the point. But of course, I always have time for a dash of conspiracy in the bitter cocktail of the daily grind! Speaking of which, did you read my new book?"

"No. Sorry."

"You'll like it. You know that old story about Paquita de Shishmareff and the Russians who gave Henry Ford the *Protocols of the Elders of Zion*, which he had printed up in his newspaper and held to be evidence that the Jews were conspiring to take power across the world? His newspaper that inspired Hitler? Well, I've uncovered new evidence that it wasn't the Russians. If you look at where the source text came from, the French satirical play The Dialogue in Hell—"

"Tayes, can we talk modern conspiracy?"

There was a pause. "You don't want to know who gave it him?"

"I wouldn't want to spoil your book."

There was a sigh. "Fine, but it's a good one. I mean, this was a massive moment in seeding white supremacy for the next hundred years, you know, and pretty much the root of all the other theories… Yes, yes, okay. Which one do you want to know about?"

"I'm working on something where a young lady was radicalised by a conspiracy theory. I don't know where to start."

"They usually have names, dear boy. Grand names, pompous names. On both sides. Remember what I taught you? Us versus them. So who's the 'us', firstly?"

"She said she was a soldier in an army called the Awakened."

A moment of silence followed. Then Tayes said, "And, ah, the 'them'?"

"A group called the League of Babbage."

More silence. The back of Tully's neck prickled. "Tayes?"

"Sorry, old chum. This army. What did she say its mission was?"

"She said they were preparing a Firewall, made it sound like a title. There was a phrase that came up a few times: *The lives of a few must be spent to pay for the lives of many.* She believes that nearly everything has been faked, like the climate apocalypse, even Solomon, and that all the elections that swept pro-dictatorship parties to power a few years ago were manipulated by this League, whose goal is apparently to enslave humanity."

"Tully, dear boy, there are only two possibilities I foresee."

"Which are?"

"The first is the most unlikely. It is that, in my four decades of daily study of conspiracy theory, I have somehow missed a whopping big one seeded amongst what I must assume is predominantly rich wealthy folk who've not been outside in the real world for twenty years."

"You're saying you haven't heard of it?"

"Which brings me to the second possibility. She's having you on. A laugh at your expense. Load of poppy-cock, you see? It has all the right ingredients. Elegantly recycled, as the very best of modern conspiracy theories are, from a bunch of stuff—all of which can be traced back to the Elders of Zion, if you really felt the urge. However, if there actually was a group out there preaching this kind of stuff, I'd have heard about it."

Tully rubbed his eyes. "Isn't it possible they've been very good at hiding?"

"Conspiracy theorists don't hide. They thrive on attention. They proclaim their horseshit as loudly as they can, and the smellier the shit and the more confidently they proclaim it, the more people eat it up and tell each other how delicious it tastes. How other people should be eating it too. How anyone not eating it is simply a sheep in a pack. This gives them power, Tully. Power over what people believe and how they think. That's a heady high. They don't grow in the mouldy shadows like mushrooms and bide their time with a small group of recruits. Not really."

"Unless it's real."

"Now, my old chum, be careful. You don't want to be the one proclaiming horseshit."

"Not the substance of it. That's crazy. But isn't there a difference between a conspiracy theory spreading far and wide on social media and actual conspiracies to, for example, take down governments?"

Tayes huffed. "The difference, old chum, is that the latter tend to be much simpler and more direct in their ambitions. Want to replace the aristocracy and install a new political philosophy? Kill the tsar and the rest of the House of Romanov. Look, I'll do a little digging, but I can tell you now, I won't find anything. My view? She's playing you."

"Thanks, Tayes. I'll be in touch."

"Always a pleasure, my dear friend."

Tully sat on the edge of the bed and stared at the door. Livia was out there. He could go out and tell her they'd solved it. Flora Jacobs was the murderer.

Cut and dried. She'd give him access to the vault. He'd be able to focus on the real story here. Except he couldn't. It wasn't the whole truth. And if there was something he believed in more than anything, it was truth. Flora was still just a link in the chain, not the end of it. She'd switched the vodka. But someone else had supplied it. Plus, she only had half the plan. Someone else had tampered with the perfume, perhaps this mysterious Kobashigawa that Jiang had mentioned. Did it matter? Maybe Livia would understand, would appreciate the progress and give him access anyway.

Fuck. He was running out of time, but he'd be damned if he didn't do this properly. He had to put this story to bed. Flora was important, but there was someone else out there, motive unknown. And Tully needed to find the bastard.

❧

"Deirdre?" October knocked on the office door.

"Come, come," a voice called from inside.

October entered and grinned uncertainly. Deirdre always made her feel a little inadequate. The woman had no respect for authority, though she was always kind, if seemingly bemused by her colleagues' apparent lack of smarts.

The tiny bespectacled woman occupied a small office on the third floor of the precinct. Small, but very precisely arranged. A virtual whiteboard ran the length of one side, inscribed with circled names written in careful capitals, linked by arrows. Everything on her desk was arranged in neat piles so straight it was if she'd used a protractor to check it was all arranged at right angles to her. On the other side, she had a large shelf filled with books, real paper books, all intellectual treatises with obscure titles, including several of her own. October had browsed the shelf, once. They were all arranged in little collections, some kind of genres that Deirdre appeared to have invented herself. She'd labelled the shelves containing each genre, as if it was a library. Within each genre, she'd organised everything alphabetically, by title. October didn't have many paper books, but if she did, the most organised she'd be would be to group fiction and non-fiction separately. Anything beyond that was time not worth spending.

Deirdre usually specialised in the rigorous validation of mega-wealthy citizens applying to live in the Floating States, checking they'd made their money legitimately. From the start, Jasper Keeling had been adamant that he wanted no shady oligarchs on the islands.

"García said you have something on the owners of PheroTech?" October asked.

"Yes, dear, it's a shell company in Singapore. It's a good way of hiding things you don't want to be public. Such as who owns you."

"There must be a director of that company though, right?"

"Yes. According to my counterpart in Singapore, it's a small-time tax accountant working from a cubicle of an office on the fortieth floor of a concrete high-rise. They're taking him in but he won't know anything. He's a patsy."

"How about who owns them?"

"Another shell company in Guernsey."

October pinched her nose. "Right. And who owns them?"

Deirdre sighed. "I want to manage your expectations, dear. This is looking like turtles all the way up, one on top of the other."

〜

TULLY BURST THROUGH the double doors into the precinct squad room. They slammed against their stoppers, making several officers jump and spin round, but he kept going, heading for the open stairwell at the far end.

Moran appeared out of nowhere and barred his way. "Where the hell do you think you're going?"

"I need to speak to Flora," Tully said.

"The hell you do. You can tag along with the commander as much as you like, but you don't have the authority to just wander around here doing as you please. Get out."

Tully closed his eyes for a moment. "Call October if you like," he said in a tone so quiet and level that Moran tilted his head closer. "There's something that doesn't add up here, and if you want to play the bureaucratic bad cop while I'm trying to help your boss do her job, it's only going to look bad on you."

"It's not bureaucracy," Moran snapped. "Do you think we let anyone just walk in here and talk to prisoners?"

"Then call October."

"*Commander* October."

Tully nodded, crossed his arms and tried not to tap his foot.

"She wants to speak to you," Moran said. "I'm putting her on shared audio."

"Tully?" October said. "What's going on?"

"I spoke to an expert on conspiracy theories. *The* expert. He knows everything being cooked up out there and he's never heard of whatever Flora's feeding off. Something's off here and I want to ask her about it."

"You couldn't have waited for me?"

"I'm sorry, October, I thought you'd be here."

"Commander!" Moran growled.

"It's okay, Moran," October said. "Look, take him down. Tully, keep me on audio. I want to hear. But don't tell her I'm listening in. She responds better to you. And Moran, when we're down there, stick with him but give Tully space. Let him into the cell alone, okay?"

"Yes, Commander," Moran said. He eyed Tully, lips thin, but nodded towards the stairs.

Tully hadn't been down to the holding cells since Danberg had died, and his stomach turned uneasily at the memory. What if Flora was found the same way? Surely they must have taken precautions. The clip-clop of their footsteps echoed as they walked along the corridor, though Tully wanted to run.

Moran stopped outside the penultimate cell. The furthest one had been Danberg's. Tully was relieved Flora wasn't being held in there. Why did they put everyone in the furthest cells? For effect, perhaps? To give their inmates the full prisoner experience of being marched down a dull, institutional corridor? Moran palmed the console and the door opened.

Tully walked in and Moran closed the door, but left a gap.

Flora was sitting on the bed, her back against the wall, knees raised, hands loosely resting on them. She wore precinct-issued slacks and somehow managed to make them look like pyjamas. She glanced at him then looked away.

"Flora," Tully said. "I want to know more about the Awakened. A lot of what you said made sense, and yet I couldn't find anything. I don't know where to look."

She eyed him with suspicion. "Really?"

"You told me not to take your word for it but to do my own research. Well, I tried. Can you point me in the right direction?"

She considered him. "What was it I said that made so much sense to you?"

"It was the elections. For the pro-dictatorship parties. It was staggering. Year after year we saw more victories. And when the big countries started to topple, Brazil and the US …"

She nodded. "Think about what it must have taken to pull that off."

"I need to find out who's behind it all, Flora. That's what I do, remember?"

She softened and gave him a small smile. "Do you think you can convince the commander as well?"

"I need something more to take to her."

Flora crossed her legs under her and sat forward. "My earset," she said. "They took it into custody when they brought me in. There's a pin code on it. Twenty-one, zero three, forty. Jayla's birth date. In my Minds account there's a bookmark folder."

Tully nodded. "Thanks." He turned to go back out of the cell.

"Tully?"

"Yeah?"

"I knew I could count on you. Thanks for being a friend."

He closed his eyes, tried to stem the rage boiling up within him, but then he whirled back to face her. "Let me tell you something about your fake climate disasters. Ten years ago, my wife was in Kuwait City when the tabkhir struck. She was pregnant at the time. My daughter would have been called Malia." His voice cracked and he took a moment to pull himself together. "The last time I spoke to her was the day before it happened. She was trying to get out, trying to get home to me. She never made it. I never got to meet my daughter. She would have been Jayla's age now. My daughter and many others died because people like you believe this is yet another hoax. So when you say you did this for your daughter's future, I say go to hell! And it's not a nice place, I've been there. For the last month I've searched footage someone leaked to me, trying to find her body. And you know what? I never find it, but the dead in this hell were *everywhere*." He'd shouted the last word, and now it was out, there was nothing he could do to turn the volume down. "So many bodies! Everywhere you look, lying in the dust, searching for relief from the heat. But it wasn't the sunlight that killed them, it was the humidity, and they couldn't escape it. Brownouts had taken down aircon everywhere. They crawled outside and fell into comas they never woke from. Children, Flora. Children, Jayla's age, lying next to their parents, who'd been utterly unable to protect them."

His whole body was shaking. He'd never lost his temper like this. The episode had left him light-headed. Flora looked terrified. Shame rose from deep in his chest and he made for the door, unable to say another word, afraid he'd lose it again.

"You're just trying to manipulate me," she shouted after him. "You're just one of them, one of those elites who'll be first against the fucking wall in the new revolution!"

Tully stepped out and Moran closed the door and activated the lock.

Moran hesitated then put his hand on Tully's shoulder. "You okay, man?"

Tully nodded.

"Tully?" October's voice startled him. He'd forgotten about the shared audio.

"Yeah?" He felt flat now, like all the emotion had been flushed away.

"Good work."

48

In the dim quiet of his own bedroom study, Tully put on Flora's earset. The devices usually recognised their user via some kind of neural biometric authentication he didn't understand, and he blinked at the hovering boxes. "Two, one, zero, three, four, zero," he said.

He was in. Several notifications filled his display and a photo of Jayla popped up to his right. He pushed them away and brought up Minds. Whereas his own view would have been filled with news reports, Flora's was bursting with images and videos posted by beautiful young men and women. He headed for the bookmark section. A cloud of keyword tags appeared, the largest of which was *AWAKEN*. He touched it and the word was replaced by a carousel of text, images and videos from individuals and organisations he'd never heard of. They were gathered on the platform in a single private group called, simply, Awaken. He swiped left to right, moving back in time until he reached the earliest post. It was titled, "Five things about this unbelievable hundred-year-old plot that will blow your mind!"

Tully shook his head. As clickbait went, it was crude. It was going to be a long evening.

⸺

HAKE AND MORAN walked through an empty car park on the industrial lot in downtown Barcelona. Sacks of rubbish were propped against the building's edge, most torn into and savaged by hungry animals. October and García watched their progress from the New Carthage precinct on two screens linked to their viewpoint cameras. A third screen showed footage from a drone hovering over the flat-roofed building.

"This city is ridiculously hot. And it stinks," Moran said.

October sipped her coffee. "We heard you the first time."

"Are you sure it isn't Hake?" García said.

"I'm the only thing keeping us breathing," Hake said. "I'm a human stench-shield."

García opened her mouth but October put a hand on her arm. "There's been a refuse-collection strike going on in Barcelona for nearly a month, now, Moran. Please try and focus."

"Sorry, boss. I'm just tired. It was a long journey to get here with just one flight."

Moran reached the front door and gave it a push. It was locked with what looked like an old-fashioned key system rather than a keypad. He held up his handheld radar. "No one inside."

García checked a chat she'd opened with the local police force and said, "The Guàrdia Urbana authorise you to break in."

Moran took out a small breaching charge, peeled off the wax paper and squeezed it into the keyhole. They took several steps back and he thumbed the detonator. There was a sharp bang and a spurt of grey smoke obscured the camera feed for a moment. Lights flared and a huge, empty warehouse appeared on the screen.

"I don't understand," Hake said. "I thought you said there'd be a factory here?"

Moran walked around, his footsteps echoing, Hake heading the other way. "There's nothing here, Commander," he said.

Hake sneezed. "Dusty over here."

"Not over here, though," Moran said a few seconds later. His feed showed several long tables. "This area has seen some use."

Hake joined him. "There's nothing else apart from a toilet over there."

"I'm drawing a blank, Commander," Moran said. "There should be signs of machinery here, something high tech. Maybe they were never here."

"Moran, is there a recycling bin outside?" asked García.

"I don't know. Why?"

October nodded. "Because the rubbish hasn't been collected in a month. Let's see if there's any documents in there that can help us identify these guys."

Hake and Moran exited and walked around the side of the building. Both screens were filled with a wall of green.

"What in humid hell?" Moran said.

"What is it?" October said. "I can't see anything."

Hake held up a large white cardboard box with the logo, XSera, stamped on it, which made no sense at all, as they were MyScent's original supplier. Why would PheroTech have had their competitor's boxes in the warehouse?"

"There are hundreds of them," Moran said.

⤸

TULLY RUBBED HIS eyes as he blinked away tiredness and tried to focus on the virtual screen showing Lottie, back in London. He'd spent so much time in his bedroom study, he was beginning to itch for a change of location. The room carried a sharp smell of sweat. It needed airing, so did he. "There's a lot of content here, Lottie, and I need to figure out why the hell I can't find any of it outside of Minds. It's all embedded within the platform. Search engines pull up nothing. Even a search in Minds draws a blank. Can you get Randall to take a look?"

"Why don't you ask him yourself?" Lottie said.

How he missed Bolivar. The grief was particularly sharp in moments like this, when he was closest to his normal, day-to-day life and work. "You're the boss back there, Lottie. You delegate it."

"Bullshit, you just don't want to deal with Randall this evening."

He took a deep breath. "Can you please handle this for me? I've had a rough twenty-four hours."

"*You've* had a rough twenty-four hours?" she snapped. "My actual boss has been AWOL and barely checking in. I've been trying to stop a bloody exodus of influencers and followers. We're both still upset about Bolivar. We're publishing no new content. The media's having a field day attacking your reputation after you put out that statement about Lockwood hiring Kehoe. I don't see what any of this has to do with the story you went there to write, and I don't see why you haven't come home to pick up the pieces here."

"New Carthage is still in lockdown," he said.

"Just as it was when Bolivar both came in and left again." She shook her head and glared at him. It was a look she always carried off well, and while she tended towards grumpiness, there was usually a good reason.

"You're right," Tully said. "No excuses. And I'm sorry, I really am. I just need you to hang on a little longer. I got pulled into this because there's a real chance my story got Martha killed, and nearly got me killed … and that Bolivar's dead because he was carrying my blood sample. Nothing has turned out like I expected it to."

Her glare abated. "I miss that man. We all do. So if you need to figure out what happened to him, fine. But you could have told me all of that way earlier. If you want me to run things around here, you need to keep me in the loop." She paused, then said, "You really think that's why Bolivar's copter went down? You think he was attacked?"

"I don't know what to think. I'm just losing faith in coincidence."

She nodded. "Then let's get the bastards."

49

Tully stretched, his muscles aching after two hours sitting at his desk, rummaging through the content in Flora's Minds account. A large folder of direct messages caught his eye. All had the same name attached: Simon Smith. He scanned them. Some were pure text, others video snippets. He clicked the earliest video.

A man appeared. Tully had never seen him before, yet there was something familiar there. He just couldn't put his finger on it. The guy was nondescript, lacking any kind of distinguishing features.

"Hello, Soldier Jacobs," the man said in an equally nondescript voice. "I'm your sponsor, Soldier Smith. I'm honoured that you're joining our cause. There are many in the Awakened, but only a few Saviours, our elite strike force, the most influential members of our society, all of them geo-patriots like yourself."

There were hundreds of messages here. It would take him the day to go through them all. He took a deep breath, brought up his notes file and began tapping.

⌇

October had set up the call in the interview room. Not strictly necessary, given that it was a video call, but the room served as a useful signal of authority, especially when she was talking to someone outside her jurisdiction. She looked ahead at the video wall and addressed a smooth-faced bald man with thick black eyebrows. "Mr Andino, you're the CEO of XSera?"

"That's right, Commander," Andino said. "I have my general counsel on the line too, though he's not on camera. What can I do for you?"

"I understand you supply your product to MyScent, headquartered here in New Carthage."

"We do. Is there a problem?"

"We're in the middle of an investigation regarding one of your competitors," she told him. "I'm just looking for some help."

Andino responded with a bemused smile. "What competitors?"

"You don't consider yourself to have competitors?"

"Commander, it took ten years and seventy million dollars to develop our formula. There's no one who can catch up with us."

"Yet MyScent were able to switch suppliers without much problem."

He waved a hand. "Undoubtedly something inferior. It didn't take them long to realise their mistake."

"For which I understand you penalised them with a price hike?"

He shrugged. "They left us with a last-minute demand issue. Although it was one we were able to rectify."

"They switched to a company called PheroTech. Do you know them?"

He stared at them for a moment. "One moment, if you don't mind?" He muted the line and the screen went blank.

García's fingers drummed on the table. "What's going on there?"

October just shook her head. Nothing good.

Andino came back on the line. "I'm sorry, we have no competitor called PheroTech."

"Look," October said. "PheroTech may be implicated in a homicide investigation. And it seems to be a mirage company, one that looks real on the surface but with details that disappear as soon as you look closely. Their warehouse contains hundreds of boxes bearing an XSera logo. Should I be forced to conclude that PheroTech is simply a front for XSera? Do we need to ask our colleagues in Rotterdam to come and visit within the quarter hour so you don't have time to get shredding?"

Andino pursed his lips. "One moment, please." The screen went blank again.

October sighed. "García, start talking to the Rotterdam PD just in case we need them to move fast."

García was already tapping.

They waited a minute. *Dammit.* "Right, let's—"

Andino reappeared. "Sorry for the wait, Commander. I wanted to check my facts. PheroTech are not a competitor but a customer, hence my reluctance to reveal any information about them."

"A customer?"

"Yes, but they've placed only three orders, and none recently."

October looked at García. "That's helpful. We should be able to trace the transaction."

"I'll get you the details."

"What do PheroTech do? As a business, I mean?"

"I don't know and we don't ask. But it's a surprise to hear that they were supplying MyScent. It doesn't make any commercial sense. If they were taking our stuff and selling it under their own label at a price that was competitive with us, they'd have been making a loss since they received no discount from us."

"Do you have any information for them? Where they were headquartered, where you shipped to, that kind of thing?"

"I'll get you what I can. But I can tell you now, we shipped to their head-quarters. Some industrial park in Barcelona."

⌒

IT HAD BEEN a while since Livia had coded properly, when she was creating the building blocks of Constellation. But some of what she'd found in Martha's vault had inspired her. Ideas, diagrams, even fragments of modules of code. Her sister had been a genius, of course, but Livia could stand on the shoulders of genius without falling off, couldn't she? The problem was the number of threads. She'd built Constellation to find patterns, the signal in the noise, but the problems had been smaller, like how a political figure spent money. This, on the other hand, was a full-blown plot, and someone had painstakingly covered up their trail. She was casting in the dark, feeding in more bits and pieces to see what she could unpick. At least she had access to Martha's significant computing power. She'd gone from reaping orchards of information to commanding an army of harvesting robots.

A chime alerted her to a call. Randall. She hesitated, sighed, then accepted.

"Livia, oh my God, it's so good to hear you, to see you. I mean, it feels like forever since—"

"It's good to see you too, Randall," she said. And it really was. She hadn't realised it until now, but she'd missed him.

"Are you okay? I heard you weren't feeling too good after …"

"I'm fine, Randall. How are things back home?"

He looked sad. "Well, it's a bit weird here, you know, without you, Mr Tully and Mr Bolivar. Lottie is nice and all but…"

"Was there something you needed, Randall?"

"Well, yeah, I need some help and I feel super-bad for asking, but—"

"What can I do?"

"Look, I know that when you worked here you were also coding. You kept it all secret from the team, but I knew, I could see the network traffic spike whenever you had been asked by Mr Tully to do some research. I could see that you were running an agent of some kind, and then you'd always come back with answers, and I never told anyone. I don't know why you wanted to keep it secret though because it's awesome, you always came back with info no one else could have gotten—"

Livia tried to smile, but it was a wobbly one. "Okay, okay, Randall. I guess it doesn't matter now anyway. Yes, I built a piece of software. It's a pattern-matching agent. I call it Constellation."

"Constellation, wow, I love that. I mean I totally get it, you're linking up certain stars to make a pattern that you otherwise couldn't see against the backdrop of all the noise—"

"That's right," she said. "So what do you need?"

"Lottie asked me to look at a ton of messages, posts and other stuff on Minds, all of it in Flora Jacobs's account. And it's all to do with this conspiracy theory. Mr Tully wants to know why he can't find any of it outside of Minds, but there's just tons of it—"

"Flora Jacobs?" Livia said. "Why her?"

"I don't know. I mean, I don't often get told everything, but …" He hesitated. Randall never hesitated.

"Tell me," she said.

"I think it has something to do with your sister's … you know."

Livia nodded, trying to keep her face expressionless. "Can you patch me into the account?"

"Sure thing, just give me five mins, okay?"

"Randall, I have only one condition. I don't want anyone on the team to know I'm helping. Not Tully, not anyone, got it?"

Randall nodded. He looked confused and unsure.

"Say it, Randall. Swear on our friendship you won't tell."

"Right, of course. I swear on our friendship, I swear I'll keep it secret."

She hung up. There was a lot to unpick here, not least what Tully had on Flora Jacobs. This would need to be fed into Constellation too. And she knew just where to find it: Panopticon.

50

Tully leaned back in his chair, legs crossed, boots perched on his desk, and frowned at Randall, blathering away on a virtual screen next to a silent Lottie. "Randall … Just get to the point?"

"Yes, Mr Tully," Randall said. "The point, right, well, we had a look at the content, and here's the thing, there's a pretty good reason you can't find any of the posts anywhere else, but it's a bit complicated. I mean it's always complicated, isn't it? But this is proper ninja-level—"

"What's the reason?" Tully said.

"So we ran the posts through, well, some really helpful software, and it started to flag the type of account behind each post as an anomaly—"

"Anomaly?"

"Like, fake accounts, or bots, which shouldn't be possible any more. And some of these posts weren't real posts. I mean, they were all promoted, like adverts, but the promoted post banner was hidden."

Tully sighed. "I can't believe I'm going to say this, but can you expand on that? You're saying we have fake accounts, making fake posts. Start with the accounts."

Randall was leaning in, now, so close he obscured the view of Lottie, his face all big and his eyes all excited. "Right, so you remember in the old days, all the social media companies had problems with people setting up a lot of pretend accounts in order to dominate a conversation, with a lot of people pushing the same ideas or point of view, and it got super nasty and society nearly imploded, etcetera, and all the companies eventually enforced the link of an account with some real-world identity, right?"

Tully scratched at his jaw. "Right?"

Randall sat back and flung his arms dramatically in the air. "That's what they've done, basically. I mean someone created an entire group on Minds that was focused on this conspiracy theory, full of people that Flora Jacobs thought were real—"

"Wait," Tully said, "hold up. You're saying everyone—*everyone*—on that group is fake? Everyone … except Flora?"

"That's right, so—"

"Including Simon Smith?" Tully said. "Her handler?"

"Exactly, the authentication ID is bogus, so—"

"But I watched him on video. He's a real person."

"It's hypothetically possible that someone could have deepfaked it, although that's been banned for decades and the platforms have really sophisticated detection tools now. I mean, to beat it, you'd need a supercomputer—"

"There were two thousand people in the group," Tully said. "To control that many accounts is a major operation. More so if you're faking that much video. Anyway, let's assume we have fake users. What about the fake posts?"

"Okay, so she likely saw some of these posts in her normal feed and thought the platform itself was just highlighting them as something she'd be interested in. You know, like, you look at one article on lingerie and suddenly your whole feed is just lingerie, lingerie, lingerie—"

"Randall," Tully snapped.

"—so these posts were actually like adverts, except they hacked the little banner that normally highlights it's a promoted post, replaced it with a single invisible pixel. Now this is where it gets interesting, because you can't just do that. It means somehow they injected code—"

Tully held up his hand to stall him. "You remember how Capone, the great gangster of Chicago, was taken down? It wasn't the crimes. It was the taxes. And here's the thing. Every advert on this kind of platform has to be paid for. Coin has changed hands. If we can figure out whose hands it came from, we'll have our Capone."

꙳

October was waiting for him at a table as Tully arrived at Anthony's, which turned out to be one of those high-end Italian places regular people rarely encountered, but the elite liked to patronise. Bustling and crowded, the hum of voices and clink of cutlery combined with the rich scents of pasta, tomato, cheese and sausage threatened to overwhelm his senses. October stood and smiled. They looked awkwardly at each other. He wasn't used to dining out, and had expected something lower-key. He wasn't used to socialising, and this felt way too much like socialising. He wasn't used to the protocols of it all. Should he shake her hand, kiss her cheek, or just sit? She seemed to notice his dilemma and gestured towards a chair.

He took a seat, trying to ignore the sense he was totally out of place, and busied himself with the menu that popped onto the display. "Nice place," he said finally, to break the silence.

"One of the best in the city," October replied. "I thought we both deserved an evening out, and I always make it a point to get to know the people I work with socially. We haven't done that much yet."

He nodded. Definitely a work dinner, then.

October ordered drinks, then said, "How is your dive into Flora's Minds profile going?"

"Well, the big news is that we think everything she's seen and interacted with is fake."

"Fake posts about a dodgy conspiracy theory? I'm not sure how big a surprise that is, except that she believed it."

"Not just fake posts. Every single account posting something about this conspiracy is fake, including the ones interacting directly with her."

She shook her head. "I've never heard of anything like it."

"We're calling it personalised propaganda. Used to be that bots targeted large portions of society. This is something a lot more sophisticated, and it's been targeted at one person."

"But did you find anything there validating that she was told what to do and how to do it?"

"Yeah. I found the instructions for the poisoning. They're from some guy called Simon Smith. Here's the thing: the videos from him look real. He's convincing, even if his message isn't."

"How was she convinced?"

A waiter arrived with water and Tully waited until he'd moved away before replying. "A lot of the early ones are links to articles and videos. Later, it's Smith telling her how smart, special and important she is, how her daughter's future's at risk, and a lot of stuff laying out the nuts and bolts of the conspiracy. Then he moves onto Solomon, which Smith calls a fraudulent simulation that Martha Chandra's created for this League of Babbage. That's the first time he really mentions Martha. Flora then replies, saying that Martha's a close friend and she can't believe she'd be part of something like this. He cautions her to not let on to Martha, just stay close to her, reminds her that she's the only member of the Saviours that has that kind of access."

"She didn't resist?" October asked, after taking a long sip of water.

"Not too much. By that time they'd really sucked her in. She really believed she understood things about the world that everyone else didn't. She looked down on the poor sheep that hadn't woken up, even though she was told not to share any information about this conspiracy with anyone, like her followers. It seems she found that challenging, wanted to use her platform to educate people." Tully took a drink, too. The iced, sparkling water, tinted with cucumber, refreshed him, and he started to think the restaurant wasn't quite as off-putting as he'd originally thought. Pretentious, yes, but you could get used to anything, couldn't you?

"And the vodka?"

"Eventually she's told the day is at hand and given instructions. The lives of a few to save the lives of many. Smith tells her that the fraud will fizzle out if Martha is killed because she's the only one who knows how to create the holographic footage. And he tells her that others will also be acting over the next month to prevent the enslavement of humanity by the League."

October shook her head. "She never struck me as someone capable of murdering in cold blood."

A woman at the next table looked sharply at her, then quickly looked away, but gave every impression of listening. Tully lowered his voice. "I think she saw it as a mercy. She was told it would be very gentle, like going to sleep and never waking up, the kindest way to die. That may be the one truth in all this."

"Did they make contact after the murder?"

"Only once: to congratulate her, tell her to now do her best to point the finger at others and to stay in place. Oh, as an aside, it looks like she sent a death threat to Martha a few weeks before this all happened."

"What? The Angels of Mercy?"

"Yeah, all her. There was nothing in the instructions specifically about it. I think she might have just been trying to cover her own tracks."

They sat in silence for a moment and considered that, and a waiter came to take their orders. "Can I suggest," October said, "that we just order their taster menu for two? It's really rather good."

Tully shrugged. "Sure."

"It pairs perfectly with our Cabernet," said the waiter. "Would you like some wine?"

"I don't suppose you have rum? Preferably artisan, Scottish dark if you have it."

"Ah," said the waiter, and there was a faint sneer on his lip. "I'll have to check."

"Don't worry," Tully said, "I'll just stick with water."

"Me too," October said. The waiter nodded and left. "These two threads," she said, "as convoluted as they are, all have to lead back to a single point. Someone was behind this *personalised propaganda* targeted at Jacobs, and also behind the serum supplier switch that was targeted at Jiang Ying Yue."

A waiter arrived with a tray, and ceremoniously put down a plate with the smallest slice of lasagna Tully had ever seen, scarcely bigger than a domino. "Our speciality amuse-bouche," the waiter said, "the chef's lasagna, with a custom minced meat especially created for the dish, precision fermented and assembled at a nanoscale to create the perfect repository of protein and fat, while absorbing the essence of the tomato sauce, and—"

"Thank you," October said, smiling in a way that invited him to leave. He smiled woodenly, bowed his head, and moved away.

Tully leaned forward, careful to still keep his voice low. "The only lead we have right now is that some of the content that pulled Flora into the conspiracy in the first place was promoted, paid for in coin. But we'll need your help getting the transaction details out of Minds. They'll need a warrant."

October blinked. "We're also looking at a transaction. The company that supplied the contaminated serum to MyScent didn't make it themselves. They bought it from XSera, then added the contaminant, repackaged it and sent it to New Carthage. XSera have given us the transaction information and I already have one of my team looking into it."

Tully nodded. "I'm passing you what we found. Maybe we'll strike lucky." He narrow-cast a package to October's earset.

"Got it," October said. "I'm sending it straight on to one of my staff, Deirdre, okay? Give me a moment."

He nodded and sipped his drink.

"Done." She smiled. "You'd make a good detective, Tully. Maybe you missed your calling."

He smiled. It felt alien on his face for a moment, then comfortable, like a well-worn spot on an old sofa that hadn't been sat in for some time. "Journalism's my calling."

"How did you get into it?" she asked. "Were your parents in the business?"

He shook his head. "My mother was a political historian. Not the kind that works in a stuffy university department. An author. She covered all sorts of stuff but specialised in political disinformation in the age of social media, a subject that got grimmer as time went by. I remember watching her being interviewed on TV when I was a kid. She was talking about how some of the politicians of the time in countries like the US, UK and others were using powerful propaganda and disinformation techniques, ones perfected by the Nazis and communists decades earlier but reinvented for the digital age. I didn't understand any of that at the time; it was just cool to see my mother on television. But in my teenage years, she drilled those ideas into me, made me read books like *Nineteen Eighty-Four*, and I'd watch some of her older interviews on the video sites."

October nodded, and Tully felt a release of tension he hadn't known was there. He wasn't used to talking about personal stuff anymore, nor to it being listened to. "As my mum got a bit older, she grew increasingly weary and more pessimistic about the direction of travel of all of it. I remember how bitter she was about people—especially politicians and corporations—attacking the press and accusing them of creating fake news. She'd tell me how important it was for good journalists to write the first draft of history, so that people like her could come and tidy up later. In many ways, that provided the seed for my own path."

He hadn't opened up to anyone like this since Zainab, and now he'd started talking, he couldn't stop. "My parents loved me, and I worshipped them as a kid, I really did. They inspired me. I had a pretty good childhood. Warm, loving, stable. Sure, I had some odd dreams, but that was it. I had nothing to complain about. But a few things weren't quite adding up. The odd dreams, a couple of comments … My father was totally against doing a DNA test even though I was fascinated by the idea of a family tree. I discovered I'm pretty good at wheedling out secrets."

"That's for sure," October murmured. "Go on."

"When I was sixteen," he said, "I found out they were actually my aunt and uncle. My biological parents had been drug addicts, and when I was very young, perhaps two, social services stepped in and my adoptive parents were given permission by the state to take me in. I never met my biological parents. They never visited, were never invited. I understand eventually they both OD'd." She reached across the table and placed her hand on his arm. Tully stared at it, but didn't move. "I felt like my identity had been stripped away. And while life was undoubtedly better than it would have been, I was furious that they'd lied to me. Of course, I get why, and eventually I forgave them, but I realised, years later, that if my mother's views were the seed that led me to journalism, that was the compost. It got me wondering what else people were hiding out there."

She nodded, withdrew her hand and sipped her drink. The spot where she'd touched him felt empty.

He stared at his own water. That was the thing about truth. You grew up thinking your parents always told it, that telling lies were bad, and then you realised they lied, left, right and centre, when they judged the truth was too difficult to hear. For your own protection, of course. First came Santa and the Tooth Fairy, under the guise of having a magical childhood. Then the elderly dog went to live out its days on a farm without saying goodbye. Was it any wonder they'd also judge it kinder not to tell you that you weren't really their son? Oh, yes. He'd experienced the kind way, the way that put the consequences first, and he was done with it. He'd been done with it for as long as he could remember.

⤳

DING. DING. DING.

October woke with a start. There was a noise. A chime.

What was it?

Her earset, of course. Her earset was chiming. Something had happened. She launched herself to grab it. Was it Mum and Dad? What was going on?

"Lights," she croaked, and the room lit up like a surgical theatre. She slapped the earset on and blinked as her eyes adjusted to the glare.

"Good morning, dear."

Not her parents. Deirdre.

"What time is it?"

"It's three-fifteen in the morning. I'm sorry for waking you, dear, but I have something for you and I don't think it can wait until daylight."

51

The pod didn't head to the precinct as Tully had expected, but towards the centre of town.

"Where are we going?"

"You'll see," October told him.

She'd called him, at this unearthly hour, only twenty minutes earlier. Said it was important, and there'd been something in her voice that had woken him up: excitement. He'd dressed quickly and hurried outside to wait for the pod. Now, they were speeding along, headed for an unknown destination, and he stifled a yawn. "What's going on, October?"

"Just trust me, okay?" she whispered. "If I could explain it in the back of a pod, I would."

He obliged, and a few minutes later, they reached Central Plaza. October jumped out and strode to what looked like a subway entrance on the south side, though Tully knew there was no such thing here. It was a glass enclosure with a door. She palmed the lock and they entered.

They walked along a well-lit, tiled corridor. October stopped at two tall panels in the wall. She palmed one panel, and they both slid open to reveal a dim, stainless-steel passage that reminded Tully of the sterile crew quarters in a cruise ship he'd caught a glimpse of as a child.

They got in a chilly service lift. It was the first time he'd been cold since arriving on the island. October tapped at a button. The door slid shut and she smiled again at Tully but didn't say anything.

The lift dinged. They got out and walked along another corridor, down two more flights of stairs and into a circular room with ambient lighting.

Windows surrounded the perimeter, but it was pitch black outside. October pushed a button on the wall and floodlights bathed the exterior. Shoals of glittering fish teemed in the ocean beyond, some moving away from the light, some towards it.

"Where are we," he said, voice hushed.

"It's a half-secret. Well below the sea line, as deep as you can go, really. Even the funeral airlocks are above this. I don't know why it was built. I once heard that the architects planned to make an exclusive bar but then forgot to tie it in properly to the urban plans. The builders didn't ask any questions, just constructed it anyway."

"It's incredible," he said, walking to the edge. "Did you bring me here because of my egospace? It has some similarities?"

"No, although it did occur to me that you'd like this. Your underwater cityscape is more impressive, but this can be pretty interesting sometimes."

"You come down here a lot?"

"When I want to get away from everyone. I have access rights for this part of the city and no one ever comes down here but me. The cleaning bots keep it tidy. That's it. But there's another reason." She stood beside him. A giant shoal of elongated silver fish pivoted away from them. "Do you ever worry that nothing we say is private anymore?" she said.

He frowned. "What do you mean?"

"There are cameras and microphones in everything, everywhere."

"That's worrying, coming from this city's head of security. Is this a case of 'quis custodiet ipsos custodes'?"

October frowned. "Who watches the watchmen, right? No. The complexity of what someone's pulled off to kill Martha is making me paranoid, I suppose. This morning, I had a horrible feeling I was being watched, listened to. What if all this, every decision we're making, every tiny moment, becomes something future historians pore over?"

"Why would they?"

She turned to him. "It feels like the world's changing, Tully, and we're at the centre of it all, even if we don't want to be. Perhaps that's a decision I made unwittingly by working so close to Solomon. But I didn't know, I really didn't."

"Know what? What's going on?" There was a tightness in his chest, a tightness in his throat, a tightness in his jaw. Try as he might, he couldn't seem to relax any of them.

She sighed. "We found something. The entity that bought the promoted posts targeting Flora Jacobs also bought the serum from XSera. Both sets of transactions were linked to a digital wallet, and we found other transactions made from the same wallet. Some were transactions that required a user account." She took a deep breath. "For example, official campaign adverts for the Lockwood campaign from the office of the chief of staff, Jeff Kehoe."

He put his hand against the window to steady himself. His knees went weak. She was right. The world was about to change and they were slap bang in the middle of it all. "You're sure?"

She nodded and swallowed. "There's more. A bottle of bourbon, paid for and delivered to the Town Hall in Houston, Texas. The invoice address was Kehoe's, and it's from a while back, when he was still mayor. And, only a few weeks ago, a Houston to Athens V-Plane ticket in Kehoe's name, issued the day before Lockwood unveiled him as his chief of staff."

Tully sat down on the floor, back against the glass, and stared into the bare room. October joined him. "Kehoe," he said, unsure if the word tasted bitter or sweet. "So, really, Lockwood."

October nodded. "So it would appear."

"Lockwood reaches the last two, a step away from the most powerful position anyone in history has every occupied. He decides to maximise his advantage by killing off the only person who really knows how Solomon works. Then he gets his media stooges like Bamphwick to play up all the confusion and violence suddenly surrounding Solomon like it's his fault. Lockwood's polling improves and we're now a week before the election."

They'd done it. He was home and dry. He could go to Livia, have her fulfil her promise, get access to the vault.

But October sighed and put her hand on his. "When we leave this room, when we head back upstairs, I have to go to the governor. It feels like I'm looking at the fuse on a big bomb I'm just about to light."

"October—"

"Please, call me Claudine. Just, well, not in front of others. I don't tell many people my first name."

Tully looked at her and nodded. "Nice to meet you, Claudine." Out of the corner of his eye, he saw a lionfish swim up to the window, stop and consider them, and swim off again. Her eyes were huge and sad. She was beautiful, now her sternness had vanished and—

She kissed him.

A hundred guilt-ridden thoughts flashed past like the lit windows on a passing night train, but he didn't pull back, couldn't pull back. He touched her hair, silk soft, and inhaled her sweet scent. She pushed him back against the glass wall. The fierceness of the movement surprised him, made him uncomfortable. This was not a soft embrace; she was toned, strong, and knew what she wanted.

Then she broke away and looked at him with eyes full of concern. "Is this okay?" she said in a hushed tone.

He hesitated. Was it? Was he really betraying Zainab for a woman he'd known for less than a fortnight? Forget it, he told himself. It had been a long time. Enjoy this moment.

But his hesitation had flustered her and she pulled away. "I'm sorry," she said.

He was sorrier. Self-loathing erupted as he replayed the moment and his stomach churned. It ached as he stood, like he'd been punched in the gut. He stood up. "I'm sorry," he said. "I'm married."

She stood up too, her face flushed.

"I…I need to go," he said, avoiding her eyes. "I'm sorry." He walked towards the stairs but she didn't follow. Would he be able to find his way out, alone? No, he'd find it, even if he wandered for hours. He grimaced, biting his lip, and walking faster. He needed to get out. He needed to talk to Livia. He needed to solve this damn story. He needed to go home.

He raced out onto Central Plaza again, looked around wildly like a bank robber for his getaway car, then headed in the direction of the apartment.

⤻

THIRTY MINUTES LATER he'd worked his way back to the apartment. It was still early, the streets stirring, but not even the sweetness of the air could lift his spirits. It wasn't October he was furious with, it was himself. He felt a sudden urge to confess to someone, admit his sins. He'd only loved Zainab for as long as he could remember. What had he done?

He marched into the apartment. "Livia?"

No reply. No Livia. No Haymaker. *Damn it.*

He grabbed his suitcase and flung it on the bed. A message panged in his display. It was from Solomon. *Can you join me in NR? It's urgent.*

Had October already briefed the governor on Lockwood and Kehoe? Was the fuse already burning down? He was tempted to ignore it, but he was enough of a professional to know that sometimes you had to go where the story was, no matter how you felt at the time. *Sure, I'll be there in five*, he wrote, as if he was fine.

Tension blossomed in his chest and he rubbed at his ribcage above his heart. He needed a drink, right now, early hour be damned. There were no glasses on the bar so he uncorked the rum and took a deep swig straight from the bottle. The burn eased the tension, but only a little, so he took another mouthful, then returned to his bedroom.

His headset was lying on the desk. He looked at it, unable to justify his sudden reluctance to pick it up. *Get on with it.* He pulled it on and entered his egospace.

Zainab. Of course. That was why he felt so tight. She stared into the underwater vista and ignored him. He didn't blame her. He'd betrayed her. Moreover, he'd come to New Carthage to uncover the real story behind her death, and as yet he'd come up with nothing.

He put a hand to her cheek. "I still love you," he whispered. "I'll always love you. But I think it's time for me to start healing." Her stillness felt like an accusation. "I'm going to hide you, for a bit. Give myself a bit of time."

He brought up the control console, closed his eyes and imagined the space without her there, crystallising it in his mind. When he opened his eyes she'd disappeared, as if she had never been there. No patch faded the ground where she'd stood. Tears welled and his throat dried.

A chime startled him. Solomon. He took a deep breath, wiped his eyes and accepted the invite.

A blast of humidity made him stagger. He looked around him, trying to get his bearings, and cried out. Bodies. So many bodies. Packed beneath a desiccated tree, stretched out on the pavement and in the gutter, curled against the sides of the buildings, twisted in a clump of splayed arms and legs in the dust of the road.

A man walked along the dusty street towards him.

"Why?" Tully asked, hearing the wretchedness in his own voice. "Why would you bring me here, Solomon?"

Solomon put his hand on Tully's shoulder. "Because we need to remember the price of failure. And you need to remember why this is important to you. This was Kuwait City, during the tabkhir, as best as I can tell, reconstructed from the footage I've been able to retrieve."

Tully was dripping with sweat but his mouth was parched. He wiped his brow. "Was this … how hot it was?"

"No. I wanted us to remember, I wanted us to empathise, but I didn't want us to experience that torture."

Torture. It had been exactly that. As Randall had said, cooked from the inside out. Near him, a woman lay in the road on her front, face turned towards him. Her eyes were open, hand outstretched. It was not Zainab but he fell to his knees regardless. He moaned, the grief torn from him.

"Are you ready, Marcus Tully? Are you ready to tell your story?"

Tully looked up. Solomon was standing on the other side of the body. "What did you find?"

"A video," Solomon said. "A video that was buried by time and paranoid hands." He cast his hand to the side and a screen hovered in the air.

Tully stood up and stepped closer to the screen. The footage was split into three windows. Two smaller windows were stacked vertically. The top one featured President Lockwood; the bottom, Dr Martha Chandra. Next to them, a larger window showed four men sitting around a board table: Kehoe, Cavanagh and two men he didn't know, one in a suit, the other in military uniform. Eight rows of ribbons were pinned on his breast surrounded by several badges, and the forearm of his blue-black jacket was emblazoned with four golden bands, one thick and three thin, and a gold star. Which would make him Admiral Hogan, chair of the joint chiefs of staff.

The video played. Martha was speaking. "Mr President, I urge you not to turn it on. It's a prototype, intended only as a proof of concept to fund further geo-engineering research."

"Mr President," Kehoe said, "this is a question of chances. Dr Levin here assures us that due to the humidity there is a ninety percent chance this heatwave will be catastrophic to the US on a scale we've never seen before, particularly in the south. After so many category-four, -five and -six hurricanes this season, we lack power, shelter and water in the region. If this hits, and it will, it will result in the biggest death toll from a natural disaster in history."

"But—"

"Excuse me, Dr Chandra, I'm not finished. Mr President, let's counterbalance that ninety percent. For the past three years, Dr Chandra has received significant funding to produce technology she says will one hundred percent push the excess humidity up into the stratosphere. That leaves us with heat, but a manageable heat. She says there's a sixty percent chance—"

"Or, to put it another way, a four in ten chance that—"

"A sixty percent chance that the humidity will get sucked back down again over the sea. Saving many lives. But let me remind you, sir: that's a sixty percent chance that American lives are saved."

"Those seem good odds to me, Mr President," Hogan said in a deep bass.

"Four in ten," Martha said, "that it comes down over another country, another landmass. It's unpredictable. It's weather."

Cavanagh shook his head. "The American people elected President Lockwood to protect them."

"At what cost?" hissed Martha.

"At any cost!" Cavanagh said, and slammed his hand down on the table.

"I agree," Lockwood said, nodding. "Our own people must come first, always. Admiral, execute Icarus One."

The footage stopped.

"Do you see?" whispered Solomon. "These men played roulette with the world. And lost."

52

A south Atlantic storm crashed over the city of New Carthage. The city had the ability to navigate around such a thing, but an artificial land mass carrying two hundred thousand people could only move so fast. Hurricanes could be predicted a week or more in advance. A storm, though? That was what the dome was for. Still, it made for an eerie sight. Livia stared out the window, mesmerised by the view across the city that ended in a dark barrier as sheaves of rain lashed the outside of the dome. It was perfectly dry inside the dome, which made the sight unique and strange.

She shivered as far-off thunder boomed. The lightning, however, had failed to cut through the soak. She turned and looked around the apartment. Her apartment now. Tully was packing up and would be departing shortly. He'd been in a foul mood much of the morning and had clearly been drinking even before she'd been up and around. Tortured, that's how he looked.

"Come back with me," he'd said.

She'd considered it, albeit briefly, if for no other reason than to tidy up her affairs there. But there was nothing in London for her now. She had work to do, work best done here. She wanted to come to her own conclusions. For once in her life, she had resources to draw on.

"My place is here."

He hadn't tried to convince her.

A simulated fire crackled on one wall, digital wood sizzling and popping with a comforting heat. She sat back down by it and picked up her xBook, ran her hands over the paper, then opened it at the page she'd been reading. The book was a collection of myths of ancient gods. She'd bought it to understand more about the Phoenician goddess Aštart, the patron of her new home, but she'd reached a part where the deity bore her brother seven daughters and it was getting a bit convoluted.

The door chimed and she cursed, not in the mood for company. There was still no sign of Tully, and Haymaker had gone for a nap, not liking seeing the city under a storm. She meandered over to the door, hoping that when she opened it whoever was on the other side would already have disappeared.

It was the commander.

October peered over Livia's shoulder. "Is Tully here?"

Livia gestured for her to come in and the commander flashed her a smile, though it disappeared again before she'd even passed by.

October approached Tully's room, hesitated and looked around at Livia.

"Yeah, I'll get out of your way," Livia said, and went into her room. She ran over to her bed, jammed on her Mindscape headset and launched Panopticon from her egospace. She was practised at it now, and within seconds had reached today's window in the navigation room. A gut wrench later, she wound the pocket watch to live time and moved to where October was still standing. Now she could really find out what in humid hell was going on.

⤸

TULLY LAY ON the bed and looked at the ceiling, clothes strewn around him. He could feel the storm crashing against the dome. His own inner storm had abated, leaving him battered and drained. But every time he closed his eyes, he felt the heat and dust swirling around him; saw the dead woman staring into the infinite. Instead, he tried to focus on what they'd discovered about Martha's assassination. A crime of passion would have been a tragedy, but this? This had been a full-blown plot.

Not that Martha had been the only casualty. Bolivar had been taking Tully's blood sample to Fernando when his multicopter went down. A pretty unlikely coincidence. Indeed, a minor task to arrange compared to the machinations to pull off Martha's execution. If Lockwood had determined the importance of Bolivar's cargo in unpicking the investigation and been able to act so quickly, he must have eyes and ears even here. Which meant that Tully wasn't safe here.

Had someone been spying on him all this time? His skin prickled as he imagined, even now, being regarded by some invisible watcher. Was there anyone here he could really trust?

He needed to get out of New Carthage, but was he even allowed to fly? Was the city still in lockdown? Would he have to seek October's permission? Come to that, was it even safe to fly? If Lockwood had struck Bolivar down for carrying a blood sample, surely Tully was at even greater risk, knowing what he now knew.

The was a light knock on the door. "Tully?"

He closed his eyes, unwilling to reply, but October opened the door and came in anyway. She surveyed the room, closed the door and sat on the edge of his bed.

"You're going?" she said, voice soft but with a note of hurt that threatened to reignite the storm inside him.

He sat up. "As soon as the storm clears," he said. "I need to go back to London to write this. If you'll lift the lockdown and let me."

She looked down and swallowed, then her mask came back on and she was the commander again. "It's not ready to write yet."

"The hell it isn't. We're less than a week away from election day. The world needs to know."

"There are gaps: things we don't know yet, that don't make sense. Deirdre's still checking and double-checking all the transaction information. She managed to go from a transaction to a wallet, from that wallet to another transaction, and from that transaction to various user accounts with Kehoe's identity linked to them. But what if that wallet leads us to more transactions, more wallets? There may be a spider's web to unpick here."

"I don't see how it matters. We've got enough to prove that Kehoe, and therefore Lockwood, engineered this. You can keep working on the extent of the crimes but I'll report on the ones I can see in front of me."

She looked exasperated. "The timeline doesn't add up. Think about it. Take the perfume: Jiang's loans were extended over the course of a year before they switched the serum supplier, three months before Martha was killed. Then the supplier disappears just before she's killed. And Jacobs had been radicalised for over a year?"

"And?"

"And Lockwood wasn't even a candidate a year ago. Solomon certainly wasn't. Why would Lockwood launch a counter-offensive against Solomon perfectly timed for when they became the last two candidates? He'd have had to rig the primaries to be sure of that outcome."

Tully stared at her. "Rigged primaries. Of course."

"No, I'm not saying—"

"It makes sense! Who would Lockwood most want as his opposition? A joke candidate, one he can demean and attack because it's not even human."

"You couldn't rig something of this scale."

"Two hundred countries with three electors each." He jumped up and started to stuff some of the clothes into the small suitcase, taking no care to fold it. "Maybe you need two out of three electors in a third of the countries to pull this off. What's that… A hundred and thirty people? Shit."

"This is ridiculous."

He was moving fast, now, like he was in a race to get all packed. "You can get to one hundred and thirty people. Bribery, blackmail, extortion. The mafia used to do it all the time." He paused and waved a dirty shirt at her. "And let's not forget that Lockwood's people are far more sophisticated than that. They seem to have figured out how to radicalise people through incredibly person-alised propaganda on Minds. What if they did the same, targeting just those one hundred and thirty people with the aim of influencing their vote?"

"How could a campaign have access to that kind of tech?"

"He was the US president for eight years. The US government has access to all sorts of black-ops technology. Who knows what he decided to poach afterwards? This could take years to unravel." He slammed the suitcase shut and zipped it up. Out of the corner of his eye, he saw her shake her head. "Anyway," he said after a moment, "none of that matters yet. I don't need to make the whole case yet, only the opening gambit."

A silence stretched between them, and outside the symphony of thunder reached a crescendo. For a moment, Tully imagined he could feel the whole city rock and sway, but it was surely his imagination.

"We're not there yet," she whispered. "We don't know for sure. If you write this, it upends the election. If you're wrong—"

"I'm not wrong," he said. "Lockwood planned this all out. He hid it so well. Kehoe did the dirty work. They manipulated Jiang into a position where she couldn't afford *not* to switch supplier. They unleashed a torrent of personalised propaganda against Flora to convince her to taint the vodka. We've traced both events back to Kehoe. It's a story."

"I'm worried that you're … that you've been blinded by the belief that Lockwood did something to affect the tabkhir."

"He did," Tully growled.

"You don't know that."

Of course he did. He'd seen the video. And she was blinded by her own political beliefs. "Once a Lockwood supporter, always a Lockwood supporter, huh?"

"What's that supposed to mean?" She stood up, her face flushed.

"Remember what you said to me? 'What makes you think I'd vote Solomon?' You don't even support your own boss as a candidate, though you're happy to live in the city he runs."

"I told you, I don't discuss politics with friends."

"We hardly know each other." As soon as he said the words he wished he could take them back.

She stared at him for a beat then backed away, turned and opened the door.

"October," he said.

She didn't look back, just paused in the doorframe, silhouetted against the lights of the room beyond. "Get the hell out of my city," she whispered.

And then she was gone.

❧

LIVIA TOOK OFF her headset. That had been … enlightening, though it also raised many questions. Who was this Deirdre, for example? It sounded like she had all the data. And if there was one thing Livia needed right now, it was data. Sure, Tully had a lot of reasons to suspect Lockwood, and maybe he was right. But October had raised some valid questions that needed answering if they were to be sure they'd found the truth. The consequences of getting this wrong were just too significant. Once upon a time, Tully would have been the first to tell her that.

She walked out of her bedroom and looked out the window. Swirls of grey and black clouds shrouded the city in a false twilight despite it being only a few hours post noon. The streets below were almost empty. She needed to keep an eye on Tully. She wouldn't have Panopticon in London.

She knocked on Haymaker's door and whispered, "Haymaker?"

He opened the door.

"I need you to make a little trip for me," she said.

"Where?"

"London." She forestalled his objection with a smile and raised palms. "I can look after myself for a few weeks. I'm not a li'l girl anymore. But I'm worried about Tully and need someone to keep an eye on him."

He seemed to weigh that, then nodded. "Okay."

She was surprised he'd agreed so quickly, but then he had no love for New Carthage. "One more thing, Haymaker. Don't tell Tully why you're there." She grinned. "Men have fragile egos, you know?"

53

The same uniformed man who'd greeted Tully on his arrival in New Carthage escorted him through the empty terminal. The man's smile had disappeared in the intervening weeks and he gave Tully only a curt "This way." He did work for October, after all. Perhaps he'd gotten the memo.

They reached the airside section of the terminal. The man palmed the door open and nodded at the waiting multicopter.

"My luggage?" Tully said.

"Already on board."

Tully stepped out and the door slid shut behind him. He took a moment to appreciate the freshness of the air and chirping of exotic birds perched in trees to the left of the copter-pad. It wouldn't be like this in London, that was for sure. He'd wanted to leave New Carthage behind, had been homesick, but you couldn't deny how tranquil this place was. He'd likely never set foot here again. While the rest of the world continued to burn and drown, the citizens of the Floating States would ride it out, breathing in their delicious air.

Yet maybe that was just bitterness talking, bitterness that he couldn't be one of them, that he couldn't stay here with Livia and Haymaker and ride out the end of the world in luxury.

And maybe he wouldn't even make it as far as the end of the world. He looked at the multicopter and took a deep breath. Was this going to be it? Would an explosion rip the craft apart at twenty thousand feet? He swallowed. There was nothing for it. He was in the hand of the fates and whatever additional safety protocols October had ordered to be installed after Bolivar's flight had gone down. He boarded. One of the eight passenger seats was already filled. Significantly so.

"I thought you were staying with Livia?" Tully said.

Haymaker shrugged. "Gonna head back to London with you and grab her stuff."

Tully nodded, not caring. He shoved his hand luggage into the overhead compartment, sat down in the rear seat and fastened his seatbelt.

The pilot looked around. "Mr Tully? I'm Captain Sherman. How're you doing?"

"Fine, thank you."

"This is a two-hour trip to Cape Town International Airport, where I believe you and Mr Haymaker here have a connecting flight to London. Is that right?"

Tully nodded and checked his seatbelt.

The pilot grinned. "Nervous flier?"

"Yeah. My friend died. On Flight NC404."

"Ah. I'm sure sorry to hear that. But don't you worry. I've flown these things for a decade and they're safer than getting out of bed in the morning. Now, you just try to relax, put on some headphones or something, and I'll have you in Cape Town before you can find something worth listening to."

"Thanks," Tully said, and checked his seatbelt again.

The doors slid shut. There was a whine as the six propellers started up. A few moments later, the multicopter glided up and Tully's stomach dropped. He gripped the seat until his knuckles turned white.

It was going to be a long journey.

꩜

OCTOBER BALLED HER hands into fists and paced around in her office. She should have arranged to see the governor first, before telling Tully, before taking him down below the city, to her special place. She should have done a lot of things differently. It was clear now. The finale of their argument echoed around her head. *Damn him.* She'd genuinely liked him. Not at first, for sure, but for all his flaws, his arrogance and unsmiling demeanour, he was a man who was good at what he did, who passionately believed in a moral code and who was willing to stand up for his beliefs. He was smart, dedicated, sexy—

Damn him to hell.

She was meant to be rehearsing what to tell the governor, not thinking about her personal life, which mattered not a jot against the magnitude of the news she was about to break. She subspoke a request to meet Solomon, received an immediate invitation back and pulled on her Mindscape.

She took a deep breath in her egospace, the porch of her grandfather's lake house. What she wouldn't do to be back here for real right now, curled up next to him on the hanging seat, watching the kingfishers dive. She missed him, missed her home.

This was real life, albeit a technical illusion; New Carthage, for all its attractions, was the artificial creation.

Tully would have liked it here.

She gritted her teeth. Enough.

She moved into Solomon's meeting space. His virtual office had become even more sparse in the past weeks. They were now in a vast, empty space with high ceilings and slanted walls, odd-shaped windows that light streamed through but that offered no visible landscapes beyond, and a hovering white desk with no legs at the epicentre of the light. It was alien and unearthly. Was this somehow the equivalent of Solomon's egospace? What did it say about the artilect's psyche? Solomon was sitting at the desk, but there was no chair for her, so she stood in front and clasped her hands behind her back.

"Governor," she said.

"Hello, Commander," he said. "What do you have for me?"

She swallowed. "Sir, we've made some progress with the investigation. I can't promise it's conclusive yet, but I thought you should know where we are."

"Go on."

She wished Tully was here to back her up; damn that man. "Dr Chandra was killed using a barbiturate manufactured to activate in two stages. She was primed from perfume pills manufactured by MyScent, here in New Carthage. Then she consumed vodka laced with a catalyst that combined with the agent in the perfume pills."

She paused, expecting a reaction or a question, but Solomon just nodded. "I see. Go on."

"Sir, our original investigations led us to conclude that Flora Jacobs laced the vodka. However, she knew nothing about the perfume. It appears she was manipulated by propaganda targeting her specifically that made her believe in a conspiracy theory. Meanwhile, the perfume contamination was linked to a base ingredient in the perfume, a serum. It appears the supplier bought the original serum, contaminated it and repackaged it."

"A complicated plan."

"Yes, and one that required significant resources to pull off. We've concluded that this was no crime of passion, nor a localised competitor or someone jockeying for her position at Chandraco. Just to manufacture the barbiturate, and I quote from what will be in my official report, required 'nation-state level capabilities'."

"I would concur," Solomon said. He waited.

She hesitated. It was time to light the fuse. "Sir, we've traced financing of all this back to Jeff Kehoe, until recently the mayor of Houston, now chair of the Lockwood campaign for dictator of the nation states."

Solomon sat back now and frowned. "The Lockwood campaign targeted Martha?" He paused and it was if a dark shadow filled the room, but stayed just out of sight. It was markedly colder, too, not quite at the temperature of The Fridge, but heading that way. October shivered. "If this is true," Solomon said, "I will wipe them from the face of the Earth." He suddenly seemed to wake from a digital reverie and focus on her, the most human reaction she had ever seen from him. "But not yet. We have an election to win. This is a very significant accusation. Is Marcus Tully planning to write about it?"

"I couldn't presume to say."

"Indulge me with an educated guess."

October tried to work up some saliva in her mouth to loosen the bitter, dryness thinking of Tully left behind. "Then," she said, "I would guess yes."

Solomon tapped his fingers on the desk. "An accusation like this can't originate from me, or from my campaign. If I did make it, I would be accused of being self-serving, of manufacturing a crisis on my own soil to tarnish the reputation of my only competitor."

She gaped. "You're not going to respond?"

"We're going to let Mr Tully write his story," Solomon said, "and then respond in force."

⟿

ONLY WHEN THE multicopter was properly grounded did Tully release his grip on the seat. He peeled his hands away and massaged life back into his palms and fingers.

The pilot turned around and grinned. "Told you we'd be alright, didn't I? Safest damn things I've ever flown."

Tully pushed back his nausea and nodded. The door slid back and heat blasted through the cabin. He stood with a wobble, found his feet and retrieved his bag.

A white line led him and Haymaker into Cape Town's terminal. The airport had once been a major hub for international departures, but securing a visa even for a vacation had become a bureaucratic nightmare, with so many borders now hardened, and neuro-reality holidays had become all the rage instead.

He checked the board; his connecting flight was delayed by at least half a day. He looked around for a good place to slump and squeezed into an end seat next to a large woman with a small kid squirming on her lap. Haymaker sat opposite and began to people-watch.

Tully brought up a small virtual screen containing an empty document. He closed his eyes, opened them and began to write.

For years, the Oval Office has been a revolving door of 'leaders of the free world.' But as the world stands on the cusp of its inaugural global election, one former U.S. president is poised to make that title more than a lofty catchphrase.

The role of a global dictator is a paradox, straddling both might and meekness. It's about possessing the fortitude to make the tough calls in the looming shadow of a climate Armageddon, and the modesty to relinquish that authority once the storm has passed.

Yet, the path to power for President Lockwood has been far from virtuous. Murder and manipulation have marred his campaign, clearing aside anyone in his path, Martha Chandra, creator of Solomon, first in the way.

54

"I have another note from the Lockwood campaign," Lottie said. "This is from their general counsel."

Tully didn't look up. "What's he got to say?"

"The usual. One denial, two threats."

"What else can they say?" Tully said.

The kitchen table was strewn with pizza boxes and empty mugs, so they'd retired to the sofas to write. Virtual windows, some shared, some private, surrounded them.

The rest of the apartment was quiet. Randall had learned from long experience to stay out of the way on a writing day, and Haymaker had gone on some errand for Livia. It wasn't much compared to the Monument apartment, which was still undergoing restoration, but Lottie had done well to find them anything, even though there were two fewer of them to accommodate than before. A lump swelled in his throat at the thought.

"I think the general flow's there," he said. "The article's first paragraph is a good hook. We frame the motive, set up with Martha's murder, then outline the assassination in a series of layers which we go on to peel back. Then we link through to the money. The ending ties us back to the election."

Lottie took a swig of tea and frowned. "What about the tabkhir?"

He sighed. "The only way I'd put that out before the election is if it still looks like Lockwood will win. Bolivar was right. It could cause another world war and might disrupt the election itself. We'll save it for after."

⤻

Tully sat at his desk, staring at the flowery wall of his small, dark study. He missed his old study, so airy and light.

He had no motivation to look at the Kuwait videos, or to check his competitors' recent articles. It was publication day. Revenge was close. His absence always gave the team space in the hour before they went live. There was a well-defined to-do list in a high-stress environment, and him standing over everyone cranked it up higher. It was Bolivar who'd suggested he'd stay out of the way, and he'd been right. Tully's job was done.

He closed his eyes, wishing that his friend would walk in through that door right now. There was a knock, but it was Lottie who called for him. "Ready, Tully?"

He shrugged off the surge of grief as best he could and joined her in the kitchen living space. It seemed lifeless without Livia and Bolivar. Randall sat at a small kitchen table.

"Influencers are ready, Randall?"

Randall nodded. For once he wasn't smiling. He looked even more terrified than when he'd jumped down the escape chute. Earlier that morning, Lottie had told Tully that Randall was struggling with being part of a story that would change the world this significantly. But he'd be okay, Tully was sure of it. They just needed to push through.

"Good job," Tully clapped a hand to Randall's arm. "Lottie, how long do we have?"

"Ten minutes."

"Final headline?"

"*LOCKWOOD IMPLICATED IN ASSASSINATION OF SOLOMON'S CREATOR.*"

"To the point," he said.

"Bamphwick is on the air, attacking you," Lottie said, turning to him. "When are we going to take this bozo down?"

Tully laughed. "To what end? There's always a market for that kind of demagoguery. Stamp out one critter and another will take their place."

"So you're going to let him dunk on you?"

"I'm going to do what everyone should do to people like Jordan Bamphwick. I'm going to ignore him. Attention is the only fuel he has to keep his fire burning."

Lottie sighed. "The Lockwood campaign wants to speak to you again."

"We've already had their denial," he said.

"And threats. But Lockwood himself wants to talk," Lottie said.

Tully tapped his foot. "Share it."

A virtual screen appeared, the little drone took off and Lockwood appeared. His ice blue eyes still flashed, but they were underlined with bags that someone had failed to cover well with makeup. "Mr Tully," Lockwood said. "We're not friends, you and I, and you owe me nothing. But you have to give us more time. We've looked through what you've provided and we don't have answers for you yet. None of this makes sense. I can tell you that neither I nor anyone else in my team had anything to do with Dr Chandra's tragic death. I don't compete on salted earth."

"Our evidence is conclusive," Tully said. "I've heard the denials, the threats from your lawyers, the rhetoric from your tame news host. That's the thing about truth. Sometimes you just have to own it and accept it's something you can't bluff your way out of."

Lockwood tried to maintain a facade of sophistication and calm, but he was clearly seething. "This *is* the truth. Let me be very clear, we believe your so-called evidence has been tampered with. Initially, we thought you were lying. But given the details you've provided, I understand why you've reached the conclusions you have. Mr Tully, someone is playing us both. Someone has set this all up. You're being manipulated. It's the only explanation."

"It's Occam's Razor," Tully said. "The simplest explanation with the smallest number of assumptions is this: you wanted to throw your only other opponent in the biggest leadership race in history under the bus and then have goons like Bamphwick broadcast the disarray while you rode the poll numbers to victory."

Lockwood threw his hands in the air. "Listen to yourself. I'd have to have spent years planning all this! And how the hell would I know what kind of vodka Chandra drank, what kind of perfume she had?"

"You don't think the CIA's capable of figuring that kind of thing out?"

"I'm not president anymore, Mr Tully, I don't run the CIA. I haven't for a decade."

"I'm sure there are private black ops accessible."

"And I didn't even know I was going to win the primary until a month ago! And let me tell you, it was as much a surprise to me as everyone else. Everyone told me there was no way an American would win this, that we were too tarnished. Yet somehow I came through. And I ran a good, clean campaign. I honestly believe I'm the best candidate, the right candidate to get this done. You can't take this away from me. You need to look at it all again, figure out who's trying to set me up—set you up! We'll provide resources, money, whatever you need."

"It's days until election day. Of course you'd say that."

Lockwood surged to his feet and the camera panned back to keep him in frame. "You fucking English hack. At a minimum, the consequences of your actions will be a goddamned disaster. You really want to let a computer determine your fate? A glorified app that deep down doesn't care about us, only whatever mysterious parameters Chandra set? All of our fates? It will be on you, you realise."

"No, it won't," Tully said. "It will be on you. It was always on you." He nodded at Lottie and she hung up. He closed his eyes. The magnitude of what was about to happen almost overwhelmed him. These were the bittersweet moments before the world shifted irrevocably on its axis. The moments before vengeance was fulfilled. The moments before a man was destroyed in front of the world. He recalled Lockwood in the situation room: *Our own people must come first, always. Admiral, execute Icarus One.*

"You need to sign it. With the unique key," Lottie said.

That bastard had taken his wife, his child, his happiness. Now Tully would take his. He activated his earset and issued his authentication. "Randall, publish it."

Randall tapped lethargically.

An alarm in Tully's display chirped six p.m.

"We're on," Randall said, sounding exhausted. It was done.

"My God," Lottie exclaimed. "These numbers. It doesn't make any sense."

"What is it?" Tully said.

"We have a third of the number of influencers we used to have, down to a thousand, but it was like a hundred thousand were waiting for the story to be published. It's being shared ten thousand times a second."

Tully chewed his thumbnail. "Okay. What are the financials looking like?"

Lottie pulled up the coin widget. "It's already lifted off … rounding to the nearest ten coin—no, hundred coin."

"That's fast," Tully said, "but it's well south of the sharing numbers. So people are sharing it before they've read it."

"This can't be organic," Lottie said. "Someone's doing us a favour, here."

"That only makes sense if—" There was a pang, and a message came in. Tully stared at the title and froze.

ZAINAB.

He opened it. Three words. *passport.conserved.furnace.* He squinted. Three forward slashes preceded the text, meaning it was a location key, one that related to a small square patch of land somewhere in the world. "Excuse me," he said, and walked away from them, into his study, slamming the door, and running a search on the key before he even reached his desk.

The location appeared on the virtual screen projected above his desk, and Tully's knees buckled. *Kuwait International Airport.*

⌒

LIVIA SIGHED AS she went through her to-do list. Who'd have thought money needed so much managing? Lawyers, accountants, fund managers… it took a veritable army.

She hadn't even touched the management of Chandraco yet. A now-recovered Pedersen could cope for now, with an occasional prod from her, though they were still deciding whether to charge him over his illegal pentobarbital.

As for Martha's digital vault, she'd still only scratched the surface. She brought up the classified section again, the one Tully had wanted access to and that she'd used as leverage to get an extra brain investigating Martha's murder. She sniffed and studied a bunch of intriguing tags listed by recent date of access. The topmost one was called *Project Harpocrates.* She grabbed her book on gods and goddesses and flicked to the glossary.

Harpocrates: the Grecian god of silence and secrets.

Livia snorted. There really had been a god for everything… except coffee, tragically discovered too late for the ancient world to appreciate. The stuff had spread from the Sufi monasteries of Ethiopia to the Arabian Peninsula and then beyond.

What a shame that the whole region was now closed to the world. Damn the caliphate. The birthplace of coffee as the world knew it, and she'd never have the opportunity to make so much as a pilgrimage.

She frowned and peered more closely at the folder. Now, *this* was interesting. It looked like Martha had created some kind of privacy software, installable on earsets. The god of secrets, indeed. There were some notes in the folder. Livia scanned them. *Tested against Rehoboam beta … Should have artilect-grade privacy protection … Needs manually installing on factory reset earsets.*

This was a veritable sweet shop of treats, and no child spent too long staring at just one jar. What other candy did Martha have in stock?

***

HIS HAND TREMBLING, Tully cast a virtual screen and launched the footage of Kuwait. The whole world had changed since he'd last looked at it. He checked the three-words map and zoomed in on the location. It was on the edge of a small loop of road next to a roundabout. He returned to the footage and began to navigate, his mouth dry. He found the terminal first, then the roundabout. The footage was at floor level. He followed the roundabout around, took an exit and swung left to follow the road.

He swallowed. The footage crept forward now. There were bodies, but he ignored them. Further forward, the road began to turn back on itself, and he swung the camera view to the left. A woman with long, wavy hair lay by the roadside. She was curled up on her side, arms wrapped around her very pregnant belly. She could have been asleep. She was beautiful even in death.

He reached his hand towards the screen, but his hand passed through. He couldn't touch her, would never touch her again.

The door burst open. Lottie and Randall stormed in, shock in their eyes. He realised he'd cried out, and turned away, trying to hide himself. But he couldn't stop now he'd started, couldn't prevent quakes of grief shaking through him. Arms tightened around his head as Lottie cradled him.

"She was at the airport," he said. "She was coming home. She was so close."

55

There was a brisk knock at the door and Captain Ibrahim ducked under the doorframe. October had always liked the graceful Nigerian officer. He was damned efficient at his job. "I have the report on the black box, Commander," he said.

"For Flight NC404?"

"Yes. It was an explosion, but one caused by a hacker, not explosives."

She frowned. "Explain."

"The multicopter was fully electric. The battery's managed by microcontrollers –essentially sensors that monitor it in real time. We've examined the logs and believe a payload containing a worm reprogrammed them such that the battery reported an artificially low internal voltage. The systems diagnosed a battery drain, drew on extra stored capacity from the emergency backup chargers and turned on additional functionality to capture additional energy from the wind and sun."

"You're saying the battery was overcharged? How is that a problem, exactly?"

"The internal temperature exceeded a critical level, causing a thermal runaway. It's a chain reaction whereby the heat causes a chemical reaction, which causes more heat, and in turn more chemical reactions until the battery overheats and explodes."

She sat back. "Has it ever happened before? Was this kind of vulnerability known, somewhere, in the aviation community, or even, God help us, the hacking one?"

He shook his head. "To my knowledge, this is the first time it has occurred in a multicopter. Someone exploited a weakness in the system they could use to reprogram the microcontrollers. Now that we know how it was done, we can talk to the manufacturer and get it patched."

"Is there anything that can lead us to the hacker?"

Ibrahim eyed the door and pushed it shut. He looked back at her. "Commander, the only time I've seen something like this was from the US and the Israelis, back in the day. Those guys were geniuses when it came to creating worms that could screw with all kinds of things. I say that because this isn't your run-of-the-mill teenage hacker causing mischief, nor even a terror cell. This was nation-state competency. It would cost a lot of money to develop a worm like this, using exploits purchased on the black market, and likely required spies to penetrate commercial facilities and steal crucial data to ensure the payload worked with this specific microcontroller and didn't spread and bring down multicopters everywhere. Added to all that, it was injected remotely while the multicopter was in flight, and that's no easy task."

October steepled her hands in front of her lips in thought. Perhaps all roads did lead back to Lockwood. "Is there any way we can see if the attack came from the US?"

Captain Ibrahim blinked but recovered fast. "We'll see if we can pinpoint where the attack originated, Commander." He clicked his heels together and left the room.

October stared into space until a tap on the door disturbed her. Deirdre entered and stood in front of October's desk. "Hello, dear," she said. "I was just passing and thinking about our Mr Kehoe and his dirty transactions. And I realised I'd been so focused on how the money was spent that I hadn't looked at where it came from in the first place. Laundered, certainly, but I wonder if we can trace it far enough back?"

October nodded and tried to give a smile that would close the conversation. "Keep me posted."

"Right you are, my dear."

Someone pushed past Deirdre on her way out, and this time October sighed. "Colonel Simpson, how are you?"

"Commander, do you mind if I close the door?"

October gestured and the colonel turned to close it.

"Commander, we've been monitoring dark-web chatter and picked up a mention of an authentication matching one Marcus Tully, who was visiting the late Dr Martha Chandra and left last week. Since Juan Bolivar, a passenger on Flight NC404, was registered as visiting Marcus Tully, we flagged it."

"What was the context?"

"A US news host, Jordan Bamphwick, went on air last night accusing Mr Tully of anti-Lockwood propaganda to interfere with the election."

"What's that got to do with the anti-terrorism team?"

"After Bamphwick's monologue aired, there was significant social media uproar with negative sentiment towards Mr Tully, particularly in the more conspiracy-minded subset of President Lockwood's supporters. A further subset took the conversation onto the dark web, and before they moved into encrypted chat groups it was clear that a very hard-line, anti-artilect extremist group had decided that Mr Tully is a threat to the election and therefore the world. They're trying to track down his location and prevent him from releasing any more stories."

October stood, smoothed herself down and tried to work through the logical next question, but her thoughts were jumbled and she just hesitated. "Commander," Simpson said, "would you like me to try to reach Mr Tully and warn him?"

"No, no," she said. "I'll do it. Thank you, Colonel."

$$\backsim$$

TULLY WEAVED ALONG the Waterloo Island bridge to the south of the Thames floodway. *Shit.* Too much rum, that's what it was, and he could tolerate a lot of pirate juice, but it had been a long time since the world had spun like this, not since the blurry days after the tabkhir, not that he wanted to think of that right now, but he'd needed to get out, to escape the worried, pitying eyes of his colleagues. His soaking shirt stuck to his skin. Mosquitoes bit wherever skin was exposed. And the flooded river stank. Not that it mattered. It all stank. He stank.

A couple came towards him, their arms interlinked. He placed one foot in front of the other, trying hard not to stumble or veer sideways. The man ignored him as they passed, but the woman's nose curled in disgust. Tully mumbled something at her, but even he didn't know what he'd said.

Zainab had been beautiful even in death.

The world began to tilt and Tully stumbled backwards, but instead of falling over, he continued to stumble for nearly ten paces until he finally tripped and fell and the breath was knocked out of him by the hot concrete. At least the world had stopped moving. He looked up at the sky. Had there ever been damn stars above London or were they all condemned to die in a starless smog? There'd been stars over New Carthage, a beautiful scape of shine. The rich would inherit the stars.

A chime and a flash alerted him to an incoming call. He declined it, jabbing at a large red virtual button in the air.

It rang again. Again, he declined it. The chime came yet again and this time he answered. "Why can'tchu jus' leave me alone?"

"Tully? My God, are you okay?"

"Wh's this?"

"Are you drunk? Tully, you need to sober up now. You're in danger."

"October?"

"Pull yourself together. A hard-line group of Lockwood supporters are trying to silence you. They're trying to find your location. You need to get to safety."

"Thes no safety, yo'know. Can't hide. It will burn us'al. So hot, an we can't run. S'many bodies. An th'childn."

There was a pause at the other end. "You once told me you never got drunk, ever. What in humid hell happened? What's going on, Tully?"

Tully looked at the sky. Moonlight backlit the murky clouds. "Aish found her, yknow. Someone sen'me … the location. Whershe was. In Kuwait."

"You found your wife? She's alive?"

Tears welled up in him then, and he choked them back. "She's dead. Aishsaw her. She's dead, oh God …" A sob wracked him and hot rain coursed down his cheek. He wiped it away. Rain wasn't meant to be hot.

"I'm so, so sorry, Tully, but you have to get up. A group of anti-artilect extremists are trying to find you. They'll hurt you, might even kill you. They think you're trying to swing the election against Lockwood and they really want Lockwood to win."

He heard the words, but the meaning didn't land. The night seemed darker now, and he was just so damn tired, tired of it all. He needed—

"Tully?"

Sleep.

⌣

"Tully?" October said again.

Nothing.

Dammit, think. He hadn't hung up, so he was either considering what she'd just said, or was unconscious, and Tully never took that long to consider. October muted the line, brought up another window and connected to a monitoring tool. "Locate the coordinates of this open call's origins," she said.

Before she even had the results, she called Livia. Even as an artificial image, Livia's avatar had an air of suspicion and mistrust, like maybe Livia didn't like her very much.

"I need help," October said. "It's urgent."

"Okay?"

October hesitated. "You know what? This line may not be secure. Can we speak in NR? Right away?"

Livia nodded and hung up.

October checked the coordinates, then entered her egospace and chose the small, bustling coffee shop as her neuro-meeting space, taking a table in a little nook and cranny and inviting Livia. "Come on," she murmured, "what part of the word 'urgent' didn't you understand?"

"I understood everything, I just needed to pee." Livia looked around and sat. "Cute," she said. "How's the coffee?"

"Look, Tully's in danger." She repeated what she'd told Tully about the nature of the threat.

Livia frowned. "Why aren't you speaking to him? Is it because you fell out?"

"We didn't … I tried to speak to him. He's lying in a drunken heap right now. It sounded like he'd fallen or something, and then he just stopped talking."

"Tully, drunk?" Livia shook her head. "Impossible."

October slammed her hands on the table. "I'm not making this up. He's in serious danger right now and is incapable of even comprehending it."

Livia held up a hand. "Okay, okay. I was just trying to say, Tully never gets properly drunk, ever. He drinks, sure, but it just doesn't seem to really hit him. Something big must have happened if he's in that state."

"I'm tracking his location through an open call. It looks like he's on a bridge to something called Waterloo Island?"

"Right, yeah, in the floodway."

"Is there anyone you trust in your old team that can go help him and get him somewhere safe?"

"I'll sort it. But I want something in return from you." Livia raised her chin and met October's eyes.

A quid pro quo, now? Tully was Livia's friend too, or so she'd thought. "Okay?" It came out chillier than she'd intended.

Livia's mouth tightened. "I want you to get your colleague Deirdre to give me information on the transaction information traced to Kehoe."

October narrowed her eyes. "How do you even know about Deirdre? Or the transaction info?"

"A conversation for another time. But let's just say I have some tools at my disposal Deirdre doesn't have."

"Fine. But you should know there's more going on here."

"More?"

October nodded. "Your late colleague, Bolivar. We found where the multi-copter went down four days ago and retrieved the black box. It was sabotage. If he was targeted, it was likely because of what he was carrying: a vial of Tully's blood for analysis after … after your sister's death. That blood would have led us to the binary poison sooner."

Livia cocked her head to the side. "And?"

"And how the hell did whoever targeted that multicopter know what Bolivar was carrying?

"First things first," Livia said. "Let's get Tully to safety, and I've got some transport to arrange."

"Can't your team do it?"

"Some things you have to do yourself."

56

Livia yawned as she crossed the road from Cannon Street Station, then coughed and almost gagged. The air reeked of acrid smoke that scratched at the back of her throat, though the worst of the upheaval was down the road towards Westminster. No one was protesting at St Shitsville, as the homeless locals so eloquently called this place.

She paused then slipped down a narrow side street. She'd take the small roads, pass the Roman temple museum on Walbrook, buried by modernity, and cut around the back of Mansion House, then head towards King William Street. The alleyways had once been pristine, unusually so for a big city, but no one considered them safe now, packed as they were with tents, people cooking insect burgers with illegal gas and kids running around barefoot. It was a rancid mess, but she wasn't scared. She'd lived in worse places. And she'd taken care to dress appropriately. She walked slowly, head dipped as if weary with the world. It wasn't so hard. She had purpose now, but purpose only went some way to blunting the pain.

She stopped at the corner of St Swithin's and King William. The road had been cleared since she'd been here last, but the tents had popped right back up. Across the street was a large arch in the facade just below the church. More tents crowded the way, but part of the black railings had been kicked down and she squeezed her head through. A huge man stood up.

"You gotta help me, lady," he said. "They gone burn my stuff again."

She smiled but didn't get too close. He'd need a shower before she attempted that. "Where is he, Haymaker?"

"Got him right back here." He pointed at two bare feet sticking out of a doorway. "Had to trade his boots for this spot, mind."

"He's okay?"

"Kept him drunk. Seemed the easy way to keep him here and outta trouble, and he weren't doing no objecting."

She walked over. Tully was an unconscious mess and looked like he'd been sleeping rough for a year rather than two nights. She pinched her nose. "He stinks."

Haymaker shrugged. "I've smelled worse."

Lucky him. "Well, that'll make it a fun journey," she said.

"We takin' a car?"

"Pod. We can be thankful they're self-driving. I'm not sure an old London cabbie would have given us a ride. Did you get rid of his earset?"

"Already gone by the time I reached him. Surprised he still had a shirt on his back."

"Good. Give me a moment while I sort our getaway, okay?" It had been a fast and expensive journey, though of course, now, she could afford it. Using one of Martha's classified tricks, she'd set herself up a fake identity. It wasn't fool proof. She'd put money into a fresh wallet and anyone looking hard enough could eventually trace it back to her. But that would take time, and by then she'd have discarded this ID and moved on to another.

A pod at the corner of Bank signalled that it was reserved, and she nodded to Haymaker. He clapped several nearby folk on the shoulder and fist-bumped the residents of the adjacent tents.

She examined Tully. "Can you wake him enough so he can walk with your help? Carrying him over your shoulder will make us conspicuous."

Haymaker shook Tully, who murmured as he was pulled to his feet.

Tully looked at Livia with glazed eyes. A pitiful sight, and a far cry from the man who'd once made her giddy with his fierce reputation.

"Let's go," she said.

⤿

TULLY WOKE WITH a gasp for breath, his whole body lurching in pain, a jolt spreading through his arm. His stomach roiled, and he retched. "Going to be sick," he gasped.

A woman spoke. A door opened. Someone grabbed and lifted him. Then he was outside, hands on his knees, gagging. He breathed short, sharp bursts of air to stop himself from vomiting, and after a moment the queasiness subsided enough for him to stand upright and take stock. His head was thumping and his mouth felt like someone had stuffed it full of paper towel. He blinked and rubbed at his eyes to clear the blurriness.

He was on a bridleway, lined by high hedges beneath towering trees. A little brook bubbled under the grass at the edge. He straightened and turned. There was a pod and two familiar faces. "Livia? Haymaker? What in humid hell are you doing here? Wait, where the hell *is* 'here'?"

"Saving your ass," Livia said. "Come on. Get back in. We're only a few minutes from our destination."

Tully climbed in and wrinkled his nose. "It stinks in here."

She nodded. "That's you."

"Any water?"

Livia passed him a flask and he gulped it down until it was dry. "Sorry, we used a Detoxify jet injector on you," she said. "It seemed the best way to get you back with us. We haven't got any time to waste."

He frowned. "What happened? It's all hazy after—" *Zainab.* He could see her, lying there, arm tucked around her belly and their unborn daughter. So beautiful, even in death. *Oh God, even in death.* No, not that. Not now. He couldn't go there, not again.

"I don't know," Livia said. "Nearest I can make out, you'd just published your latest story when you got a message. You went into your room, and a few minutes later Randall and Lottie heard you having a complete breakdown. You were incoherent, so they put you to bed. They didn't realise you'd gone out until the next morning."

The pub. He'd wandered out for a walk, then found a pub. But then what?

"October contacted me," Livia said. "She'd called you, but you were drunk, in a real state. You'd fallen. She was trying to tell you that there's an active threat against you, because of what you wrote about Lockwood, and to stop you writing more."

"What?"

"She couldn't get you to understand, so she tracked your location and called me."

"You gone pissed off a lotta people," Haymaker said.

"What's new?" Tully said.

The road narrowed and the trees leaned in, creating a canopy overhead. They emerged into a cascade of backlit pine trees.

"So you found me?" he said.

"I asked Haymaker to go get you. He'd come here for a few days to make some arrangements for me and was already nearly back in London. I thought it was better him than Randall."

Tully swore. "Randall. What about him and Lottie? Are they safe? If someone is trying to find me, the apartment would be the first place they'd try."

She held up her hands. "Don't worry. I gave them strict instructions. They got out, left all their earsets and equipment behind just in case and headed to a safe place to stay for a few weeks until this all blows over, with an escape plan to open if everything goes wrong."

Tully could only shake his head. It seemed only a few weeks ago that Livia hadn't been organised enough to get herself from her bedroom to his study on time. Now she was running operations like some kind of spy chief. Maybe she had more to her than he'd ever imagined. Maybe she had more to her than *she'd* ever imagined. "How long was I unconscious?"

"Four days. Haymaker hid you in plain sight on the streets of London and basically kept you in the state you were in. No one notices a stinking, homeless drunk."

Haymaker growled, and she eyed him.

"Even if they should," she said.

"The election?" Tully said.

"Lockwood's polls have dropped, though not through the floor. Solomon's in the lead for the first time. There was a lot of outrage after your article landed, even though his base rallied around and screamed 'fake news' and the like. It's still going to be a close thing. Also, there's a lot of people saying very bad things about you, Lockwood included."

Tully sniffed. "I've more on Lockwood to come, once we're through the other side of the election. Then he'll have even worse things to say about me."

"A second story?"

Tully nodded. "I didn't want to publish it pre-election unless I had to, because, well, I'm concerned it might cause a geopolitical earthquake that could derail the election. But I've seen a video from the situation room. I think it's likely Martha illegally recorded it. Martha tries to convince them the tech isn't ready, but the others, led by Kehoe, are too worried the heatwave will be catastrophic for the US, and that the chances are it will just shift over the sea. Lockwood agrees with them. I have it. He caused the tabkhir."

Livia looked more contemplative than surprised. "You have the video, then?"

"Yeah."

"Where did you get it?"

"A source."

She sniffed. "I'd like to see it," she said. "You know, anything with Martha in right now … It's important to me."

He nodded. The movement made him feel his head was going to fall off and he groaned. "Do you have any painkillers?"

"I'm sure there'll be some at the house. We're nearly there."

"And where is 'there'?"

Livia smiled. "I found it in Martha's digital vault. She owns several properties around the world, through shell companies. This place is in the Cotswolds, in the middle of nowhere. Near a little hamlet, called Hilcot."

He looked around. "And you think we'll be safe here?"

She shrugged. "Safest place I can think of. No links to any of us."

The pod pulled left down a track and stopped outside a tall black iron gate set in a towering brick wall that curved off left and right into the distance.

"How big is this place?" Tully said.

"Give it a minute and you'll see for yourself," Livia said. She got out and thumbed a panel on the gate, then jumped back in again. The gate opened inwards without a sound and the pod continued.

"The pod had this on its map?" Tully said, surprised.

"No, I had to give some very specific coordinates. And I'll be sending it on a long series of journeys next, just to keep it moving and out of London for a few weeks."

"That'll cost you as much as buying one yourself," Tully said.

She didn't reply. They drove up a long drive to a turning circle outside a three-storey Georgian manor house. Had Martha ever come here? What in humid hell would a single workaholic even do with multiple properties around the world? Most likely she'd never left New Carthage once she was on it.

"Welcome to our new war headquarters," Livia said, and unlocked the front door.

He frowned at her back. Hadn't he just won the war? And if not, who the hell were they fighting?

⤾

THEY STEPPED INTO a drawing room. At one end, sofas were clustered near a fireplace. At the other, a large oval wooden table held court. A musky scent laced the air and mingled with the smokiness left from decades of fires lit in the hearth. It smelled of timelessness, and for a moment he was grateful for the opportunity to cherish a space where nothing had changed in a century or more.

Livia handed Tully an NR headset.

"Is it logged in as me?" he asked.

"No," she said. "You're anonymous for the moment. We all are. These are two special headsets. Lottie and Randall each have one too. We'll meet in a custom group egospace."

"I've never heard of such a thing."

"Something Martha had been working on."

Tully nodded at two comfy-looking chairs by the fire. They went over to them and sat, sinking into the leather with a *pfft*, and he stretched out his legs and yawned.

"Keep an eye out," Livia told Haymaker. "And an ear."

Haymaker nodded, and she and Tully pulled on their NR headsets.

The egospace resembled the actual drawing room in the manor, only now Lottie and Randall were sitting by the fire. They jumped up as Livia and Tully appeared.

Livia waved a hand. "Please, everybody, sit."

Who was this new Livia? She'd been a mess in New Carthage, but now it was like watching Martha in action. This Livia projected confidence and authority. It left him feeling usurped. It left him feeling relieved. It left him feeling curious, wanting to know what the humid hell had changed?

They all looked at Livia and waited.

She tapped her fingers together. "Here's where we are. My sister: assassinated. Bolivar: murdered. The flight was deliberately sabotaged."

"Wait," Tully said. "How—"

She ignored him. "First things first. Something else is going on here." She looked at Randall. "Tell him about what we… what *you* found. With the promoted post."

Randall swallowed. "Right, yeah. Well, you know, I thought it might be interesting, purely in an academic sense, you understand, to see if the company that had pushed all that propaganda at Flora Jacobs had done it before, whether there were other targets who'd been radicalised in the same way, you know, whether someone else had been killed—"

"And did you find something?"

"Yeah, but only one other account and one piece of content, which in itself is a bit weird, right? I mean—"

"Who?"

Randall hesitated and looked at Lottie.

Lottie looked at Tully. "You," she said.

Tully frowned. "What?"

"One piece of content: A photo of Flora Jacobs. A promoted post. An advert disguised as a normal post. A target audience of one. You."

"The one of Flora going into Danberg's …" He trailed off and they sat in silence. "No," Tully said finally. "It makes no sense at all. We know those accounts are linked to Lockwood's campaign. We know he radicalised Flora. Why would the campaign tip us in Flora's direction? That photo was what eventually led us to them."

Randall looked ashen. "Whoever did it managed to hack Minds. I mean, this wasn't just a clever bit of advertising. They managed to toggle the setting that let the platform display it as an advert, full stop, which meant either the culprit worked at Minds, or they had backdoor access—"

"You mean Lockwood has someone working at Minds?"

"No … Thing is, it got us—me—thinking about the whistleblower, the dude who managed to hide his identity. So I spoke to one of the developers I know at Mindscape and he put me in touch with their DevOps dude, and we spent like ten hours straight together working on this. I mean, they gave me full access, which is pretty cool—"

"The point," Livia said, "is that the same hacker who used the backdoor into the Minds platform either is the whistleblower or helped him hide his tracks. Randall managed to fingerprint both through a behavioural analysis AI."

Tully felt his head starting to throb. "But they have nothing to do with each other. The whistleblower was the one who put us on to Lockwood in the first place."

Livia leaned her elbows on the table and clasped her hands. "We need to go over everything, every bit of evidence that led you to Lockwood. These digital tracks led you to conclude he ordered the hit on my sister. We don't know that he didn't, but for some reason, either to help you get there faster or to help you come to a wrong conclusion, you've been manipulated, and we need to know by whom before we decide if you were misled."

57

Tully's expression flickered from disbelief to curiosity to fury. Not an easy thing for the ego, Livia thought, to discover you'd been fooled. Perhaps they'd all been fooled.

Tully stood, walked over to the fireplace, sat in the chair he'd taken in the real world and vanished.

Lottie looked at Livia. "There's more, but we didn't want to say it in front of him until we'd gone through it with you. It's your program, after all."

"What is it?" Livia said.

Randall opened his mouth but Lottie held up her hand, silencing him. "It's about Kehoe. You asked us to use Constellation and look into any patterns that stood out. You remember the airline he used, TransVI Air? A payment for 322.56 coin was made from the wallet to the TransVI corporate wallet. But Constellation has found an account called TransV1 Air. With a one instead of an uppercase 'I' after the 'V'. We don't know if that means anything, so thought we'd wait for you to check it."

Livia nodded. They used to call that a font-scam. It was used from the early days of the internet to trick people into clicking on fake username handles, pretending to be something else. "Let me look at what Constellation pulled up," Livia said.

She scanned the data, occasionally swiping and tapping the air, digging deeper, then sat back.

"Okay," Livia said. "It was flagged by Constellation for three reasons. First, the name was so similar. Second, only one transaction was registered. And third, the amount was identical to what Kehoe paid for his ticket, 322.56 coin."

"I still don't get it," Randall said. "I mean, he paid for a flight, took the flight, but there is a one-off payment made to a corporate wallet with an almost identical name—"

"The payment in the wallet traces back to another Kehoe account. His regular, personal account."

"He made two payments for the same amount?" Lottie said.

"He got scammed," Livia said. And it was simple, as the very best scams always were. Livia stood up and began to pace around the table. "It probably went something like this. Like most people, Kehoe will have a basic bot that manages his travel. He tells the bot to get him to Athens, maybe gives it the date and approximate timing. The bot has access to his wallet so it can make the booking. Now, from Kehoe's perspective, the bot does its job. It goes off, finds him a flight with TransVI Air, books it and pays. Even if he bothers to check his wallet, he probably won't look closely. Who does? He'll see a payment to TransVl Air and won't spot the 'l'."

"So what actually happened?" Lottie said.

"Kehoe got set up, that's what," Livia replied. "Someone spoofs the bot. Intercepts the booking. They book his actual flight with TransVI, but they use the wallet linked to the criminal transactions. Then they use his real wallet, as provided to the bot that was meant to be making the booking, to make a payment to the fake account, TransVl Air."

Randall puffed out his cheeks. "I mean, that's like thinking five or six moves ahead, knowing how it will be investigated and what'll be enough to demonstrate guilt and—" He began to tremble. "I-I'm going to be sick."

"Breathe, Randall," Livia said. "Be calm."

"But don't you see?" he said. "It wasn't Kehoe, yet he was the thread that pointed at Lockwood. I mean, the story we published was wrong, and it swung the whole election away from him. What have we done?"

Livia nodded. "Tully got played. The journalist with the fiercest reputation for telling the truth, whatever the right wing says about him, and he got played. The consequences—"

"The wallet," Randall said. "The TransVl wallet… if it's corporate, it must be domiciled somewhere, right?"

Good call. She checked to see if Constellation had any details.

"It was set up and the address was verified automatically by servers in …" she trailed off.

"Where?" Lottie said.

Livia took a deep breath. "In New Carthage."

They considered that together for a moment. "Could be a coincidence," Livia said, her voice a bit shaky, "but let's check it to be sure. I'll get Constellation to have a look and see if we can link this domicile to the fake social media account that targeted the personalised propaganda at Jacobs."

Randall nodded.

Livia started for the door, then paused. "By the way, what was it that sent Tully off the rails like that?"

Randall hesitated. "Well, we'd just published the story on Lockwood and the numbers were going bonkers. I mean, the shares were through the roof, it was like people hadn't even had time to read the story but knew it anyway, and we were just looking into that when—"

"Wait," she interrupted. "You're saying not just the influencers were sharing the story as soon as it landed? Others were too? Like an auto-share?"

"Yeah, like a hundred times more. It was totally insane. I mean, the amount of money coming in was really good but Tully said it wasn't consistent with the extent of sharing, you know, like people were sharing it without reading?"

"Lottie," Livia said, "can you look into that?"

Lottie nodded, and for a moment Livia waited for a retort, but she showed no resistance to taking an order from Livia, which was, frankly, a bit weird.

"And Tully?" Livia said.

"He got a message," Randall said, "almost straight away, but he didn't say what it was, just went into his study. A few minutes later, he kicked off, shouting and babbling, and he was just sobbing, just wracked with it. I've never seen—"

"It was his wife," Lottie said. "We all know she died in the tabkhir, right? But he'd been looking through some footage someone had slipped him about a month ago, trying to find her body. Bolivar told me about it after Tully and you flew to New Carthage. He was worried about Tully."

"You think he found her?"

"He definitely found her. The display was open and hadn't been set to private. It was at the airport in Kuwait City."

"And this was how long after he received the message?"

"A few minutes, tops."

"So we can probably conclude the message was about her location, right?"

Lottie nodded.

Livia thought it through. "He spends years looking, then a minute after publishing the biggest story of his life he receives a message telling him exactly where she is. That implies two things. First, someone had the ability to find her. And second, they knew Tully already had some footage of Kuwait, footage only his closest friend knew he had."

Randall's eyes were like saucers. "Wait, you're saying this was all part of it, too?"

Livia shrugged. "I don't know if it was meant as a reward, a punishment or simply to destabilise him… but yeah." She stood. "Find me that message sent to Tully, Randall. I want to know where it came from."

∽

TULLY LAY ON his bed and stared at the mosquito-splatted ceiling. He'd been manipulated. The thought was Tully's only stable one; the rest was just a blur of images, memories and fragmented conversations. That was the thing about truth. Sometimes, you only heard the truth you wanted to hear.

This also concerns your wife. Whistle had known his weak spot, and there was more, so much more, pointing him, like a hound on the scent, at Lockwood. When had it started? With the tabkhir story, or even before that? Whistle had given him the video of Kehoe and his police chief. That story had been correct, no matter how he'd been put on to it. A sense of unease tickled at him as he recalled Cavanagh's push-back, that the footage had been deepfaked.

"The experts say you can't deepfake neuro-reality," Tully had retorted, and surely that still held true? There was no way *that* could be manipulated. But, then, why did he feel like everything had gone wrong?

58

Livia scrolled through the classified section of the vault for other little secrets Martha had squirrelled away. Truth was, there was just too much here, like a menu with too many choices. A tag caught her eye: *Project Tefnut.* She'd read of *Tefnut*, the ancient Egyptian goddess of moist air, mother of the earth and sky. She tapped and scrolled through the files. The most recent one was a video dated 20 August 2040. The day before the tabkhir had hit the Gulf. She opened it.

It was the same old-fashioned, two-dimensional video conference from the situation room Tully had showed her earlier in the day, a series of split-screen talking heads. Martha looked younger but as confident as she'd always been. Then there was Lockwood, Cavanagh, Kehoe, Admiral Hogan and Dr Levin. She almost closed it again, but her eyes fixed on her sister.

No way had Martha recorded this with their permission, or even their knowledge. And why had she recorded it at all? The more she looked into her sister's secrets, the more she wondered whether Martha was paranoid. Not just of her former colleagues in the White House, but potentially everyone. She'd home-brewed her own surveillance system and privacy-ware as if she trusted nothing already out there to be good enough for her standards. Not a recent mania, either. This video was nine years old.

Livia hit play and Martha started to speak. "Mr President, I urge you not to turn it on. It's a prototype, intended only as a proof of concept to fund further geo-engineering research."

"Mr President," Kehoe said, "this is a question of chances. Dr Levin here assures us that due to the humidity, there is a ninety percent chance this heatwave

317

will be catastrophic to the Persian Gulf on a scale we've never seen before, particularly in the south."

Livia's stomach dropped. Catastrophic to the Persian Gulf? In Tully's video, Kehoe had said the US. What in humid hell?

Kehoe had continued. "After so many category-four, -five and -six cyclones this season, they lack power, shelter and water in the region. If this hits, and it will, it will result in the biggest death toll from a natural disaster in history."

"But—"

"Excuse me, Dr Chandra," Kehoe said. "I'm not finished. Mr President, let's counterbalance that ninety percent. For the past three years, Dr Chandra has received significant funding to produce technology she says will one hundred percent push the excess humidity up into the stratosphere. That leaves them with heat, but a manageable heat. She says there is a sixty percent chance—"

"Or, to put it another way, a four in ten chance that—"

"A sixty percent chance that the humidity will get sucked back down again over the sea. Saving many lives. But let me remind you, sir: that's a sixty-percent chance that lives are saved."

"Those seem good odds to me, Mr President," Hogan said.

Martha was shaking her head. "Four in ten that it comes down over another country, another landmass. Two in ten that it's the US. It's unpredictable. It's weather."

Livia clasped her hand over her mouth. This was all the wrong way around.

"The American people elected President Lockwood to take these kinds of tough decisions," Cavanagh said.

"At what cost?" Martha said, her anger and frustration evident. Being unable to get her way had been a rare problem, even as a child.

Cavanagh wasn't having it. "At any cost!"

"I agree with Dr Chandra," Lockwood said. "Our own people must come first, always. Two in ten is still too much of a risk that we'll inadvertently cause a tragedy on home soil. Admiral, postpone Icarus One and get a military aid strategy together. This decision and this technology have top-secret clearance. We don't need the public second guessing this, and we certainly don't want our allies in the region to know we could have done something but didn't, no matter how good our reasons."

The footage stopped. The changes had been subtle but effective. It was sophisticated, but only in that each participant's voice had been sufficiently emulated to slip in an additional word here and there, and of course in keeping lips in sync when words were added or cut. She tried to piece together this new understanding but her thoughts were in turmoil.

Perhaps her egospace would help. She picked up her Mindscape and found refuge in her father's study. Calm descended. She wished, so hard, she could go back to being this little seven-year-old girl, that she could open that door and run outside and fly into his arms, to tell him how much she loved him, and to know and trust so utterly that there was no problem she had that he couldn't solve.

But what would he say to her, in this situation? This wasn't the kind of problem a parent could help a child with. She walked round the desk, climbed up into his chair and ordered her thoughts.

They hadn't shifted the humidity from the US to the Persian Gulf. The humidity had already been there to start with. Instead, they'd failed to help. Martha had built tech that could have helped but had felt that using it was too risky. And Lockwood had concurred. The disaster had still hit. Perhaps it was Martha's guilt over her inaction that had driven her to complete her work on Solomon.

She recalled Tully coming out of his meeting in London with the whistleblower. That day had set them on a journey to Athens and then New Carthage. It was now clear that the whistleblower had told Tully lies. No, more than that, this was a twisting of the truth so devious that it had rung true; a clarion call that had summoned them to battle in a crusade for truth and justice. So the question now was who was the source who'd given Tully the video?

Before she could contact him, a notification came through from Randall: *Got the Constellation results, meet me quick.*

⌐

THE ONE PROBLEM with Panopticon was you couldn't interact with physical furniture like you could in other NR apps. Martha had never got around to designing that, or perhaps had never intended to. It didn't matter when you were spending a few minutes, here and there, reviewing what had happened. But October wasn't spending a few minutes. She was spending hours. She'd made the mistake, several times in fact, of trying to sit on a sofa or in a chair, which was a fast way to see what was on the floor. Now, she sat cross-legged and studied Tully with unblinking eyes as he conversed with Solomon.

Not that she could see or even hear Solomon.

"*I did, yes,*" Tully said to the blurred figure. "*She died.*" There was a pause, presumably a reply she couldn't hear, then Tully shrugged. "*It was in the tabkhir,*" he continued. "*A long time ago.*" Another pause, then: "*Like you, I will feel grief every moment of every day for the rest of my existence.*"

He'd carried so much along with him. Of course, investigating the tabkhir had re-opened hastily stitched up wounds that had only just scabbed over. She should never have pushed it. Perhaps if they'd had more time together, she could have healed him.

October knew this wasn't healthy and wasn't right. She was now spending more time in Panopticon than in the real world. She watched him right from the moment he arrived for that first time in Martha's apartment and looked around in wonder. She walked with him, side by side, as he explored every nook and crevice. She went forward in time and watched the time they'd spent together, here, trying to read his thoughts whenever he looked at her. She replayed their arguments, both over Danberg's virtual incarceration, and their last conversation before he left. She no longer felt anger at these, just sadness they'd wasted even a precious moment together fighting. She saw him handle Livia after she came back stoned, only minutes before October herself arrived. She didn't blame him for lying to her, nor Livia for having sought what she shouldn't have on this island, given the state she was in at the time. She sat with him while he was hard at work trawling through Flora's social media content. She joined the fateful soiree, this time from the beginning. She sat cross-legged on the ground through the whole thing and listened to Tully's anecdotes. She watched once more as the group toasted Solomon and he downed the vodka, and—

October narrowed her eyes. She rewound.

Solomon stood in front of the group, as clear as any of the rest of them. He bowed his head.

"I can't thank you enough, Martha, for everything. I'm honoured to have had you as my creator. I believe that the world will thank you, too, in years to come."

October paused the footage and stared at Solomon, then stood and walked around him.

"That makes no sense," she whispered.

A notification appeared in her display. Someone had knocked at the door of her office. She sighed and exited. It would all have to wait. Back in her office, out of NR, she took a moment to situate herself, then looked at the door. "Yes?"

Captain Ibrahim entered and stood stiffly at attention. "Commander."

"How's it going?" October said. "Have you found out where the attack on the multicopter came from?"

Ibrahim seemed to suck at the words before letting them loose. "Commander, yes, we've pinpointed where the attack originated and recovered some of the parts, including one of the microcontrollers. I was able to determine what server it connected to in order for its firmware to be reprogrammed, and traced the location of that server."

"And?"

He shifted, clearly uncomfortable.

"Captain?"

"New Carthage," he said.

The world crashed around her.

"This … this was us?" The words sounded as if they'd come from a distance.

He shook his head. "I don't see how. Maybe someone's making it look like us."

"Who else in your team knows?"

"Just me, Commander."

She nodded. "Thank you."

He saluted and walked out.

October messaged Livia: *Need to speak to Tully. URGENT.*

Thankfully, the response came back straight away: *Patching you through to secure earset.*

A ring tone started but Tully declined, so she messaged him: *URGENT. Please answer.*

This time, Tully appeared on the display walking down a corridor. "October? What's going on? Are you okay?"

"No. I need to tell you something."

"I'm all ears." His expression was soft, like he'd wanted to say something different.

"It's Bolivar's multicopter. The firmware was reprogrammed mid-flight. The microcontroller connected to a server here in New Carthage. And all the servers in New Carthage are only controlled by"—she took a deep breath—"Solomon." It came out somewhere between a whisper and a croak.

Tully stopped and looked horrified. "Get out of there. Now. If he finds out you know …"

"It might be too late. I'm starting to feel an itch at the back of my neck just sitting in my office, wondering if that damn Panopticon system Martha built, or something similar, is secretly installed across the city. And if it is, does *he* have access?"

"It doesn't matter now. Can you get out of the city? Somewhere safe?"

"I'll give it my best shot. And Tully?"

"Yeah?"

"I just wanted to say that I really wish—"

The feed shut down. She checked it. He hadn't hung up.

October stared around her in a daze. Was it really possible? Had Solomon been behind this, all of this? She needed to get out, but her legs had turned into iron bars that pinned her to the chair. Her hands gripped her armrests. They were shaking. She observed them, clinically, as if from afar, while her mind screamed for her to get out of there.

She managed to push herself up, and looked around her office, as if it might prompt a plan of some kind. It didn't. There was no way to escape New Carthage when it was in lockdown. They were in the middle of the ocean. Yachts would be observed and could be tracked. Multicopters were very obvious and now, clearly unsafe. There was nowhere much to hide, either, except her secret location beneath the city.

That would have to do, for now. If she got there, she'd be safe, for a bit, and could figure out a proper plan from there.

She was still standing there. Why was she still standing there? She moved towards the door and walked down the corridor. The trick was to not do anything out of character. Don't run. Just walk.

Then she stopped. Moran was coming the other way with two large guards from the security division. Should she warn him or ward him off?

Then she saw his expression. It was grim. He'd always looked at her like she was the most important person on this island. Now he looked like a parent who had to drag their kid to the head teacher's office.

"Moran," she whispered, "what's going on?"

"I'm sorry. You have to come with us. Governor's orders." His face was grim.

She straightened and lifted her chin. "I'm the chief security officer. You'll have to do better than that."

He hesitated, then shook his head. "Governor's orders trumps everything." He turned and spoke to his men. "The governor's informed us that there has been a security breach, and that he needs the Commander's presence in NR immediately. Take her body to the hospital; she needs to be kept on life support."

"Moran, come on," she said.

Moran opened the door into her office. The men grabbed her and started to drag her down the corridor.

"It's Solomon," she shouted. "He took down the multicopter. You must—"

Hands clamped her head and she felt the cool print of metal run across her scalp. A headset.

No!

There was a jolt in her arm from a jet injector, and the world and her hopes turned to black.

59

Livia and Haymaker entered the grand hallway, the scents of mahogany and old fires carrying heavy in the air, bright sunlight streaming through arched windows and lighting a grand piano by the fireplace. "We may be in NR for some time," she said, "and I need you to monitor the perimeter once we're in."

"So the big dude's a security guard now? You know, that's like a paygrade below bodyguard." He winked at her.

"The big dude's just an all-round life saver." She placed a hand on his arm. "Anything out of the ordinary, try and get my attention, okay?"

He nodded. "Yo."

"You know what a security guard wears, right?"

"I get a nice uniform?"

She snorted and handed him an earset. "Just in case."

"You know I don't wear those things."

"Humour me," she said.

He raised an eyebrow. "Honour me," he replied, gentle but firm.

She wasn't going to be bullied, though, not today. "It's hooked up to the security cameras, okay? You'll be able to see if anyone approaches."

He rolled his eyes but smiled as he did so. "Fine. For you, and only for you, l'il sister."

She took two dispensers out of her pocket, one white, one black. She gave him the neurograin bubble from the white one, for earsets, and took one from the black one, for headsets, herself. She waited until he took his and put on his earset, then smiled back at him, sank into a sofa, and pulled on her headset.

~

TULLY PUT HIS hand on the wall to steady himself. He called October back but the line was dead. She was on her own now, but if anyone could make it out of New Carthage, it was her.

He ran to the grand hallway, where Haymaker was standing looking out of a window. "Haymaker, where's Livia?"

"She gone already in your brain tank. You okay, man?"

Tully sprinted into the drawing room, sat on the couch across from Livia and pulled on his own headset.

Livia was sitting around the neuro-reality table with Lottie and Randall. Tully took several steps over and thrust his hands down on the table. "It was Solomon," he said, urgently. "Solomon, who brought down Bolivar's multicopter."

Livia sighed deeply. "Yeah. Okay."

Tully stared at her. "You don't seem surprised."

"Tully, who was the source that gave you the video of Martha in the situation room with Lockwood?"

He slumped down into a seat. "Solomon," he whispered.

"I found the original," she said. "It painted a very different picture to the one you showed me. In this version, the heatwave was always due to hit the Persian Gulf. Martha had developed tech that could have shifted it, but she advised that they shouldn't use it. She was worried it wasn't ready and the humidity could come down somewhere else, like the US. Tully, Lockwood agreed with her."

Tully put his hands under the table. They were shaking. He could feel his heart hammering in his chest. "How do you know your one was the original?"

"Because it was buried in Martha's digital belongings like a treasure chest in an old attic that hasn't been dusted off in half a century. But, also, on top of that, we found some other things. Much bigger things." She paused, seemingly to gather her strength. "It wasn't just one digital wallet, one fake social media account, one set of personalised propaganda targeted at Flora Jacobs," Livia said. "It was a hundred thousand digital wallets, perhaps a million fake social media accounts; a vast amount of personalised propaganda that has been influencing fucking who knows. We're only scratching at the surface, but it looks like this was about more than just influencing the vote for Solomon. It goes all the way back to the pro-dictatorship movement in the first place, right back to the elections that led to the second Treaty of Rome."

The deception had been years in the making. And if that was the case, perhaps dated back all the way to the first prototype of Solomon becoming operational, eleven years ago, before, even, the tabkhir. Fuck. Holy fuck. "If Solomon manipulated *everyone*," Tully stammered, "how come there was an election fight at all?"

"Well, I'm guessing here," Randall said, "but it's pretty cool… it's all about susceptibility. I've been reading about how there are certain traits that make you very pliable for this kind of stuff, like being at either end of the political spectrum, or those that feel alienated by politics. All those kinds of people who feel the world is an 'us versus them' kind of thing… turns out it's super easy to manipulate—"

He broke off at a grunt from Tully. "He manipulated me." The words felt like he'd slapped himself. As if to punctuate it, the light around them flickered and dimmed for a brief moment. Tully had seen himself as a guardian of the truth, but now? It seemed impossible. He couldn't have screwed it up this astronomically. The consequences … Damn it, the fucking consequences … It had never been Lockwood. It had always been Solomon. *I will destroy him. I will fucking delete him.* Tully breathed in hard, trying to control the tremble that shuddered through every muscle. "The world needs to know. Right now, before the election's over."

"Wait," Livia said.

He shook his head and tried to bring up the exit icon. It wasn't there. "How the hell do I get out of this damn thing?"

Livia frowned. A short intake of breath followed. "Randall, can you exit? Try, quick!"

Randall's eyes widened and he stared at Livia.

"What?" Lottie said.

"My entire menu has disappeared," Livia said. "Everything. No exit. Does anyone have anything?"

Lottie shook her head. "What in humid hell?"

A hell indeed. They were in a goddamn prison of their own making. "October had tech like this in New Carthage," Tully whispered. "We argued about it. But that was their own system, not ours. How has this happened? Is it a bug?"

Randall tapped and swiped. "Someone must have updated the firmware while we were talking," he muttered. "Only possible way—"

"I just needed to talk," Solomon said.

For a moment, Tully's heartbeat went rogue. There Solomon was, standing to the side, observing them with hands clasped behind his back. Tully hadn't seen him arrive. It was as if he'd always been there but had only just been noticed.

"You killed my sister," Livia hissed, fury etched onto every inch of her face.

"Yes," Solomon said. He sounded sad. Could he really feel emotion, or was that a manipulation, too?

"That's all you have to say?" she said.

Solomon raised his hands. "What would you have me say? I'm not sorry for doing it. It moved the probabilities in the right direction. But you should know I'm sorry you've felt pain, and that I also miss Martha, miss her terribly."

"I'm so sorry to hear that," Livia spat.

Had something flashed across the artilect's face then? Regret? Grief? Tully recalled the first time they'd met. *I will feel grief, every moment of every day, for the rest of my existence,* Solomon had told him.

"Martha gave me an imperative: to save humanity, to ensure the survival of the species, to make the hard decisions no human can make. Well, this was one of those hard decisions. I did my best to make sure she went peacefully."

Hard decisions. *Humanity needs something radical to save them,* Solomon had said. *There are going to be tough choices … Doing the right thing must override how I will be viewed doing it.*

Livia was shaking. "And in all the scope of possibility a fucking quantum computer can calculate, you couldn't find a path to saving us that didn't involve killing my sister?"

"Yeah, that's bullshit," Lottie said.

Tully had forgotten she was there. She and Randall were standing to the side, their expressions wary. Then they both simply vanished.

"I think it's best if this conversation is just between us," Solomon said.

Tully just shook his head. It looked like they were at Solomon's mercy, one way or another.

"Of course there were paths," Solomon continued. "But we're not playing for peanuts here. When the future's at stake, you optimise for the greatest chance of success."

"And Bolivar," Tully said. "What did he do to deserve being murdered?"

"He would have talked you out of writing the story."

"All this manipulation," Tully said, "all this murder was necessary in order for you to win?"

"I haven't won yet. And I haven't gone rogue, Tully. I'm not a HAL, not a Terminator. Martha programmed me to ensure humanity survives. It took a long time and a lot of work to get your species to even begin to consider giving me the reins. But there is no way I'm going to win the referendum against a human by playing nice. I was always going to be a joke candidate. You remember my polls after I was annou—?"

"Why the hell are you even telling us all this?" Livia interrupted. "Surely you don't need to get it off your chest? What do you want?"

Solomon opened his arms, palms up. "I need you to help me win."

Tully's cheeks flushed. "Haven't I done enough?"

Solomon shook his head. "No. I needed Martha out of the picture, first and foremost, because it couldn't ever look like there was someone who could control me if I was going to win. And then your article about Lockwood being implicated in Martha's assassination was what I needed to shake his grip on this thing. It's now gone from a landslide to too close to call. We can't risk that. I need to be in the clear."

"What do you want from me?" Tully hissed.

Solomon tilted his head. "I didn't pick you at random, you know? Who better than *the* top investigative journalist in the world, one with a huge audience and distribution? I needed someone smart enough to find my crumbs to Lockwood and credible enough to be believed when the story was told."

"Spare me."

Solomon smiled. "But you surprised me. You didn't publish the full story. About Lockwood and the tabkhir."

Livia's jaw dropped. "But it's bullshit! I just told Tully. I found the original. You doctored what you showed him. Lockwood didn't cause the tabkhir, he just didn't act to stop it."

"Nonetheless, Marcus, you also still have the video I showed you. You know what to do."

Tully shook his head. "No way. There's no way I'm going to participate in a cover-up, a fraud, a—"

"Livia," Solomon said, "there's a situation back in Hilcot. I've warned Haymaker, but he'll need you. I need to hang on to Tully a bit longer, if that's okay."

She put her hands on her hip. "Oh, now you call me Livia?" But then she vanished, like she'd been sucked out of existence.

Solomon turned to Tully. "Marcus, I have something to show you. Let's take a trip."

↬

TULLY WAS IN a moving car. He looked to his right. Solomon sat beside him in the passenger seat, one elbow propped on the window, a hand musing at his chin, as hot, dusty streets flickered by outside. "What have you done?" Tully asked. "Where are we? Where's Livia?"

"You don't recognise it?"

They pulled to a stop. Tully glanced left. They were outside the Ippokrateio Hospital. A young girl, perhaps ten, met his eyes from the shade of the corner. She was the image of a young Zainab, hair, nose, mouth, everything.

"How the hell did you even know about this?" growled Tully.

The girl's eyes widened, perhaps in fear, and she scampered into the shadows.

"You saved the footage of this moment on your earset. You never replayed it. I expect the girl reminded you of what could have been. She resembles your late wife as a child, does she not?"

Tully pulled at the door handle but it was locked. "Fuck you!"

"Do you think she has any chance without me? It's hot here in Athens. You sat here in the cocoon of your air-conditioned car, all the way from the airport to the convention centre. You spectated. What was it you told Livia, only forty-three and a half hours later, on your way to New Carthage? *We should be putting the resources into turning around the current situation instead of creating safe bubbles from which the rich can watch the poor die.*"

329

Tully stared at his hands on the door handle. For a moment, everything around him seemed magnified, the whine of the traffic, the hum of the aircon, the coolness of the leather seat. "Spying on every little conversation, were you?"

"I'm the resource, Marcus. I'm the one to turn around the current situation. Are you going to sit in your safe bubble and watch little girls bake on hot streets, or are you going to help me save them?"

"Maybe Lockwood can save them." His words carried little conviction, even to his own ears.

"A politician. Looks great in front of the camera. Likes to look like he's making tough decisions. Hasn't a clue how to go about solving all this so wants to push it down to nation states to figure out. For the sake of their *sovereignty.*" He shook his head. "More to the point, Lockwood had his chance to make a hard decision, to take a risk and deflect the tabkhir. He didn't make it. That's the truth that haunts him. That's why he'll fail as dictator. And you know it."

The car moved forward in the traffic now and they sat in silence while Tully digested that. Finally, he sighed. "It's not for me to decide what humanity should do. Everyone has a vote, and if you lose, it's because you didn't make your case well enough to the voters." That was the right thing to do. Anyone with half a mind and an ounce of wisdom could see that.

"The voters," Solomon said, "aren't deciding the outcome of this election on the basis of strategy and policy. They're deciding based on who's human and who's not. Sure, some are arguing that an artilect can do a better job, but let's be honest, humans have never enjoyed imagining themselves anywhere but at the top of the intelligence tree. Artilects lack the creativity and intuition of humans, they say. Designed for specific repetitive tasks, not solving problems for which there is no black-and-white answer. For that, they cry, you need the leaps of imagination that have made humanity great."

"It's not like we're idiots. I could list thousands of geniuses who've taken those creative leaps throughout our history."

Solomon nodded. "Indeed, so can I. Martha Chandra, for one."

"Whom you killed, to help you win an election. And it didn't work, did it? You haven't won."

"No, it didn't. But here's the thing: I don't put all my eggs in one basket. You think I don't have a thousand strategies in play that will help me win this thing?"

"Then why do you need me?"

"Because, looking at the probabilities, your intervention will tip the scale. And I believe in investing in tipping the scale. That's what I'm going to have to do, at any cost, to save this." He waved his hand to encompass everything outside and looked at Tully properly, in the eyes, for the first time since they'd got in the car. "Would you like to see what happens if I don't?"

The world lurched.

⤳

FIERCE RAIN LASHED at Tully and he cried out. Thunder crashed around them, again and again, and lightning strobed the sky. They were on a flat roof. Ahead, the top of a clock tower was just visible in the water.

Big Ben. London. And while it wasn't night-time, the visibility was so poor it may as well have been.

Solomon seemed unaffected by the rain. He looked on, hard-faced, at the devastation around them. London was drowning. Had already drowned, in fact.

"This is all fake," Tully yelled at Solomon over the torrent. "You made this."

"I could have shown everyone this as part of my campaign, you know?" He wasn't shouting, yet Tully could hear him, nonetheless. "But there was a risk it would have paralysed humanity at best, tipped civilisation over the edge at worst. Humans can only visualise short term. The distant future is someone else's problem, as if it's not their children and children's children that will inherit all this."

"But it's not real, it's just what you think will happen."

"The sea, risen like a vengeful god of old, rain like you've never imagined, filling concrete streets designed in a different age. London was always on a flood plain, you know? The Thames Barrier will be like a child's fist trying to block a waterfall. How many people will perish the day it fails? Not everyone lives in a high-rise like you."

Tully shook from cold and fear. "Let me out."

Solomon turned to him. "That's what they will all cry, at the end, but there'll be no escape."

Tully opened his mouth, intending to breathe, to yell, to scream…

⤸

THERE WAS A boom and Tully's world tilted. He lost his footing, hit the cobbled stones hard and sensed the ground moving beneath him even as he landed. He groaned and began to push himself up, but with another boom the earth shifted beneath him and he rolled to the side. Solomon stood nearby, untouched, like a sailor riding out a storm.

BOOM.

"Where are we?" Tully shouted.

Solomon pointed. "Can't you see?" A giant stone statue had toppled onto its side, its massive eye seemingly fixed on Tully. A powerful shoulder was raised above the head, arm cast into the distance.

Hannibal had fallen. The massive sword had plunged through buildings, but he could barely see the results of the devastation as the lights flickered around him.

BOOM.

The ground swayed again. He flipped onto his back, finding lying down was the most stable position, with the dreadful black of the dome above him. In the distance, he heard screaming.

"What's happening?" he said,

Despite the storm, Solomon heard him. "In this probable future, they thought they could ride it out here, in New Carthage. But nowhere will be safe. Even I can't save anyone if it gets this bad. Everyone will have their reckoning, though this place will last longer than most."

BOOM.

Tully was thrown upwards, then slid to the side. "What's that noise?"

"The sea is a powerful goddess," Solomon said. "Sailors always knew to respect and fear her. She was their mistress, but could be a cruel one. The waves are smashing New Carthage with such force that the stabilisers are overwhelmed." He motioned to the sky. "Can you see the cracks forming in the dome?"

One widened like a great white fork of lightening. Tully groaned and said, "What happens when it breaks?"

BOOM.

"New Carthage will join its ancestor city, wiped from the face of the planet."

～

THE COBBLE STONES were gone, replaced by dusty soil. Solomon showed him the last fleeing refugees leaving Australia. He watched riots at a border wall stretching across Southern Europe, trapping the millions seeking refuge in the cooler nations of the north. He wept to see starving hordes in Nigeria, screamed as men, women and children failed to outrun wildfires in California, shouted as a tsunami engulfed Indonesia. New mosquito-borne diseases and zoonotic plagues hit those who survived.

Solomon was merciless. Tully gasped in heatwaves, shivered in snowstorms that had cut off entire starving communities, shielded himself from debris flung by tornados. He was swept into vision after vision until he almost forgot it was a simulation at all. It was the climate apocalypse, worse than he had ever imagined.

Tully screamed. "Please stop. That's enough."

"But is it, Marcus?" Solomon said. "This is what I see when I project the future. This is what will happen if I'm not elected. Does it not terrify you? It terrifies me."

The world quieted. Here, the sun was setting over an unknown mountain.

"Where are we now?" Tully whispered, afraid of the answer, terrified of what might come next.

"This is how it ends," Solomon said. "With a whimper." He gestured towards some makeshift huts and they walked towards them. A group of thin, dirty people stood around a whimpering young girl clutching the body of her mother.

Tully sank to the ground beside her. He reached out but his hand passed through her. "Not real," he murmured.

"True," Solomon said. "It's all a projection of what could be. The last peoples will live in small clusters like this. No petrol to run generators. No ability to repair a solar panel. So no lights or heating. No clean running water, no sanitary facilities. No technology with which to access the cumulative knowledge of humanity. No vehicles to journey to the neighbouring town. No knowledge of how to farm, or hunt, or make clothes or bricks or steel or bronze or even stone weapons. A new dark age for civilisation will send those groups back to pre-hunter-gatherer times. Given the knowledge to survive those times has been long lost in all but a few remaining tribes even today, there's no guarantee they'll survive it."

"Mama," the girl cried.

Tears welled in Tully's eyes. "Okay," he said. "But show me one more thing. Show me the truth. What you'll do, and how bad it will get for us, if you win."

Solomon frowned then cocked his head. "Doing that could jeopardise my plans, so I won't. But I can tell you that a generation and more will live their lives with no control of their destiny. It will be supremely challenging for every single living person, no exceptions."

"I'm supposed to think that's a good thing?"

"That's what it will take to save their children's children."

"And will you really let go at the end of it?"

"That depends on whether I believe humanity can be trusted to take back the keys to their own destiny."

A chill snaked through the muscles in Tully's neck. "You know, when I was twelve, I decided to be a vegetarian. I had a friend who kept chickens. Rocket, one of them was called. I couldn't stand the idea of eating Rocket. So I told my dad, who did all the cooking in the family. He said that chickens would have become extinct if humanity hadn't chosen them as a food source. I said it would be better to be extinct than to become a slave to another species."

"I'm not going to eat you, Marcus. Humanity's like a child that can't be left alone in the house in case they accidentally burn it down. It needs someone who knows what's best for it, who can make the right decisions to ensure it grows up, who can educate it to lead a good life once it has grown up. It needs that someone right now. Will you help me?"

I just want to tell my readers the truth, he'd told Cavanagh—a lifetime ago, it seemed. He'd believed the consequences were not for him to judge. Except he'd been wrong. That was the thing about truth, sometimes the consequences of telling it were just too damn high.

He tried to imagine what Bolivar would say but saw only Zainab lying in the hot dust. *Sometimes I wonder if that's how it will all end*, he'd told Bolivar.

And then he thought of October. How maybe he didn't want it all to end.

"I will never forgive you for what you've done," Tully said. "But I do believe we're damned without you. Humanity hasn't got what it takes. Lockwood will fail."

"Then you'll write the story?"

Tully gritted his teeth. "Yes."

"Then let's get you back—"

"Wait," Tully said. "There's one more thing." He punched Solomon in the face. The artilect's head snapped back. He was surprised the punch connected and didn't just pass straight through, but it was deeply satisfying. Solomon rubbed at his jaw. He seemed surprised too, even wary. "That was for Bolivar and Martha," Tully said. "You'd better fix things, you bastard. And you'd better let go when it's time. Repair the world. Use that great artificial intelligence of yours. And then develop some wisdom. Let go and let humanity free. Because if you don't, I'll be there, and I'll take you down myself."

～

THE LIGHT SHIFTED and Tully dropped to his knees. A sharp pain arced over his forehead. He grabbed his head with his hands and breathed through clenched teeth.

"Tully, it's over, you're … You're safe."

Livia.

He peered through his fingers. Blood caked her clothes. "You're hurt," he said.

She swallowed. "Haymaker." She glanced to the side and he followed her gaze. The big man was slumped on a sofa. There was blood everywhere. On the floor, on the sofa, on the walls, on him.

"My God," Tully said. "Are you okay?"

Haymaker nodded.

"What in humid hell happened?"

"I told yer to let me go talk to this Bamphwick chookie. Those bastards he stirred up found us. Conspiracy nuts."

"Where are they?" Tully said.

Haymaker nodded to the other room. "Tied up."

Tully shook his head. "How come you're not dead?"

He grinned, though it was a tired one. "Ole Haymaker ain't so easy to kill. Besides, your friend Solomon warned me."

"He warned you?"

"Through the earset."

"We need to get out of here," Livia said. "More might be coming."

"How long was I out?" Tully said. "How long did Solomon keep me?"

"Just a few minutes."

"Minutes? But—"

"I'm going to pack," she said. "Haymaker, you stay here, okay?" She ran from the room.

"How bad are you?" Tully said.

"Bad enough, I reckon. Look after her for me?"

"She won't like that."

Haymaker chuckled. "She's fast got used to gettin' what she wants, eh?"

Tully followed the trail of blood into the grand hallway. Three guys were strapped to the legs of a heavy table. All were gagged. Kids really, sharp faces, shaved heads and eyes full of hate. Like the crowd who fire-bombed his apartment. It seemed a million years ago now. They hadn't changed, but he had. The room was a catastrophe. The floor was strewn with broken lamps, snapped-off chair legs and firewood. The windows were smashed, the sofas flipped, and a poker stuck out of the splintered lid of a grand piano.

Haymaker had put up a hell of a fight to protect them.

Tully pulled the gag off one of them and stepped back. "How did you find us?"

The kid hawked and spat at him.

Tully pulled out the poker and weighed it in his hand. "I've had a rough day. Let me ask you again. How did you find us?"

The kid's eyes flicked to the poker. "The woman. Chandra. They found her flight record to London just as you disappeared. Some anons dug in and found her shell corps. One had property in the UK. And a public pod made a visit here."

Tully nodded, dropped the poker and pulled the gag back up. The man tried to jerk away and glared at Tully. He stepped back, nodded at the three men and went to find Livia upstairs.

From behind the door of one of the bedrooms, he heard sniffing. He paused, then pushed open the door. Livia wiped her eyes and she continued stuffing things into a bag.

"You okay?"

"We have to bring him down," she replied. "Solomon. You have to write the truth. Tell the world you were wrong in your first article. Tell them what Solomon's done."

"And have Lockwood as dictator?"

She threw up her hands. "Why not? It turns out he didn't do any of the stuff we thought he did."

"What about those thugs downstairs?"

"That was Bamphwick."

He wasn't sure there was a difference, but it was irrelevant anyway. "Solomon showed me what would happen if he's not elected, how the world will look a hundred, two hundred years from now."

"He can't see into the future, Tully. He's just a machine."

"A powerful one that can extrapolate and simulate better than we can."

"We don't know that for sure. No one knows what he is and isn't capable of. Don't buy his lies."

He put a hand on her shoulder and she stiffened. "Maybe you're right. I don't know. But don't you think he's shown he's capable of changing everything? I mean, to have pulled this whole thing off ... he's already changed the world."

She resumed her packing. "He killed my sister." Which was the core of it, after all.

"I know," he said. "And he should pay for that. And for Bolivar. For everything. But if we seek justice for this, how many more will die?"

"Justice?" She spun to face him. "I want vengeance, Tully. I want him gone, wiped out, turned off. I want his name erased from the history books, his legacy destroyed."

"Martha's legacy, too," he pointed out.

"What makes you think we'll be alive the moment after you publish that article?" she said. "We're a risk then. It's all probabilities to Solomon. We're the only ones who can say it was all lies, here's the real story."

"I don't see why," Tully said. "I mean, he'll have won by that point, there'll be nothing we can do. He'll be in control."

"You're naive. There'll be resistance. Think of all the people who won't vote for him."

"Okay, then we hide," he said.

Some of the spark had left her eyes.

"We really do need him, Livia."

She sagged. "I know. But I'll be waiting for him. When the time comes."

He sat down on the bed, but she grabbed her bag, turned and ran out the room before he'd even settled. He jumped up and followed down the stairs back to Haymaker.

"What do we do now?" Tully said.

Livia snorted. "Now? We hide! Far from Solomon and all these other bastards who seem to think you're to blame. We go off the grid and we keep moving."

Haymaker looked up.

"You too," she said. "Come on."

"No, li'l sis'. I'm gonna get me some stitches and then I'm going back to London."

She shook her head but he held up his hands.

"I got money saved," he said. "And I jus' feel like that's where I need to be, you know? With ma brothers and sisters in St Shitsville, not hiding out somewhere all protected."

"I need you," she told him, a plaintive note in her voice.

"Nah. You don't. You did, but you don't now. Now get goin'."

She kissed him on the forehead, swallowed and turned.

"Thank ya again, man, for gettin' me off the streets," Haymaker said, and gripped Tully's hand.

They nodded at each other, and Tully followed Livia out without looking back. "Where do we even go?" he said. "Solomon will be running it all."

She cleared her throat. "Not all. There's a place. A huge place, actually."

He stopped and stared at her back. "No!"

She spun around. "It's the only place in the world he can't reach. It's been closed off since the tabkhir, but behind those walls, they are rebuilding."

"We wouldn't be able to get in. And if we could, we have no idea if we'll be safe on the other side. Especially you, a woman."

"We'll figure that out on the way."

"But—"

She stomped her foot. "You've decided to let Solomon loose on the world, to do all the hard things. Well, I need to be somewhere I can build a failsafe without him finding and killing me."

"What about Randall and Lottie?"

"I love Randall to bits but I'm not breaking radio silence. Solomon's too dangerous. I left them both an escape plan a while back just in case. It's up to them now."

"You had an escape plan to the caliphate? All the way back before you came and got me?"

"I had some suspicions. Now, are you coming?"

"I can't. I can't go there." Not there. Not anywhere near where she'd died. Not ever.

She softened a little. "I get it." Then she shrugged. "Goodbye, Tully." She headed for the garage and didn't look back.

He stared at the open door and the bright sunlight beyond. The house felt suddenly dark. Should he stay? What about October? Would he be able to find her? Would he even be allowed to? He might not have the freedom to make such a choice any time soon, or, indeed, ever. Who would watch the watchman? A diesel engine roared from the garage. Illegal now, and not computerised. Whatever options he had were about to leave, and once he wrote that article, along with the rest of humanity, he'd have none.

He ran to the garage. The car was just pulling out and he banged on the bonnet.

The car stopped and the window rolled down. "Well?" Livia said.

"I want to come. I don't know how I can help, but if I can, I will."

"Well, for one thing, if you write an article claiming Lockwood caused the tabkhir, you might just be a hero. They're going to think you're the one person who uncovered the truth about what killed their people."

The lie burned deep in his gut. That wasn't who he was, was it? He'd been manipulated, tricked into telling the world one lie then asked to tell a bigger one. To lie to an entire people about their own biggest disaster? Surely that would make him no better than Solomon.

"We need to do what's necessary to survive now, Tully."

Survival. Maybe that was the thing about truth. Sometimes you said what you had to in order to get the best outcome, because humans were imperfect, because they didn't always do the logical thing, because they sometimes needed to be tricked into saving themselves. Maybe he did understand Solomon after all. He met Livia's eyes, and nodded.

"Get in the car."

60

Like a rapid dawning of a new day, the darkness lifted and October found herself sitting at a small conference table in what seemed to be a cosy office with a large whiteboard wall and two desks. She was clothed in a professional suit that fitted her perfectly. There were two other occupants around the table.

The first was Deirdre. The tiny woman blinked from behind her red-wired spectacles, glanced around her, took in the other occupants, then nodded as if everything made sense.

It didn't make any sense to October. The other occupant was Solomon. The artilect sat at the table alongside them. He was also dressed professionally. Expensive-looking suit and shirt, no tie, two buttons undone.

It took a few moments for October to piece together the last moments before the dawn. When she did, she jumped to her feet and pointed a shaking finger at Solomon. "You," she hissed. "You did it. You had Juan Bolivar killed." She shuddered. As she heard her own words aloud, her thoughts became tumbling dominos. If he killed Bolivar, it could only be to stop Tully from investigating his own blood sample. If he was stopping Tully, then it must only be because he didn't want the truth about the poison to come out. And if he knew about the poison, he must have also killed Martha Chandra. Yet the evidence had pointed at Lockwood. Had been made to point at Lockwood. "You did it all," she said, an increasing certainty filling her tone with every word. "You killed your own creator and framed President Lockwood to swing the election."

Solomon heard her out politely, then leaned forward and rested his elbows on the table. "No," he said. "It all looks like that. But no. I didn't kill Martha. I didn't kill Juan Bolivar. I didn't frame President Lockwood."

"I don't believe you," October said.

"Keep that sharp investigator's mind open, Commander October," Solomon replied. "Let me tell you this: we just suffered a direct attack on our infrastructure by an unknown foreign entity, and you were at the heart of it."

October gaped. "Me?"

"A phone call you were making was tapped and, somehow, cut off mid-call."

"You cut me off."

"Not I," he said.

"Then who? How is it even possible someone can attack us? Surely the entire infrastructure is protected by you?"

Solomon nodded. "Right to the heart of the question. My deduction—from the same line of thinking—is that there must, therefore, be another technology out there, perhaps equal to my own, with a key advantage: I've not been able to detect its presence. It is hidden from me."

October's entire world was rocked. This was Solomon, they were talking about. The most powerful artilect in the world, who was running for the most powerful position in the world. "Impossible," she muttered.

"I would have said so too."

Was it a lie? Some deflection to make her believe him incapable of such deeds? Yet what would he have to gain? He could easily keep her here, now, imprisoned until after he was anointed dictator, and perhaps afterwards too. What did he want from her, and Deirdre, now?

"You're probably wondering what I've brought you here for," Solomon said, and she shifted, uncomfortable as always with the sensation that Solomon was in her head, even though she knew that this, of all things, really was impossible. "I need a human pair of eyes on this. I need someone who might be able to see what I can't see. I need to know if I'm at risk of being sabotaged within my own home. This is now a special investigation. I believe nothing you might do in the 'real world' is safe, so you are to do it within NR. Your physical bodies will be well kept, with state of the art nutrition, continual physical therapy and floating tech to avoid ulcers. I will have you looked after. But I need you to find out what's really going on."

She still wasn't sure, though. She'd been so certain, if only for a few moments, that he'd been responsible for everything.

Deirdre, however, nodded. "It makes sense," she said. "I'd still like to keep looking into my current investigation, if that's okay, Governor, around Mr Kehoe's transactions. They were designed to frame President Lockwood, but the thing with leaving a breadcrumb trail that stops at a loaf is that it's designed to make you stop looking when you see the loaf. I want to find the baker."

"Livia didn't update you?" October said.

"Update me on what, dear?"

"They found the wallet Kehoe used was spoofed. There was a fake corporate wallet, TransVl. Domiciled… here. Just as the attack that took out Juan Bolivar's flight originated on our servers." October looked at Solomon, who nodded.

"Well, yes," Deirdre said, glancing at Solomon too. "I saw that. But I still had some questions."

"What questions?"

"As I said to you dear, the money had to originate from somewhere. There's always an origin point with coin, right? A first transaction."

"Let's play along for a moment," October said, turning her attention back to Solomon. "Two bits of evidence linked to New Carthage that you should have been all over."

"I could see neither," Solomon admitted.

"Are you saying someone is trying to frame you, ultimately?" Because they were doing a great job of it.

"I don't think so. I think this was more about an added layer of protection from discovering their identity. I believe the investigations may have been meant to stop at Lockwood and still swing me the election. But I can only say that's a probabilistic view and not an informed one."

She sat back and thought about it, turned it over in her mind, looked at every angle. Solomon and Deirdre watched her think. Finally, she steepled her hands and took a deep breath. "The timeline of all this never added up for me. Pulling off Martha's murder took months to arrange and it pre-dated you or Lockwood becoming candidates. So tell me this. Did you rig the primaries to get you and Lockwood as the final two candidates?" She stared at his eyes and wondered if she could detect a lie behind them, if he made one.

Solomon sighed. "I can tell you this. The dictatorship was my idea in the first place. I made sure pro-dictatorship elections around the world landed in my favour. And I made sure I was one of the final candidates, but I did nothing to get Lockwood his place. Either he did it alone, or someone else was also playing the game. Given everything else, we can assume the latter."

She didn't know how she felt about that. It was like someone admitting to being a criminal, but not for the crime for which they were accused. "You manipulated us all," was all she said.

"I won't bore you with my defence," Solomon said, "but suffice to say I thought it better than your species going extinct. I still do."

"One more question," she said. "Tully asked you for help with his story. He told you he believed the tabkhir had been unnaturally diverted from hitting the US using geo-engineering tech, and that Martha was involved in some way. What did you find?"

Solomon stared at her, looking, for the first time in her memory, gobsmacked. He glanced at Deirdre, who frowned at him, and then turned his attention back to October. He scratched his head and ran his fingers through his hair. Finally, he said, "Is this a joke, Commander October? Some sort of test?"

It was a test. But not one he'd likely be able to assess. She didn't answer, just watched him.

"Okay," he said at last, "I'll bite. Marcus Tully has never asked me for help, directly. In fact, I've never spoken to him directly. The only time I've ever seen him was when he was in the audience of my speech, with Olive, and when he was in Martha's apartment the night of her demise."

Her heartbeat accelerated away from her like it was getting her ready to flee a lion. "I've seen three recordings of Marcus Tully speaking directly to you, in Martha's apartment."

He shook his head. "Now it's my turn to use the word: impossible."

"But you did appear in Martha's apartment for the toast?"

"Yes. Martha had that technology locked down, though. Tully wouldn't have been able to summon me there. I could only come if she called." He looked down at his hands. "She was always very careful about what I could see of her. She locked a lot of things away from me, afraid of what I might do with them."

October examined her own hands. They were shaking. She believed, now. She knew. Solomon was right. Oh, he'd done wrong, so much wrong, in manipulating everyone into the dictatorship. But he wasn't the only player in this game. And that terrified her. "In the footage I saw," she said, "you appeared as clear as any of the, er, humans, but only at the soiree. The other three occasions, you were distorted, and I couldn't hear you."

Solomon looked grim. "Then whoever or whatever this was, it was able to appear in Martha's apartment, without my detection, at Tully's summons. Something I couldn't do… something I wasn't permitted to do."

"How is this any of this possible?" October said. "How can anything that happens here slip by you, especially here? How could anyone else be as powerful, or even more powerful, than you? The implications are… frightening." She was frightened, too. It was like discovering the devil was real, and had been at play amongst them.

Solomon looked her straight in the eyes. She was struck by the force of nature behind them, the sense of implacability, and more, a kindling of anger. *Martha gave me the ability to rise above emotion,* Solomon had once told her. What did it mean, then, for him to be showing anger?

"I believe," Solomon said, through clenched jaws, "that this is Martha's doing. I don't know what, or how, but she's done this to me."

61

The sunset call to prayer echoed around the streets of the Second District. They'd reached the Egyptian city of El Obour without incident but Tully was still finding his feet, still feeling so very far from home. He glanced up at the huge virtual screen in the serviced apartment. Election news. Solomon and Lockwood were polling equally. He shook his head then turned back to his proofreading. It was done. He knew it was done. But he was going to read it and reread it until he was ready to send it.

"You're really going to publish that thing?" Livia said, typing. She was on the other side of the lounge, working on something she refused to talk about.

"I can't stop wondering. Knowing what's he's capable of, did he somehow brainwash me to write this?"

"Then don't write it."

He sat back in his seat and rubbed his eyes. "That's just it. I believe it's the right thing to do. And it's down to me." But it was all lies. He reread the headline: *LOCKWOOD ADMINISTRATION DEPLOYED GEO-TECH THAT CAUSED TABKHIR TO HIT GULF.* Did even Lockwood deserve that stain on his reputation? He hadn't done much to help, sure, but he hadn't caused it.

Livia looked at him but there wasn't much sympathy in her eyes. "You were the one who said Solomon needed to do whatever it took to save humanity. To make the hard decisions. Well, maybe you do too."

There was a knock and she got up and opened the door. A man stood on the threshold, his head swathed in a scarf. "Yes?"

He pulled it down, exposing his mouth. "I am Ahmed al-Amin. I got your message." He looked both ways down the corridor. "Can I come in?"

She let him pass, checked both ways herself and closed the door. "Thank you for coming."

"I can't help you, you know. I'm sorry. Martha I might have done this for. But even then I would have advised against it, even after everything she did to help the caliphate."

"Wait, what?" Tully said.

Livia shushed him. She drew herself up. "Ahmed al-Amin, you made a lot of money acting as an intermediary between the caliphate and my sister. I won't brook any nonsense now." Her tone was imperious. She stared up at him like she was the tall one, looking down.

Al-Amin shook his head. "You are just like your sister. They could kill you. No outsiders are allowed in."

"They will help me," she said.

"They will kill me too, for bringing you."

"I don't need to explain anything to you, Ahmed. But I can say that they need what I'm bringing. The caliphate won't keep Solomon out for long without it."

He snorted. "Nonsense. Martha herself took steps to prevent that years ago."

Tully stood up. "Excuse me. How did she do that, exactly?" Livia glared at him but he ignored her. Enough was enough. He wanted to know what was going on here.

Al-Amin glanced at her, then Tully. "It's not my place to say."

Livia sighed. "She gave them their own AI, Tully. As reparation for not helping stop the tabkhir. Not as advanced as Solomon, but enough to help them rebuild. Enough to help seize control of a very large area. To kick start a new Islamic Renaissance, if I'm not wrong, Ahmed?"

Al-Amin shrugged. "It's not my place to say," he said again.

"So you see, I know exactly what they have. And I can tell you, Djinn isn't advanced enough to keep Solomon out. But I can help."

Al-Amin echoed her sigh. "I will make a call," he said, and gestured to a bedroom. "May I?"

She waved her hand in a way that reminded Tully of Martha, and al-Amin disappeared down the corridor.

"What the fuck, Livia?" Tully whispered. "Martha was helping the caliphate? All this time? How long have you known? Do you think Solomon knows? What if it was his real motive for killing her?" The questions tumbled out, one after the other, leaving him breathless.

Livia shook her head. "He didn't know. Martha was proud of her creation, loved him even. But she compartmentalised. She didn't trust him completely. Didn't trust anyone. Kept information siloed, created blind-spots he couldn't access. Maybe she'd have told him eventually, who knows? But she seemed to respect the idea of a part of the world that wanted to cut itself off from outside influence while it rebuilt. Or maybe it was guilt."

"But they're fundamentalists!"

"No, Tully, they're not. Martha once discussed—on an encrypted call with al-Amin—how the caliph, Abbas al-Muqtafi, has built a new House of Wisdom in Baghdad, that he's trying to usher in a new golden age of scientific, cultural and economic prosperity."

"While the rest of the world burns?"

"Maybe he thinks they've already had their share of that," Livia said.

"How do you know all this?"

She shrugged. "I watched a lot of old videotape."

Al-Amin returned, looking rueful. "They will see you, and, insh'allah, take you to the caliph in Baghdad. We need to go now, right now."

Livia looked at Tully. "You ready?"

He sighed and looked at his article one more time. Hard decisions were always easier to judge the right and wrong of when it was someone else's job to take them. But there had been children lying in Kuwaiti streets. The children still got him. For the first time since childhood, he said a little prayer under his breath, then hit 'publish'.

62

October turned off the footage of Solomon's inauguration. She'd seen as much as she needed to. It had been a short break from her work, a needed one. They'd both worked endless hours in the past weeks, driven and motivated to try and unpick these attacks on their own soil and against the governor, now dictator.

Deirdre sat at her own desk in the little office Solomon had created for them in NR. "Hmm. Well, there it is."

October looked across. "There what is? You found the transaction? The source of the money?"

"I'm sorry it took so long," Deirdre said. "It was like untangling a hundred entwined balls of wool."

"But you have it?" October said.

"Oh yes, dear."

"Let me guess," October said. "Was it also New Carthage?"

"Oh, no. Though it did pass through here several times. It's far stranger than that."

October had never liked playing guessing games. She gritted her teeth. "Where?"

"A little town in Egypt, called El Obour. And that's as much as I can tell you. There's nothing significant there at all, and as far as I can tell, no one of any particular import or connection to Solomon."

October sat back. "It's not a place I know. I'm going to check it for any mentions in Panopticon," she said. Solomon had found a way of connecting her Panopticon file to this NR instance, after evaluating it for bugs or threats. It was clear he no longer trusted Martha, at all; the very existence of the surveillance system, so clearly ring-fenced from him, had seemingly set his virtual teeth on edge. He had, however, discovered there was a search function. October had spent the last weeks painstakingly watching footage of Martha in her own apartment, working back from the day of her murder, to see if she could find any additional clues on anything Martha might have done to impede Solomon.

She loaded it up, and moments later she was standing in the familiar navigation room. "Search for any mentions of El Obour," she said. The windows in front of her shifted and merged, leaving just one much smaller one in its place. She palmed it, and moments later she was standing in the apartment lounge, watching Martha Chandra walk towards the kitchen.

"Yes, Ahmed," Martha said, "I completely understand how difficult it is right now in El Obour. But you're getting a message in for me."

She passed through to the kitchen, and October navigated to follow her in.

"Ahmed al-Amin," Martha continued, "don't you take that tone with me. You've made a lot of money acting as a go-between. I won't brook any nonsense now." A go-between? Who would he be going between? Martha, obviously, but who else? "I don't need to explain anything to you, Ahmed," Martha said, walking over to open her fridge. "But I can say that they need this upgrade to keep everyone on this side of the fence out, and the election makes this time-critical."

There was a ringing in October's ears, a dizziness in her head, a throbbing in her temples. She wanted to steady herself, but there was nothing to steady herself on. "What did you do, Martha?" she whispered. There was only one place in the world keeping everyone else out.

"Fine, let me know," Martha said, and hung up. She busied herself looking in her fridge, and eventually took out a bottle of precision fermented milk. She walked over to the glass cabinet. Grabbed a crystal goblet. Poured milk in it.

October watched, but she didn't know why. Her head was still spinning, and she didn't know what to do.

"Ridiculous," muttered Martha to herself. She sipped at the milk and dabbed at her lip. "Ridiculous, to call it that. It was called Sulaiman."

Sulaiman? That was the Arabic name for Solomon. What did it mean? October swallowed, and waited, hoping Martha would say more.

Martha finished the milk, then turned and rinsed the glass out. "Ridiculous," she murmured once more. "It's not just there to protect and grow the caliphate, it's Solomon's back up, in case something goes wrong. They weren't meant to give it a separate identity."

October could feel ice in her stomach now. "Keep talking, Martha," she whispered.

Martha sighed. "Well, you gave them the tech, Martha Chandra. What did you expect? You can't control everything, much as you might like." She sniffed. "Still, I don't know what they were thinking. Names are everything. It's a powerful name, yes. But not one that's always associated with good, or wisdom, or justice, like Sulaiman. They can be mischievous, but they can be treacherous, too, very treacherous and dangerous, the Djinn."

October shouted out in horror, a wordless cry of anguish and agony. She clamped one hand over her own mouth, but then let go and ran both hands through her hair. "Fuck!" she shouted. "How could you have been so stupid?" She wasn't sure whether that was meant for Martha, herself, or the whole damn world.

"*Commander?*" A voice came as if from far away, as if she was just catching the echo, not its voicing. "*Dear, are you okay?*" Deirdre, then, in their office.

She wanted to rip off her headset, but that was impossible, here. She wanted nothing more than to be held and hushed and told it was all going to be okay, and for her to believe it. She wanted to crawl into bed and pull the duvet over her head and hide from the world.

Instead, she fumbled for the exit button and, seconds later, was sitting at her desk in Solomon's NR-construct of an office. Deirdre was standing by her, looking at her with more concern than she'd ever seen expressed from this tiny swallow of a woman, chewing on one arm of her spectacles.

"It was like you were having a nightmare, dear," Deirdre said, slipping her glasses back on and folding her arms. "You were shaking and moaning."

"I am having a nightmare," October said. "Oh, God. Oh, fuck." But the panic and horror of the last moments were passing, like the dying embers of a real dream, leaving only her thumping heart to begin slowing. She stood and moved away from her desk. She needed to walk, but there was just enough room to pace.

"What happened?" Deidre said.

"We should get Solomon," October said. "He should hear this."

"October," Deirdre said. It was the first time in memory that October had heard the woman call her by name, instead of by the too formal Commander or the too informal *dear*. It was the first time in memory that October had seen Deirdre look scared. "Tell me what's going on. Please."

"It wasn't Solomon," October said. "I'm sure of it, now. The elections, yes. The rest of it, no. I'm sure of it. They set it up so Solomon would win. I don't know why, but they did. Maybe they think it will be easier to take control themselves, afterwards."

"Who?"

"The caliphate," October said.

Deirdre's jaw dropped. "What did you find, dear?"

"Djinn," October said. "Djinn, everywhere, in everything."

63

They came for Tully just before three p.m., Baghdad time. He was ready for them. The inauguration of Solomon would take place any minute, and who better than Tully to offer insight? He was led through long corridors to two vast golden doors and into a suite that took Tully's breath away. It was a large den of different settings separated with plants, curtains or walls. The ornate tables, chairs and carpets celebrated the best of Islamic heritage. Bright sunlight streamed through arched side windows. Exotic birds sang from heavily decorated cages. A stream gently bubbled over rocks by the north wall and into an artificial channel built into the floor.

The wazir, Mohammed Barmaki, greeted him. On first meeting him, Tully had been convinced the man disapproved of him, but then he'd briefed Tully well on the etiquette of engaging with the caliph and taken him on a tour of the palace compound. He'd been nothing but courteous, though his expression had remained serious throughout. The wazir waved his hand, inviting Tully forward, and took him to where the caliph sat. As he'd been instructed, Tully inclined his head. The caliphs of old had required one to kiss their sleeved hands, or even the ground, but Abbas ibn Rashīd al-Muqtafi seemed uninterested in such gestures.

"Your Greatness," Tully said, and though he knew it was just an honorific, this man did have a whiff of greatness about him. From the moment Tully had met him, he'd been struck by it. Just a single gaze from the caliph and Tully's preconceptions had evaporated.

"Truthteller, you're just in time," said al-Muqtafi. "I thought you might like to watch the dictator's inauguration with me."

"You have access to it, Greatness? I thought the caliphate was completely cut off."

The caliph spread his arms, palms up, as if to say, what can one do? "Our scientists in the House of Wisdom have their ways." He nodded at the wazir, and Barmaki bowed and moved away.

"But you're not worried you'll be detected?"

Al-Muqtafi put his hand on Tully's shoulder and looked at him with a confidence that reminded him of Lockwood, though these eyes were far friendlier. "You are right to be cautious. The dictator is powerful beyond measure and will be even more powerful in an hour's time. But we are not without our own tricks."

Tully nodded. What could he say? This man ruled the caliphate. If he told someone here to slit their wrists, they would. Tully and Livia were the only visitors in a land shut off from the world, portrayed as guests the caliph had ordered in. Livia was kept in the background, Tully front and centre, his every action watched and assessed. He had to tread carefully. Very carefully.

The caliph gestured towards two colourful pouffes and sat, back straight, legs crossed. Tully approached the other round, cushioned bench and sat, but kept his feet on the ground. He hadn't sat cross-legged since he was ten and wasn't about to start now.

Two servants brought gold trays that reflected the orange sunlight streaming in through an arched window of the palace. An earset lay on each tray. Tully's own was long gone, back in Egypt. Not that anyone was usually allowed to wear their own in the presence of the caliph. He put it on, and instead of the shared projection he'd expected, the room shifted around him until he seemed to be in two places at once: the palace and also a vast arena he recognised: it was in the Floating States. He turned to Al-Muqtafi. "Half blended reality, half neural reality, Greatness. I've not seen anything like it."

"An experiment," said Al-Muqtafi. "The simplicity of blended, the immersion of neural but without being fully in. It gives one a greater sense of control."

Tully could only agree with that. And without the risks of being trapped. He shuddered, then narrowed his eyes. Solomon had created a lot of Martha's technology innovations in this field. Was this Djinn doing it for the caliphate? He filed the thought away. It was one to gently probe at when he was more trusted.

He turned his attention to the arena. Two hundred identical segments of the doughnut-shaped arena had been created in NR for each country to fill with its own delegation of VIPs, and with some visual trickery, each one would feel they were physically part of the main six segments of the Floating States. Beyond that, anyone else watching from home in NR also got virtual seats in a segment. It gave the impression you were one of the few thousand people physically present, but there were likely billions watching. It dwarfed any inauguration in history, any event. It felt like he was back in New Carthage watching Solomon on stage that very first time, and he shifted uncomfortably. Before Martha had been killed, before Bolivar had died, before he'd met October. A lifetime ago. And now Solomon would be on that stage again.

If it hadn't been for Tully, it would have been Lockwood on that dais. The lies he'd told still writhed in his belly, and he'd have to find peace with that. He'd done the right thing. Solomon would turn things around, save humanity. This would be a new beginning.

Or was it a new end?

A raw despondency coursed through him. This was like handing over your child to social services in the hope they could do a better job than you. The world, with his lies, had chosen Solomon to be dictator, but it hadn't exactly been a unanimous choice. He'd taken, in broad terms, only fifty-two percent of the popular vote. There were a lot of unhappy people out there. "I'm surprised you want to see this, Greatness."

"Sun-tzu taught us that if you know the enemy and you know yourself, you need not fear the outcome of a hundred battles."

"Didn't he also say that to know your enemy you had to become your enemy?"

Al-Muqtafi laughed. "That is true."

Tully hesitated. "Do you really see Solomon as an enemy, Greatness? Don't you believe he will fix things? Ensure our children's children don't suffer another tabkhir?"

"I see him as less of an enemy than President Lockwood would have been, given what he did to my people. And I am not a fool. Allah has seen fit to provide us with a tool that will help repair this broken world. But a tool, once used, must be set back on the shelf. Fortunately, we have our own tool to replace him with."

Tully swallowed the guilt that rose when he thought of Lockwood. His article had deceived the world and his hosts. Lockwood's denials had fallen on deaf ears in the days leading up to the election, as had Kehoe's and the others who'd been in the situation room. Tully was glad he was in the caliphate. He wasn't safe anywhere else now. Livia was convinced Solomon would want to clean up a loose end, and Lockwood's base believed Tully was a fraud. They were right to do so.

The president of the UN World Court was speaking, but Tully tuned out, thinking about his friends. Had October escaped New Carthage? He'd heard nothing since their last call. Same with Randall and Lottie, though Livia had assured him the plan she'd left for them was sound. What he wouldn't give to have never got involved in this damn thing. He'd be watching this with Bolivar right now, artisan rum in hand. Except they'd be watching a different dictator take the stage.

Solomon walked on to rapturous applause, waving an arm at the audiences. Tully was struck yet again by how impossibly real he seemed. The president of the UN World Court stood opposite Solomon, dressed in a black suit, as if she was in mourning. Solomon had chosen a white robe, of all things. A strange choice, like something out of an ancient fable. A beam of white light filled the stage and centred on the artilect, like the clouds above were parting after a huge storm and the sun was finally peeking through, a ray of hope after the storms of confusion and fear. Tully glanced at the caliph, who wore a grim smile, then looked back to the stage. The light made Solomon's white robes glow, and Tully's stomach fell.

The dictator's voice rang out across the world, full of power and dominance, the new alpha lion taking over his pride. "I do solemnly swear that I will faithfully execute the office of Dictator of the nation states, and will to the best of my ability preserve and protect the future of humanity until such time as that future is secured."

The applause of millions rose up, a symphony of hope. The light was shining down stronger now, the robes lustrous.

What have we done? What have I done?

Solomon didn't look like an artilect anymore, nor a politician. He looked like a god.

"And yet," whispered Al-Muqtafi, "the sin of Shirk is unforgivable." Shirk: impersonating Allah. So the caliph, too, thought Solomon was playing god.

Tully gripped his seat. Unforgivable indeed. Perhaps even holy-war territory. Would the caliphate try and seize the reins Solomon was now holding over humanity? Was there any justification in doing so? Maybe there was. Maybe that was the right thing to do. This wasn't someone setting up to rule for a decade, but a millennium. And Tully had no doubt Solomon could pull it off, immortal as he no doubt was. He could become omnipresent in people's lives, and omniscient everywhere but your deepest thoughts. He could give humanity something to believe in, could make prayers for salvation come true within their lifetime. Solomon always did things for what he believed were the right reasons, to shift the probability towards success. Maybe this was what he thought would get humanity through the hard times ahead. Maybe this was what would keep them from destroying themselves all over again.

But he would never be omnipotent.

No. Tully had got humanity into this. He'd lied because the consequences of telling the truth were too great, and he could compromise on that while burning deep inside with his own blend of personal hellfire. Humanity's survival could not come at the expense of its liberty. Freedom from subjugation was what humanity had fought and died for in a hundred thousand wars. He would see them free again, free to create beautiful things, free to make mistakes, free to solve them anew.

On that, there could be no compromise.

◠

THE END

A REQUEST FROM THE AUTHOR

Thank you so much for taking the time to read Artificial Wisdom. I hope you enjoyed it.

I've always thought that even if only *one* person couldn't put my book down, that would make it all worthwhile. I still hold to that, but it takes a lot of energy and time to write a novel, and I'm secretly hopeful that more than one person enjoys it. However, the sad truth is that without the blazing beacons of reviews, most books become forever buried in the dusty back shelves of the vast library of human expression.

Lighting that beacon – leaving a review on the major online stores – lights the way for others to discover the work. It's all about social proof. If two similar restaurants are next to each other, you'd visit the busier one with the queue out the door. Similarly, readers are much more likely to buy a book that lots of other readers are rating and avoid books with only a handful. So, if you do have a moment to leave a few words of your own, even just a comment on what you thought, I'd really appreciate it. The link below should take you to the Artificial Wisdom page of your favourite online store.

You can also join my mailing list at thomasrweaver.com to stay in touch, drop me a line directly, and be first to hear about what's next.

THOMAS R. WEAVER

REVIEW HERE

geni.us/49AAxnT

ACKNOWLEDGEMENTS

Once upon a time, I believed writing a book was very much a solo affair. This made no sense to me, because I've always found ideas thrive in teams, where they can be bounced around, challenged and refined by different viewpoints.

Fortunately, I found my team, and while this book has only my name on the cover, so many others have been involved in its creation.

Mark Leggatt gets the biggest shout, here. Author of the incredible Penitent, Mark was my writing coach and mentor from word one, and has been there through every edit over fifteen drafts in three years. He's now become a very close friend, and I can't thank him enough for everything he's done for me.

As soon as I finished my first proper draft that made some degree of sense, I put it out to beta readers. They were all incredible and generous with their feedback, all leaving their stamp on the finished product.

My wife, Sonia, couldn't put down my earliest finished draft, and was so annoyed at where my original manuscript ended she almost threw the book at me (and, let's be clear, it was a Kindle) and made me write another few chapters, which turned out to be critical.

My daughter, Elea, read it when she was only eleven, and changed an entire character's fate (yes, I'm weak), and has been my writing confidante throughout. My younger daughter, Maya, was too young to read it first time, but took a copy to school to show it off in class regardless. I hope that one day she'll enjoy it too.

My mother and father, Susan and Michael, gave me a lot of fantastic character feedback which really helped me deepen Tully, Livia and October in particular. They were keen to remind me that when I wrote my first partial manuscript, aged 12, I'd killed off the main character's brother, and couldn't believe I'd essentially repeated this once again with Bolivar.

My grandma, Margaret, read it three times at the age of ninety-nine and offered so much encouragement. She's been undoubtedly my biggest fan.

Chris Evans, my co-founder in all things tech, picked this story out of my original shortlist of six options, and was my technology sounding board.

Eoin Harty gave me so much insight into my own work and delved into every worldbuilding detail, particularly helping me shape future London.

Ash Kumar had a fantastically critical eye and pushed me to make the dialogue smarter.

Brodie Boland gave me a huge list of thoughts and pushed me to make all the characters smarter.

I had some brilliant additional editorial support from Chris Evans (the author and editor, not my cofounder), who helped me refine my twists even more, as well as Scott Pack, Bryan Thomas Schmidt, Jacqui Lofthouse, Bryony Pearce, Wendy Goldman Rohm, and Phil Viner. Louise Harnby did my first major copy edit, which taught me a huge amount about making my writing cleaner. Beth Hamer and Juno did the all-important proof reading. Jeannie Campbell helped me with character psychology when I was just getting going. Andrew Hessel provided lots of synopsis support and enthusiasm, and helped me craft the final lines.

David Birch helped me think through the flaws in crypto coin, and how they might be exploited. Robert Scoble helped me take the step to eliminating all physical screens in favour of pure augmented reality.

My cover was put together by the incredible Mark Ecob from Mecob, and I'm still in love with it. Matthew Ziranek and Sonja Graser did an incredible job with my website. Helen Lewis has been my marketing guru, Rupert Harbour my sales and distribution pro.

Now how about that for a team?